THE PATHS BETWEEN WORLDS

THIS ALIEN EARTH BOOK ONE

PAUL ANTONY JONES

THE PATHS BETWEEN WORLDS

Print and eBook formatting, and cover design by Steve Beaulieu.

Published by Aethon Books LLC.

ALSO BY PAUL ANTONY JONES

Published by 47North

Extinction Point

Extinction Point: Exodus

Extinction Point: Revelations

Extinction Point: Genesis

Toward Yesterday

Published by Good Dog Publishing

Extinction Point: Kings

The Darkening

Ancient Enemies (Dachau Sunset - short story)

This book is dedicated to:

Meredith Emerson, whose bravery inspired the lead character of the series.

And to the memory of Dr. Gerald "Gerry" Henseler. As good a man as you could wish to meet.

PART ONE

THE LONELY ALMOST-DEATH OF MEREDITH GALE

The soul becomes dyed with the color of its thoughts.

—***Marcus Aurelius***

ONE

I GOT the letter kicking me out of Berkeley the same day Oscar Kemple's mom called to tell me she'd turned off his life support.

It'd be easy to blame everything that happened after that on those two coincidental events, but the truth is, I was already on a downward spiral; I just didn't see how close I was to crashing face-first into the ground. I can guess what you're thinking: *Meredith, don't be so hard on yourself. You weren't to blame.* And that's mostly true, I suppose. After all, the asshole driving the Ford F150 is where my life really changed. But here's the crazy thing, the one thing that surprises me the most—even knowing what I know now—if I could go back and change what happened, I don't think I would.

But I'm getting ahead of myself. Let's start with Oscar.

Oscar is, or rather *was*, my best friend. There had never been anything romantic between us, just a really strong connection that started the moment we bumped into each other in the junior high library. He pulled the book I wanted (the latest Harry Potter, if I remember right) and must have seen the look of disappointment on my face because, without a moment's hesitation, he smiled and handed it to me. Turns out, we shared a lot in common. We liked all the same stuff; the same music, the same movies, the same books. And, to cap it all off, as we each grew into our teenage years, I liked guys and so did he—so it really was a friendship made in geekdom heaven. We made it through junior high school together, suffering all the associated ignominy of that period of our young lives; me the relentless target of bullying for being a 'copper top,' 'little orphan Annie,' or 'freckle face,' and finally, every school bully's favorite go-to insult for redheads, a 'soulless ginger.'

Oscar, for who he was attracted to.

On my fifteenth birthday, Oscar handed me a small package neatly wrapped in shiny silver wrapping paper with an orange-ribbon bow. Inside was a copy of *Anne of Green Gables* he'd picked up from a second-hand bookstore. That night, after the few friends I'd had over to celebrate left, I'd sat in my room and begun to read the book and the adventures of its eponymous red-headed heroine. I finished it in one sitting. The next day at school, I'd rushed up behind Oscar and delivered a quote from the book, "Kindred spirits are not so scarce as I used to think. It's splendid to find out there are so many of them in the world."

Oscar had laughed, hugged me, and without even thinking about it, I'd kissed him. It wasn't a romantic thing, not in the boyfriend-girlfriend sense, it was just an expression of my absolute love for my *friend,* my very best friend. It was... *natural.* He was my first kiss and I his, and when we pulled back from each other, we were both beaming like the proverbial Cheshire Cat and his doppelgänger.

"Well, that was unexpected, Carrots," he said, calling me by the same nickname Anne's eventual Green Gabel's love-interest had given her. And from that day onward, I was officially 'Carrots,' and every time he called me by it, I smiled. *That* moment... It's the best memory I have, and I hold on to it like it's the most precious thing I possess of my old life. Because it *is.*

After high school, Oscar was quickly accepted to Caltech and graduated as a materials scientist with a job offer from Dow Corning that would have set him up for life. By the time I found myself sitting at my first UC Berkeley Law school class, I'd spent four of the previous six years as a mild-mannered receptionist by day, and five evenings a week at my local community college to earn an Associate Degree. Add to that another two years to earn my Bachelor of Science, and you can pretty much see why I'd stayed single for most of those six years, except for the occasional brief romantic fling. I hadn't ever *really* wanted to be a lawyer, but I thought it would be a good foundation for a move into the political arena, which was where I felt my true calling in life really lay. Still, at that moment in time, my future looked brighter than I could ever have hoped for... right up until it didn't.

Fast forward to Christmas 2015, and I was one year in at Berkeley Law. Oscar and I hadn't seen each other in almost six months, so when he called to tell me he was going to be home visiting his parents at the same time I was on winter recess, I could barely contain my excitement. We had a lot to catch up on. So that's how he came to be a passenger in my beat-up Toyota Camry driving home early from a Christmas party that'd turned out to be nowhere near as exciting as it'd promised to be. Oscar, never one to let a moment of happiness slip by uncelebrated, sat in the front-passenger seat blasting Beyoncé's *Single Ladies* from the car stereo. We were both giving the Queen B a run for her money, serenading her at the top of our voices, Oscar moving and grooving to the rhythm as he drummed out the song's beat on the dashboard with his hands. He'd had a drink or three, and he was happy and relaxed. I'd stuck to Diet Coke. Despite my sobriety, the drive home was turning out to be more fun than the party that evening; an evening that should have become nothing more than a vague memory for the both of us.

That was not to be.

The last memory I have before both our lives took a sharp right turn was stealing a glance at Oscar as he sang and bopped to the beat of the pounding music. So young. So happy. So full of potential and promise, his face smiling back at me as the Ford F150 ran the stop sign, its headlights flooding the car's interior, creating a momentary halo around Oscar a second before the two-ton truck slammed into us at fifty-five miles-an-hour.

The next thing I remember was waking up in a hospital bed, three days after the crash with a concussion, broken wrist, and a fractured femur that left me with a permanent hitch in my step. It was Oscar who got the grand prize; he spent the final year-and-a-half of his life in a hospital bed, hooked up to a bunch of machines, in what the doctors classified as 'unresponsive wakefulness syndrome.'

The uninsured asshole in the F150 walked away without even a scratch. I've always thought it was a sign of just how screwed up our existence is when a single second of time can divert your life for better or for worse, depending on what side of a decision it falls. A moment's delay here or there and your life is suddenly moving down a completely unexpected road. It was only much later that I would truly understand the implication of that simple observation, how a simple choice can quite literally save or end a universe.

Again, I'm getting ahead of myself.

So, two surgeries on my leg followed by four months of outpatient treatment and physiotherapy later, I was on my feet again. The Oxycontin my doctor prescribed after I'd been released from hospital took the edge off the residual pain enough for me to get back to my classes at Berkeley. Then my insurer decided they wouldn't pay for the pain meds anymore and I was suddenly, and irrevocably, cut off. I wasn't particularly worried. I had enough pills to last me the rest of the week, and when they were gone, I'd do as my doctor suggested and just switch over to Tylenol and leave that period behind me. Done. Over. Deep breath; time to get on with my life.

But a half-a-day after I'd swallowed my last pill, I started feeling the first uncomfortable effects of withdrawal. As the day went on, the discomfort graduated to a pain so intense even my bones hurt. Tylenol had no effect whatsoever, and by the time that first evening rolled around, I was at a bar, searching for anyone who could hook me up with something, *anything*, to take away the terrible sensation I had of rotting from the inside-out. It wasn't hard to find him, and from that day on, my habit was fed mostly by cash transactions in the bathroom at the local Denny's.

I won't bore you with too much of the gory details, but as my habit got worse, I started missing classes. Just one or two at first, but within a matter of months, I was spending more time in my apartment getting high than I was at Berkeley. Then I stopped going to class altogether. I told myself I could always catch up; the faculty would understand. After all, I was traumatized. I needed the downtime. Everything would be just fine. Everything *felt* fine... until reality finally caught up with me.

Which brings me to earlier this afternoon.

With not a dime to my name and out of Oxy, I'd woken around mid-day with the red-hot grip of withdrawal already beginning to melt my insides. My mind refused to focus, constantly slipping from thought to thought as I tried to come up with a way, *any* way, to scrounge up some money, but my friends wouldn't loan me another dime; I'd burned those that had stuck around one too many times, already. I'd sold or pawned everything I had of any value. Rent on my apartment was due in two days, but I'd already spent that. I had nothing left. I was twitchy, constantly pacing back and forth from bedroom to living room to bathroom to kitchen, my mind a fog of disjointed thoughts, paranoia, and fear. Finally, unable to deal with the constant feeling of uneasiness, I walked out to the street. A couple of fliers sat in my mailbox... and a letter from the university.

For the attention of Meredith Jane Gale, the envelope read in laser printed letters above my mailing address, Berkeley's return address in the upper left. I was seized by a sudden sense of hope; there had been a clerical error, and inside this crisp white envelope I'd find a nice little check. Just sixty bucks or so would be enough for me to score some Oxy and get my head straight again for a day or two. That'd buy me enough time to sort myself out, get myself back on track. My heart began beating faster, saliva filling my mouth. A smile sprang to my face, and I felt a surge of anticipation. Tossing the fliers, I tore open the envelope, pulled out the neatly folded sheet of paper within and read it:

Dear Miss Gale,

Despite numerous attempts by our staff to contact you, we hereby notify you that your position within the Criminal Law curriculum has been revoked due to lack of attendance. While we understand that there have been mitigating circumstances... blah, blah, blah...

If you feel this decision has been reached in error, you may appeal by... blah, blah, blah...

Sincerely...

The air became suddenly heavy... abrasive against my skin as a growing pressure pushed against my chest. I let the letter slip from my fingers. It fluttered to the sidewalk, where a gust of wind caught it and carried it down the street. I stood motionless, watching as it tumbled away, taking with it the last vestige of my future and everything that I had worked so damn hard for since leaving high school.

Above the roof of my apartment building, angry rainclouds scudded across the sky toward me, dark and menacing, bringing with them a promise of chaos. I watched their approach with a growing sense of foreboding as, with each passing second, the pain in my chest became sharper as though the storm were attracted to the swelling desperation within me like some kindred force. Unable to look away, I might have remained transfixed for eternity if I hadn't felt my phone vibrating against my thigh. Without taking my eyes from the sky, I slowly reached down with a hand that seemed to be encased in molasses and slipped the phone from my pocket.

"Yeah?" I mumbled.

"Meredith? Is that you?"

I recognized the voice instantly; Oscar's mom, June.

After the accident, Oscar's parents had transferred him to a hospital near their home in Studio City so they could be closer to him. They had never forgotten the friendship their son had with me, which I was thankful for, even though it was always they who called me. It had been a long time since their last update, and I was glad to hear her voice, mainly because they were good Christian people. Generous to a fault. Which was just what I needed right then because I hadn't ever hit them up for any kind of a loan and I knew they were well-to-do. I took a deep breath, pushed the swelling panic within me down into the darkness and tried to make my voice sound as normal as possible. In the back of my mind, I was already concocting a sob story about how I'd been robbed and left penniless with no way to pay my rent or buy food. I felt that warm, nagging glow of anticipation return. I was beginning to feel better already.

"Hi, Mrs. Kemple, how are you?" I said, finally dragging my eyes from the ominous clouds. "How's Oscar doing?"

There was a long pause before June spoke again and my paranoid mind thought that maybe, just maybe, she'd somehow figured out what I was up to. When she did speak, June's words were like a sledgehammer against my heart, somehow able to batter their way past all the pain and the incessant needling of my addiction.

"Oscar passed this morning, honey," she said, her voice hushed and slow. "I... I wasn't sure if anyone had told you yet."

"Wh... what?" I stuttered. My head swam, and a fog descended over my vision. My legs suddenly unable to hold me up, I crumpled to the sidewalk, my free hand resting on the side of the mailbox to stop me from tipping over completely.

"I'm sorry, Meredith. It was, well... it was just time. We couldn't let him go on like... like *that*."

At the sound of those last two words, the image of Oscar lying in his hospital bed the last time I had visited him flashed into my head: surrounded by machines, tubes coming from his mouth and his sides. The only sound in the private hospital room the constant *beep, beep, beep* of the monitors. And the smell, that antiseptic, unmistakable hospital scent that barely masks the scent of dying and despair.

June continued, "Richard and I... well, we decided it was for the best." She paused for what seemed like forever waiting for me to say something, but I found no words to fill the expanding emptiness. The knowledge that they'd ended my best friend's life, my *only* friend, without even giving me the chance to say goodbye drove an invisible spear through me, skewering me to the spot.

"Meredith, are you there?" June eventually whispered. I

could hear the barely hidden river of her agony flowing behind the words.

I'd tried to blame myself after the accident, but June and Richard refused to allow me to, placing the blame squarely on the driver of the F150. But secretly, I knew I was still the one to blame; if I'd only taken a different route or stayed and talked to a couple of our friends for a few minutes more, everything would have been oh-so-different. None of this would have happened. Oscar would still be alive, and I would still have been me, not this strung out, drug-addled addict. That one extra minute would have made all the difference, and this version of the universe would have never existed. Everything would have been... right.

"I'm sorry," I managed to whisper, my voice cracking.

"It's not your fault, sweetheart. You know we don't blame you. And it's all for the best," June's voice whispered in my ear.

I felt tears slip down my cheek.

I'm not sure if I was crying because of the news of Oscar's death or the letter kicking me out of law school or the pain of the withdrawal that was already turning my body and mind into mush. I guess, if I'm honest, I'm going to go with the withdrawal pain because that was symptomatic of what I had become back then; selfish, negligent, and, ironically, considering the source of my addiction, in almost constant pain from the residual effects of the accident. But this news about Oscar, well, it was a pretty close second. The combined weight of it all broke me. Somewhere inside, an invisible dam buckled, crumbled, fell. And the reservoir of self-loathing and despair it held back spewed its poison into me.

"Fa... fa... thanks for letting me know," I sniffled and hung up the phone. I hadn't offered a single word of comfort to June, and that's something I'll never forgive myself for, but at that moment, I felt utterly empty. And that emptiness was a relief, because even the withdrawal pain was gone, replaced by an emotional void, black and infinite. I felt as though I was just a sack of skin, inflated by the fumes of that toxic, black nothingness. *Dead.* And if this was what it felt like to be dead, then I welcomed it, because there was no pain, no guilt, no caring, nothing.

It was already late afternoon, and the shadows of the trees lining the street stretched across the road, reaching for me like skeletal-fingers. I pushed myself to my feet, stared at my apartment building, then staggered off in the opposite direction just as the first plump drops of rain began to splatter on the sidewalk.

I was soaked through within the first minute, but I didn't care. *Couldn't* care, not anymore. So, I kept walking, my eyes cast downward, permanently fixed to the continually unwinding concrete pavement just a few feet ahead of me.

One step. Two steps. Repeat.

I don't know for how long I walked, have no real memory of the journey, but by the time I looked up again, the sun was setting, and my familiar neighborhood was gone. Ahead of me, I saw the lights of the Oakland side of the Bay Bridge stretching out into the San Francisco Bay, the city lights of the bay's namesake glowing in the darkening sky beyond. What should have been a beautiful ethereal sight was nothing but pain-inducing to my bulging eyes. A walking path extended across the span of the bridge, and I followed it, the oncoming lights from cars heading to Oakland slicing through the gathering darkness just a few feet from where I staggered through the rain falling in ice-cold sheets.

The emptiness within me shifted like a living thing, as if the void sensed the approach of night, growing restless as the sun's last rays vanished from the horizon.

Blackness within. Blackness without, I thought.

I continued walking the footpath, black and shiny with pooling rainwater. When I reached the center of the Oakland span, I stopped. In the distance, the lights of the Golden Gate Bridge sparkled and scintillated. Unlike its infamous sister, the Bay Bridge had no safety nets to catch a jumper who was willing to simply climb over the waist-high metal security fence and step off into the freezing waters of the San Francisco Bay.

Until this moment, I hadn't fully understood why I was here, why my feet had led me to this place. Now it was all perfectly clear; there was *nothing* for me; no one who cared for me; no reason to stay. The final frayed ties to this life were all broken. *This* was the *place.* Here was where all the pain would end. I was about a mile or so out over the bay, almost at the midpoint of the Oakland span.

Far enough, I decided.

I stopped and grasped the freezing, rain-slick metal of the bridge. Movement drew my attention back to the path: a cyclist was approaching along it toward me, his head bowed to keep the rain out of his eyes, water spinning off his bike's wheels.

Somewhere within the blackness that had once been me, a small spark of hope sputtered into life and began to gradually expand; a dim light weakly illuminating the void. This had to be a sign, it told me. A final attempt by a seemingly indifferent universe to grab my attention; to give me a chance.

"If he stops, it means he cares," I muttered to myself. It means I *matter*.

The cyclist rode by without even glancing up at me.

The spark sputtered and vanished.

All I wanted now was an end to this *torture.*

I grasped the safety-barrier with both hands, ignored the jagged chill that ran up my arms, swung my legs over, and lowered myself down onto the thin lip of concrete extending out just a couple of inches, my back pressed against the railing.

Below me was nothing but a black mirror; the only evidence there was anything other than oblivion down there, the refracted light of headlights on the shore-road bouncing off the waves of the bay. If my eyes could have pierced the darkness and driving rain into the glassy waters of the bay what would I see? Bright red hair pulled back into a bun, unruly tendrils falling around my face. Blue eyes peering back at me, surrounded by darkly shadowed skin, puffy and lined from lack of sleep. I'd lost about twenty pounds over the past couple of months, and it showed mostly in my face; I was almost twenty-eight, but I wouldn't have blamed anyone for thinking I was closer to forty.

I teetered on the edge, the rain pounding all around me. A numbing wind gusted in from the east, cutting into my soaked and rapidly freezing skin. My teeth began to chatter. My fingers were quickly turning numb against the icy metal. I leaned back to take some of the strain from my arms, let go of the barrier, and pressed the palms of my hands against my thighs, eyes tightly closed.

"Now," I whispered.

It was *so* simple. Just step off.

My body refused to obey me.

"Now," I repeated, the first tears of frustration beginning to run hot over my freezing cheeks.

"Now!" I screamed, urging myself to do it. All I needed to do was take a step, a single step, and it would all be over. I began to lean forward...

...and stopped.

I reached blindly behind me for the safety of the guardrail as the emptiness within me vanished as though it never existed. What replaced it was an explosion of overwhelming panic, then terror at my utter stupidity, and a wild undeniable desire to *live*.

There were people who *loved* me.

I could *get* help.

All I had to do was reach out to someone, *anyone*. My heart thudded loudly in my chest, adrenaline pushing back the fear and the discomfort and pain. Everything could be fixed, but first I needed to get off this bridge, *now*!

Ever so carefully, I turned back toward the safety that lay just on the other side of the barrier. Shuffling my feet inch-by-inch while I swiveled my body to face the walking path, my fingers now totally numb and barely responding, the cold eating into my bones, slowing my muscles. I'd managed to get my left leg up onto the safety rail when a violent gust of wind flashed across the bridge, slamming into me head on. My right foot skated on the slick concrete lip like it was ice. I tried to keep my balance, overcorrected, felt my foot whip out from beneath me... and I slipped. My chin smashed into the railing knocking my head back. I felt teeth and bone crack as my jaws smashed together. Hot blood filled my mouth. Pain exploded through my body. My vision swam, my fingers released their grip on the railing. I began to slide off the side of the bridge, stopped from plummeting straight into the bay only by the fact that my body, from my right heel all the way up to my armpit, scraped agonizingly across the lip of concrete I'd been balanced on. As I dropped, my hands smacked against the railings... and the fingers of my right hand locked onto the metal. I would have screamed, but the blood in my mouth clogged my throat, choking me. I couldn't even draw enough air to breathe let alone cry out for help.

I'm going to die. Oh my God, I'm going to die, my mind screamed. *This can't be happening. Oh my God! Oh my God! Oh my God!*

A fresh wave of panic exploded through my body, taking hold of me and refusing to let go. I whimpered like a baby as the fingers of my right hand began to cramp.

I gasped out loud at the sound of someone's voice nearby.

"*Candidate 13, do you wish to be saved? Answer yes or no.*"

I couldn't tell whether the voice belonged to a man or a woman; it was flat, emotionless. It *sounded* like it was coming from the walkway, about two-feet above where I dangled over the drop into the freezing bay water, suspended by one hand. And for a moment, I thought I was saved. I looked up, expecting to see feet or a hand reaching for me... but no one was there.

Then the disembodied voice spoke again, crackly and with a distinct electronic edge to it, like you hear in a movie when some kidnapper is trying to disguise his identity from the Feds. "*Candidate 13. Meredith Jane Gale. In thirty seconds, you will be beyond my ability to save. Do you wish to be saved? Answer yes or no.*"

I blinked several times in quick succession. "What?" I managed to slur through lips that felt like they were made of cotton. I felt warm blood spill over my chin with each word. "Help me. Please."

"*Meredith Jane Gale,*" the voice continued. "*Born August 7th, 1990 to Norman and Doreen Gale. Attended El Camino High School. Your best friend was Oscar Kemple. He expired today, contributing to your advanced state of depression. You lost your virginity to Richard Pollard at age sixteen and seven months in the rear seat of his Ford Explorer. The color of the walls of your childhood bedroom was purple, a color your mother objected to. This afternoon you received a letter stating you have been removed from your law course at Berkeley University.*

Candidate 13, in eight seconds, you will lose your grip and fall. You will break numerous bones upon impact with the water, but you will not die from the fall. You will, however, drown six minutes and eighteen seconds after impact. The pain during that time will be intolerable. Once you are deceased, high winds and a stronger than normal swell will sweep your body far out to sea. It will never be recovered. I can save you. Answer, yes or no."

Just how the voice knew all of this, I did not know. "Please, help me," I whispered, blood clogging my lips. "You have to help—"

"*Answer,* yes *or* no," the voice interrupted in that same cold, almost-electronic tone.

I started to answer, but before I could get the words past my shredded lips, my fingers gave way, and I slipped from the bridge, and I fell.

"Yes!" I screamed, my eyes tightly closed as I dropped toward the waiting abyss. Whether the words were in my mind or I actually managed to say them, I don't know, but a millisecond later, there was a bright flare of orange light, and my world ceased to be.

TWO

DARKNESS WAS REPLACED BY DAYLIGHT.

I had a fleeting moment to realize I was still falling, dropping through the air like a stone. My legs kicked wildly in a vain attempt to halt my fall, arms windmilling as though I might suddenly learn the secret to flight.

I started to scream, but the cry never came. I crashed into water, swallowing a mouthful of it instead. *Seawater*! Its briny taste unmistakable as it flooded down my throat and into my lungs, choking the breath from me. I spewed it back out just as my head broke the surface.

Gasping for breath, panicked and confused, I began treading water as my brain struggled to make sense of what had just happened. This wasn't the San Francisco Bay. There was no sign of the bridge. No sound of a distant city and no way for me to explain how night had, in an instant, been replaced by this insipid daylight.

A gauzy mist hung just a few inches above the water, rising high enough that I could see no more than a few feet of the surface. Something splashed into the water close by. It took me a moment to realize it was a piece of the walkway from the bridge. It sank instantly. My cellphone bobbed on the surface a few feet away from me, and I made a vain attempt to reach it, but then it too disappeared into the murky water.

Born and raised in California, I'm a fairly decent swimmer —I should be after a childhood spent playing on the beaches up and down the West Coast. I knew I wasn't going to drown, I could tread water like this for hours if needed. I willed my body to relax, fighting to regain control of it from the panic-induced rush of adrenaline still surging through my veins. Minutes passed, and I switched position to float gently on my back, staring upward into a sky filled with leaden clouds.

It was raining hard, the downpour pounding the water's surface and my face as I tried to relax, blinking away fat, stinging raindrops. I began to regulate my breathing to match the gentle bobbing of my body—in through my nose... out through my mouth—gathering my wits, my stomach-acid-raw throat burning with each breath I exhaled.

I flipped myself upright and began treading water again. Gray, foamy water the same color as the slowly dissipating fog surrounded me. The surface was calm, like that of a lake, but the mouthful of water I'd swallowed was definitely seawater, which meant I was in an ocean. Fog blocked my view beyond just a couple of feet, and the rain blurred my vision. The sun was a barely perceptible ghost, haunting the invisible sky, hidden behind the mask of angry cloud.

The mist began to fade, gradually revealing more of my surroundings. The hazy outline of a distant coast appeared, maybe six or so miles away. Suspended above it, rising high into the troposphere was a tower-like structure.

It was *huge*. Just how huge, I couldn't tell because its upper section was hidden by the cloud. But, like the stem of a wine-glass, the tower tapered downward, narrowing as it drew closer to the ground. It was too far away for me to be able to make out much detail besides its immensity, but the way the light reflected off its surface suggested the tower was constructed of flat planes, placed together at differing angles, like the facets of a diamond.

I stared open-mouthed at the unbelievable monolith for more time than I can remember while my brain tried to process it, all thought of my predicament temporarily gone from my head. But then reality came crashing back again as I realized I had been deposited so far from the shore of that distant coast there was little chance I would be able to swim to it. I simply wasn't strong enough to make it that far. I rotated slowly, shivering as the chilly water finally made itself known.

"Yes!" I hissed. An island sat about fifty feet away, its beach covered in white shale and gray-and-black pebbles. Beyond the beach, a swath of tall grass swayed in the breeze. And then a line of trees that could be palm or maybe coconut reached skyward before the craggy outline of a mountain jutted high into the air, dominating the island, its pinnacle hidden within the thick gray clouds that owned the sky.

A shrill cry of panic drew my attention back to the ocean. *There*! I saw the face of a young Asian woman about thirty feet to my left, her long black hair streaming all around her head just before she vanished beneath the surface. She popped up a second or two later, spluttering and spitting water. She yelled something in a language I didn't understand before sinking again.

This time she didn't resurface.

I swam quickly to her, and dived down, searching blindly, the water so murky I could barely see any further than my hands. I pulled myself deeper into the darkness, feeling for the woman. *Nothing*. With a kick, I propelled myself to the surface, sucked in air, and dove again... but the woman was gone.

By the time I surfaced for a third time, the fog had almost

completely dissipated except for a few wisps, allowing me to see that I was not alone. There were *more* people in the water, many more, some splashing frantically, others treading water like me. Still others swam for the island. There had to be at least a hundred or more, stretched out in an arc that roughly followed the contour of the beach, as though we had all been deposited into the ocean in a neat line. Objects floated around them; baskets, hats, bits of wood, other things that were nothing more than indistinct blobs to my irritated eyes. I spotted a couple of horses heading for the safety of the island, one with a rider still seated in the saddle, another, riderless and panicked, foam bubbling from its nostrils and mouth as it fought its way up onto the beach and stood there, panting. I caught movement near where the riderless horse stood nervously pawing at the ground. The horse spotted it too, squealed in terror and galloped away in the opposite direction.

I gasped in astonishment as a figure, nine feet tall, humanoid in shape but definitely *not* human, rose up from the beach, sand and stones falling from its body, and strode down the beach toward the shoreline.

It was a machine, I realized as it got closer to the water... a *freaking robot*!

Two small electric-blue eyes sat on either side of a narrow, concave bar that floated unattached to the bump that was its head. A **V**-shaped torso tapered down to hips protruding almost as far from its body as its broad shoulders. A black triangular latticework or grill sat in the middle of the machine's protruding convex chest. Two arms, made up of multiple flat oblong-shaped segments, swung at the machine's side, each segment hinged in some unseen way to the next. Its legs were human-like, long with muscular metal thighs and calves, the illusion of humanity only ruined when I saw the robot's feet; they were claw-like and articulated with six-joints on each of the three elongated 'toes.'

A single, fourth spur jutted backward from each heel, kicking up gouts of shale with each step as the robot moved closer. Its body was either painted gold or was actually *made* of gold.

The golden robot reached the shoreline but did not stop; striding into the water, never faltering for a moment as it continued toward me, a wake trailing behind as its massive body pushed through the water to where I bobbed helplessly. Only as it drew closer to me did I realize it was speaking, repeating the same words over and over again like a stuck record: "*Welcome, children of Earth. Do not be afraid... Welcome, children of Earth. Do not be afraid...*"

Less than five feet separated us by the time the robot drew parallel to where I floated, gaping in shock and amazement and fear at this impossible creature.

"*Welcome children of Earth. Do not be afraid,*" it repeated, its eye-bar shifting left and right before facing forward again as it pushed further and further out. It vanished beneath the surface with only a ripple and a few bubbles to mark that it had ever been there at all.

As if a hidden switch had been thrown, the people still floating all around me simultaneously began screaming, their words and pleas merging into one incomprehensible voice. Exertion, shock, and the cold water had begun taking their toll. My muscles were starting to stiffen. If I didn't try to get to the beach now, the chances were good that I'd end up like the unfortunate woman I'd tried to save.

I struck out for the beach, trying to conserve my dwindling energy. Others did the same, and by the time I pulled myself up onto the stony shore, shivering with the cold, arm and leg muscles spasming, twelve people had made it there before me. Eight men, the rest women, all with the same wide-eyed look of confusion in their eyes. One woman looked as though she'd stepped out of an eighteenth-century period drama, her long dress clinging to her body. Her auburn hair had been tied back in a bow, but it had come half-undone and flopped over her face. Another, a man this time, was dressed in robes, or maybe it was a toga. Another wore an expensive looking suit, and another some kind of military uniform. Others looked to be dressed in similar attire to my sweat-shirt and jeans, but there was something about the style that seemed dated to me, though I couldn't put my finger on exactly why.

While I lay there catching my breath, shivering hard now from the cold, two of the men I'd seen pull themselves from the water—and who I assumed must know each other—grabbed the woman dressed in the eighteenth-century attire and dragged her screaming up the beach toward the forest. Another man scrambled after them, yelling in a language I didn't know. They disappeared into the trees before I could even find the energy to push myself to my knees.

Behind me, the others still struggled to make it to the island. Allowing myself ten seconds to gather my wits and energy, I forced myself to my feet and waded out into the surf.

Grabbing anyone I could find, I helped as many as I could ashore, depositing them one-by-one on the beach where they collapsed, feeble as half-drowned kittens. Some looked at me with obvious terror in their eyes but were too weak to resist my help, and I wasn't in the mood to take no for an answer. Others seemed grateful; obvious words of thanks spilling from their water-wrinkled lips. I thought I caught what could have been a couple of words in French mixed with a recognizable word or three of Spanish or Italian. But for the most part, their speech was unintelligible to me.

Then someone *did* yell in English.

To my right, about a hundred feet away, I spotted a small head bobbing in the water, raised hands waving in an attempt to catch someone, *anyone's* attention. It was a young boy, twenty feet offshore and he was being dragged further out to sea.

Riptide.

Instead of allowing the riptide to carry him along until it dissipated, the boy was fighting it; trying to swim directly to shore. That was a sure way to quickly exhaust yourself and drown. A surge of adrenaline pumped through me, and I stumbled down the beach, pebbles crunching beneath my sneakers until I was parallel to him. I considered dumping my clothes but thought better of it. I waded out as far as I could, hoping I could simply grab his hand and pull him to shore, but by the time I got close enough, the boy floated face down in the water, ten feet still separating us.

The riptide tugged greedily at my legs. Instead of resisting, I allowed it to take me, relaxing as it pulled me out until I was parallel to the boy. Once within arm's reach, I grabbed his still body by the collar of his jacket and flipped him over while I trod water.

He was no older than ten I guessed. I pulled him close and leaned in until my ear was against his lips; he was unconscious but still breathing, thank God. I maneuvered myself behind him, rolled onto my back, slipped my hand beneath his chin to keep his head above water and allowed the riptide to carry us further out. Eventually, I felt the grip of the riptide slacken, and I began to backstroke the two of us toward land.

My feet touched the shoal of the beach, and I heaved myself and the boy up into the surf as far as my weakened body was able. I collapsed, unable to move another inch as waves lapped at my elbows, lifting me gently from the ground then depositing me back down again. I flopped back, gasping like a fish, staring up at the leaden sky, my vision darkening as exhaustion overcame me. Muscles cramping, I closed my eyes and tried, again, to regulate my breathing, but my mind was racing uncontrollably as it tried to process the impossibility of everything that'd happened.

I heard footsteps crunching across the beach toward me. I opened my eyes and tried to push myself upright, but for the second time that day, my muscles refused to obey, and I simply lay there, unable to do a thing. My eyes closed again.

The footsteps stopped near my head.

My eyes fluttered open, and I found myself looking into the face of the most beautiful woman I have ever seen.

"Are you an angel?" I croaked, pain gripping me, squeezing me like an iron fist.

The angel looked down at me quizzically, her head canted to one side, her eyes narrowed while she processed what I'd just said. Then she laughed, a bubbly melodic laugh, and said something in a language that my addled mind could almost understand; words that were almost, but not quite, English. Her voice was sweet, intoxicating, like wine.

"Okay," I said, "sounds good." Then I closed my eyes again and slipped away into blissful unconsciousness.

PART TWO

CHILDREN OF EARTH

THREE

WHEN I CAME to my senses, it was to the stinging smell of woodsmoke in my nostrils, the thrum of rain against leaves overhead... and darkness; a darkness only held at bay by a campfire that crackled and flared brightly a few feet from where I lay. The air was thick with moisture and the dank smell of rotting vegetation. My mind was a blur of incoherent thoughts. The last thing I remembered was... Oscar? No, that wasn't right. I was on a bridge... there was... a voice...?

It all came roaring back to me: the double-barreled blast of soul-destroying news; the pall of depression that had possessed me; the bridge; the voice; falling; and then the events on the beach. The memories returned one after the other, each one like a punch to my gut.

I had *no* idea where I was or how I'd gotten to this forest. I knew I hadn't lit the fire, which meant someone else must have. With that in mind, I forced myself to remain absolutely still and allowed my mind to work backward over my recollection of the events, trying to decide whether what I *thought* I remembered was what had *actually* taken place, or whether it was all just some kind of an awful dream. It *had* to have happened, I decided. It was all just too real.

I allowed my eyes to move slowly to the left then right, trying as surreptitiously as I could to get a better look at my surroundings. Whoever had made the fire knew what they were doing. A ring of large stones had been arranged in a rough circle, the branches and twigs used as fuel formed into a pyramid, tee-pee-like. The flames created a halo of orange illumination for about four feet around the fire before the absolute darkness beyond stopped it.

The ground was littered with twigs and bushes and a layer of wet leaves in various states of decay, and the trunks of several large trees were just visible within the perimeter of light, the largest one just a few feet away. Whoever had built the fire had managed to find a spot beneath its heavy boughs, the sprawling limbs giving enough protection that the rain I heard smacking above was funneled off to the left and the right, leaving the area around the fire quite dry.

Directly across from where I lay, on the opposite side of the fire, I saw the woman I had thought was an angel. She sat on a short rotting tree trunk, leaning forward, elbows placed against the top of her knees, the palms of her hands supporting her chin, her fingers pressed against the light brown skin of her cheeks. I thought she was looking at me, but after a few seconds had passed, I realized she was staring deep into the flames of the fire, lost in her own thoughts.

To the right of the angel was the young boy I'd pulled from the water. He sat cross-legged on the ground, his back against the dead tree trunk, also gazing into the fire. He had something in his hands that glinted in the light of the fire. They clinked together with a glass-against-glass sound as he absentmindedly transferred them from one hand to the other.

Near my feet, stretched out on his back next to the kid lay

the body of a man who was either unconscious, asleep... or dead. That question was answered a few seconds later when he exhaled a deep groan of pain and grasped at his right arm resting across his chest. The arm was wrapped in a crude sling. He struggled to sit up and failed, then tried again, moaning loudly. With his good arm, he reached for a wide piece of torn material on his forehead. His pale face illuminated by the flames, I saw he had a nasty-looking ragged gash about five-inches-long running from just above his left eye, over his temple, stopping just below his hairline. Flakey, dried blood had caked around the wound, and a scab had already formed.

The angel jumped to her feet and moved to the man's side. She was tall, around six feet. She wore a white blouse and matching skintight pants that accentuated her athletic figure but looked impossibly clean given we were in a rain-soaked forest. A voluminous cloak of the same white material reached down to just below the top of a pair of knee-high black boots. The inner lining of her cloak scintillated like Mother-of-Pearl in the fire-light. The hood of the cloak was pulled down, revealing the long thick black braids of her shoulder-length hair and the finely cut features of her face, her mocha skin contrasting perfectly with the pure white clothing. High cheekbones, full lips, an aquiline nose, and a slim jawline gave her face a proud yet gentle look. But it was her eyes that truly held me: large and expressive, they seemed to glow with a deep ice-blue in the light of the fire. Thin purple strokes of what could be makeup but might just as easily be tattoos below and above each of her eyes only served to emphasize their intensity. She moved with an assuredness and grace, like a ballerina floating across a stage. She was, as I might have mentioned, the most stunningly beautiful woman I have ever seen in my life.

The angel dropped to her knees beside the restless man, clasped his shoulders in her hands and gently eased him back down to the leafy ground. She murmured something to him I couldn't hear, then picked up the makeshift-bandage he'd removed from his forehead. She dipped the bandage into what looked like a large clamshell filled with water, twisted it to wring it out, and placed the bandage back over the man's head-wound. Her patient groaned then slipped back into unconsciousness, his chest rising and falling rapidly for several seconds before returning to a more natural rhythm. The angel hovered over the man until she seemed sure he wouldn't try to sit up again, then pushed herself to her feet... and noticed me watching her.

The angel smiled and said something in the same beautiful language she had spoken on the beach. I still had no idea *what* language it was; couldn't even take a guess at her accent, but that was okay because the tone of her voice conveyed her concern for me.

I smiled weakly back at her and tried to sit up.

Major mistake, and one I instantly regretted as my brain felt like it was being bounced around the inside of my skull. My vision swam violently, and I felt myself sway, as my sight grew misty. Muscles cramped like I'd just finished a five-hour workout, every joint throbbed. A headache pounded above my right eye, probably from dehydration judging by my chapped lips and swollen tongue. My stomach felt twisted and overflowing with nothing but bile. Above all of that, prowling through the hinterlands of my nervous system was the ravenous beast of my opioid withdrawal. It clawed at my mind and insides. Every cell of my body felt like it was alternately on fire or frozen. Every nerve-ending vibrated agonizingly. My body itched as though it was crawling with ants. A greasy sweat peppered my skin, and my mouth was as dry and rough as a sheet of sandpaper.

I need a fix, right now, the beast screamed at me, demanding I give it what it desired.

I'm ashamed to say that, at that moment, if I had been given the choice of saving the people collected around the campfire or downing a single pill of Oxy, I would have swallowed the pill in a heartbeat, never giving a thought to the well-being of my three companions. Shit, I would have sold my own soul for half a Percocet.

Now, please, don't make the mistake of thinking I enjoyed being an addict. No, that would be the furthest thing from the truth. After the accident, I never *asked* for the pills. Was never warned of just how addictive they were. Jesus, until the crash that sent my life careening down this detour I'd never even tried marijuana. Before all of this, I'd known *exactly* where my life was going, had it all mapped out; I would graduate from law school, pass the California Bar Exam, get picked up by some big law firm, and work my way up the ranks. After five years or so, maybe I'd dip my toes into the political waters. If nothing got bit off, I'd aim for the DA's office. Maybe higher.

This junkie version of me was something I had not planned on or for. It had been *inflicted* on *me*.

I turned on my side and vomited nothing but bile toward the fire. A few seconds later, I threw up again, which made the throbbing behind my eyes even worse. When I was done, I rolled over onto my back, gasping from the ferocity of the pain.

The kid got to his feet, a grossed-out grimace on his young face, and I felt a moment of shame at him seeing me this way. Even through the haze of pain and self-loathing, I registered that the boy was dressed in what I thought was a school uniform: gray pants, a light blue shirt made of some rough looking material, and a black, threadbare blazer. He was a skinny little thing; narrow faced, unruly brown hair, a larger-than-average nose, and hazel eyes.

"Is she alright?" the kid said, with a very British accent. I could still hear the quiet *click-clack* of whatever it was he was holding as he moved them from hand-to-hand.

The angel was halfway to where I lay squirming on the ground, she looked back over her shoulder at the kid, flashed him a smile and said something that sounded reassuring. The kid sat back down as though he'd understood her, but continued to stare at me with wide eyes, worry lines creasing his pale forehead.

Then the angel was kneeling next to me. This close to her, I could see just how perfect her features were. Most everyone I've met has some kind of blemish or scar or out of place feature when you get close enough to them, but there wasn't a single mark on her skin. She picked up something from the ground near the roots of the tree we sheltered beneath. It was another shell that she had placed close enough to the tree to collect rainwater running off the bark. She leaned in close, gently placed a hand behind my neck, and raised my head, bringing the makeshift-cup to my mouth.

The water was cold and tasted slightly woody as it spilled over my lips, dripping onto the front of my sweatshirt. I drank deeply, gulping the liquid down. My throat unclenched, and I pulled my lips away momentarily to whisper a 'thank you' to the angel. She smiled, nodded, and lifted the cup back to my mouth. When I was finished, the angel lowered my head just as gently back to the leaf-covered ground. I felt better, enough that I tried to sit up again, slowly this time. The angel took both of my hands in hers to help me, easing me to a sitting position.

I grimaced in pain as my guts suddenly twisted, cramping violently as the beast gnawed and gnawed and gnawed away at my insides. I flopped back down again, trying hard not to throw up. The angel's forehead creased in concern and she reached out and took my hand in one of hers, squeezing it gently while whispering what could only be words of comfort.

I tried to relax, to focus on the angel's touch rather than the waves of pain. Eventually, as the pain eased, my eyes drifted away from her, to the thick trunk of the tree we sheltered beneath. The light from the fire illuminated enough of the trunk I could make out the lowest branches, about eight feet or so above the ground. Miniature rivers and tributaries of rainwater ran down the bark. The *pitter, patter, pitter* of random drops hitting the canopy was soothing, and I felt my anxiety begin to subside a little.

My eyes swam in and out of focus before fixing on something... well, I wasn't quite sure what it was I was looking at. Two pinprick green dots of light glowed on the tree trunk, midway between the lowest branch and the one just above it, burning like tiny jade fires. I blinked a couple of times, not sure if what I was seeing was real or if maybe it was light from the campfire reflecting off rainwater as it ran down the trunk. I continued to watch, trying to focus my eyes on the lights. The two jade dots looked strangely out of place against the sinister backdrop of trees and darkness, sitting just within the penumbra of illumination cast by the fire, and I was sure they had not been there moments earlier... but the way my head was pounding and my sight fading in and out, I couldn't be certain they hadn't been there all along.

My heart jumped as, without warning, the lights moved. Just a couple of inches first, then after a few seconds, with a rapid spurt of movement, traveling down to the leaf-choked twist of roots at the base of the tree. They leaped the final foot or so onto the forest floor, vanishing momentarily into the detritus of leaves, before popping up again and moving quickly toward the dead log the angel had been sitting on. The lights disappeared behind the log. Both the boy and the angel were focused on me, so neither noticed the two little lights.

I tried to say something, but my tongue was stuck to the roof of my mouth, all my saliva having dried up. I chided myself to focus, but my mind was just too foggy, as another wave of nausea knotted my stomach. I managed to tilt my body on its side, so I wouldn't choke, and heaved up most of the water the angel had just fed me. Rolling over, I saw the jade eyes (that was what I was convinced these things were now, eyes) reappear on the top of the dead log. They began to move slowly toward where the boy stood watching me. The eyes came to an abrupt stop. And as they did, I got an immediate and unshakable feeling that behind those two jade sparks, someone or something was watching us intently, surveying our little camp. Then the eyes were off again at twice their previous speed, leaping from the end of the log down to the forest floor, heading directly for the boy's feet.

I managed to raise my hand from the floor and weakly point a limp finger in the direction of the eyes. "Look... out..." I mumbled.

Both the boy and the angel followed the direction my finger pointed. The boy's mouth began to open in a yell of surprise as he saw the lights just a few inches from the heel of his shoe. He took a step away, but before his foot could even leave the ground, the angel was beside him, traveling the six or seven feet so quickly she became a blur. She swept him up with one arm while simultaneously reaching for something on the ground with the other. I had a moment to see the thick branch in her hand as she raised it over her head and smashed it down onto the two glowing eyes.

There was a popping sound followed by a hiss, and then the two lights flickered, dimmed and vanished.

Immediately, I began to question what I had just witnessed, because this woman I had thought of as an angel had crossed the space to the boy, grabbed him and the makeshift club, and dispatched whatever the eyes belonged to in what seemed like only a second. No one should be able to move that fast.

It must be me, my inner voice whispered, *I'm not well.* It really shouldn't come as a surprise that I'd be seeing things weirdly. Still...

The angel swung the boy to her left side, carrying him on her hip as though he were a toddler, before lowering him to the ground. The boy's mouth hung wide open, either from fear or from awe at the way the angel had just dealt with whatever those eyes belonged to. This last choice seemed most likely given the look of admiration on his face, his eyes following the angel as she moved closer to where she had dealt her killing blow to the jade-eyed *thing*.

The angel dropped to her knees, prodded with her club at something I couldn't see in the carpet of leaves. She reached down and picked that same something up with the thumb and forefinger of her left hand, raised it to eye level and examined it closely for a few seconds, twisting whatever it was back and forth before finally dropping it into the palm of her other hand. She stepped closer to the fire to get a better view of what looked, to my strained eyes, like a shapeless lump lying on her hand.

"Can I see?" the boy said, stepping in closer to her... and let out a little gasp of astonishment. "What *is* it?" he whispered.

The angel's eyes left the crushed object in her hand to look at the boy. She flashed him her dazzling, reassuring smile but didn't say anything, just shook her head in what was an obvious gesture to convey *I have no idea*. She continued her examination for a few more seconds before coming around the fire to where I lay, followed closely by the boy. The angel lowered herself to the ground near my head and sat cross-legged. Slowly, she extended her open hand to me until it was a few inches from my eyes. Then she tilted her head inquisitively as if to say to me, *You got any idea what this is?*

I blinked several times in succession to try and clear the thin layer of mist blurring my vision. It didn't help, so I reached out and pulled her hand closer, bringing it into focus. Now it was my turn to gasp. Resting in her upturned hand was what looked like a large bug—a stag beetle is the name that came to mind. It was about seven inches long, completely black, with six articulated legs, two of which still moved weakly, pedaling through the air in slow circles. The legs were attached to a carapace that was split in two, two delicate-looking wings lay just beneath the chitin covering. Two large compound-eyes sat on either side of a broad flat head from which extended a dangerous looking set of pincers that resembled the horns of a deer. It looked like any other bug for the most part. Except for the inch-long crack along the belly of the carapace. Instead of spilled goo and insect-guts, I saw tiny gears and pulleys and levers, all working in perfect synchrony, moving the two still functioning legs.

It was a *machine*!

A nightmare of a thought suddenly elbowed its way through my pain to the front of my befuddled mind; what if *we* were machines? What if whoever the voice on the bridge had belonged to had taken my soul, my essence, whatever you want to call it that makes me *me* and placed it in a new body, a mechanical body? Like the suicidal robot I'd seen on the beach. What if all *my* guts and innards had been replaced by cogs and wheels and pulleys and God-knows-what-else. I felt hot tears begin to roll down my cheeks as panic swept over me. My sudden emotional turn seemed to surprise the angel. She pulled her hand, and the mechanical beast it held away from me, moving it out sight as though that was the cause of my tears.

I realized she must think the dead robo-bug had scared me. But there was still enough of my brain functioning that I had already figured my panic was nothing more than the far-fetched imaginings of a paranoid brain and a body suffering through withdrawal. The unconscious man lying just a few feet away pretty much disproved my theory that we were anything other than human. The gash across his skull bled what was obviously real blood. Which meant he was human. And if some evil genius had decided to place my mind in an android's body then why leave me with all this pain? Why not just give us new, perfectly functional robot-bodies, instead? No, this was definitely the same body I had before the voice had saved me from my own stupid half-hearted attempt at suicide.

I started to try to explain my idea to the angel and the boy, but before I could muster the strength to get the words out, the night sky exploded.

FOUR

ALL HEADS SWIVELED SIMULTANEOUSLY toward the forest's canopy. Bursts of red, green, blue, yellow, and every color in between cascaded through gaps in the branches above us. Flashes of color streaked across the sky, saturating everything in a kaleidoscope of shimmering hues, illuminating the heavens like the Aurora Borealis on steroids. It was a beautiful but disturbing light-show that gave no hint or clue as to what could be causing it. I saw from the confused expression on the angel's face that she was as surprised as I was. The boy, on the other hand, seemed absolutely ecstatic at the incredible aerial show. He stood, face turned skyward, wide-eyed, mouth fixed in an 'o,' staring at the shimmering ribbons of color.

The aurora sliced through the darkness around us, pushing it away, painting everything with a surreal blast of color.

I noticed something even more curious floating through the air all around us; tiny motes of what I assumed to be dust. Not much bigger than a pinhead, these tiny particles glowed and pulsed with a small but intense white light of their own as they swirled slowly through the air.

If you've ever shaken a snow globe and watched the imitation snow swirl, it looked just like that. If the aurora hadn't revealed them, I doubt any of us would ever have known they were there.

I inhaled a deep breath of air... and tightly shut my mouth again as I sucked several of the glowing particles into my mouth. A moment of fear followed as I wondered whether they might be dangerous before I realized that we must have been inhaling them from the second we arrived here. Certainly from the time the angel and the boy had brought me into the forest. It was, I reasoned, probably just some kind of particulate matter from the layer of rotting leaves and vegetation that was reflecting the light from the aurora somehow. But whatever these tiny motes of lights were, they were everywhere. The entire forest, for as far as I could see, glowed with their otherworldly presence. Even the branches and trunks of the trees were outlined by this weird glowing pixie dust. It lay in a thin layer all over the ground, too; a sparkling carpet of tiny white lights.

The boy shifted his feet as he moved to get a better look at the aurora, kicking a puff of the pixie dust into the air. He didn't seem to have noticed its presence yet, his attention focused entirely on the small gap of sky visible through the forest's canopy.

The angel, on the other hand, definitely saw them. She followed a single glowing mote as it traveled across the space between us. She raised one eyebrow when she saw me watching her watching it as if to say, 'Well, this is weird.' I was in the process of shrugging back my amazement in answer to her when a violent boom shattered the silence of the forest, shaking the ground and sending leaves spinning from their branches. I jumped in surprise. The boy yelped in shock, and the angel took a step backward, shaking her head as though she'd been slapped. At the same time, the aurora grew momentarily more intense, and I felt the strangest sensation pass through my body. It was like a low-voltage electric shock, mildly discomforting but not painful. It lasted for only a few seconds, but every muscle in my body jerked in response. I suddenly felt very warm, as though I'd developed a low-grade fever. Raising my hands to eye-level; I saw they were flushed red. Sweat popped on my forehead, my arms, my legs, and my breathing became very rapid as I gulped in huge lungfuls of air.

And then it was over as abruptly as it had started, melting away as though whatever God ruled this place had thrown its off switch.

Darkness hemmed in our little camp once more, held back only by the light of the campfire. The pixie dust continued to glow for a little longer before it too faded away, disappearing as though it had never been there, even though I knew it still must be, floating invisibly through the air.

The three of us remained silent and motionless for several long heartbeats. I think we all half-expected the sky to ignite again, but it didn't. And as the shock of what had just happened began to fade, I realized the pain that had permeated my body was also gone, vanished, as though it had never been there.

I sat up, slowly.

There was none of the vertigo I'd experienced just a few minutes before the aurora. In fact, apart from a stomach that felt as empty as I knew it was, I felt... fine. *Better* than fine. I was... invigorated. Not even a creaky muscle from lying on the damp ground for so long. Tentatively, I got to my feet and stretched. Gone were the muscle aches and cramps. Gone was the sense of alternately being on fire and encased in ice. Gone was the knife-wielding headache, the nausea, the sweating. I took a few steps. The limp I'd had since the car crash, *that* was gone too. It was... miraculous and terrifying at the same time.

"Wow!" I said, quietly. "Wow!"

At the sound of my voice, the angel turned and looked at

me, smiled, then said in perfect English, "Well, you're certainly looking better."

I blinked three times in quick succession.

The little boy stared, too. "I can understand you," he said, matter-of-factly to the angel.

The angel froze mid-step. She turned to the boy, turned back to me. "And, apparently, I can understand you, too," she said, enunciating each word slowly as though she was double-checking each of them as they left her lips.

We stared wide-eyed at each other.

"This is very... peculiar," the angel said. "Until this moment, I have been unable to understand anything you have said. I recognize that your language is an old one, but there appears—"

Before I could ask what exactly she meant by 'old,' we were interrupted by the injured man who had been lying unconscious next to the fire.

He sat up, slowly shaking his head from side to side, as if waking from a deep sleep. The blood-stained bandage fell from his head into his lap.

I gasped: the ugly gash across his forehead I'd seen just minutes earlier had vanished, replaced by a thin line of fresh, pink skin where the wound had been.

The man blinked several times, squinted at each of us in turn, and said in a thick Midwest American accent, "Where the hell am I? And who in God's name are you people?"

FIVE

WE STOOD ROOTED to the spot; four strangers stunned into silence, the only sound the constant hiss of rain, each of us expecting—*hoping*—for the other to say something, *anything*.

When no one did, I spoke up.

"My name is Meredith Gale," I told the man, "and these others are... well, you know, we haven't actually been introduced." I looked at the angel, raised my eyebrows questioningly.

The woman stared back at me, an odd expression on her face. It wasn't so much a look of surprise, more like she recognized something when I told them my name.

"What?" I asked after a few seconds of her staring at me.

It took a couple more seconds before the angel answered me. As if she was carefully weighing her reply, she said, "My name is Weston Chou. I am—or rather, I *was*—the *Security and Research Officer* for the exploratory vessel *Shining Way*." While her words were obviously English, Chou's accent was still exotic and unrecognizable to me.

'Security and Research Officer' seemed like a particularly contrary mix for a job title, especially for someone who I assumed worked on some kind of a privately funded ocean-going research vessel. Or maybe she was part of a foreign navy, which would explain the strange accent. I didn't mention any of this; my mind already had enough to think about, and I was trying to remain as present as I could, considering the utter weirdness of what had just happened.

The angel, or rather the woman who now said her name was Weston Chou looked to the boy. "And you, little one, what is your name?"

"I'm Albert," the kid stuttered, "Albert Edward Glanville." Then after a short pause, he added, "Schoolboy." Albert nervously shifted the small objects he held from hand to hand, and now I saw they were glass marbles. He noticed me looking at them and held them out for me to inspect. They were larger than the ones I vaguely remembered owning as a child and quite lovely.

"They're beautiful," I said.

"You can have one if you like," Albert said, sheepishly, holding all six on the palm of his extended hand.

"No, it's okay, you keep them safe." I tried not to smile but couldn't help myself. The kid was just too cute. Between his obvious wide-eyed admiration of Chou and his English accent, well, he was just adorable.

The man nodded each time we identified ourselves, and when we were done, he stood there as if assessing us. "Okay, well that's good. Now what I want—"

"And your name?" Chou interjected.

The man looked taken aback. "It's Phillip. Phillip Yeoman. Where the hell am I?"

Chou said, "When we found you on the beach, you were unconscious. You had a broken arm and a head laceration, possibly some internal injuries. Albert and I did what we could to stabilize you. Moments ago there was an... event. That event appears to have healed your injuries."

Phillip chewed his bottom lip. "Beach? I don't remember any beach. I don't remember anything at all after—" He stopped talking as though he had been on the verge of giving away some personal secret.

"When we arrived," I said, "I saw stuff falling out of the sky around all the other people in the water. I think parts of the bridge I was on arrived here with me. Maybe you were hit by something heavy that came through with you. It'd explain the broken arm and head wound."

"There are others?" Phillip said.

"Yes," said Chou. "I estimate there were at least two-hundred others in the water upon our arrival."

"Well, where are they now?" Phillip demanded.

I said, "They all panicked and ran away into the forest. It was pandemonium for a while."

Phillip turned slowly, looking out into the darkness as if he expected to see some visual clue to where he... where *we*... were. "There's no shelter nearby? No town? A village maybe? Nothing to tell us where we are?" he said. I presumed he was talking to us because he didn't bother to turn and speak to us directly.

Chou smiled. "There was no time to inspect the area."

"Well, don't you think it would be a good idea if we looked for some shelter? We could be close to a town and not even know it," he said, looking back over his shoulder at us. "And I'd prefer not to spend the rest of my night out here."

"Without some form of portable illumination," Chou said, her voice low, "anyone foolish enough to venture further into the woods will quickly become lost. And it was obvious when I carried you here from the beach that there is no shelter other than the trees within the immediate vicinity."

Phillip turned to face Chou. "*You* carried *me*?" he said, condescendingly. "Look, lady, I'm thankful for your help, but I hardly think you're capable of carrying someone my size more than a few feet."

I have to admit, I found the idea a little farfetched too, at that point. Phillip was easily one-hundred-and-eighty pounds, maybe more. Chou was tall and obviously fit but couldn't have weighed more than one-twenty. No way was she going to be able to carry a full-grown man too far.

"She did," the boy, Albert, said. "I saw her pick you and Meredith up and carry you both here."

Phillip didn't look convinced. He stared at Chou for a few long moments.

Chou held his stare. She threw more twigs into the fire. It crackled and bloomed, sending sparks floating high into the canopy, reminding me of the pixie dust I'd seen earlier.

"Did you see the tiny lights during the..." I searched for the right word to describe the light show that had swept over us only minutes earlier, "...aurora?"

"I saw them," Albert said excitedly. "They looked like tiny stars floating through the air."

"Huh?" said Phillip. "Aurora? What lights?"

"You were still unconscious when it happened," I said, and quickly explained what had occurred while he lay senseless, adding, "and when it was done, that's when you woke up. Your head wound had vanished, and it looks like your broken arm has healed too. And I... well, let's just say that I feel a lot better than I did when I arrived here."

Albert said, "And we can understand each other now, as well."

Phillip looked at the boy. "So, you're saying that before this... aurora happened, none of you could understand each other?"

"Well, Albert and I could understand each other, but we

couldn't understand Chou, and she couldn't understand us," I said.

Phillip eyeballed me with such incredulity I wanted to punch him. "It's true," I said.

"Well, I certainly don't intend to wait around here all night," Phillip said eventually, his gaze moving over the darkened canopy of the forest. "Can't even see the damn stars from here." He turned back to Chou. "Which way is the beach?"

Chou pointed to her left. "That way. But if you're thinking of leaving, I would advise you wait until the morning. We have no idea where we are or what's in these woods."

Phillip shook his head. "Well, as I said, lady, I have absolutely no intention of—"

We froze as a sound, half-snarl half-growl, echoed through the forest from somewhere close by.

"Is... is it a wolf?" Albert said, suddenly at my side, his two hands clasped tightly around the fingers of my left hand. I instinctively drew him closer to me.

"Maybe a coyote?" Phillip said quietly, though I knew from the tone of his voice he didn't believe his own words.

Living all my life in California, I'd heard coyotes on an almost nightly basis, and whatever creature that bone-chilling snarl belonged to was most definitely *not* a coyote.

"Probably just an owl or... something," I said, not wanting to scare the boy any more than he already was.

"Shhh!" said Phillip, "listen." He took a quick step back as something large moved through the undergrowth beyond the light of the fire. "Jesus!" Phillip hissed. He stumbled backward, narrowly escaping falling into the fire.

"Quiet, all of you," Chou whispered, staring into the darkness beyond the range of the fire as though she could see whatever was moving there. She picked up the heavy branch she had used to club the mechanical bug with, gripping it firmly in both hands. Not daring to move, we remained where we stood for several minutes, listening helplessly as the thing prowled through the darkness around the perimeter of our camp.

From somewhere even deeper in the inky blackness, the unmistakable sound of a woman's high-pitched scream reached us. It was followed by a man's panicked yell, his words unintelligible.

Our visitor gave a few short snorts that were quickly followed by the sound of it padding away through the underbrush, presumably drawn by the screams.

"It's gone," Chou said with certainty after another minute had passed.

Despite the sureness of her words, I wasn't convinced the thing wouldn't come back and said so.

Chou said, "I will stand watch and keep the fire burning all night. I believe that will keep it at bay. You should rest."

Phillip, his face pale in the orange glow of the fire, turned and said, "I think you have a point about waiting until morning." He grinned sheepishly, and I couldn't help but smile back, relieving some of the fear I still felt.

"You should all try and sleep," Chou announced. "Tomorrow, we should leave as soon as the sun rises. Whatever that creature was might be less fearful of us in the daylight, and we should find more defensible shelter as quickly as possible."

Despite the myriad questions still clamoring for answers in my brain, I knew Chou was right. How we had all arrived here on this island was confusing enough, but the events of the past hour made everything before them pale into insignificance on the Weird-Event-O-Meter in my head. There was no guarantee any of these strangers knew any more about what was going on than I did.

The rush of adrenaline that had saturated my body began to

fade, replaced by a growing exhaustion. I sat down close to the fire and watched my three companions.

Phillip didn't seem like he was likely to slit my throat in the middle of the night, and Chou had been the one who saved all of us. We would all undoubtedly be alone or dead if she hadn't shown up on the beach when she did. And little Albert? Well, he was just a scared kid.

"Come on over here," I said, beckoning Albert. He did as he was asked and sat down beside me. "I won't let anything hurt you," I promised him. He laid down next to me with his back to the fire, one hand cushioned between his head and the now dry leaves surrounding the fire. I did the same, facing him. Over the next few minutes, I watched his eyes gradually close and the slow, intermittent flare of his nostrils as he succumbed to sleep.

Phillip sat with his back against the tree trunk. He pulled his windbreaker tightly around him and closed his eyes. It wasn't long before he too was asleep.

Chou leaned against the log and stared deep into the campfire's flames.

That was the last thing I saw before my eyes closed and I drifted away too.

SIX

I WOKE WITH A START.

Albert still slept beside me, curled up in a tight ball like a kitten. The campfire burned weakly. A dull gray light permeated everywhere. Phillip lay asleep on his side just a few feet away, his back toward us. Chou stood off to the left, her cloak pulled tightly around her shoulders, looking out into the woods.

We'd made it to morning.

The rain had, thankfully, stopped, but the cloud-choked sky, visible through the treetops, was as dull and gray as the insipid light, painful to my eyes.

"Good morning," I said quietly, hoping not to rouse Albert or Phillip.

Chou turned and smiled at me. "Hello. How are you feeling?"

"Good," I said, shooting a weak smile in her direction. I actually felt much better than I had in, well, forever. My mind was surprisingly clear, free of its usual clutter. My muscles felt strong, energized like I'd spent a week on a beach somewhere rather than a few hours of sleep on a damp mattress of rotting leaves in the middle of an unknown forest.

Phillip suddenly sat bolt upright like he'd been pricked with a pin, making me gasp and jump. He looked left then right, as though he had no idea where he was. When he saw me and Chou, he relaxed a little.

"Wasn't sure last night wasn't just a bad dream," he said. He pushed an unruly tongue of hair out of his eyes, scratched his head, then added, "Unfortunately, it wasn't."

I knew exactly what he meant. This was all so... out there. I mean, that didn't even really begin to describe the events of the last twenty-four hours. But maybe today we would get some answers.

Phillip stood, stretched, then began to walk away from the camp.

"Where are you going?" Chou asked.

"I need to take a leak. That okay by you?" he said, before disappearing behind a tree. A cloud of steam appeared a few seconds later, and he exhaled a contented sigh.

"I'm hungry." I turned to see Albert getting to his feet, rubbing the sleep from his eyes.

"Makes two of us," Phillip said, rejoining us, wiping his hands on his windbreaker.

"Here," said Chou. She handed each of us several large pieces of something woody-looking and white. "Coconut," I exclaimed, taking a bite. "Oh my God, it's delicious."

"There's water over there." Chou pointed at the two conch shells full of water resting on top of the dead log.

"Where'd you get this?" Phillip asked, sniffing at the coconut.

Chou nodded back in the direction she had said the beach was.

"You snuck off while we were still asleep?" Phillip said.

"And snuck back. I have enough supplies for us for the next twenty-four-hours if we limit ourselves. There will be little time to waste today. We must find permanent shelter soon. We will not be able to survive long in these woods if the weather turns."

"You mean we need to find a settlement or a village," Phillip continued.

"I do not believe that we will find anything of the sort on this island," Chou said.

"What? Why?" Phillip said between chewing pieces of his coconut.

"A suspicion, at this point," Chou said. "But one which I believe will be proved correct."

"Well, are you going to share?" Phillip said.

"Not yet. When I am certain, I will."

I said, "No matter which of you is right, we can't live on coconut and rainwater forever."

"You are correct," Chou said, "we need to find a water source and food, too."

"I don't expect we're going to find a 7-11 anytime soon," Phillip said gruffly.

"What's a 7-11?" Albert asked.

I looked down at the kid, surprised he'd never heard of the favorite store of pot-heads and road-trippers and weekend drunks of all ages. But then, he was British, so I guess that would explain why. "It's a store... a shop."

Albert nodded as though he understood, but I wasn't really convinced he did.

"Maybe we should head to the mountain?" I suggested, turning my attention back to Chou and Phillip. "If we can get above the forest's canopy, we might be able to see where we are, or maybe we'll spot signs of civilization. We should at least get a better idea of the size of the island."

"I vote we head back to the beach," Phillip said, matter-of-factly. "There will probably be rescue boats or planes or something looking for us."

"I don't think so," Chou said.

"Don't think we'll be rescued or that we should head back to the beach?" Phillip said.

"Both," said Chou. "Meredith's idea is the better one. We do not know where we are or..." she paused as if she had been about to say something then thought better of it. "We should head to the mountain."

I kicked dirt over the fire, extinguishing it.

"Are you ready?" Chou said to Albert, smiling and reaching out a hand for him to take.

The kid nodded enthusiastically and took hold of her hand.

"As I'll ever be," I said.

"Now wait just a damn moment," Phillip blustered.

Chou walked away. "You may do as you wish Phillip Yeoman, but *we* are going this way."

Looking back over my shoulder, I saw Phillip stand his ground for a good ten seconds or so. Then he grumbled something under his breath and jogged after us.

We'd only walked about ten yards from the camp before Phillip stopped abruptly and said, "Holy sh..." He glanced at Albert, finishing his sentence with, "...Shmoly! Would you look at that." He pointed down at the ground in front of him.

A set of tracks, paw prints to be exact, ran in an arc through the wet earth of the forest floor back in the direction of our camp.

"Were those made by our visitor last night?" I said.

"Undoubtedly," said Chou.

I knelt and placed my hand inside one of the prints. It was easily four times the size of my hand and three times as deep. Big *and* heavy. The print showed the outline of four distinct toes, each with a deep indentation at the top of them, presumably from a claw.

"It must be huge? Do you think it was a bear?" I asked.

Chou didn't respond, her head was on a swivel, turning left and right as she scanned the forest looking for any sign of whatever the prints belonged to.

"It'll be a big son-of-a-bitch if it was," Phillip said, his decorum momentarily lost.

Albert pushed closer. "Bears have five toes," he said, "this one only has four."

"Really?" I said.

Albert nodded enthusiastically, then added, "But tigers have four toes and a dew claw, like a dog's, so the tracks might be a from a tiger."

"Oh, that's just great. That's just freaking great." Phillip turned rapidly from left to right, his eyes jumping up and down the trees as if he expected to spot the beast watching us. "So, we're being stalked by a big cat? Freaking wonderful."

"The tracks are heading away from us," Chou said. "I don't think whatever predator these belong to is still in the vicinity, but we shouldn't test my theory. We should continue onward and place as much distance between us as quickly as possible."

"Agreed," Phillip said, for once not looking to argue. He took Albert's hand in his and started off again.

The forest floor was mostly flat, apart from the occasional mound pushed up by the deep roots of the trees. Still, it wasn't exactly easy going, winding our way through the tree trunks and brush, but we made decent time. There was no sign of any of the other humans who had arrived offshore with us. If it hadn't been for the screams last night, I might have begun to doubt I'd seen anyone at all. But the forest *was* alive with life; birds of every size and color, odd-looking rat-like creatures that burrowed deep into the leafy forest floor when they sensed our approach or scampered up the trunks of trees. I even saw what I thought might have been a monkey high up in the branches overhead but it moved so quickly through the upper-canopy of the forest I couldn't be sure.

We'd not taken more than two-dozen steps away from the prints before a large bird with breathtaking plumage exploded from a nearby bush with a clap of frantic wings, sending all of us a foot into the air in surprise.

"Well, that doesn't make any sense," Albert said after he watched the bird fly up into one of the nearby trees.

"What doesn't?" I asked.

"The trees are all wrong," the boy said. "And the animals, too."

Chou stopped and knelt before the boy. "Explain," she said, gently.

"Well, *that's* a California Redwood," Albert said, pointing to a huge tree towering over everything else. He pointed at another growing just ten feet away from it. "And *that's* a Manna Ash." Then he pointed at another tree I'd assumed was just a run-of-the-mill conifer. "That's a Mountain Hemlock. And there were coconut trees on the beach." Albert walked over to a large bush and gently pulled off one of the long tongue-shaped leaves from it and brought it over to us. "And I think this is a Glossopteris."

Phillip sighed, "So? So, what?" He turned to Chou. "Is there a point to this zoology lecture?"

"Dendrology," Albert shot back. "Zoology is the study of animals."

Phillip rolled his eyes and said, "You're making my teeth itch, kid. How the hell do you know all this stuff, anyway?"

Albert smiled broadly, showing all of his less-than-perfectly-straight teeth. "Books," he said. "I like to read."

"Go on," Chou encouraged, a smile forming on her lips; not

condescending, but one a teacher might use when a pupil has finally grasped a concept that had eluded them.

"Well, that bird we saw just now, I think it might have been a Monal, and I definitely saw a Leithia running up a tree."

Chou didn't take her eyes off the boy. "Tell us, why this is important," she whispered.

"Most of these trees, and I don't recognize all of them, they shouldn't be growing together at all, especially not in this climate. They all come from very different ecologies around the world; cold, hot, humid. They shouldn't thrive here, not together."

"At the risk of sounding like I'm repeating myself," said Phillip, "So, what?"

Albert's cheeks grew red at the older man's dismissive tone, but Phillip saw the daggers I was sending him, and some of the condescension evaporated. He wasn't a bad man. He was just a guy who was under a shit-ton of stress and wasn't handling it quite as well as the rest of us.

"Sorry," Phillip said, throwing a pained smile at the boy, and ruffling his hair gently. "Tell us the rest."

"And this," Albert said, holding up the leaf he'd just pulled from the bush, "is a leaf from a Glossopteris."

"Okay," Phillip shrugged.

"It went extinct during the Great Permian Extinction. And the bird we saw, I think it was a Himalayan Monal which lives in Nepal and shouldn't be here."

"And what about that other thing? What did you call it, a Leika?" I asked.

"A Leithia. A giant dormouse; it's extinct, too."

Phillip took a step backward. "So, just let me see if I've got this straight? You're telling me that we're walking in a forest full of impossible trees, filled with bushes and animals that went extinct before man even walked the Earth? Oh, and did I forget to mention the thing that was apparently looking to add us to its meal plan last night?"

"Yes," said Albert, smiling happily.

Phillip gave the boy a confused stare for about three seconds, then shook his head and turned back to Chou. "What if the kid's wrong?" he said.

"He's not," Chou said.

"But what if he is?" Phillip insisted.

"He's not," Chou repeated.

"No sense. This makes absolutely no damn sense at all," Phillip muttered and began walking again.

As the day wore on, the meager afternoon daylight grew even weaker, and it became apparent we would not even reach the foot of the mountain by the time darkness came around again. Although there was no way to accurately measure how far we'd walked or how far we still had left to travel, Albert was convinced we must be getting close.

"The ground's been slowly rising for a while now. It's getting steeper, so we must be close to the mountain."

"We should make camp soon, then," Chou said, "before it gets dark. We will strike out again in the morning."

"No argument from me," I said.

"Or me," said Phillip, and with that, he leaned his back against the trunk of a nearby tree and allowed himself to slide slowly down it until he was in a sitting position. "Wish I had a damn cigarette," he mumbled as he patted the pockets of his jacket. "Damn lighter's vanished, too."

Albert gave a little gasp and reached into his pants' pocket. He pulled out a silver-colored Zippo lighter and held it out to Phillip. "It fell out of your pocket when Chou was carrying you to the forest."

Phillip reached out and took the lighter from the boy's hand.

"Thanks, kid. Don't suppose you have my cigarettes in there, too, by any chance?"

Albert shook his head.

Phillip sighed, then, with practiced ease, began to rapidly flip the lighter's lid open then closed. "Weird thing is, I've smoked since I was fifteen, but today I don't even really want one."

"Those things would have killed you anyway," I said, wondering if his tobacco addiction had been cured just like my pain-killer addiction had.

"Bit late for that, sweetheart," Phillip replied. "Truth is, I think it might be a bit late for all of us."

We gathered dry wood and stacked it at the foot of a tree whose wide branches and dense leaves we would spend the night beneath. It would provide cover if the cloud-packed sky made good on its threat of more rain.

Albert got on his knees and swept away leaves with his hand until he exposed the fertile soil beneath. He quickly gathered together a pile of small pieces of wood and dry leaves, then topped it off with a pyramid of larger twigs. Phillip handed him his Zippo, and the boy used it to ignite the kindling, then blew gently into the kindling, encouraging the flames until they bloomed and ignited the larger sticks.

"You are such a cool kid, Albert," I said.

He looked up at me, confusion on his face. "Now we have the fire none of us will be cold," he said.

I glanced across at Phillip who simply raised his eyebrows quizzically.

"No, I mean you're *cool*... you know, never mind."

Albert went to hand the lighter back to Phillip.

"You know what, Meredith's right," said Phillip, "you are a very cool kid. You keep it."

The little boy beamed as though he had been handed a pound of gold, threw his arms around a surprised Phillip, hugged him then headed over to where he had set aside four long, straight branches. He brought the branches to the base of the tree, sat in the natural pocket made by its roots, and began to carefully examine them.

"You'll poke your eye out with those things if you're not careful," Phillip said, then added, "Hey, where'd you get that from?" when he caught the glint of a small blade, about three inches long in Albert's other hand.

"It's mine," said the boy, as if one of us might try to take it from him.

"Don't worry," I called to him, "it's okay. Just be careful with it."

I followed Albert out of the corner of my eye as he used the knife to strip away the bark from each of the branches, exposing the soft virgin wood beneath. He used the knife to whittle the end of each branch into a sharp point, then, one after the other, he placed the sharpened end into the embers around the edge of the fire.

I observed him in silence, fascinated by what the kid was doing.

"The fire hardens the tip of the spear," Albert said, as he pulled the first branch out of the embers. "See?"

The tip of the branch had turned black. Smoke rose slowly from it into the evening air.

"We'll take your word for it," said Phillip, but I could tell he was impressed by Albert's knowledge. "Where'd you learn to do that, anyway?" he added. "Wait, don't tell me... books."

Albert nodded enthusiastically. "I like to read. Here." He

handed the sharpened branch to Phillip. "It's a spear. We can use it for hunting and spear-fishing."

"That is one hell of a pig-sticker," said Phillip, no longer trying to hide how impressed he was with the kid's handiwork. He flicked the spear's tip with the nail of his thumb and nodded as if it had passed some kind of inspection.

Albert handed Chou and me a spear each.

"Thank you," said Chou. "We do not know what other predators live in these woods. This will offer us a modicum of protection. You have done well, Albert."

Albert glowed at Chou's praise. "I can make bows and arrows, too," he offered, as if it was something he did every day, which, for all I knew, he did. "But that will take a bit longer, and I'll need special materials."

Night had closed in fast while we watched Albert work; shadows crawled almost imperceptibly between the tree trunks until, finally, all that remained visible of the world was contained once again in the protective orange ring of light extending out from the campfire.

"We will need to post guards tonight," said Chou. "I will take the first watch. Phillip, will you take second?"

Phillip nodded, still inspecting the spear—which I think had relieved some of his feelings of vulnerability.

"And you, Meredith, would you take the third watch?" Chou asked.

"Of course," I said. I'm a naturally early riser, so getting up a few hours earlier than normal wouldn't affect my energy much. I mean, I'd barely gotten any rest last night and my energy and focus had been better today than they'd been in years.

We gathered closer to the fire and silently watched the flames for a while. Over the crackle of the burning wood, I heard things moving in the woods: strange animal calls echoing around us, the rustle of leaves and branches in the trees as things crept from limb to limb, the scratch of claws on tree bark.

"I didn't notice how alive the forest was last night," I said.

"Well, we were kind of preoccupied, but it's a whole other world out here," Phillip answered.

I caught Chou's gaze move in Phillip's direction, as if he'd said something deeply profound, but she said nothing, just continued eating the last of her coconut ration.

Phillip must have sensed the weight of her attention too because he said, "So, come on Chou. You've hinted all day that you've got some kind of a theory about all of this. You've obviously been chewing it over since we arrived. You going to share your insights about what the hell you think is going on here?"

Chou looked up slowly, her gaze moving from me to Albert to Phillip. She paused as if she was still considering whether to speak, words poised on her lips, then said, "Tell me, Phillip Yeoman, what language do you speak?"

We all looked at her a little oddly. It was perfectly obvious to the rest of us what language he was speaking.

"English," Phillip said slowly, as though he'd been asked a trick question. "But then I assume you already know that as—"

"And what year were you born?" Chou said, with that same soft tone.

"My birthday? Look, I really don't know what any of these questions have to do with—"

"Please, answer my question," Chou insisted.

Phillip bristled. He outweighed Chou by a good fifty pounds, was in decent shape, and Albert's gift of the spear seemed to have returned some of his earlier arrogance. But there was just *something* about Chou's bearing that screamed that it would be the biggest mistake of his life to screw with her. Phillip must've sensed that too, because he answered her, albeit grudgingly. "October 30th, 1966."

Albert reacted like he'd been slapped hard, his head whipping first to Phillip then back to Chou. And I understood why—or thought I did, at least. Phillip Yeoman looked to be no more than a couple of years older than me. I'm twenty-seven, and there was *no way* he could have been more than thirty-five, tops. And yet I was born on August 7th, 1990. Which meant Phillip was twenty-four years older than me. That put him around fifty-two.

"You've got to be joking," I blurted out, unable to contain my surprise. "Whatever exercise program you're on, you have to let me in on it." I laughed briefly at my sad little joke.

Phillip just looked at me oddly. "What *are* you blathering about?" he said.

Before I could answer, Chou said "And that would make you how old... *precisely*?"

Phillip sighed as though he were answering an imbecile. "I'll be thirty-three this coming October." He must have seen the look of disbelief on my face because he added almost slyly, "Why?"

Chou ignored his question, turning her attention to me. "And you, Meredith; when were you born?"

I gulped, my mouth suddenly dry, then told her my birthdate.

Now it was Phillip's turn to be taken aback. "That's ridiculous," he said, "look at you! You look like you're the same age as me. You should just be a child, younger than Albert even. It'd be impossible for you to—"

Chou cut him off again. "And you, Albert. When were you born?" her voice was now soft, comforting.

We all turned to look at the boy who suddenly seemed very vulnerable and confused under the weight of our combined gazes.

"I don't... I... I," Albert stuttered.

I walked the four steps to his side, sat and placed an arm around his shoulder. I squeezed him gently. "It's okay, kiddo," I said. "Take your time."

Albert drew in a deep breath. "I... I'm twelve years old. I was born on January 5th, 1898."

Phillip jumped to his feet and stared at Albert.

I did the math quickly in my head. That would make him around... one-hundred-nineteen years old. *I've changed my mind*, I thought, *I need whatever diet the kid's on*.

Phillip finally found his voice. "That's just... I mean... no way. Just no way. Is this a joke?" he hissed. He sat back down again and stared into the flames, not pressing for an answer.

"And what about you?" I asked Chou. "When were *you* born?"

Chou turned her ice-blue eyes in my direction. "I was born in March of 2253. When I entered stasis, I was almost one-hundred-and-twenty-two years old."

Phillip's head lifted momentarily from the flames to look at her then drifted slowly back again.

Albert started to quietly cry.

I blinked hard, several times. But you want to hear something weird? I *absolutely, unequivocally* believed her. *Believed* all three of them. Because, unless these people were professional actors, there was no way they could come up with such outrageous fabrications and deliver them so believably. No *damn* way! And when I took into consideration everything else that'd happened since that strange voice had asked if I wanted to be saved, well, there was no doubt in my mind that I had wandered so far off the normal path I'd taken up permanent residence in the Twilight Zone. And *everything* that had happened since the Bay Bridge had begun with that question: *Do you wish to be saved?*

A question of my own burst in my mind like a firework.

"Hey," I said. "Right before we ended up... wherever this place is, did any of you hear a voice? Did it ask you a question?" I couldn't believe I hadn't thought to ask it before.

"How did you know that?" said Phillip.

Chou nodded slowly. "Yes, I did."

Albert said, "A voice asked me if I wanted to live."

I turned to Phillip, trying to frame the question I had in my head as succinctly as possible. "Can you tell me what led up to the voice talking to you?"

For a moment I thought he wasn't going to answer, his gaze already focused deep into the fire again, but he pulled his eyes away and spoke.

"I was on a sabbatical. Truth is, I hadn't been able to write a thing in over a year. So, I decided to leave Los Angeles and head to Argentina for a road-trip. Just something to try and grease the cogs again." He tapped two fingers of his left hand against the side of his temple.

"You're a writer?" I asked.

He nodded. "Author. I left my son in my ex-wife's not-so-capable hands for six weeks, pocketed my passport and hopped on a plane to Bolivia. About a month later, I'd made it to Argentina, and I was heading through the *Los Glaciares National Park*, remotest damn place I've ever seen. Beautiful. Cold. Snow and ice everywhere. I think I hit a patch of black ice, lost control of the rental car, headed off the road and took a nosedive into an ice lake." He paused for several moments as he recalled what happened next. "Everything seemed to... I don't know... slow down, like when you put a video-recorder on slow-mo." Phillip took a deep breath. "Then a voice came over the radio just as the car was about to hit the water. It spoke to me by name. Told me I was about to die. It started to tell me all these things about my life, *personal* things, things no one else could have possibly known about me, not even my family. It said my body would never be found. And then it asked me again if I wanted to live, yes or no? I said 'yes.'" His voice trailed off.

"I'm... sorry," I said, lost for words.

Phillip shrugged. "Don't be. At some point, I'm going to wake up and find out this is all a bad dream. Right?" He gave me a half-hearted smile. "I just hope my boy's okay."

Turning to face Chou, I asked, "What about you, Chou? What's your story?"

"I had been placed in deep suspension onboard the *Shining Way*. Several years into our mission, my husband alerted me that he had detected a catastrophic problem with the ship. He woke me to help assess the situation. There had been some kind of malfunction with the life support system, and it was only a matter of hours before the ship's atmosphere would be exhausted, and I would die. We were still over a million light-years from our destination when the—"

"Wait a second. Wait just a damn second," said Phillip, interrupting her. "Life support? A million light-years? You're telling us you were on a *spaceship*?"

"Have I not made that fact obvious?" Chou asked. "Yes, the *Shining Way* is an interstellar research vessel. Our mission was to reach and study an area of dead space. We would spend an estimated eight years there before returning to Earth with the information we gathered. But I suspect that our mission may have been sabotaged. There were factions back on Earth who did not believe fully in the mission. A failure of our ship's system was close to impossible. Outside interference is the only other possibility. Either way, there was nothing that could be done. I was doomed."

"*You* were doomed?" I said. "But you said your husband was on the *Shining Way* with you, too. What about him?"

Chou's head tilted slightly toward her shoulder, as though I was asking her the strangest of questions. "Ah, of course," she said, "the bonding of human and non-corporeal intelligences is not yet possible, let alone legal, in your times."

"Wait," I said, "you're telling me your husband was... an artificial intelligence?"

"A Non-Corporeal Intelligence," she insisted. "For our mission, my husband was, for all intents and purposes, the *Shining Way*. His personality once merged into the ship's system core would allow him to pilot and control the ship while I, upon reaching our destination, would carry out all of the required scientific experiments."

Everything Chou had just said should be completely unbelievable. And yet, I believed her. And if she really was from three-hundred and fifty years into my future, it also explained why her language had been so utterly unrecognizable to me.

"A few seconds before the atmosphere became unsustainable, my husband asked if I wanted to live. Confused, I said of course I did. My next memory was plunging into the ocean offshore of this island."

Phillip seemed overwhelmed by everything he had just heard. I decided to shift the topic back to him.

"You said you were an author," I said, touching Phillip on the forearm. "Write anything famous?"

Phillip nodded slowly. "I wrote *Last Stand at the Maple Leaf Lodge*." He delivered the line as if that would explain everything I needed to know.

"Don't know it," I said. "Sorry."

"*Really*? You've never heard of it?"

He seemed quite taken aback, bordering on hurt.

"It was on the *New York Times* bestseller list for like twenty months. Have you been living under a stone?"

I know writers have fragile egos, but his reaction seemed a little much. He continued, "They made a movie out of it that won three freaking Oscars. Jeff Daniels played Lazlo. He said it was his defining role. You never heard of it? *Really*?"

"When was the book published?" I asked.

"1994. The movie was released in '96."

I shrugged. "Sorry." And even though it wasn't true, I added, "But then I'm not much of a reader." Still, it did seem weird that the book's title didn't ring any kind of a bell with me. And while I *did* like to read, I *loved* to watch movies, especially old movies from the eighties and nineties, so I was sure I would have remembered *Last Stand at the Maple Leaf Lodge*; especially if it had really won as many Oscars as he said it had.

Phillip turned his head toward me. "What about you? What's your story?"

"Suicide," I said, matter-of-factly. "I got some bad news, and I was dealing with some personal problems, so I decided to jump from the Bay Bridge into the San Francisco Bay."

I welcomed the momentary silence that descended over us. It allowed me a few seconds for all the new information to sink in. Then I said, "So, what seems perfectly obvious to me is that we were moments away from dying when the voice contacted us. What we don't know, is who the voice belongs to and why they chose us."

No one appeared to have an answer to that question, so we retreated into silence. Chou placed a couple of branches into the fire. The wood, still damp from the rain, hissed and spat, but eventually caught and the flames rose higher. The warmth was welcome, comforting.

"I believe," said Chou, eventually, her eyes still staring deep into the flames of the campfire, "that whoever has brought us here did so for a very specific purpose. An intelligence capable of plucking each of us from our own specific time, depositing us together at this same point in time, must have access to incredibly advanced technology. The energy required to move just one person must be incredible, but to move the several hundred I saw arrive on the beach with us would require access to massive stores of energy. And if the people on this island are not the only ones that have been brought here..." She allowed her words to fall away.

I got the impression Chou was talking more to herself than us, and though I had questions, I didn't want to break her train of thought to ask if she'd also seen the distant continent the day we first arrived. Or the huge structure towering over it.

Chou continued. "Energy so immense it could only come from..." Her words faded again as her eyes drifted skyward, they lingered there before returning to the fire.

"But who on earth would be able to do something like that?" I said when I judged she was open to questions.

"Who said anything about the voice being from Earth?" said Phillip. "Maybe it was aliens."

Chou looked at him. "In my time, we have established colonies in many of the nearest star systems, explored even further than that. But we have never encountered or seen any evidence to suggest there is any alien presence elsewhere in our sector of the galaxy. The likelihood of aliens being responsible for this, seems... improbable. Although it cannot be ruled out completely."

"Well, if it's not aliens, then who is it?" Phillip sounded put out that Chou had shot down his idea so quickly.

"I don't know," Chou admitted.

"So, then it could be aliens."

Chou smiled slightly, "Yes, Phillip, I suppose it *could* be aliens."

Her acceptance of the possibility was enough of a victory for Phillip. He quietened and went back to staring into the campfire.

"But why would they bring us *here*? And where on Earth *is* here exactly?" I said.

"How do you know we're on Earth?" Albert said quietly as if the question might get him into trouble.

We all stared at him.

It hadn't even crossed my mind that whatever intelligence had transported us through time might also have the ability to move us through space, too. And judging by the look on Phillip and Chou's faces, neither had they.

"That is a *very* astute observation," said Chou. She flashed him one of her smiles, and he instantly beamed with pride. "And one I should have thought of, considering how far away from Earth I was at the time of my... translocation. You are correct, Albert. Currently, we have no way of ascertaining exactly where we are. The storm and the forest canopy have obscured our view of the sky; hopefully, when we reach the mountain, I will have a clear view of the stars and be able to make a judgment as to our location."

Chou got to her feet and stepped closer to the trunk of the tree we sheltered beneath. She ran her fingers over its crenelated bark.

"Having said that, this tree appears to be an oak. And as you have already pointed out, Albert, the forest is full of trees and animals that originated on Earth. That data alone suggests that we are still on earth."

"But," said Albert, apparently unwilling to let go of his position within the discussion, "couldn't the..." He paused, searching for the right word. "...couldn't the *force* that brought us here also have brought the trees and animals too?"

Phillip nodded, enthusiastically.

Chou remained unconvinced. "Again, the amount of energy required to bring just us here would be—"

"And yet, here we are," I said, interrupting her.

Chou turned to me, the edges of her mouth betraying a slight smile. "Yes, Meredith, here we all are, indeed."

"If our assumptions are correct," Chou continued, "and we were brought here for a reason, I would expect there to be some form of sustenance easily accessible to us. But, I would also have anticipated a more... welcoming arrival. It does not make sense for us to be dropped here with no access to food or water or shelter."

I leaned forward. "But if whoever's controlling all of this really had our best interests at heart, why drop us so far offshore of the island? I saw at least one person drown."

Chou pondered the question. "I do not know," she said eventually. "As I have already stated, I would have expected a more accommodating reception on our arrival. However, I do agree that it does run contrary to the theory that there is a structured plan behind all of this."

Albert spoke up again. This time his voice was quiet, frightened. "Maybe we aren't really alive," he said. "Maybe we are all dead, and this is hell."

"Do you see any demons, kid?" said Phillip, sarcastically.

"Well... well, *maybe* this is purgatory, then. Hot tears began to fall down the kid's cheeks.

I put my arm back around Albert's shoulders and pulled him closer to me again. "It's okay, kid."

Chou continued. "I do not believe that this place is either 'hell' or 'purgatory.' While whatever or whoever is behind these events has what we would conclude to be god-like powers, that does not mean that they are a god. No, I am confident that the explanation for this lies somewhere other than ancient extinct religions."

Albert seemed unsure of what to say to that, so I said, "Hey, listen. Why don't you tell us about how you got here? Can you do that?"

The boy looked up at me, his eyes, glassy, distant. "There was a fire at my boarding school," he said, his voice barely above a whisper. "I... I was trapped in my room, and I couldn't get out. And the fire got closer and closer, then—"

Before Albert could finish his sentence, Chou jumped to her feet. "Quiet!" she hissed.

"What's happening?" Albert whispered.

I answered by pulling him closer to me. The hairs on the back of my neck suddenly erect.

"Something's not right," said Chou, rising slowly to her feet.

She was correct; the forest had fallen suddenly and completely silent.

Phillip started to say something then his mouth sprung shut with an audible cracking of teeth as somewhere nearby, the same terrifying snarl we had heard the night before bellowed from out of the darkness.

"It's close," Phillip said, slowly turning on his heels.

"Look out!" I screamed, as a shadow suddenly exploded from the greater darkness and catapulted itself at Chou. I kicked my heels into the ground, pushing myself backward, dragging Albert with me by the collar of his shirt.

In what seemed like slow-motion and with the kind of high-definition detail only a mind drenched with adrenaline and fear could coolly observe, I watched a huge creature, all fangs and claws, leap over the fire.

I estimated Phillip was at least six feet tall, probably closer to six-two or six-three. *This* thing was three-feet longer than him, and that didn't even take into account its tail. It resembled a tiger with the same orangish coloring as tigers I'd seen on a visit to the LA Zoo, but its fur was longer, more like a Husky's, as though it had evolved to live in colder climates. Its fur was covered in black stripes and mottled with black and brown patches, similar to a leopard's. Its paws were as big as Chou's head, and the four toes on each foot ended in a claw that I had no doubt could rip us open like we were nothing more than a wet paper bag. And its head... its head was *huge*. Spittle flecked from between the gaping jaws, which looked more than capable of swallowing all four of our heads at once. Its eyes burned with a merciless intensity and the cold cunning intelligence of an apex predator. But it was the two huge incisors that curved downward from its upper jaw to below its lower jaw that really set it apart from any other big cat I'd ever seen.

If the tiger-thing had aimed for anyone else but Chou, it would have easily sunk those teeth and claws into its intended victim and carried them off into the night.

Chou, however, was something else entirely.

She leaped right, her cloak billowing around her as a monstrous paw swooped through the empty space she had momentarily occupied. The tiger-thing hit the ground, kicking up leaves. It turned to look back at us, yellow eyes flashing in the firelight, snarling as it repositioned itself to face us.

I felt Albert's grip on me tighten. The boy was attached to my side as though he were a new limb, his arms wrapped around my waist. I looked down. He was pale as a ghost, his eyes fixed on the tiger-thing. He whispered something, over and over.

I leaned down to hear him.

"Smilodon's are thought to have had excellent night vision and to be able to see up to six times better than humans. They could grow to weigh up to eight-hundred pounds or more," he mumbled, the words coming out so fast I could barely process them. "Popularly known as a sabre-tooth tiger, the smilodon is not truly related to any modern big cat and evolved from a separate genus." He was obviously reciting the words directly from memory, perhaps as some kind of nervous reaction.

"Shhh!" I whispered and placed my hand gently over the boy's mouth.

Phillip seemed stunned, his limbs frozen in mid-motion, trapped by the hypnotic, monstrous eyes of the big cat. He too was mumbling something under his breath, and I strained to catch what it was: "Good kitty. Nice kitty," he whispered over and over.

The monstrous cat seemed conflicted. It had four targets to choose from and seemed quite happy to take its time in deciding which of us it was going to make a meal of first.

Chou seized on its indecision and reached blindly for one of the spears Albert had made earlier, lying close to the fire, her eyes never leaving the creature. Her fingers found the spear's shaft, and she dragged it to her. The weapon looked almost comically toy-like compared to the thousand-pounds of muscle, sinew, claws, and teeth she was facing down. But there was nothing childlike about the pose Chou struck, placing herself directly between us and the tiger... between us and the sabre-tooth *freaking* tiger. She crouched low, her feet set in a wide stance, the spear thrust out in front of her.

Chou took a step toward the tiger. Then another. And another.

The sabre-tooth squared its body to Chou and roared, its mouth so wide I saw past the rows of teeth into its black maw.

Chou appeared unfazed. She advanced another step then thrust the spear at the sabre-tooth's head. It batted at it with one of its huge paws, but Chou was too quick for it. She dropped the tip of the spear then thrust upward just as the cat's paw passed above it.

The sabre-tooth yelped in pain and surprise as the hardened tip of the spear penetrated the paw. Blood dripped from the puncture wound, but rather than dissuade it Chou's attack only seemed to enrage it. Its attention now fully focused on Chou, the giant cat lunged forward, trying to snag the spear in its bear-trap jaws. Again, Chou's reactions were faster, she pulled the spear back so the sabre-tooth's jaws locked on empty space, then thrust forward with a deep lunge, aiming for the cat's left eye. But the sabre-tooth anticipated the attack, it dodged its head to the right, avoiding being blinded but not fast enough to completely avoid injury. The hardened tip penetrated its left ear, pushing all the way through to the other side of it.

The saber-tooth bellowed, wrenching its head away which caused the spear to rip through its ear, slicing it open in the process, leaving a ragged bloody tear. Now the creature roared in real pain.

"I think you're just pissing it off," Phillip hissed. He was moving again and had grabbed his own spear which he now held out in front of him like Chou. He swallowed hard and moved quickly to Chou's side.

The sabre-tooth took a step backward. Its eyes had lost some of their confidence. It batted at its head, then backed up another step. Perhaps it was the injured ear, or maybe it was the fact that there were now two of these pesky two-legged creatures willing to do it harm; either way, the promise of an easy meal had turned out to be a lie, and I saw the confidence leave its eyes.

"Yahhhhh!" Phillip suddenly screamed. He leaped forward, thrusting the point of his spear ahead of him in quick short jabs.

Chou jerked, almost as surprised as the sabre-tooth at Phillip's strategy... but it worked. With a final snarl, the cat turned and leaped behind a tree, then sprinted away.

Phillip, panting hard, watched it disappear into the darkness.

Silence descended again over the camp.

The buzz and drone of the forest's nightlife slowly returned.

Phillip slumped onto his butt, buried the tip of his spear into the ground, wrapped his hands around its shaft and leaned his forehead against his knuckles. "Jesus! Did we really survive that... that..."

"Smilodon," said Albert, peeking from behind my midriff.

"Sabre-toothed tiger," I said, then repeated it, more to convince myself than anyone else. If there had been any doubt in my mind up to then that we were somewhere very, *very* strange, the past four minutes had completely removed it. I looked down at my hands. They were covered in minor nicks, cuts, and grazes from pushing through bushes and climbing over trees, but they weren't shaking. Which also surprised me, because inside I was nervous as a long-tailed cat in a rocking chair store.

Chou took a knee in front of Phillip. "Are you hurt?"

He looked up and, surprisingly, smiled. "No, no. I'm fine. As stupid as it sounds, I actually feel more alive than I have in forever."

Chou smiled back and laid a hand on his shoulder. "You were very brave," she said.

Phillip released one hand from his spear and covered Chou's with it. "I wouldn't go that far, but thank you." He glanced in my direction. "Are you and the boy okay?"

"I'm good," I said and looked down at Albert. Slowly, ever so slowly, he was releasing me from his death grip. He took a step away from me, then one toward Chou and Phillip.

"You alright, kiddo?" Phillip asked.

Albert nodded. "That was frightening."

"Yes, yes it was," said Phillip.

"Will it come back?" Albert asked.

"I don't think so," said Chou. "I think it has learned its les—"

Before Chou could finish the forest lit up like a Christmas tree, as streams of multicolored light rained down through the canopy, soaking everything in color.

"It's happening again," said Albert, the sabre-tooth forgotten already as the aurora illuminated the forest.

"My God," Phillip said, experiencing the aurora for the first time. He used the spear to push himself to his feet. "It's *so* beautiful." He glanced back at me and said, "I'm sorry I didn't believe you." Then he gave a little twitch as a billion tiny white lights sparked into life around us.

"The pixie dust," I whispered, reaching for a cloud of the tiny motes of light floating in front of my face. I wasn't afraid this time, only a little nervous. I forced myself to breathe in deeply and sucked in the cloud of light.

"Everything's covered in it," Phillip said. "The trees, the grass, everything. Why can't we see them any other time?"

Before anyone could answer, all four of us gave a little shudder. A feeling of absolute well-being spread through my body, and, judging by the expression of pleasure on my companions' faces, they were experiencing the same sublime sensation of deep relaxation too. As it washed through me, I felt the day's aches and pains and stress drain from me.

"Woah!" Phillip giggled. He staggered a little. "That's some *good* shit!"

And then, just as it had the night before, the lights in the sky faded to nothing, and the pixie dust dimmed into invisibility again.

"Wow!" said Phillip. "I feel... great. Absolutely invigorated." He sounded stoned. "What the hell are those things?"

Chou said, "I believe that the lights Meredith refers to as pixie dust are a form of highly advanced nanotechnology. Are you familiar with nano-tech?"

"Yeah, it's like little-robots that can be used to repair stuff, right?" I said.

"Yes, that approximates their use, I suppose." Chou moved her hand through the air as if she could still see the particles I knew must still be floating invisibly all around us. "In my time, the healing of minor wounds can be accelerated over the course of a matter of days; broken bones, such as your arm, are healed and fully functional again in a week to nine days." She turned her attention to Phillip. "Last night, while you were unconscious, we witnessed the healing of your broken arm and head wound in a matter of seconds."

"Look," I said, holding my hands out and turning them slowly so everyone could see where the scratches and grazes I'd accumulated over the course of our journey had vanished, completely healed, leaving only fresh, pink skin behind and a fading warmth. "It's amazing. Like magic." After a second, I added, "Last night, I think the aurora cured my addiction, too."

"It is impressive," Chou said, inspecting her own hands in the glow of the firelight.

"Do you think it's going to happen every night?" Phillip asked.

"Perhaps," Chou replied. "Two nights does not establish a pattern, but it could be the beginning of one."

"Okay," said Phillip. "I follow this nano-tech can heal us, kind of, but how does it explain how we can understand you, Chou? I mean, it's not like language is something that can just be fixed like a cut, right?"

Chou paused briefly. "I believe that the nano-tech also rewired our brains to be able to understand each other's language. We have been *augmented* so as to be able to communicate with one another, which indicates to me that we will be *expected* to cooperate. However, it does not make *who* is responsible any clearer to me."

I said, "But I thought nano-tech was supposed to be like really tiny? What I saw looked like it was the size of a pin-head. Shouldn't they be invisible to the human eye?"

"Yes, you are correct, but I think the lights represent bundles of nanites, grouped together for efficiency."

"Bundles? But doesn't that defeat the idea behind nano-sized technology?" Phillip asked. "I mean, these little mechanisms are microscopic for a reason, right?"

"Yes, under controlled conditions and certain applications small would be desirable, or if the nanites were to be, say, swallowed to aid in curing an illness you could keep them at their normal size. However, it would appear that this island is supersaturated with the nanites, and, like anything that exists in the wild, there is much to be gained from roaming as a pack; efficiency and survivability being the two most obvious. All it would take would be for you to swallow a single bundle and you would be 'infected,' so to speak. The nanites can then utilize your body to replicate."

"Wild nanites?" Phillip said. "Roaming bands of do-gooder robots that heal us and change our brains. Sounds great on the surface, I guess, but our permission wasn't asked for any of these changes, and until I know who's behind all of this, I would never have said 'yes' to any of it."

"Except you already did," Chou said.

I nodded my agreement with her. "She's right. The voice was very specific when it spoke to me. I got the impression it wouldn't do a thing to help me until I answered 'yes' to its question. So, technically, you did give it permission."

Phillip nodded slowly, "I guess I did, too, except none of us were told up front what we were getting ourselves in to."

"Beggars can't be choosers," I said. "And think about the alternative."

Chou continued, "I presume we have been breathing in bundles since we first arrived here. The energy storm that we have witnessed for the last two nights... the aurora as you named it... is probably a way to energize the bundles and provide the nanites with the power they need to carry out their tasks. Although, it does seem like a massively inefficient way to go about it."

Throughout most of the conversation, Albert had remained silent, his eyes following whoever was talking.

The poor kid must be utterly confused, I thought. Here he was sitting in a forest in the middle of the night with three virtual strangers talking about technology that couldn't have even been dreamed about in his day. It was confusing and scary enough for me, God knows what he must be going through.

"Albert," I said, "are you okay?"

The kid nodded.

I patted the ground next to where I sat. "Why don't you come over here and sit with me?"

Obediently, Albert joined me.

"Don't worry," I whispered to him, "I know it sounds confusing, but I'll explain it all to you."

Albert nodded again and yawned.

I put an arm around his shoulders. He leaned into me and closed his eyes. I felt his body relax. There was no way to tell what time it was, the night sky was still invisible, hidden beyond the darkness of the treetops.

"I think perhaps you and Phillip should follow Albert's example and try and get some rest," said Chou. "I'll keep watch while you rest."

I did not disagree.

SEVEN

THE CLOUDS that had held permanent sway over the sky since our arrival had vanished by morning, revealing patches of blue between the high, thick limbs of the forest's canopy. Somewhere within those branches, birds sang a vibrant morning chorus greeting to the newly born day. A light mist moved across the ground, and I breathed in the heady smell of wet leaves and damp soil, bringing back memories of childhood camping trips.

Phillip crouched near the dying campfire, warming his hands against the morning chill, he smiled and nodded. "Good morning."

"Where's Albert?" I asked. The boy wasn't anywhere to be seen around camp.

"He is urinating behind that tree," Chou said, matter-of-factly, pointing at a large oak about twenty feet away.

Hearing his name, Albert's head appeared around the tree trunk, a look of mortification on his face. I suppressed a laugh by pretending to cover a yawn, turning my head away as the red-faced kid walked back to the camp.

A short time later, we were on our way again, determined to reach the mountain as quickly as possible.

We walked in a loose group, chatting quietly back and forth. Over the next hour or so, terrain that had begun as a gentle incline grew gradually steeper and more taxing. I was about to suggest we stop for a short rest when Phillip said, "Hey! Listen. Hear that?"

"I think... it sounds like water," I said. I could just make out the faint hiss and burble of running water. "It's coming from that direction." I pointed to our right.

We changed course and followed the sound until it increased to a roar.

Chou pushed ahead of us through a cluster of tall, thick bushes. "Careful!" she said suddenly, throwing out her arms to stop any of us from passing.

"Woah!" I whispered as I saw why she had stopped us so abruptly. We stood at the highest point of a horseshoe-shaped cataract, just inches from its edge. I leaned forward and peered over. A quarter of the way down, a steady torrent of water gushed out of a ragged crack in the rock, cascading the remaining sixty or so feet into a large natural pool of the clearest water I'd ever seen. The pool, in turn, fed a creek that zigzagged downhill in the direction of the beach.

I felt Albert's hand suddenly clasp my arm while his other pointed to something near the pond. "Look," he whispered.

"Ho-lee shit!" Phillip hissed.

I simply stared.

At the far edge of the pool, a group of five deer lapped at the water. I've followed the Pacific Coast Highway along the California coast, up through Oregon and Washington state a couple of times, and I've seen more than my fair share of deer along the way. But the creatures lapping at the water and ruminating on the abundant vegetation growing along the bank were unlike anything I'd seen on any of those road-trips. These were *huge.* They stood at least seven feet tall at their shoulders and must have easily weighed a thousand pounds each, if not more. The single buck among them, larger again than the females, sported a pair of antlers almost as long as his body from tip to tip. But rather than the branch-like antlers of normal sized deer, this creature's formed a single structure that reminded me of a giant bony maple leaf.

"They are magnificent," Chou whispered.

And quite intimidating, too, I thought, even though I knew they were unlikely to attack us unless we got too close. Those antlers looked like they could snap bones.

As if sensing our presence, one of the females looked up, her head tilting to one side as she locked eyes with me. For three breathless seconds, the doe held eye-contact with me, then, with a high-pitched warning bellow to the others, she darted off into the woods, the other deer right behind her.

"Well, at least we know there's a good supply of fresh meat," Phillip said. "Hell, one of those would feed us all for a month or more."

"Indeed," said Chou, "but what concerns me more is that if there are herbivores such as those, then they will undoubtedly attract predators such as the sabre-tooth. We should remain even more vigilant from now on."

We cautiously followed the edge of the cataract down to the pool. The water was crystal clear, bubbling over rocks and stones rounded from years of shaping by the creek's constant caress. I scooped up a palm-full of water and drank it down. It was ice cold and delicious. Small fish, about an inch or so long and far too tiny to make much of a meal, swam through the reeds and stones. There was no sign of any larger aquatic life.

"So now we also have access to a fresh water supply," said Phillip, splashing water over his face. "This day is shaping up pretty nicely."

"Yes, but the water is a valuable resource," said Chou, "and there may be survivors who will be willing to do others harm to keep it for themselves."

I scooped another palm-full of water into my mouth, shook the remaining drops from my hand then joined the others as we continued our journey again toward the mountain.

"We have to be getting close," Phillip said, pointing to scattered rocks and larger gray boulders sprinkled between the trees.

"I can see the edge of the forest," Albert said excitedly, not long after. Ahead of us, through the thinning lines of trees, I could just make out a cold gray scree of pea-gravel and some larger boulders.

We picked up our pace, panting a little as we jogged up the growing incline and crossed from the forest out into the open air.

"Wow!" I said, panting. I stood with my hands on my hips, the sun's rays kissing the back of my neck as I stared up at the mountain. It was much, much bigger than I remembered from my brief glimpse of it that first day on the beach, the craggy and snow-capped peak starkly visible against the washed out blue-gray backdrop of the sky.

Phillip let out a long whistle. "It's got to be nine, ten thousand feet," he said, reverently. "Wish I'd brought my damn climbing gear." He was panting lightly from the jog, too, a hand shading his eyes while they acclimated to the sudden change from dark forest to daylight.

This side of the mountain rose steeply upward from where we stood, the pea gravel quickly transitioning to larger rocks and stones then boulders and finally, slabs of granite and craggy outcrops.

"We are still well below the forest's canopy," said Chou.

"We will need to climb higher if we are to be sure to spot any signs of civilization."

"I think we should aim for that outcropping," Phillip said, pointing at a large slab of flattish rock jutting out from the mountain, another hundred-and-fifty feet or so further up from where we stood. It created a ledge which looked like it would give us an unobstructed view over most of the island back in the direction we came from and a pretty good view over either side of it, too.

Phillip handed Chou his spear, then reached down and swept Albert up onto his shoulders. "Come on little man, the going's a bit too rough to trust you won't slip."

With Phillip leading the way, Chou and I followed him from boulder to boulder until, sweating profusely, we reached the ledge.

"Up you go," said Phillip, hoisting Albert off his shoulders and onto the ledge before pulling himself up alongside the boy. He turned back to face me and extended a hand.

"Grab ahold, and I'll help you—"

Phillip's words faded away to silence. His eyes grew huge shifting from me to over my shoulder, then skyward. "Holy shit!" he hissed. "Holy. Shit."

I was in a precarious position, my left hand grasping onto a crevice in the lip of the rock ledge, the rocks, and loose gravel beneath my sneakers making it dangerous to turn too quickly without the risk of falling. As carefully as possible, I repositioned myself until I was looking back over the tops of the forest in the direction we had come from... and almost slipped from my perch.

"Oh, my God," I whispered. "Someone tell me this is a joke."

In the far distance, the gigantic multi-faceted edifice I'd briefly seen in my first few minutes on this island towered over the coastline, vanishing into the clouds collected around its upper portion. From this vantage point, I could see that the coastline did indeed run for hundreds of miles along what I assumed must be the eastern horizon, as I had suspected. The sun hung above it, making its slow climb toward its azimuth. *Except*, this quite obviously wasn't *our* sun. This *couldn't* be Earth's sun. This star was larger, brighter, and rather than the golden-orange light I had taken for granted all my life, *this* star burned with a dark orange that bordered on red.

A glowing net of lights filled the sky, encircling the sun within a framework of concentric rings. There were *hundreds* of rings, each filled with thousands-upon-thousands of pinprick-sized orange lights. It looked like millions of fireflies had surrounded the star, only to be frozen in place, trapped in a permanent orbit around the glowing ball of gas. It was obviously *not* natural... and it was obviously *not* human-made. At least, not by any human from my time.

"My God!" Phillip said, then repeated himself several more times.

Chou said nothing, but her face reflected the shock we all felt.

I felt a tugging on my wrist and looked up to see Albert facing in the opposite direction to the caged sun. He pointed up toward the summit with a trembling hand.

"The moon," Albert stammered, "what's wrong with the moon?"

We turned to look in the direction Albert pointed. To the west, emerging from where it had been hidden behind the mountain's snow-capped peak, the remains of what very well could have been the twin of our own moon described a slow arc across the blue sky. I couldn't be absolutely sure, but I thought I could make out what looked like structures or maybe even buildings peppering the moon's cratered surface, or, at least, what was *left* of its surface. *This* moon looked as though some giant space-faring monster had taken a bite out of it, then vomited up its undigested meal. I estimated about a third of the moon had broken away from the main satellite, and now trailed behind it in an extended tail of debris. Other, larger chunks orbited the dead planetoid, moving in never-ending circles around their mother as it continued *its* never-ending journey around this planet.

It all felt so dreamlike. And, as if that dream insisted on forcing me to accept this new, strange version of reality in one mind-boggling minute, my attention was drawn first to the northern horizon, then to the southern. Rising high above each, sunlight glinting off the quartz-like facets of their sides were exact duplicates of the monolith so clearly visible above the distant coastline to the east.

Struggling to exert *some* control over this information overload, my mind drew the logical conclusion that if I could see through the thousands of feet of mountain obstructing our view, there would be a fourth structure dominating the western horizon, too. Which made four monoliths, each standing guard like giants over this hemisphere.

"I... I don't see any settlements," Phillip murmured, his voice barely audible over a gust of cold wind rolling down from the summit.

"No," I said, just as quietly, "no signs of civilization."

Phillip breathed in deeply, held it for a New York minute, then exhaled a long sigh, as though he was finally resigned to the fact that this world was not his, not any human's.

"So, what do we do now?" he said, looking to me and Chou.

Chou considered the question. "I believe this confirms that our chances of rescue have been reduced to zero. Our immediate objective should, therefore, be to focus on establishing a permanent, defensible shelter."

Another gust of wind swept down the mountainside, blanketing us with freezing air.

"Let's get down off this mountain before we either die of hypothermia or get blown off it; both of which are beginning to appeal to me," said Phillip. He picked Albert up and lowered him down to my waiting arms.

"Stay close," I ordered Albert. I took the boy's hand in mine and followed behind Chou who was already gingerly making her way back down the mountain in the direction we had come from. As relieved as I had been to finally get out of the forest and see open blue skies, I was twice as relieved when we crossed back into the woods again; to have everything the skies had revealed hidden from me once more.

Phillip picked up his pace, striding past us as if he was trying to outrun what we had all just seen up on the mountain.

"Is Phillip alright?" Albert said.

"Absolutely. He's just... confused," I said, but for all I knew, Phillip intended to keep on walking until he couldn't walk anymore and leave us all behind. "For God's sake, Phillip, hold up," I called after him. He didn't stop, but he did slow enough for us to catch up to him.

"Hey!" I yelled. "Stop! Phillip! Just stop, would you?" I let go of Albert's hand, reached out and grabbed Phillip tightly by the bicep, forcing him to either stop or drag me along with him.

Maybe it was the hint of desperation I heard creeping into my voice that finally made it through the panic I knew he must be feeling, I'll never know, but Phillip stopped and turned. His face was a mask of shifting emotions and confusion.

I understood exactly how he felt, of course. I mean, it wasn't *his* reality alone that had just been shattered, it was *ours* too.

He exhaled a long sigh. "I'm sorry, it's just that—"

I saw the object fly out of the shadows behind Phillip. It traveled with a *swooshing* sound in an arc and pierced Phillip's shoulder with a sickening *thud* before I could even shout a warning. Phillip grunted like he'd been punched, blinked twice and tried to turn his head to see what had hit him.

I gasped as I saw the shaft of an arrow buried almost down to the feathers of its fletching in Phillip's right clavicle.

Phillip reached weakly for the arrow, but before his fingers could close around it, there was another *thud.* He staggered under the impact, coughed, sending a gobbet of blood spilling over his lips, and toppled forward. Phillip collapsed face down into the ground, a second arrow sunk deep into his back, just below his left shoulder blade.

He twitched, then lay motionless.

I started to reach for him... and froze.

Behind Phillip, deeper in the forest, two men stepped out of the shadows. Both were dressed in leather armor and chain mail. They looked like extras out of a movie about ancient Rome or medieval England. One held a bow, the other carried a small round shield, the edge of which was ringed with metal studs. In his other hand, he carried a large sword with a curved blade that grew thicker toward the end. He raised the sword high above his head, let out a bloodcurdling cry and dashed toward us.

EIGHT

"RUN!" I screamed.

I grabbed Albert's hand tightly in my own, and we took off like frightened rabbits, zigzagging between trees so our pursuers couldn't get a clear shot. I didn't know if Phillip was alive or dead, but what was obvious was that if the two men caught us, they *would* kill us, without hesitation. *Why* though? And who were they? I chanced a quick look over my shoulder and saw we hadn't put any extra distance between us and them, despite the heavy leather and chainmail armor they were wearing. Albert's legs were just too short for us to outrun them. Chou must have reached the same conclusion because without missing a step, she leaned down and plucked the boy from me and pulled him in close to her chest.

"Put your arms around my neck," she ordered the boy. Albert did as he was told, clutching tightly to her. Now he was looking back over Chou's shoulders at our attackers. Chou increased her pace, moving from a fast jog to a sprint, despite her now carrying a sixty-pound child.

I struggled to keep up, her long legs eating up the uneven ground in huge strides. I knew she was holding back, that she could have easily outrun our pursuers but wasn't willing to leave my slower ass behind.

"Look out!" Albert yelled.

Chou ducked to her right. An arrow whistled past us and thudded into the trunk of a tree, missing Chou by just a couple of feet.

"Our only chance is to lose them in the trees," I yelled, panting hard already.

"Yes," Chou yelled back, leaping over some dense undergrowth, then zagging to her right.

"We need to—"

I should have kept my eyes fixed on the ground ahead of me rather than on Chou, that way I would have seen the knot of roots at the foot of the tree we were sprinting past. Instead, my foot snagged on one, twisted painfully, and I went sprawling to the ground with an *Ooof!*; the air knocked from my lungs.

Chou yelled at me: "Get up! Get up, Meredith!"

I tried to push myself to my feet, but my ankle wouldn't support my weight.

Chou stood close by, both she and Albert glancing down at me then back in the direction of the fast-approaching men, the *clink-clink-clink* of their chainmail getting closer by the second.

Chou flinched as an arrow streaked past her. "Get up!" she yelled at me again.

I managed to push myself to my knees, then scramble to my feet, but the second I put weight on my injured ankle I screeched and collapsed to one knee. I pushed again and limped a few steps but quickly knew my ankle was at best twisted or sprained, possibly broken. Either way, my running was over for the foreseeable future... maybe forever.

I stole a look back; the two men were less than sixty feet from us, closing fast. They'd be on us in less than ten seconds.

Without missing a step, the archer slipped his bow over his

shoulders, then pulled a long dagger from a belt around his waist. Both men were sweating profusely, but the look of cruel triumph on their faces told me everything I needed to know about their intentions.

"Go!" I hissed at Chou. "Take Albert and run. I'll try and delay them long enough for you to get away."

With Albert still clinging tightly to her, Chou wordlessly assessed her choices, then sprinted away... only to stop at a nearby oak and lower Albert to the ground behind its wide trunk. "You must be a brave boy and stay here," I heard her tell him.

Albert nodded, his eyes wide with fear.

Chou spun around, ran back to where I lay, and placed herself between me and the attackers. She took a long, deep breath, exhaled slowly... and launched herself at our pursuers, moving faster than I had ever seen anyone run in my life.

The two men, suddenly faced with a six-foot-tall Amazonian warrior charging at them, stumbled to a confused stop. The swordsman took up a defensive stance, his sword held out in front of him, while the archer dropped back ten feet and began pulling his bow from around his shoulders again.

Chou surged across the last few feet, dodged right, leaped into the air, and used the trunk of a tree to propel herself at the swordsman. She held the spear Albert made for her above her head with both hands as she crashed knee first into the swordsman's face, sending him sprawling to the ground in an explosion of dirt and dried leaves. Chou landed next to him, used her momentum to roll away, leaped back up and lunged at the swordsman's back with her spear.

The man's reactions were almost as fast as Chou's, and he managed to bring the flat of his weapon around in time to deflect Chou's attack. Jumping to his feet, he brought his sword up in a whirling attack aimed at Chou's neck that was so fast the blade became a blur of liquid silver.

Chou ducked under it and rolled away.

The archer had unslung his bow, an arrow nocked and ready; the bowstring pulled back to his shoulder, ready to let fly the second his friend was free of the woman who ducked and dived so nimbly around him. The archer's face was a picture of frustration as he moved the bow left and right, trying to draw a bead on Chou, but she was just too fast... and too close to his friend for him to be able to risk a shot.

Chou feinted at the swordsman's face, waited for her opponent's move to block her attack, then twisted the spear past his guard and drove the tip into the man's unprotected leg, just above his right knee.

The swordsman screamed in pain, teetered, but remained standing. Reversing his swing, he slammed the rounded base of the sword's pommel against Chou's temple, sending her staggering away.

Chou picked herself up, wobbled as if she was concussed and moved back a couple of feet, lowering her spear. The sword-wielding man took two quick steps toward her, a smile of victory on his face as Chou took another small step backward, her eyes moving left and right. She wobbled and dropped to one knee.

I looked on in horror as, with both hands wrapped around the pommel of his weapon, the swordsman raised the sword above his head. He held it for a second, took another step forward and began to bring the blade down in a swooping arc that would remove Chou's head from her shoulders.

Chou turned to face her attacker, and the look of defeat melted away. Her mouth set in a wicked grin, I instantly understood she had lured him into the overconfident move. The swordsman tried to sidestep, but it was too late, he was committed to his attack, the weight of the sword and its momentum carrying him forward.

In one lightning-fast movement, Chou leaped up and forward, placing herself almost nose to nose with the swordsman, and thrust the spear up in a short jab, driving the fire-hardened tip into the man's unprotected chin and then up into his brain.

The sword flew from the man's hand and landed in the leaves near the archer as the swordsman's lifeless body continued forward, colliding with Chou and knocking her to the ground, covering her in a spray of arterial blood that gushed from his neck.

Chou pushed the dying man's body away and jumped to her feet. Her face fixed in a grimace of determination, made all the scarier to me by the blood splattered across her clothing and smeared in long stripes over her cheeks. She placed a foot against the man's leather-clad chest and pulled her spear from his body, took a step toward the archer... then screamed, knocked back as an arrow struck her above her left hip. Chou stumbled then collapsed to the forest floor.

The archer dropped his bow, pulled his knife from his belt and advanced on Chou.

Chou forced herself to a sitting position, grimacing as the shaft of the arrow thumped against her knee, sweat dripping from her forehead. She gripped the spear with both hands, holding it out in front of her like a lion-tamer keeping an unruly beast at bay.

"Leave her alone, you son of a bitch," I screamed at the archer.

He glanced over his shoulder, sneered at me, and backed away from Chou. For a moment, I thought he was coming to slit my throat. Instead, he ran to where his friend's weapon had fallen, searched amongst the fallen leaves, found what he was looking for and hefted the sword. Striding confidently to where an immobilized Chou sat, he knocked the spear from her weakened hands with the flat of the sword and kicked her hard in the solar-plexus, forcing her onto her back. He pinned her to the ground with one sandaled foot on her chest, switched his grip on the sword, so the tip of the blade faced down, and lifted the pommel to eye level, preparing to drive it point-first into her heart.

I flinched as two deafening explosions split the air a half-second apart behind me, their echoes moving through the woods like restless spirits. Two corresponding spurts of blood erupted from the archer's torso. He grunted and spun sideways, the sword dropping from his hands point first into the ground where it swayed back and forth. The archer's body crumpled next to it, twitched once... twice... and was still.

As the echoes of the two gunshots faded, I heard Albert's desperate sobbing from behind the tree where Chou had left him. I scuttled crab-like on my butt, my throbbing ankle all but forgotten, repositioning myself to face where I thought the shots had originated.

Around fifty or so feet away, a man sat on a horse. The horse was a brown and white dappled male, young and strong looking. Beautiful to behold. As if it had psychically sensed my silent compliment, it whinnied fiercely and raked at the ground with a hoof, kicking up leaves. The rider looked like... well, he looked like a cowboy, complete with a black, wide-brimmed hat that hid his eyes in shadow. He sported a thick straw-colored mustache and long shoulder-length auburn hair, not as red as mine but just red enough to guarantee he would stand out. He wore a dark green frock coat that stopped just above his knees, beneath that a white frilled shirt. In his hands, he held a lever-action rifle, smoke rising from the muzzle. The rifle was pointed at me.

I held my breath, waiting for the stranger to shoot me, too. Instead, the cowboy slid the rifle into a leather sheath on his saddle. He kicked his heels gently into his mount's flank. The horse trotted in my direction, stopping when it was ten feet away. The cowboy silently looked us over, then he pinched the front brim of his hat between thumb and forefinger and nodded.

"Morn'in," he said in a deep, gravelly voice, thick with a heavy mid-western accent. "Name's James Hickok, but you ladies can call me Wild Bill."

NINE

"COME on out from behind that tree, boy," the man who said his name was Wild Bill Hickok yelled; not unkindly, but still with a tone that conveyed he expected to be obeyed.

I was still processing this latest insanity, but the fact that the stranger who had just saved our asses shared the same name as the legendary cowboy was not lost on me, but at that moment, it was the last item on a pretty long list of craziness.

"Come out, Albert," I called, wincing at the pain in my ankle. "It's safe. I don't think this man's going to hurt us."

Albert hesitated for a few moments, his hands planted firmly against the trunk of the oak he was hidden behind as if it were his mother's skirt, then he ran to where I sat, his eyes never leaving the cowboy.

"That's better," said Hickok. "Are there any more of you hiding around here?"

None of us said a word.

Hickok sighed. "Do any of you speak American?"

I nodded. "Yes."

"I speak English," said Albert, quietly.

"No," said Chou, grimacing with pain.

Hickok gave Chou a look that said he thought she might be a little loco.

"Well, alright then." He looked directly at me. "Would you mind kindly answering my first question: Are there any more of you that I should know about?"

"Just... just our friend, Phillip." I nodded at the bodies of the two men who had attacked us. "I think they killed him. He's back that way." I pointed. "Please, you have to let us go check. He could still be alive."

The cowboy pushed the rim of his hat up an inch then pulled it back down again, looking through the trees in the direction I'd just indicated, but said nothing. He pulled the rifle from its leather holster, then, to the accompanying creak of oiled leather, dismounted, dropping nimbly to the ground. Wild Bill walked to where Chou lay. She'd crawled to the same oak Albert had hidden behind and now sat with her back resting against its trunk. She tried to get to her feet, but the pain was too much for her and, wincing, slipped back down between the roots.

"Ma'am, there ain't no reason for you to get up right now. I don't mean you or your friends any trouble. I've had compadres who been stuck with arrows before, maybe I can help, if you let me." He nodded in the direction of the two dead men. "Now, those bandits don't look like no Sioux I never seen, but I'm guessing the idea's the same." He nodded at the spear Chou clutched to her chest. "Are you going to stick me with that thing if I try to take a look?"

Chou hesitated, then placed the spear on the ground next to her within easy reach.

Hickok knelt beside Chou and traced the shaft of the arrow with his fingers. There was a tearing sound as he ripped the fabric of Chou's pants around the arrow's shaft and leaned in to examine where it had penetrated her flesh.

Albert continued to stare openmouthed at Chou and Hickok. I tapped the kid on his thigh to get his attention. "Help me up," I said. Albert crouched down, and I used him as support to pull myself upright, then as a crutch to lean on while I hopped closer to Chou and the cowboy. Albert gasped when he saw the blood spatter on Chou's chest, sleeves, and hands.

"Most of it is his," Chou said between gritted teeth, nodding at the body of the dead swordsman.

Only a small amount of blood trickled out of the wound where the arrow had penetrated her hip. I don't have any medical training to speak of other than general first aid and CPR, but I was confident lack of bleeding was probably a good thing.

"Alright. Now, next, I'm going to have to roll you over just a little and check your back." Hickok didn't wait for Chou to answer. Instead, he placed one hand on her butt and moved her slowly onto her right side.

Chou hissed in pain, clenching her teeth so hard I thought they would crack.

"Almost done," said Hickok. He moved the palm of his other hand to her lower back and began to slowly move it around as though he were petting a dog. "There she is," he said a second later. He tapped at a slight bulge protruding from the material just above her left butt cheek. "Arrow head's out your back. That's a good thing, at least for when we get around to removing it. Can't speak to what it's done to your insides, but there's folks back at the garrison that can take a shot at patching you up. I'd bet a month's wages you're gonna be just fine."

"Back at *what* garrison?" said Chou. Her words came out from between her clenched teeth like gas escaping from a pipe.

Hickok leaned back on his haunches. "So, you do speak English?"

"No," said Chou, "I do not."

Hickok closed his eyes for a second. Shook his head slowly from side to side as if he was trying to clear it, then stood up and turned to face me. "You said you had a friend who might still be alive?"

I nodded. "He's back that way," I said, pointing again. "About a quarter mile, maybe. Near where the forest ends."

Hickok looked in the direction I was pointing, then turned and walked over to his horse. He swung himself into the saddle. "I'll go check on him." Then with a "Ha!" and a kick of his heels, he rode off to look for Phillip.

I watched until Hickok and his horse disappeared in the trees, then turned to Chou. "How is it?" I asked urgently, not knowing what else to say.

"Painful," said Chou, more calmly than I would have if it'd been me impaled by a two-foot-long arrow. "I believe the arrowhead may have clipped my hip bone."

"Can you walk?"

"Probably as well as you can without Albert's assistance," Chou replied.

I frowned. "There's no way we can outrun that guy. He has a horse," I continued, then asked, "Do you think he really is *the* Wild Bill Hickok?"

"Yes," said Albert, as though the question had been directed at him. "He looks like the pictures I've seen of him in history books of the wild west."

Chou raised an eyebrow. "On any other day, I would vehemently argue the probability of that being possible. But, given the three of us..."

I stood up. "This is all just so... crazy. What do we do when he comes back?" I was torn; part of me wanted him to come back because he had that gun, the other part of me wanted to just vanish into the trees because, well, *that* gun. "I guess he did save our asses," I said, finally.

"He has not shown any aggressive behavior toward us," said Chou. "And none of us would be able to escape him and his animal."

"It's a horse," I said. "If we can't get away from him, unless he's willing to just leave us be, I suppose we'll have no other option but to go with him to this garrison. Whatever that is."

"It's like a fort. A kind of military outpost," Albert piped up. "He said there were people that could help Chou. We should go."

"I don't know," I said. I wasn't feeling particularly confident about either choice we faced.

"It's not like we have any other option," Chou said. "Unless this arrow is removed, and I receive medical treatment, I will, in all probability, expire. And you, Meredith, you are barely able to walk. Albert is too young to be able to help us. I see no other way. We will go with him when Wild Bill returns."

As if the mention of his name had summoned him, the silhouette of the cowboy materialized from the trees, moving through the forest in our direction.

"Your friend is dead," Wild Bill said when he pulled up alongside us, with only a hint of emotion in his voice. "Here." He tossed something at Albert, who caught it deftly, despite me still leaning heavily on the boy's shoulder. It was a bundle of clothes. *Phillip's* clothes.

"What!" I hissed. "You stripped him?"

Wild Bill dismounted and began to rummage through one of his saddlebags. "Well, he ain't gonna need 'em no more," he called back over his shoulder.

"That's... that's..." What exactly *was* it? I finally came up with "Sacrilegious." The word sounded dumb even as I spoke it, but it got my point across.

Wild Bill turned and looked at me. "Ma'am, if you have any idea where we are, how we got here, or when we can expect to find civilization again, especially given the peculiarities of this locale that I am sure you would have to be blind not to have noticed..." he jabbed skyward with his right index finger "...or when we're likely to find an outfitter capable of replacing your clothes and sundries, then I'd suggest that you make a habit of picking up *anything* you think might be useful to our well-being and comfort. And seeing as you have no problem already dressing like a man, I figured you might want your friend's clothes, too." He didn't say any of this with any kind of arrogance or malice; it was all delivered in a very matter-of-fact way, as if he were explaining it to a child. As Wild Bill talked, he strode over to where the body of the archer lay sprawled on the ground. He undid the belt holding the man's knife and slung it over his shoulder, then began removing the dead man's chainmail and leather armor. "Now, I'll take what I can from this hombre, and I'd suggest you and the boy do the same to that other fellow, over there." He nodded at the body of the dead swordsman not ten feet from where Albert and I stood. "When we're done, we'll get your friend here situated, then I'll take you to the garrison." He continued pulling pieces of clothing from the dead man.

He was right, of course. We still had no idea where we were or even *when* we were, but after my first look at that sky, one thing had become very clear to all of us: this could not be Earth. And drawing from that obvious conclusion, dear Toto, we most definitely were not in Kansas anymore, so to speak. Which meant that unless I was right, and whatever intelligence had brought us here had plans for us and had made some kind of provision for our well-being, we were on our own. Or, at least, we were on our own along with a couple of hundred or so other humans who had been dropped on the island alongside us. Better to err on the side of caution and expect the worst.

"Okay," I said. "Albert, stand still for a second, will you?"

Albert nodded.

I kept my right hand on his shoulder, then eased a small amount of weight onto my injured foot. There was pain in the ankle, but it wasn't as bad as it had been, which gave me hope. I took a tentative step, winced, which made Albert (bless his heart) throw an arm around my waist to support me. I smiled and shook my head at him.

"I think I'm okay," I said.

He backed away but stayed close enough that I could reach out to him if needed. I took another step toward the dead swordsman. This time, I was ready for the pain and kept as much weight on my good leg as I could. I took my hand from Albert's shoulder and walked a couple more steps, Albert shadowing close by. I smiled to myself. *My hero*. There was still pain but I could walk. I stood by my earlier self-assessment that I wouldn't be doing much running for a while still, but I'd lucked out and was in better shape than I thought.

"How you holdin' up, over there?" Wild Bill called out to me.

I gave him a thumbs up and even threw in an "I'm fine, pardner," using my best Clint Eastwood voice. In return, Wild Bill gave me a bemused look before turning his attention back to undressing the archer, which I can assure you looked as weird as it sounds. My attention turned back to the body of the dead swordsman. He looked a little younger than me. His deeply tanned olive skin was already beginning to pale. His eyelids were half closed, his mouth agape showing lightly stained teeth. He had a full beard the same color as his black wavy hair. His beard was twisted into four long braids. Each braid had three colored beads (red, green, and brown) threaded onto it. Even though his eyes were half-closed, I could see they were intensely green. A light blue eyeshadow had been applied to his eyelids and swept across to each temple. The makeup was actually quite scary, creating a mask effect across the upper portion of his head. He had been a good-looking man, I would have even said he was attractive if the little bastard hadn't tried to kill us. I unbuckled his knife belt then began to undo his armor which was a lot harder than it sounds thanks to some really weird fastenings that took both me and Albert almost a minute to figure out how to release. By the time we were done, I was looking at the body of a young man in his early twenties who would not have looked out of place lounging in a park reading the latest Steven King novel. While his sinewy body was certainly more muscular than my own, he wasn't that much bigger than me.

What a stupid waste, I thought.

A question still nagged at me: why would they want to kill us in the first place? It wasn't a stretch to think that these two men had been offered the same choice Albert, Chou, Phillip, and I had been given. So why try to kill us all on sight? It made no sense to me. And if this man, who said he was Wild Bill Hickok, hadn't shown up...

"Don't forget his sword," Wild Bill said, looking approvingly at the pile of armor and underclothes lying at my feet.

"It's a scimitar," Albert said. "I'll get it." He quickly located the sword from the undergrowth where it had landed and carried it back and handed it to me—a little reluctantly I noted—pommel first. Surprisingly, the sword was a lot lighter than I expected. I gave it a couple of half-hearted swings in front of me. The meager light that managed to make it through the treetops bounced off the curved interior edge of the blade, glinting as I swept it back and forth.

Yeah, I thought, *I could get used to using this*. In fact... I eyed the body of the dead man again; he *really* wasn't that much bigger than me. I could probably fit into his armor. I resolved to give it a try once Wild Bill took us back to this garrison he had talked about and Chou was safe.

"Albert, could you hand me the sword's *thingy*, please." I pointed at the long envelope of leather fastened to the dead man's belt.

"Scabbard," Albert said, as he handed it and the belt to me. I fastened the belt around my hips and slipped the sword, somewhat awkwardly into the scabbard.

"Why don't *you* take this?" I said to Albert, holding out the dead swordsman's dagger to him.

The kid's eyes lit up. "Really?"

I smiled, extended my hand a little more. "Sure. Go ahead."

He took the knife, slipped it from its scabbard and moved it slowly in front of his eyes.

"Just be careful you don't cut your fingers off with it. Or anyone else's for that matter," I said, only half-joking.

Albert nodded enthusiastically, undid the belt holding up his pants and threaded it through the two slits in the back of the scabbard. We gathered up the clothes and armor then limped over to where Chou sat. Her eyes were closed, and I didn't like how pale her skin had turned. I could see her chest rising and falling steadily, so I decided to simply let her rest. Albert and I placed the armor we were carrying next to the archer's armor and equipment Wild Bill had left near his horse.

Wild Bill was working nearby. He had cut down a bunch of long low-hanging branches which he was lashing together with twine from a roll lying in arms' reach of where he knelt. He then used the branches to build a flat triangular trellis that measured about nine feet long.

I said, "Albert, go stay with Chou while I speak with Wild Bill." He nodded and ran to Chou's side, then began examining his new knife.

Wild Bill was engrossed in lashing more branches horizontally across the trellis.

"What *is* this?" I asked, looking at the mesh of branches he was working on.

Without looking up, he said, "This here's a travois. We'll put your friend on it, fasten it to Brute over there, then get her back to camp. Camp's a good four hours east of here through these trees, probably longer seeing as we'll be taking it slow. I'd say we should make it back by early afternoon, but the hell if I know how long a day is in this place." He finished up fastening the last branch from his pile, clasped the apparatus with both hands and shook it violently, to make sure it wasn't going to fall apart, I guess.

Happy with his work, Wild Bill got to his feet and announced, "There, we're good to go. You take the other side." He picked up the side of the travois nearest to him and waited for me to do the same with the other. Together we dragged it over to where his horse Brute waited.

Brute gave a low huff as we approached pawing at the dead leaves and branches beneath its hooves with a long muscular front leg.

"Careful now," Wild Bill said, as we got closer, "that horse is nothing but fifteen-hundred pounds of hate. Don't want to get on the wrong side of him. And let me tell you, most every side is the wrong side of this old son of a..." He cut his words short, replaced them with a shy smile.

While I held the travois upright for him, Wild Bill used more of the twine to fasten the left and right side of the travois to the stirrup leathers on either side of the saddle. When he was sure it was securely fastened, he unfurled a rolled-up horse blanket and laid it over the travois.

"Let's go get your friend," he said. We walked to where Chou still lay, either asleep or unconscious, I couldn't tell.

Albert looked up as we approached and smiled.

Kneeling at Chou's side, Wild Bill placed a hand against her forehead and said, "She's running a nasty fever. Sooner we get her back to the garrison the better." He gently shook Chou by the shoulder. "Hey! Wake up now, you hear?"

Chou's eyes fluttered open.

"That's better," said Wild Bill. "Now listen, the boy's going to go get my horse and bring him over here." He nodded sharply at Albert. "Go on now," he said. Albert took off to where the horse waited and began untying the reins from around the branch it'd been fastened to. "Then your friend and me are going to get you to your feet. Now I'm not gonna lie, it's gonna hurt like a son-of-a-bitch, but if you could try and stay conscious, that'd be a big help. Okay?"

Chou nodded and said, "Yes."

"You know," said Wild Bill, turning to look at me, "for someone who says she don't understand English she sure does understand a lot of English."

"Long story," I said. I turned back to Chou, as Albert led the horse to us. "You ready?" I asked her.

Chou nodded.

I positioned myself on Chou's left, Wild Bill her right, each of us taking an elbow. "Okay," I said, "on three we lift."

Wild Bill nodded.

"One... two... three..." Together we hefted Chou to her feet. Chou grimaced but didn't utter a word of complaint.

Slowly, we helped Chou one painful step at a time over to the travois, my own ankle still spasming. We positioned her at the widest end which lay against the ground, then gradually lowered her down onto the blanket. She lay there with her eyes closed, panting hard, her brow covered in perspiration.

Wild Bill took a long length of rope from his saddle and cut off a piece about six feet long with the knife he kept in his boot, then used it to tie across Chou's chest and under both arms, before securing it to the travois framework.

"Grab those fellas' belongings, if you'd please," Bill said to Albert and me, nodding to the two piles of armor. We did so, bringing the two sets of armor and assorted bits and pieces to him. He placed what he could in his saddlebags, securing the rest to the travois with more twine.

I leaned in and took Chou's hand in mine. "You doing okay?" She opened her eyes, looked at me and shook her head. "Something... does not... feel... right," she whispered. She coughed once then closed her eyes again.

Without another word, Wild Bill Hickok, a man I was sure had been murdered in a saloon over a hundred years before I was born, urged his horse in the direction of the garrison, and Albert and I followed behind.

We had been walking for what must have been at least three hours. My ankle still hurt every time I put weight on it, and my legs felt a little tired. Apart from that, I felt good, despite the fact that for the six months before I ended up on this island, the closest thing I'd gotten to exercise had been when I left the apartment to score more pills, or I got up to pee. I should be breathless, barely able to move, but instead, I was breathing evenly and I'd hardly even broken a sweat. I began to suspect that more changes had been made to us than just the ability to understand each other's language. I remembered the sensation I'd felt the previous night when the aurora had streaked across the sky. When it was all over, I had felt completely refreshed; like how I'd imagine an athlete who ate right, never drank, and was in bed by ten every night for a full eight hours of sleep must feel. My body was invigorated...

renewed. And if Chou was right, it was all down to the pixie dust; the nanites.

The forest had grown denser, trees and shrubs crowding in all around us to the point we found ourselves almost constantly having to adjust our course to avoid some new obstacle.

"Maybe we should head down to the beach and follow the coast; we'll make better time," I suggested.

"It'll also leave us exposed," Wild Bill said, without turning to look back at me. "We'll make too plump a target for anyone who makes the mistake of thinking we're an easy mark. Better we stay hidden in the trees for as long as we can." He hesitated, then came to a complete stop. "Say, have either of you eaten anything today?"

Albert and I both shook our heads.

"I guess I must have left my manners back in Arizona," Wild Bill said. He reached into his saddlebag and pulled out a small brown sack. From the sack, he took two long strips of something that looked like mummified hundred-year-old skin and handed one each to me and Albert.

"It's beef jerky," Wild Bill said, smiling when he saw us both staring blankly at what he had given us. He pulled another strip from the bag, took a bite out of it, then raised his eyebrows in mock pleasure and said, "*Mmmm! Mmmm! Mmmm!*"

I took a tentative nibble of my jerky. It was tough to the point that it took me several seconds of levering it back and forth between my tightly clenched teeth to actually tear off a piece, but it tasted not too bad. Albert started on his too, his eyes widening in obvious pleasure as he chewed. For the next twenty minutes, we did nothing but walk and gnaw our way through the jerky. By the time I was done, my jaw muscles ached from the exertion.

Chou lay motionless on the travois. She had grown paler, her hair now stuck to her forehead by a sheen of perspiration.

Her chest rose and fell slowly and steadily, and occasionally, she would let out a little moan, but at least I knew she was still alive. I asked Albert to stay back with her while I walked quickly to where Wild Bill guided his horse between the trees.

He turned and looked at me as I drew alongside him.

"Thanks for the jerky," I said, by way of an ice-breaker.

He pinched the tip of his hat and nodded at me. "You're welcome."

I dove straight in with my questions. "You mentioned a camp? A garrison, right? How many of you are there? Did you all arrive here together?"

He gave me a reproachful look. "That's a whole lot of questions for one breath," he said. I wasn't sure if he was being serious or not, but then his face cracked into a smile and I breathed a silent sigh of relief.

"Yeah, sorry," I said, not really knowing what I was actually apologizing for. "I just... when I arrived, I saw probably two hundred people in the water heading for the beach. I just wondered how many you've found."

Wild Bill nodded solemnly, his eyes searching the ground ahead as he continued to negotiate the best route through the trees. He gave his horse a friendly stroke along its neck. "When me and Brute hit the water, we managed to swim to shore easy like. Helped as many folks as we could, but most everyone we saw was skittish as a runover 'coon. We fell in with a couple of others and, well, we just kind of started to pick people up. Found a place near the river—"

"There's a river?"

"Uh huh," he said. "We started the fixings for a camp near it."

"How long until we get to there?" I asked.

"Not too much further. Look!" He pointed through a gap in the trees ahead of us where the forest had begun thinning.

Through the gap, probably a quarter mile or so away, I saw the river Wild Bill had spoken of. "We just need to follow it downstream until we find the garrison. I'd guess it ain't too far now."

As if Wild Bill pointing it out had suddenly made it real, the sound of the river reached us. By the time we stood on its stony bank, the trees had thinned sufficiently that we could walk in a mostly straight line.

"So, you're the boss of the garrison?" I asked Wild Bill.

He laughed loudly. "Me? No, not me. I don't have the disposition or preclusion to such a position. I'm too attracted to the more immoral of life's ways: gambling and such."

"Who is then?"

"Fellow by the name of Edward Hubbard. An Englishman; says he's from the future. Said the last thing he remembered was being involved in some mighty war that killed so many people, they'd lost count how many exactly."

The idea of some futuristic warrior holding sway over the island's population was, on the one hand, kind of enticing. If Wild Bill had no qualms about following this William Hubbard, then he must have some redeeming qualities. On the other hand, if Hubbard was from the future, then who knew what kind of deadly advanced weapons he might have. That could be why Wild Bill seemed so nonchalant; there was simply no chance of fighting and winning, so it was better to be on the winning side.

"Did this Hubbard guy say which war he fought in?"

"Yes, miss," Bill answered. "Said it was the European War. Someone else said, where they came from, it was known as the Great War."

I exhaled a slow breath and tried to conceal the smile of relief that went with it. While I'm not exactly what you would call a history buff, I'd paid enough attention during high school history to know those were two names that would be replaced over time by the name World War I. I'd not considered that the whole of the twentieth century would be the future for Wild Bill. Same went for Albert, and anyone else from the nineteenth century, too. I'd bet my last dime that Chou was the most chronologically advanced human on this island right now, which would give our little group an advantage.

"Look, yonder," said Wild Bill.

A half-mile in the distance was a clearing where several small groups of people sweated under the glare of the afternoon sun.

"They've been busy while I was gone," said Wild Bill, a note of genuine pride in his voice. "Come on, let's go introduce you to the boss man."

TEN

CLOSER TO THE GARRISON, I counted eight small structures that formed a horseshoe-shaped arc around a large campfire. A woman was in the process of stoking the fire with wood from a stack of nearby branches. A gray-black pillar of smoke rose straight up into the air, undisturbed by any breeze.

A hundred or so steps closer and the structures resolved into lean-tos; simple shelters made of a single panel of woven branches about eight feet by ten feet, similar in design to the travois we carried Chou on. The panels were propped up at a forty-five-degree angle by two supporting branches at each corner. They wouldn't win any design awards, but they would provide decent shelter from the elements.

To the right of the camp, near the edge of the forest, two men stood on either side of a tall oak tree. Both held axes in their hands which they methodically swung back and forth, alternating each swing in precise time as they chopped at the tree. Suddenly, the two men scurried away, and the tree slowly toppled over, kicking up dust and debris as it crashed to the ground. The stumps of at least twenty others marked the path of the men's progress into the forest. The lumberjacks paused to wipe sweat from their foreheads, then moved on to the next tree. Near them a pile of felled oaks waited for a group of four men and women to finish the job of stripping off the remaining branches before cutting the trees into ten-feet long sharpened stakes. The completed stakes were, in turn, being carried by two men to the outer edge of the camp where they set them into pre-dug holes to create a stockade. The stockade was already forty-feet or so long and would, judging by the number of empty pre-dug holes, enclose the entirety of the camp, save for a six-foot gap at each cardinal compass-point, which I guessed would be used as entrances.

Three burly looking men stood guard at the south, east, and northern points of the camp. Each cradled a spear like the ones Albert had made for us.

Between the campfire and the stockade, a man and two women worked on putting the finishing touches to a large log cabin. Thick branches had been used to form the beam-like supports of the roof, and the two women stood atop them while a tall, thin man passed them bundles of long-grass which the women then used to thatch the roof.

The woman I'd seen tending the fire earlier was now walking back from the river. She struggled with a large brown vase-like container that was almost half her height, supporting it with both hands like it was a fat, struggling baby. Water sloshed over the container's rim, soaking her front and leaving small puddles behind her, as she half-walked half-staggered back toward the campfire.

The guard at the northern approach spotted us, raised a hand to shade his eyes, then yelled something back in the direction of the camp, waving his arms above his head until he got the attention of the slim man working on the cabin.

The slim man looked toward us as he was handing another bundle to one of the women doing the thatching. She stopped, tapped her workmate on the arm and their heads turned in our direction too.

"That's Edward, the boss man," said Wild Bill. "The two girls are Sarah and Jacquetta." There was something about the way the cowboy spoke the last woman's name. He had a wistful smile on his lips that made it obvious he had a bit of a 'thing' for this Jacquetta. I looked back at the camp before Wild Bill could see that I had noticed. Hubbard said something to the women, then stepped away from the cabin, wiped his hands on his trousers and trotted toward the guard who had alerted him to our approach. Sarah and Jacquetta watched us for a few more seconds before turning back to their work.

We reached the guard about the same time Hubbard did.

"Welcome back, Wild Bill," Edward said as we approached, an honest smile of happiness on his face. "I see you brought some friends." Like Albert, Edward had an obvious English accent, but it was rougher than the boy's. But the rich timbre of the Englishman's voice made his words sound soft, rounded like pebbles smoothed by a river. And his quiet, even pitch made his delivery gentle and measured. I was struck by a distinct but impossible feeling that I knew Edward from somewhere. He had the most intense hazel eyes, short brown-bordering-on-black hair, and a complexion which suggested he hadn't seen much sun in a very long time. He was dressed in a worn and patched brown/gray military uniform. The right elbow of his tunic had a large green patch inexpertly sewn to it.

"Welcome to the garrison," Edward said looking directly into my eyes. He reached out a hand, saw that it was covered in dirt and grime, smiled apologetically and wiped it clean on his pants, then extended it again, his smile widening. "Honest dirt from an honest day's work."

I shook Edward's hand and told him my name, still unable to shake the feeling of déjà vu. He seemed *so* familiar to me.

"And this young man is...?" Edward said.

"I'm Albert."

"Your son?" Edward asked.

I shook my head. "No. We met on the beach."

Edward smiled again, started to say something, then noticed Chou on the travois. His expression became serious. "You have a casualty?" he said, walking to the travois, the flat of his right hand running down the flank of Brute as he did so.

"We had a run in with some... unfriendlies," said Wild Bill, joining Edward and me.

Chou was conscious, but her skin was even paler, and she looked to be in a great deal of pain.

"Hello," Edward said quietly, kneeling just off to the right of Chou, his attention drawn to the arrow protruding from her hip. "We're going to get you to the surgeon and have him take a look at you."

Chou said nothing, she just stared at Edward through half-closed lids. There was definitely something seriously wrong with her, and I worried she might be bleeding internally... or something worse.

Edward turned to face Wild Bill. "Let's get her to Bull." He turned back to face me and Albert, "I expect you'd like to stay close to your friend?"

"Yes," I said. "Thank you."

"Come with me," Edward said. We followed him through the stockade entrance into the camp then he guided us toward the lean-tos I had seen on our approach.

The stockade wall was taller than I had thought; a good thirteen feet high. At our approach, men and women looked up from their work, smiling or nodding at us as we walked through what was effectively a construction site toward the horseshoe of lean-tos.

"Doc Bull!" Wild Bill yelled in the direction of the two

lumberjacks working on felling another oak. "Doc! Hey, Doc Bull, you got yourself a patient," he yelled, louder this time.

One of the two lumberjacks, a large man, his belly extending over his dirt-smeared trousers, stopped mid-swing and squinted in Wild Bill's direction.

Wild Bill waved his arms above his head and yelled the man's name again. "Doc Bull, we need you right now."

Bull turned to his workmate, said something to him, then leaned his ax against a tree stump. He dusted off his hands and quickly walked to where we waited.

"Got a patient for you, Doc," Wild Bill said, as the man I would later find out was named William Bull approached us. Bull was overweight, but there was also clearly muscle beneath the top layer of fat, and he carried himself with a confidence bordering on cockiness. He was a squat, fireplug of a man, and reminded me of a neighbor's Bulldog. He had a thick, drooping mustache the same color as his curly blond hair. He didn't say a word to anyone, just eyeballed me and Albert as he passed us on his way to where Chou lay, the smell of sweat and wood sap wafting behind him.

He knelt beside Chou, raised one of her eyelids and stared deeply for several seconds, before doing the same for her other eye. Bull took Chou's left forearm in his hand and measured her pulse with a pocket watch he'd pulled from his waistcoat's breast pocket. He tutted to himself, then gently moved the clothing from around the arrow's shaft so he could get a better look at where the arrow had penetrated Chou's hip.

"Wild Bill, take her over to the fire and get her off this sled... carefully." Bull sounded American, Boston, or New York maybe. His voice had a cultured accent I wasn't familiar with, and although the precise delivery of his words conveyed a deep intelligence, there was an aloofness that didn't sit well with me.

"Edward, if you would set some water to boil while I fetch my medical bag."

While Albert and I followed Wild Bill, Edward jogged through the space between two of the lean-tos and spoke to the woman I had seen working on the fire and fetching water from the river. She immediately grabbed more fuel from the supply of branches and leaves and fed it to the fire.

Edward picked up a large iron pot from near the fire and filled it with water from the same vessel I'd seen the woman bringing from the river (a big brown amphora with a chunk missing from its lip). A tripod made of thick, straight branches lashed together by vines stood over the fire. Edward hung the pot from a long piece of metal shaped like a hook that had been attached to the tripod.

I helped Wild Bill unhitch the travois from Brute, and we dragged it as slowly as we could to the lean-to closest to the fire, then gradually eased Chou off it and under the lean-to.

Bull came back with a big black leather bag secured by a brass clasp similar to a woman's purse. He laid the bag on the ground, undid the clasp, and pulled out a roll of tanned leather. Kneeling, he unrolled the piece of leather, next to Chou. Attached to the roll by pockets of more leather stitched to its interior were a variety of medical instruments. Some of them—like the scalpel, scissors, and stethoscope—I recognized, the rest, I had no idea about. He also took a small metal container from the bag that reminded me of an antique cigarette case. Inside the case were eight thin glass vials swathed in cotton wool. Each vial was about three inches long and contained a reddish-brown liquid. Bull took one of the vials, popped the tiny cork seal, lifted Chou's head with his free hand and moved to tip the contents of the vial between her lips.

"Hey!" I said, grabbing his wrist. "What are you giving her?"

Bull looked completely taken aback.

Judging by the dark gray wool trousers, what had once been a white cotton shirt was now almost as gray as the waistcoat he wore over it, I'd already reached the conclusion that the last holiday Bull had celebrated had been sometime around the end of the nineteenth century. I guess being challenged by anybody would come as a bit of a surprise to him, more so if it was by a woman.

Bull gave me what could've been considered a hard-stare.

"I asked you what you intend to give to my friend?" I tightened my grip.

Bull flushed red, the jowls of his cheeks began to tremble like a volcano about to erupt.

I had no illusions about his ability to break free of my grip, but he'd look like a good old-fashioned buffoon to everyone if he did. And there was no way I was going to let him administer whatever was in that vial to Chou until I knew *exactly* what it was.

"Well?" I continued to stare at him and wait for his answer.

I heard a chuckle behind me, followed by Wild Bill's unmistakable gravel-road-crunch of a voice. "You two better learn to play nice," he said. "Doc, I figure Ms. Meredith here has a right to know what your intentions are with her friend. Now, in the spirit of us being a welcoming community and all, why don't you just tell her, so we can get this over and done with. The sun isn't much longer for this world, and I'd like to water Brute before dark."

Wild Bill placed his hand lightly on my right shoulder. I held Bull's wrist for another second, just to make my point, then released it.

Bull continued as if nothing had happened, but his face remained flushed. "In order for me to extract the arrow, I need to sedate your friend." He held up the skinny glass vial. "This is laudanum. It is a soporific and analgesic."

"Isn't that opium?" I asked.

"Of sorts. It's a tincture of approximately twelve-percent opium," said Bull. He appeared grudgingly impressed, giving me a little nod of acknowledgment, some of his brashness falling away. "You've had some experience in medicine?"

"In passing," I said. I was surprised at my reaction to the drugs. Not so long ago, I would have *killed* to get my hands on Bull's doctor's bag if I'd known they were in there. Now there wasn't even a tinge of interest. Whatever changes the nano-clusters had made to me, it had been done proficiently and completely.

"May I continue?" Bull said, his eyebrows raised while he waited for my answer.

"Sure, go right ahead."

Bull placed the open end of the vial against Chou's lips and slowly poured the laudanum into her mouth. I watched, still expecting some kind of reaction from my own body, you know, like a starving dog watching someone devour a big juicy burger, but I felt nothing. Chou, however, was an entirely different matter; within a few seconds, her body visibly relaxed as the drug took effect. I watched the small muscles in her face loosen and begin to droop.

"We can proceed," Bull said with a slight smile at the corner of his mouth. "Mr. Hickok: if you and the young... *lady* would be so good as to help me turn the patient on to her right side... gently now... that's it."

Despite being loaded up on laudanum, Chou still moaned as we slowly eased her onto her side.

Bull took the scalpel from the leather roll and slit through the fabric of Chou's trousers, exposing the arrowhead where it had exited her back. The barbed head of the arrow was coated in what I first thought was congealing blood, but it looked too black and too thick.

"What in heaven's name?" Bull said. He leaned in closer and touched the black viscous fluid with the tip of a finger, brought the finger to his face and sniffed. He wrinkled his nose, then touched his finger lightly to the tip of his tongue. Bull spat three times in quick succession into the grass, then turned to face me. "I believe your friend has been poisoned."

"What?" I said. "You can't be serious?"

"I assure you, I am," Bull continued. He held the finger with the black goo on it in front of my eyes for a second then wiped it off on his trousers. "While I can't be completely sure, the smell leads me to believe that this is, in all likelihood, a plant-based poison, possibly from the *Genus Helleborus*." Then with barely hidden urgency, he said, "We need to remove the arrow immediately. Continued exposure will only worsen her symptoms."

Bull turned to me and said, "If you would support her shoulder here, please." He placed his hand on Chou's left shoulder where he wanted me to put mine. When I did so, he grasped the shaft of the arrow about six inches above where it entered Chou's body. "And Mr. Hickok, if you would do the honors and cut the arrow just below my fingers."

"Be my pleasure, Doc." Wild Bill reached down and pulled the large-bladed knife from the inside of his right boot. One side was a regular knife blade, the other a serrated edge. Gently, he began to saw away at the arrow's wooden shaft just below where Bull held the arrow. It took about a minute of careful work on Wild Bill's part, but finally, the arrow shaft snapped off. Bull tossed it to Edward, who examined it thoroughly before tossing it into the fire.

"Meredith, stay where you are and support her back. Mr. Hickok, when I give you the nod, if you would be so kind as to slowly remove the arrowhead from your side of Ms. Chou. And do not let it come into contact with your skin." As Bull gave us his instructions, he rummaged in his bag and removed two squares of cotton gauze and a roll of three-inch wide bandages along with a small brown glass tub with a gold lid. The words ZINC OXIDE CREAM were handwritten on the lid.

"Now, Mr. Hickok, please."

Wild Bill took a pair of worn leather gloves from his belt and leaned over Chou. He wrapped the leather glove around the head of the arrow, grasped it with his right hand and began to slowly pull it out.

Chou moaned quietly but did not regain consciousness.

The end of the arrow shaft popped out of Chou's back with a wet slurp that made me want to gag, but I managed to resist the urge. Blood began to trickle out of both entry and exit wound.

Bull leaned in close to Chou and inspected first the wound in her front, and then her back. "I don't believe it has damaged anything vital to her survival, but only time will tell. Our priority, now, is to keep her comfortable and ameliorate the effects of the poison as best we can." He beckoned to Edward, "The hot water, if you please."

Edward ran to the fire, unhooked the pot of hot water and brought it back to us. Removing a large handkerchief from his pocket, Bull dipped it gingerly into the steaming water and used it to clean Chou's wounds. He took the roll of bandage and handed it to Wild Bill, then set about smearing some of the contents of the Zinc Oxide tub onto each piece of cotton gauze, which he placed over the entry and exit wounds. "The Zinc Oxide will help prevent infection and promote healing," he said to me specifically. He beckoned for the roll of bandages from Wild Bill. "Now, very carefully lift her an inch or two from the ground." Wild Bill and I complied without a murmur from Chou, and Bull fed the bandage under her then around her abdomen twice, covering the two pieces of gauze. He cut the bandage and tied it off. "You may lay her down now," he said finally, after he had inspected his work.

We lowered Chou down onto her back.

Bull placed his materials back into his bag and stood up. "She's in God's hands now," he said.

"What?" I blurted out. "Is that it? Don't you have antibiotics or *something* you can give her in that bag of yours?"

Bull looked at me quizzically, an eyebrow raised. "I've done as much for her as I can. I'm sorry," he said slowly, then he walked back in the direction of the tree stump where he had left his ax.

Albert sat cross-legged with his back against the lean-to's sloped wall, his elbows resting on his legs, his chin in his hands, silently looking out at the camp and the people working there. His face was drawn, his expression glum, his eyes shaded by worry.

"She'll be okay," I said, smiling at the boy. The truth was, I had no idea if Chou would survive or not. I felt absolutely useless. The poison was obviously working on her, and there was nothing any of us could do to stop it. The only hope we had was that she lived long enough to make it to tonight's aurora. But, while I knew the aurora could mend bones and heal cuts, I had no idea whether it could negate the effects of poison.

I sat down next to Chou and did the only thing I could think of that might help; I began stroking her forehead. Chou's skin felt hot, clammy beneath my hand. Occasionally, her eyelids would twitch then become still again as if she was deep in a dream. I don't know how long I watched her like that, but eventually, I felt a hand touch my shoulder. I turned and looked up into Edward's face.

"We should probably let her rest," he said quietly. "Why don't you both come and get something to eat?"

Food! In the days since we'd arrived, we'd gotten by almost exclusively on coconut, except for Wild Bill's jerky. Now, at the mere mention of an actual meal, I felt how empty my stomach really was.

"Yes, please," said Albert, nodding enthusiastically. "I'm starved."

"Well, young man, you're in luck. Come with me." Edward winked at Albert, smiled at me, then helped us both to our feet and led us over to the campfire. He sat us down on one of four large logs, each about ten feet long that had been placed in a square around the edge of the fire. He pulled a sharpened stick from where it had been poked into the ground, then proceeded to prod the ashes and cinders around the edge of the fire until he found what he was looking for. He flipped a misshapen brick of mud from the ashes onto the ground, then poured water on to it from a coconut-cup. The mud brick hissed and steamed. Edward continued to pour water until the steam subsided then gingerly tested the brick's temperature with his fingers. Satisfied it wasn't going to burn him he made his way back to where we waited, tossing the brick back and forth between his hands.

"Watch this," Edward said to Albert.

Sitting cross-legged in front of us Edward dropped the mud brick to the grass and pulled what looked like a cross between a set of brass knuckles and a butcher's knife from a sheath on his belt. He gave the brick of dried mud a couple of good thwacks with the knife's hilt until it cracked along a seam then pried the two halves open like a clam.

A scent of pure deliciousness wafted into my nostrils. My stomach growled like a dog and my saliva glands immediately tried to drown me as the unmistakable smell of cooked fish filled my senses.

"Salmon," said Edward. He nodded in the direction of the river. "The river and lake's teaming with them. Other fish, too.

Here." He separated the two halves of the mud brick and used them as plates for us. "Just watch for bones."

It took all of my self-discipline to first pull the tiny, fragile white bones from the salmon before eating it, but it would have been a real shame to come all this way only to choke to death on my first real meal. Edward helped Albert debone his portion, then, as if he was the head-chef of some fine French restaurant, sat back and watched us with a look of expectation on his face as we ate.

It was quite possibly the most delicious thing I had ever tasted. The smoky, oily salmon flesh melted in my mouth, filling my senses with pleasure. Albert grinned from ear to ear, juice and oil shining on his lips and chin.

"Good, eh?" Edward sat back on his haunches, smiling broadly, apparently pleased with our reaction. "Let me get you another," he said, as we made short work of the first. He returned to the fire and repeated the process of pulling a brick from the embers, cooling it and cracking it open. He also brought us a canteen of water.

As I ate my second helping of salmon, I added another tick to my growing list of things pointing to someone or something having brought us here for a reason. I'm no mathematician, but I'm pretty sure the probability that there could be salmon on a planet other than Earth without someone transporting it there was only a couple of digits shy of next-to-impossible. No, this was just another indication that whoever, or whatever, was pulling the strings behind the curtain of this world, had plans for us. They didn't want us to starve, which meant, logically, at some point they were going to have to put in an appearance and make those plans known to us.

"I really need to check on Chou," I said after finishing my meal. I felt a pang of shame at having left her for so long.

"Of course, of course," said Edward. "Go, be with her. I'll

watch over this little rapscallion." He ruffled Albert's hair playfully.

I thanked Edward and moved to Chou's side, wiping pieces of fish and oil from my mouth.

Chou lay on her back, chest rising and falling slowly, rhythmically. She was still in her drug-induced sleep. I placed the back of my hand against her forehead.

"Shit!" I hissed quietly. Chou's temperature was definitely higher than earlier. I bit into my lower lip with concern.

A slim, elegant-looking woman approached from behind the lean-to. She was a little taller than me, her round face free of any wrinkles or blemishes, with the kind of cheeks I imagined aunties would have felt the need to pinch every time they visited. Her thick light brown hair was pinned back on either side of her head at the temple by two metal hair clips. I guessed she was somewhere in her early thirties. Her clothes looked like they were circa nineteen-forties or fifties: blue pants and matching jacket over a white blouse, which, although a little worn-looking was business-like and clean save for a few muddy splotches. She wouldn't have looked out of place in an office or welcoming you to an LA art gallery. I recognized her as the woman I had spotted tending the fire and fetching water from the river when we first arrived at the garrison.

"Hello," the woman said, with a distinct New York accent. "I'm Evelyn McHale."

"Meredith," I replied, shaking her offered hand. "This is Chou, and the little boy is Albert."

"I'm going to assume you all arrived here from different times?" She paused, then, with a smile, said, "Aren't those just the strangest words you've ever heard?"

I nodded in agreement. "I'm from 2017. Albert's from 1910 and Chou says she's from 2374."

I expected the dates to leave Evelyn speechless. Instead, she nodded and said, "You and Ms. Chou are by far the 'oldest' of us, if I may use that term. Before you arrived, that title belonged to Tabitha; she's from 1977. My last stop before whenever we are now was 1953."

I suddenly felt intolerably overwhelmed by the absurdity of our situation. How was any sane person supposed to deal with this? How? I gave a brief snuffle and threw my hand to my mouth to stifle it.

"Oh, honey! What's wrong?" Evelyn said, she stepped in close to me and wrapped a comforting arm around my shoulder, her hand slipping down my arm to hold my hand. She squeezed it reassuringly. "Tell me what's wrong. Are you okay?"

I nodded, gave a little snort and pulled myself together as best as I could. "Sorry," I said, embarrassed. "It's just... all of *this*." I fluttered my hands around my head.

"Oh, my dear, it's nothing you should be apologizing for," Evelyn said, stepping back but not letting go of my hand. "I've felt like falling apart ever since I arrived. If it hadn't been for Edward, well..." her voice trailed off, and her eyes seemed to briefly focus on a point far away. Then she was back again, smiling at me. "Tell me, how's your friend doing?"

"I don't know," I answered honestly, hearing my voice falter again. A small red dot of blood had appeared on the gauze Bull had placed over Chou's wound. "Bull says he thinks she's been poisoned and... and I think it's getting worse." It had only been three days since Chou, a total stranger, had dragged my ass off the beach, but in that short time, she had saved my life twice. This last time, putting her own life on the line to save Albert and me when she could have easily outrun our two pursuers and left us behind. The idea of losing the one person in this world I felt I could trust was terrifying.

Evelyn leaned over and placed the back of her own hand against Chou's head. After a moment or two, she pulled it away, nodding in agreement with me. "Well, don't you worry. Doc Bull's a fine physician. Bit abrupt for my taste, but I'm not going to hold that against him. I'm sure your friend'll be just fine." She did a pretty good job of sounding convinced.

I seized the moment to change the subject. "You all have made a lot of progress in just three days." I took a good long look over the camp.

"That's all Edward's doing. He's been unstoppable since we arrived. We landed in the water together, and he helped me get to shore; then he went back in and rescued as many souls as he could. Everyone was just so confused and frightened, but not Edward. He took charge, organized us into scavenger groups and had us search the shoreline picking up anything useful that washed ashore and looking for anyone else who made it to the beach. Most people were just as terrified as we were and ran away, but some were grateful and decided to join us. When we found the river, Edward said we should consider making a camp along it as we wouldn't last long without a source of fresh water. We followed it upstream and found this clearing. We spent the first night sheltering from the rain as best we could. Then the lights in the sky came, and everyone felt so much better. It heals you, you know?"

"Yes, we know," I said. "I'm counting on it curing Chou... if she can just hold on." I felt tears force their way to the corners of my eyes. I'm not sure I've ever felt so useless in my entire life as I did then.

Evelyn grasped my hand and gave it another brief squeeze. "Now, don't be silly. Of *course,* she's going to make it. You have to have faith."

I nodded, knuckled the tears away and said, "Please, go on."

"Well, now, where was I? Oh, yes. The next morning, when we all saw how strange the sun was, it became obvious we were not on Earth anymore. Edward stopped us from panicking. He said he believed we'd been brought here for a good reason and he was sure that reason would be revealed to us at some point. Until then, we needed to survive and to do that, we needed shelter. He gave us all something to live for, a purpose."

It seemed like Chou and I weren't the only ones to believe that whatever intelligence was behind transporting us to this planet had an as-of-yet unrevealed plan for our future.

Evelyn continued, "Edward had us make the lean-tos, so we had somewhere dry to shelter. Then he got everyone involved in creating the garrison. Except for Wild Bill. He asked him to go scout out the island and report back what he found."

"Luckily for us," I said.

Evelyn gave my hand another squeeze. She pointed at the almost complete cabin that Edward and the two women had been working on. "Benito showed us how to make the cabin, which was difficult, seeing as he doesn't speak any English. Thank goodness for Peter, he speaks more languages than you can shake a stick at. We're going to have a fine village here soon. Somewhere safe for all of us."

"You said Benito doesn't speak English?"

"Just a dialect of Spanish, as far as we can tell."

"Not even after the aurora... you know, the lights that come at night."

"Aurora. I like that name," said Evelyn. "But to answer your question, no, we still have to rely on Peter to translate. Why?"

I gave a moment's thought to making up some story as a cover but thought better of it. The world I came from thrived on deceit and mistrust. We had a chance to change that and now seemed like as good a time for me to get on board. I took a deep breath and said, "Because Chou doesn't speak English. And up until the first night's aurora, we couldn't understand each other at all. Now, when she talks, I hear her words as English and when anyone else speaks Chou hears it in her language."

"Oh, my Lord," Evelyn said. She turned to where Edward sat chatting with Albert by the campfire. "Edward, you need to come hear what Meredith has to say," she called out.

Edward got to his feet and brought Albert with him, his right hand resting on the boy's shoulder as they continued whatever conversation they were so engrossed in.

"Meredith just told me something amazing," Evelyn said. "Go ahead dear, tell him."

I dutifully repeated my story for a second time.

"It's all true," said Albert, when I was finished.

"Chou said she thought it was the nanites... the pixie dust... that's what we call those little specks of light the aurora illuminates. She says they are actually really tiny but powerful machines that have reprogrammed us in some way, so we can understand each other."

"Pixie dust... I like that name, too," said Evelyn, cheerfully.

"Chou is convinced these little machines are responsible for healing us. I know it probably sounds impossibly farfetched to you, but in the time I come from, they're beginning to work on that same technology. And Chou said that in *her* time they're commonplace, just not as advanced as the ones on this planet. Which I guess makes sense if she's really from several hundred years into my future."

Edward's brow furrowed. "I'll admit, it's hard to get my mind around. If I hadn't seen what they can do with my own eyes, I would be skeptical." He paused momentarily, then said, "Tell me, Meredith, why do you think only your group was given this ability to translate?"

"Until now, we didn't even know we were the only ones affected. We just assumed that because we changed, *everyone* on the island must have too. Why were *we* singled out? I honestly have no idea."

"How do you know it changed *all* of you?" Evelyn said.

"Couldn't it have just affected one of you? And who's to say it only works when it's translating between English and whatever language it is Chou speaks. Do you think it works with other languages, too."

"Wow!" I said. "That hadn't even crossed my mind." I thought the idea over for a second. "There's only one way to test that theory. Maybe we should go talk to Benito and see what happens?"

"That's a good idea, but we'll have to save it for later, I think," said Edward, "I don't want to pull him from his work right now."

"Well, one thing is for certain," said Evelyn. "Whether it's all of you or just one of you that has this ability, if it works on other languages too, it's going to make you very, very valuable."

"What do you mean?" I asked.

"Oh, my dear, just think what it means if you are able to translate *any* language? There are hundreds of people on this island, and I'll bet you dollars to buttons most of them don't speak English."

It was a keen observation on Evelyn's part. In this strange new world, it would be what you could *contribute* on a personal level, your skills, knowledge, abilities, and willingness to learn which would be the yardstick by which your worth was measured. There could be *hundreds* of different cultures from throughout time represented on this island alone, some of those languages would inevitably be so old they would be a complete mystery. I could only imagine how valuable someone who could communicate with all those cultures might be... and how coveted they might be by those who pursued power. And if there were more humans on that distant continent to the east, there could be thousands of different cultures, millions even.

"That's concerning," I said.

Edward stood, subconsciously brushed dirt from his pants,

and looked over to where the two women were still working on the cabin. "I really should get back to work. That roof isn't going to finish itself. Perhaps later we can put your theory to the test," he said. "In the meanwhile, make yourselves comfortable. I'll introduce you to everyone when we're done for the day."

"We'd like to stay as close to Chou as possible," I said, placing my arm around Albert's shoulders.

"Of course," Edward said. "Evelyn, would you do the honors?"

"Don't you worry, I'll look after them," Evelyn offered with a smile.

Edward said goodbye and walked off toward the cabin.

"Well, young man," Evelyn said, sitting down, "why don't you come over here with me and tell me all about yourself." She patted the ground next to her. Albert joined her. I turned my attention to Chou while Evelyn kept Albert occupied with stories of her own childhood adventures growing up in Washington D.C. and Tuckahoe, New York—which he seemed fascinated by. They chatted enthusiastically, laughing as they bantered back and forth.

Thankful for a few minutes to myself, I checked Chou's temperature again; she seemed unchanged, but I noticed a line of drool running from the corner of her mouth. It had a slight red tint to it.

My thoughts drifted back over everything that had happened since morning. I hadn't even had time to really think about Phillip. Poor, poor, Phillip. Although I had known him for only a few days, his violent murder had rocked me to my very core. Despite his outer gruffness, he'd been a good man, and his affection for Albert had been apparent. It was a painful loss.

I felt a swell of panic rising within me as I realized how close we'd all come to dying. If Wild Bill had not been near enough to hear the fight, or if he had arrived a few minutes later, then the chances were good Albert, Chou, and I would be lying dead alongside Phillip. As it was, Chou had risked her life to save us and had paid a painful price; might even pay the ultimate price. The idea of losing Chou, too... well, that was too painful to even allow myself to consider.

"He reminds me of my boy," Evelyn said.

"What?" I said, suddenly pulled back to the present. "I'm sorry, I was thinking back over... never mind."

A look of concern passed across Evelyn's face, like a cloud moving in front of the sun. "Albert, he reminds me of my own son, Malcolm. He's about the same age. A good boy. A very good boy." Evelyn's mask of abundantly cheerful energy slipped momentarily, a lopsided smile hinting at a deeper pain lying just beneath the surface like a toxic pond. It hadn't even crossed my mind that some of these people might have families they'd left behind. That everyone on this island had their own story to tell, their own pain and worries and fears that were easily equal to my own, if not even more so. This was no time for me to wallow in self-pity and fear.

"I'm so sorry," I managed to say.

"Oh, that's alright." Evelyn reached out and patted my knee affectionately. "It's not like my ending up here was anyone's fault but my own. Others arrived here because of a bad flip of the coin, but I'm the only one responsible for my fate. No one to really blame but me."

I was about to ask what she meant by that but thought better of it. I sensed there was a lot of pain hidden behind the beautiful façade that was Evelyn McHale.

"How many kids... I mean children, do you have?" I asked, trying to redirect the conversation back to something more cheerful.

"Just Malcolm," Evelyn said, her smile returning as she recalled her boy.

"Don't worry, I'll protect you," said Albert, throwing his arms around Evelyn's neck and hugging her tightly.

Evelyn laughed, a cute, girlish giggle, obviously genuinely moved by the boy's show of affection. "That is a *wonderful* thing to say, Albert. You are a *very* chivalrous young man."

"He's also a very *brave* kid," I said.

Albert blushed.

Evelyn cocked her head in exaggerated curiosity. "Oh really? It sounds like there might be a story of knightly gallantry behind that sentence." She spoke her words with no hint of adult condescension. She pulled Albert to her and held him tight, rocking back and forth as she stroked his hair. Finally, she set him down again. "I swear to you, my fine young knight, that just as you have promised to protect me, I will *never* let anyone harm you. Do you hear me?"

Albert nodded, tears appearing at the corner of his own eyes.

"Well, I guess now is as good a time to share my own story," I said. "If you'd like to hear it?"

A dip of Evelyn's head indicated that she would, and I spilled everything that had led up to my arrival on this world, leaving out none of the gory detail.

"You don't look as though you're shocked or surprised," I said when I was done. There was perhaps even a hint of understanding in Evelyn's eyes.

"Time might separate us, but society's problems rarely seem to change," she said. "We're more alike than you would imagine. I knew several people who were frequent users of illicit drugs, and more than a few who were addicted to Horse. We're all just human, after all."

"Horse? What's horse?" I said, a little confused, and thinking she might be referring to a gambling addiction.

"Heroin," Evelyn whispered as though the long arm of the

law might have an interplanetary reach. She flushed red and gave that same innocent giggle she had earlier. "Racehorse trainers used to dose their horses with heroin to give them a little extra pep, if you know what I mean. So... Horse." She smiled, and I laughed along with her.

"Oh, my! Wherever did the time go?" said Evelyn. She stood up. "I'm supposed to be preparing the evening meal," she went on. "Do you feel up to lending a helping hand?"

"Sure," I said. Sitting around fretting wasn't going to help Chou, so the idea of having something to distract me was enticing.

Evelyn turned to Albert and said, "I need to show Meredith something down at the river, would you be a gentleman and watch over your friend Chou for a little while?"

Albert, ever eager to be of assistance, nodded.

"And if you need him, Edward's right over there at the cabin." Evelyn reached out and touched Albert's cheek tenderly. "You're a good boy."

Albert blushed a deep crimson, walked over to where Chou lay and sat next to her, clasping one of her hands in his own.

"Come on," Evelyn said, setting off toward the river. "I need to check the traps."

"Traps?" I asked as I followed her.

"You'll see," Evelyn said.

At its widest, the river stretched two-hundred feet from one side to the other. It moved languidly, like liquid diamond; slow enough that lily-pads grew in clumps below its banks, along with tall bulrushes and wispy reeds, and lined with poplars, oaks, and willows that dipped their weeping branches into the water like fingers trailed behind a boat.

I followed Evelyn along a rough path she must have been responsible for beating, pushing through curtains of bamboo, past trees and bushes heavy with red and black and orange berries until we reached a natural bay, formed at the elbow of the river where it curved to the left, altering its route through softer soil.

"Here we are," said Evelyn. She placed a hand on my shoulder for balance, kicked off her shoes, rolled her pants legs above her knees, and waded out into the water of the bay, moving toward three tall bamboo canes rising up from the water about twenty feet from the earthy riverbank I stood on. The water was shallow enough that, by the time Evelyn made it to the first bamboo cane, the water was still only just above her knees. She reached down, and after a moment or two of feeling around, pulled out a cone-shaped object about four feet long, made from bamboo lashed together to form a cage.

"Fish trap," Evelyn called over to me, grinning from ear to ear while holding the trap above her head so I could see the four large Salmon thrashing within.

She waded back to where I waited for her on the shore, before returning to the other markers to bring back two more traps full of fish.

"Jorge showed us how to make these," Evelyn said, anticipating my question, as I helped her haul the last fish trap out of the water. A wide mouth at one end of the wickerwork trap gradually narrowed to a much narrower hole. It allowed fish to swim in and become trapped in the back section of the cage. The salmon thrashed dementedly as the water spilled from the basket. With a sharp tug, Evelyn dislodged the inner part of the trap from the main basket, laid it at her feet then reached in and pulled out a fish. Dropping to her knees, she placed the salmon on the grass, held it in place and reached for a thick piece of wood from where she had evidently stored it between the roots of a tree. "And we use this," she said, brandishing the piece of wood like a club, "to kill them." She smacked the salmon on the head with the club. The fish, understandably, stopped moving.

Shocked, I gave out a little gasp at the sudden act of brutality.

Evelyn seemed not to notice. She started to hum a catchy upbeat tune to herself as she worked, singing a chorus about 'Rum and Coca-Cola' and 'working for the Yankee dollar' while she proceeded to kill the remaining fish one after the other.

"Now we have to prep them," she said. She pulled a knife from inside the waistband of her pants and set about expertly gutting the fish, tossing the innards out into the river.

"You, uh, look like you've done this before," I said, trying not to allow the revulsion I felt show in my words.

Evelyn glanced up from her butchering, regarding me with raised eyebrows. "Nothing I haven't done on a regular basis for dinner for my family."

"I buy my fish frozen from the supermarket," I said.

"Supermarket?"

"Really, really big stores that sell, well, everything."

"Oh, like a Safeways? I've heard about them out in California. Sounds... easy," Evelyn said as she finished gutting the last fish. There was no judgment in her voice.

"It is... or I suppose, it *was*."

Evelyn picked up the fish and walked back down to the river's edge. I followed. "This next part's a bit, well, messy," she said.

I wondered what could be messier than pulling the entrails out of a fish.

"Here hold these." She dumped the gutted salmon into my outstretched hands where they slipped around like they were still alive. As I fought not to drop them, Evelyn began pulling large handfuls of mud from the river bank until she formed a large mound on the grass between us. "Let's try that big one first," she said, plucking one of the fish from my hands. She immediately began to cover the salmon in the mud, plastering it on until it was an inch deep all over and resembled one of the bricks I had seen Edward pull from the fire earlier. She did the same for two more, then said, "Now you give it a try." She took the remaining fish from me, and I proceeded to try to duplicate the procedure.

"Ahhh," I said as the fish slipped through my hands and onto the grass with a splat. "It's a lot harder than you make it look." Getting the right consistency of the mud so it would stick to the fish scales and not my hands was easier said than done.

"Just add a little water to the mix," Evelyn said, guiding me.

I did as she instructed, molding the more pliant mud around the fish.

"There. Perfect," she announced when I finally had a finished product that somewhat resembled hers.

Perhaps it was my earlier candidness that made Evelyn feel at ease, or maybe it was just that she needed to say what she had to say aloud to someone, I don't know, but as I worked on the next fish, Evelyn took a deep breath, looked me straight in the eye and said "I prefer women to men. That's how I ended up here." She sounded almost apologetic. Her eyes dropped to the ground, and she flushed red. "There I said it." Her eyes rose back to my face, obviously expecting to see judgment in them.

"You mean you prefer women in the romantic sense, right?" I said, cautiously.

Evelyn bit her bottom lip and nodded.

I smiled warmly, and said, "Well good for you." I raised my right hand and waited for her to return my high-five. An awkward three seconds followed of her staring, confused, at my muddy hand before I finally dropped it and gave her a light tap on the knee instead. "But that doesn't really explain how you ended up here." Now I put both hands up in the classic gesture of surrender. "And I completely understand if it's just too personal and you don't want to talk about it."

"You mean how did my preference for women lead to me standing on the bank of a river teaching a woman from the future how to gut fish?" Evelyn said, with only a hint of irony. "No, it's okay, I need to get this off my chest because it's all a bit of a jumble in my head right now."

She placed the fish she had been working on down next to the others we had already prepped, and continued, "I met the love of my life in 1943. We were at war, and I'd joined the Women's Army Corp to do my bit for the effort, as we all did back then. I was stationed in Jefferson City, Missouri, of all places. Her name was Caroline, and she is... *was*... perfect."

A sad smile haunted Evelyn's lips, and a tear began to roll down her right cheek, but she exorcized them both with one muddy hand, leaving a streak of dirt behind.

"Those two years were the best time of my life, but when the war came to an end, I knew there was no way we could carry our love affair into the real world. I was tormented by confusion and self-loathing, and, may God forgive me, I left Caroline without even saying goodbye. I moved to New York, got a job and met a man, married him, had my sweet baby Malcolm by him. Everything seemed... bearable, and for a while, I convinced myself I'd put all of that other foolishness behind me. Then a year after Malcolm was born, I received a letter from Caroline: she had tracked me down and wanted to talk. I met with her, of course. How could I not? But it was with the intention of telling her that there was no chance for us, none at all. I had a husband, a child, a *life*. But, oh, when I saw her sitting at that cafe table, I knew that none of that mattered. I loved her; *that* was what mattered. For the next eight months, we would meet at her apartment every chance we could, planning how we would spend the rest of our lives. And maybe it would have all worked out if my husband hadn't cottoned to what was going on. How he found out, I can only guess, but when I got home one night, my bags were packed and waiting for me on the porch, and no amount of pleading or crying was going to change his mind. I don't know how it is where you're from, but women don't fare so well in divorces in my time. I lost my child, my home, my job. And, my God, the *shame* that was heaped upon me."

"I can't even begin to imagine," I said quietly.

Evelyn smiled sadly, and continued, "Caroline begged me to come away with her; we would move somewhere quiet and live as spinsters, the only acceptable way for society to cast a blind eye to two women living together. But I was inconsolable; I knew everything was my fault and nothing Caroline could say or do was going to make a difference. So I threw myself into the Potomac. It was just as the river pulled me under that I heard a voice offer to save me, to take me someplace where having to worry about who I loved would play no part in my life." Evelyn paused for a second and looked around us. "This wasn't quite what I thought they had in mind for me." She laughed with a heavy dose of melancholy laced through it.

At some point during Evelyn's story, I had taken both of her hands in mine. I squeezed them now and smiled a matching sad smile. We picked up the fish-bricks and began to retrace our steps slowly back along the river bank in the direction of the garrison.

"You can imagine my surprise when I found myself swimming in what I thought was another river that first minute after we arrived," Evelyn said. "I suppose it would have been the ultimate cosmic joke to have drowned in the process of being saved."

I nodded and said, "Well, here we both are then: two suicides given a second chance. If God or the universe or whatever is willing to forgive us for that, then I don't think either are going to be too interested in judging us for who we choose to love."

When we reached the campfire, we began carefully burying the fish-bricks under the glowing cinders.

"Where I come from..." I paused, realizing I would have to change the tense of my memories from this point on. "In the *when* I come from, most people don't have a problem with two women being in love. In fact, they live together openly and can even get married if they want to."

"Married? Really?" Evelyn seemed incredulous.

"Really. People *can* change, Evelyn. Civilization is like a river, it changes people whether they want to or not. It just takes time, that's all."

Evelyn took a moment to consider my words, her head tilted to the right, the ghost of a smile returning to her face. "Well, if you're right," she said quietly, "maybe there's hope for us after all."

ELEVEN

FOR ONE HEART-STOPPING MOMENT, I thought Chou was dead. Then her chest rose and fell, and I exhaled a silent sigh of relief along with her. The afternoon was making way for evening agonizingly slowly. With several hours left until the aurora, I could only hope that Chou was able to hold on until then. I knew this woman from the future was astoundingly strong, but I didn't know if that would be enough to save her from the poison coursing through her body.

Albert had fallen asleep next to Chou, his hand still entwined with hers. I woke him, whispering for him to follow me over to the fire where Evelyn watched over the evening meal.

Long shadows were edging their way across the garrison, and I wondered what time the rest of the camp would quit for the day. As if they'd heard my thoughts, I saw Edward and the rest of his people begin to make their way over to the campfire.

Edward, sweat-stained and dirty, smiled as he approached us. "I see you've had a productive afternoon," he said, eying the fish-bricks baking in the fire's embers.

"Food feeds friendship," Evelyn said, beaming.

"You guys have been pretty busy too," I said. In the time since we had arrived, Edward and his two helpers had all but completed thatching the cabin's roof.

Edward looked back over his shoulder at the cabin. "Tomorrow, God willing, we'll have it finished. It'll be nice to have a proper roof over our heads again, and somewhere secure to store our food and supplies." We spoke for a minute longer, then Edward said, "Well, I could talk your ear off all night, but I think there are a few others here who would like to meet you. Are you ready?"

"You bet," I replied.

Edward got to his feet and called out loudly, "If you'd all gather around, please." He beckoned everyone over to us, and once the last person had arrived, he continued. "I'd like to introduce you to our latest arrivals: Meredith and Albert." I smiled and gave a little wave, Albert leaned into me, suddenly shy. Edward continued, "Their friend Weston was injured earlier today, but she's under Dr. Bull's care now. We're sure she'll make a speedy recovery."

I was glad Edward was confident of Chou's recovery because I certainly wasn't.

A murmur of greetings and nods came from the gathered group. Albert and I smiled back. I did a quick headcount. Not including Chou, Albert, and me, there were thirteen other residents of the garrison, or as Edward liked to call them Garrisonites. The people looking back at me were mostly Caucasian, but there were two heavily muscled men and a strikingly pretty young woman who I guessed were either from South America or perhaps somewhere in the Mediterranean. The two men both wore heavy-looking shirts and thickly-woven pants, stained with sweat and dirt, the sleeves of their shirts rolled up past their elbows, exposing thick, strong forearms. It was obvious these men were used to manual labor, their strength gained from daily hard work, rather than from hours spent at a gym. The young woman, her long black hair pulled up into a tight bun on the top of her head, wore a beautiful dress; a white bodice with intricate embroidery of flowers and beading, the skirt red with black embroidered flowers and beads. She regarded me through half-closed eyes as she stepped closer to the fire, smiling a little nervously.

The rest wore what looked to me to be a mixture of twentieth-century clothing: three of the women wore skirts and blouses and a mixture of jackets or sweaters tied around their waist. The men wore pants and shirts you could've picked up in just about any store in my time. Two also had jackets folded over their arms. Everyone was dirty and smeared with sweat; their skin covered with splashes of dirt and mud. They all had scrapes and cuts and grazes of some kind on their arms and faces. And they all looked tired. And collected together, their body odor was... well, let's just say it was pungent.

A woman appeared from inside the cabin and walked over to me, wiping her hands on a dirty cloth. She thrust out a hand and said in a clipped English accent, "Hello, I'm Jacquetta Hawkes. Very pleased to meet you." She was dressed in light-brown riding jodhpurs tucked into calf-high black boots and a cotton blouse, the sleeves rolled up to show off her tanned arms. The blouse had been white at some point, but it was now stained tea-leaf brown with dirt.

"Pleased to meet you," I said back, and we shook hands.

And finally, there was Peter Freuchen. He looked like he was eight-feet tall and weighed about the same as a fully-grown grizzly bear. He had a head of thick, black, disheveled hair. A matching fuzzy beard hid most of the lower half of his face. A pair of bright, intelligent eyes peered from beneath eyebrows that were so bushy they looked more like fur. He regarded first me, then Albert with equal interest. He strode toward us, and I half expected the ground to shake beneath his feet. Stopping in front of me, his face cracked into a smile.

"Hay-lo," he said in a voice that was surprisingly gentle but heavily accented by what I would later find out was his Danish origins. "My name is Peter, but everyone just calls me Freuchen. I'm very glad to make your acquaintance." He offered his hand, and I automatically took it, my own hand swallowed up in his meaty paw. He wore a thick leather belt with a machete hanging from it. In his other hand Freuchen carried a large wooden-handled ax, and when he caught Albert's eyes straying to it, he chuckled loudly and said, "Don't vurry, little vun I only use this for chopping the trees. You are safe." He gave the ax a playful swing above his head.

Edward stood between Freuchen and Jacquetta. He clapped Freuchen loudly on the back and squeezed Jacquetta's shoulder affectionately. "I see you've made your introductions already. Peter and Jacquetta are our resident translators; and thank God for them, too."

"I speak most European languages," Freuchen said, matter-of-factly and with no sense of boastfulness. "I have traveled the vurld many times over, so it has come in quite useful." He smiled modestly.

Jacquetta said, "And I am fluent in Spanish, French, and German. I can also hold a decent convo in Latin and Ancient Greek. Oh, and I have a passing familiarity with several Arabic dialects." Unlike Freuchen, there was a distinct sense of pride in Jacquetta's voice.

"Jorge, Benito, and Evita don't speak much English," Edward said, looking across at the two men and the woman I had seen first walk back into camp. "Without Freuchen and Jacquetta's help, we would have had a devil of a time understanding each other." Again, I was reminded that whatever *alterations* had been made to me, or Albert, or Chou the previous night that allowed us to communicate so fluently, had not happened to anyone in this group of strangers.

"How is your friend?" Freuchen asked, looking over my shoulder to where Chou lay beneath the shelter.

"She's holding her own," I said.

"Edvard has told me that both you and your friend—"

"Chou," I said, "her name is Weston Chou. Just call her Chou; she seems to like it."

Freuchen nodded. "Sure. Sure. Edvard told me that both you and Chou are from the future. I very much look forvard to talking vith you both, at some point."

He was like a little child; eager to learn as much as he could. The idea that I was, to all of these people other than Chou, some version of a futuristic time traveler had never crossed my mind. All the questions I wanted to ask Chou about what the future was like must be burning just as strongly in these people too.

"Come with me," Edward said, taking me by the elbow. "Let's go introduce you to everyone else. You too, Albert." We walked back toward the fire where the rest of the group had settled, sitting on the logs placed around the fire to act as benches, drinking water from the pots we had seen filled earlier while chatting amongst themselves. Everyone looked exhausted, but apart from their clothing, they all looked so, well... unremarkably *normal*. Certainly not what I would've expected of a group I suspected had been hand-selected for some higher purpose by the *Voice*.

"Alright, everyone, please gather around," Edward said again. Heads turned in our direction, and people moved in closer. "We're going to be seeing a lot of new faces joining us over the coming weeks, I'm sure, and the first of those are here with us this evening. This is Meredith, and the little chap next to her is Albert."

Freuchen began to repeat Edward's words but stopped a half-sentence in, a puzzled expression on his face; an expression echoed on the faces of the three non-English speakers Jorge, Benito, and Evita as they looked first at Edward then Freuchen, then to the rest of the group.

"Is something wrong?" Edward asked Freuchen.

Freuchen seemed confused. "I... you understand vat I'm saying to you?" he said to Edward.

"Yes, of course. Why?" Edward replied, and I felt a sense of déjà vu wash over me.

"He's not speaking English," Albert said, beating me to the answer.

Edward looked puzzled, glanced at me, then across to Freuchen, raising his eyebrows questioningly.

"The boy is correct," said Freuchen. "I am speaking Spanish. At least, I *think* I am."

"This is what you were talking about earlier, isn't it?" Edward said to me. "You said you thought the aurora made some kind of a change to you so that you could understand Chou and she you."

"Yes, but I guess this means it was either me or Albert that the changes were made to. Peter, can you say something in another language?"

"And now I am speaking in French," Freuchen said in perfect English.

Jorge, Benito, and Evita regarded us intently, everyone else seemed mildly confused as to what was going on. I smiled at Evita and stepped forward, extending my hand. "Hello," I said, "I'm Meredith, can you understand me?"

Both Jorge and Benito looked at each other as though I was setting them up somehow, but Evita smiled warmly and said, "Yes, your Spanish is perfect."

I glanced back over my shoulder at Edward and Freuchen. "I hardly speak any Spanish."

Jacquetta's face broke into an amused smile. "This is *very* strange, very *interesting*, but mostly *very* strange. The question would appear to be which of you is the one responsible for this... psychic translation."

"Let's find out," I said and walked away from the group. When I was about fifty feet away, I waved my hand and waited as Freuchen, Edward, Jacquetta, and Evita talked amongst themselves. I was out of earshot, so saw only their mouths working silently and then the shrugs and raised hands that seemed to indicate they could no longer understand each other.

Freuchen waved me back, and I jogged over to them.

"Well?" I said.

Jacquetta answered, "As soon as you moved away, only Freuchen and I were able to understand anything that was said."

"I can understand you now," said Jorge, nodding sternly.

"Now, I too can understand you," Benito added.

Evita smiled and nodded enthusiastically. "As can I."

"Vell," said Freuchen, "it seems ve have an answer to who our new interpreter is."

"Let me try something else," I said. "Keep talking until you can't understand each other anymore," I said.

Edward nodded and began to recite aloud to Evita a poem that seemed familiar to me.

I began to back away from the group, taking one step at a time and pausing. Around thirty feet, as Edward's voice became muffled and indistinct, I saw Evita's head tilt sideways in puzzlement, her smile turning into a look of confusion and mild amusement. Edward turned toward me and yelled for me to come back.

"It looks like I have to be close to you for whatever this effect is to work," I said. "As soon as I can't hear you, the translation ability stops. It's like I'm some kind of human Wi-Fi router." I realized by the puzzled looks directed at me that no one but me knew what a wireless router was. "A radio transmitter. It's like I'm a radio transmitter, but with a very short range." That explanation seemed to do it for the majority of the people to grasp the concept.

"This is incredible," Freuchen said, but I barely heard him. My mind was occupied with wondering why I had been singled out to receive this... ability.

"So many questions," I said.

"Excuse me?" said Edward.

"Oh, nothing. Just thinking aloud. Look, we're obviously not going to get any answers as to why I have this ability any time soon, so we might as well make use of it." I turned and smiled apologetically at Freuchen. "Sorry to put you out of a job, big guy."

When Freuchen laughed, it sounded like thunder echoing down a valley. "That is fine vith me. I have other things I could be doing."

Edward nodded slowly. "Let's get on with the introductions then, shall we?"

As I'd noted earlier, the Garrisonites were just every day, normal people. Jorge was an Argentinian fisherman who had drowned during a storm at sea in the winter of 1908. Oliver Schwartz, a tall, gaunt-looking man in a gray business suit, was an architect. The *Voice* had plucked him from his time when the private airplane he had been piloting alone to Bermuda had crashed into the ocean just before Christmas of 1965.

Benito Bella was a lumberjack who'd been in the process of bleeding to death after an accident with his saw in the Venezuelan rainforests in late 1898. Tabitha Keenan, a strikingly beautiful Irish botanist, said she died of malaria while on a solo expedition to the Amazon in 1958. Sarah Harmon, a veterinarian, had chosen to end her own life for reasons she was not willing to talk about. And Jacquetta was an archaeologist.

"I had a bit of an accident while exploring a tomb in Egypt in 1941," Jacquetta said, by way of a cryptic explanation as to how she had ended up here with us.

Caleb Doggett, a haggard, stone-faced man of very few words told me he had been close to burning to death after his Texas homestead had caught fire sometime around 1902.

And last but not least was Evita Samaniego; the quiet-spoken woman from Mexico in the beautiful red and white dress which, it turned out, she'd made herself. She was a seamstress from San Pedro. Evita thought she'd probably died from tuberculosis, as her husband and three young children had already succumbed to the disease weeks earlier, leaving her alone. The last few weeks of her life were still so foggy within her mind, she couldn't be sure. All she remembered for certain was the *Voice* offering to save her.

Everyone remembered the *Voice*.

There were no geniuses among them. No great leaders (at least that I knew of at the time) and, apart from Wild Bill, no one I recognized as standing out in history. But when you considered them as a *group*, they all had very specific skills or knowledge; knowledge that would be really useful for sustaining a civilization... *or* maybe for starting a new one.

As darkness settled over the garrison, and the shattered moon rose deathly-white to haunt the sky, we pulled the salmon Evelyn and I had prepared out of the fire's ashes. We ate as a group gathered around the fire and talked for the next couple of hours about our own times, safe within the campfire's lambent glow, burning furiously now as it was fed more branches. When everyone had eaten their fill, Edward dispatched Wild Bill and Benito Bello to stand watch on the perimeter of the camp.

The fire pushed back the darkness far enough that I could see all the way to the edge of the camp in one direction and almost to the bank of the river in the other. Overhead, the sky was cloudless and already buckshot with stars, the likes of which I had never seen before. Thousands upon thousands of them peppered the black canvas, mingling almost imperceptibly with the mysterious network of lights between us and the sun. I could not recognize one constellation amongst them. The moon, its tail of debris dragging behind it, crawled across the night sky. I strained my eyes to try to see the structures I thought I'd spotted on its surface earlier, but all I could make out now were shadows and craters. I would need a decent pair of binoculars or a telescope to be certain there was anything really there or whether it had been a trick of the light.

I noticed Bull kneeling next to Chou and excused myself from the group. The doctor held Chou's hand in his own, the back of his other hand placed against her perspiration covered forehead.

"I fear your friend has taken a turn for the worse," Bull said, looking up as I approached. Chou was soaked with perspiration. Her skin pallid, almost the color of chalk. Her eyes moved constantly and rapidly beneath her eyelids, and she groaned deeply as though she were caught in a nightmare she couldn't wake from.

A wave of panic spread through me. "Isn't there *something* you can do for her?" I begged, clutching Chou's hand.

Bull shook his head slowly. "I *am* sorry," he said, by way of a final prognosis, then, head hung, walked slowly away.

I felt a deep sense of frustration at my inability to help the woman who had undoubtedly saved my own life the previous night, and then again today, potentially at the cost of her own. I mopped the sheen of sweat covering her forehead with a water-soaked rag. Beneath Chou's lids, her eyes would occasionally jerk left and right. And twice I could have sworn I heard her mutter what I thought was the word 'husband,' but I couldn't be sure, her voice was so fragile, barely even qualifying as a whisper.

I continued to gently stroke Chou's hair until she quietened again.

Shadows leaped across the camp in a synchronized dance with the flames of the campfire, pushing back the darkness then allowing it in again as the flames rose and fell. I watched my new compatriots talk and eat together, my translation ability passively allowing them to finally converse freely. I felt a faint sense of pride that I was, at least, able to do this for these people, but again I wondered why me? What was so special about *me*? But my mind was too exhausted with worry for my dying friend to hold onto the question for longer than a few seconds.

I stretched out next to Chou. If she was going to die, I was going to be right here at her side when it happened. It was the very least I could do for her. I cast my eyes skyward; the aurora *couldn't* be too far away now. She just needed to hold on a *little* longer.

Chou breathed raggedly, then slowly dropped again. Once, twice more. A wheezing, high-pitched whistle escaped from between her lips, then Weston Chou, pilot of the starship the *Shining Way*, the woman who I owed my life to, took one final breath and then breathed no more.

TWELVE

"CHOU!" I cried out, shifting position from my side to my knees. "Chou! Wake up," This time I yelled the words, but still, there was no response.

Her mouth hung open, exposing perfect teeth tinged with blood, her eyes stared sightlessly at the roof of the lean-to through half-closed lids. I glanced over at the Garrisonites, but no one noticed me, the crackle of the fire and their energetic conversation covering my words, the shadows hiding my frantic movements.

"No. No... no." I leaned in close to Chou's mouth, listening for any sign she was breathing. There was nothing. I placed two fingers against her neck, checked for a pulse, but felt none.

"You can't die. I won't let you," I hissed into her ear. I'd taken a first-aid course, years ago, and I wracked my brain for the memory. I'd checked her pulse, checked her breathing. I had to get her heart going again.

Leaning in, I tilted Chou's head back, pinched her nose shut, and placed my lips over hers which were already blue around the edges. Was it three or five puffs? I couldn't remember. I settled on four and quickly breathed them into her and was rewarded with a corresponding inflation of her chest, but the second I stopped, she did too.

"It's okay," I said to myself, "you can do this." I placed one hand on top of the other, interlaced my fingers and laid them over the center of her chest. The instructor had told me the easiest way to remember the correct rate of chest compressions was to follow the beat of the *Bee Gee's* song *Staying Alive*, so I started singing it to myself now as I pushed up and down on her chest.

One-two-three-four.

One-two-three-four.

"Oh God, I'm sorry. I'm so sorry," I cried when I felt one of Chou's ribs crack beneath my hands while trying not to lose count of how many compressions I'd completed. When I reached thirty, I stopped and gave her two more quick breaths then went back to the chest compressions.

"Meredith?"

I looked up and saw Edward and the rest of the Garrisonites standing around me, their faces marked with concern.

Albert clung to Evelyn, his eyes as large as saucers. "Is... is Chou going to be alright?" he barely managed to mumble through the tears rushing down his cheeks.

"Yes," I said, "I just... have to keep... this going... until the—"

A thunderous boom cracked apart the silence of the night, and everyone turned to look skyward.

Albert, Chou, and I had been deep in the forest every night prior to this one, so clouds and the forest's canopy had blocked most of the sky and the aurora from us. We'd caught glimpses of it, of course, but tonight, here in this clearing, I had an almost completely unobstructed view. I looked up in time to see a column of blue-green light shoot into the sky far off to the east; the same direction as the first monolith that dominated the horizon in the daylight hours, I noted. More light columns exploded skyward from the west, south, and north.

There was a collective gasp of amazement from almost everyone as, in a split-second, the light columns split into branches that traveled across the firmament high above our heads, tendrils of color shooting off from larger bolts to create smaller light trails (smaller at least in comparison to the main bolts. These lesser off-shoots must still have been tens of miles in length). In graceful arcs, the aurora crisscrossed the sky from all four cardinal directions, converging on a central point, as though seeking each other out. They *had* to have originated from the monoliths; it couldn't be coincidental. Right? I mean, what were the chances?

All around us, tiny spots of brilliance flickered into life, just as they had in the forest, suspended in the air and covering every object and building; energized it seemed by the aurora's raw, naked energy.

"Pixie dust," I heard Evelyn say.

The nano-particles that had, until now, floated, invisible in the air around us glowed and pulsed, shifting on the night's warm eddies and currents. Within a matter of seconds, everything was aglow with their strange ethereal luminescence. The trees around the perimeter of the camp were turned into lamps, their trunks and branches ignited with the tiny motes. The lean-tos glowed like Christmas decorations. My hands were covered in hundreds of tiny glowing dots, shimmering with an intensity that was quite beautiful, unthreatening.

Chou too was covered in the tiny specks of light, but unlike those on my hands, hers were moving in what appeared to be a very deliberate fashion. A gentle stream of particles drifted across her chest, then over my hands as I continued to administer chest compressions, as they moved toward the wound in her hip. More lambent streams flowed into her mouth and nostrils.

The Garrisonites had all turned to stare at the sky, gripped by the awe-inspiring show playing out above us. Sarah and Evita stood together just outside the next lean-to. They moved their hands through the air, shifting the glowing pixie dust like they were water droplets, a look of almost mystical awe on their faces. With each passing second, the aurora grew brighter but other than the initial crash to announce its arrival, the event was silent. As the light grew in intensity, I felt an electric tingle move across my skin. It was like the feeling of pins and needles you get after a limb goes to sleep, but this was a pleasant sensation, almost soothing. I hadn't realized how badly my neck and back ached from the continued exertion of trying to resuscitate Chou until I felt the dull throb of pain fade away as a wave of relaxation washed over me.

Beneath my hands, I felt a growing warmth; it came from Chou's skin! The warmth quickly grew to heat, intense enough I had to pull my hand away. I looked down again at Chou and gasped in amazement. She was almost completely cocooned in the nanites, radiating so intensely it hurt my eyes; the heat was emanating from them as they worked whatever magic it was they did.

"Please," I begged, "please work."

I felt the full power of the aurora wash over me. I stumbled to my feet, unable to look at Chou, the light was so bright now. The sensation flooding my system was almost but not quite as good as my first opiad-induced high. Every muscle in my body relaxed, and after a few moments, I felt... rejuvenated. I took a couple of steps away from the lean-to my attention pulled skyward by the maelstrom of light coursing across it.

Edward stood next to Albert and Evelyn, their backs to me, faces turned heavenward. "It's so beautiful," Edward said, turning to look at me. The light played across his face and, again, I was struck by the notion that I knew him from *somewhere*, but from where continued to elude me.

"The most beautiful thing I've ever seen," I said.

Albert turned at the sound of my voice. His eyes locked on mine, then shifted focus to a point behind me. A huge smile spread across the boy's face.

"Hello, Chou," Albert said, beaming now.

I spun around.

Chou was sitting up, blinking hard as the light of the fire played across her face. Pixie dust still moved over her skin and clothing, but with less urgency. She shook her head, blinked a couple of times, then gave a little shuffle of her shoulders as if trying to get rid of a knot in her muscles.

She rose unsteadily to her feet and looked around at the people staring back open-mouthed at her, a slightly confused expression on her face. Spotting Albert and me, Chou smiled and said, "Hello, Meredith. Hello, Albert. I'm very hungry. Do you have anything to eat?"

"How's it taste?" I asked Chou as she picked apart the last of the salmon. She washed the last mouthful down with a gulp of water before answering.

"Delicious!" she replied, smiling back at me.

Cold Salmon is hardly something I would ever describe as *delicious*, but hey, under the circumstances, I got it. "I cooked it myself," I said, which got a raised eyebrow from Chou. "I'll explain later. Now, will you please tell me how you're feeling?"

Chou pondered the question for a second while she licked her oily fingers clean, then said, "Very good. I feel... very good." She pulled up the hem of her blouse and pushed down the waistband of her pants to expose her left hip. The arrow wound had completely healed leaving only an area of fresh pink skin much like I had seen on Phillip's head wound.

"Miraculous!" said Bull, leaning in closer to get a better look. "Absolutely miraculous!"

Edward stood to my left. Crowded behind him were the faces of the rest of the camp, all fascinated by Chou's miraculous recovery. "What kind of technology can bring the dead back to life?" Edward asked.

I paused as I tried to think of a way to articulate the complexity of how the nano-clusters worked (not that I had anything but a rudimentary idea myself), but Chou beat me to it.

"From what Meredith has told me, I was not truly dead; at least not for long enough."

"You were 'only mostly dead,'" I said, smiling to myself at the *Princess Bride* reference.

But Chou actually nodded. "You are correct, in a way, Meredith. Your resuscitation efforts managed to keep my heart pumping blood and oxygen to my brain long enough for the pixie dust to rid my body of the poison arrow's toxin and repair the damage it had caused. So, to answer your question, Edward: Advanced technology. Very, very advanced medicine."

Bull said, "Does this mean that we are immortal? If we die, will the..." He screwed his face up in obvious disgust at having to say "*...Pixie dust...* bring us back to life?"

Chou shook her head. "There are too many variables. But I believe it will depend on the extent of the wounds or illness that caused the fatality. And, most importantly, how long before the aurora's arrival the deceased perished. I think I was both lucky to have expired close to the aurora and to have such a determined friend." Chou looked up at me and smiled, and I grinned back at her.

"I still can't believe it," Evelyn said. "I had scratches on my hands, just small ones, but they're gone. It's like magic."

"Same here," said Oliver, the guy who had crashed his plane. "Had a three-inch long cut on my arm. It's vanished. See!" He extended his right arm and showed me the line of pink skin where the laceration had been.

"And I feel so refreshed," I said. "Like I got a really great night's rest."

People nodded enthusiastically.

"It's like I've spent a week at the seaside," Edward said.

"Yes," rumbled Freuchen, "that is exactly vot I feel like; as though I have had a relaxing holiday."

Chou continued, "It seems that whatever brought us to this island—"

"Avalon," Albert chimed in. "We should call the island Avalon."

"Ver King Arthur sleeps eternally," Freuchen said. "Yes, I like that idea very much."

"A ship with shields before the sun, six maidens round the mast. A red-gold crown on everyone, a green gown on the last," Edward recited quietly.

"That's William Morris," I said, impressed. I had to think for a second before I remembered the poem's title. Then it came to me, "Near Avalon," I said, pleased I'd remembered.

"Indeed," said Edward, who seemed even more impressed that I knew it.

"Yes, Avalon," said Chou, smiling and dipping her head to the boy. "Whoever is responsible for bringing us all here to Avalon desires that we stay alive and healthy."

"You think there's an intelligence behind this with a plan, too. Don't you?" I said.

Chou nodded. "All evidence that I have observed would point to that being the most likely conclusion, I believe."

I felt a warm glow of vindication in my chest. I hadn't had time to tell Chou that I seemed to be the one behind our ability to communicate in each other's language, but I did so now.

"Interesting," Chou whispered when I was done. "That would seem to increase the probability that we were brought here with a very specific purpose in mind."

Edward stood up. "Could it be," he said, "that we are here to populate this planet? It makes perfect sense to me. Why else would you relocate so many doomed people to this island, heal them, give them abundant food and water sources, if not to have them start humanity over? We were all going to die, right? But we didn't. We all accepted the offer the *Voice* made. Now we've been given a second chance on this world... to create a brave *new* world." He looked down at Albert and smiled, "A chance for the metaphorical Arthur to rise from this island and reclaim that which he was sworn to protect and hold dominion over. Begin all over again. Afresh."

While I appreciated the romantic notion of Edward's theory, if anything, it sounded *too* altruistic.

Chou got up and walked to the fire. Everyone else followed along with her as though she were the Pied Piper. "I do not believe this to be a new world, Edward," she said.

"Why?" said, Jacquetta, the archaeologist. "Surely, to make that kind of a statement, you must have some evidence to back up your assertion?"

Chou dipped her head in acknowledgment. "You will have all noticed the net-like structure that surrounds this world's star, yes?"

"It's hardly missable," said Bull, glancing up at the dots of light that peppered the night sky.

"I believe those lights are part of a structure known as a Dyson Swarm."

"What on God's good green earth is a 'Dyson Swarm?'" asked Edward, stepping closer.

Chou thought for a second. "Think of it as a way of harnessing vast amounts of energy collected from the sun. Millions of mirrors are placed in rings orbiting a star, collecting unimaginable amounts of energy; all the energy needed to power a highly advanced civilization's technology."

"Like a windmill?" said Jorge.

"Or a waterwheel," Freuchen added.

"Similar in principle, yes," Chou said, "but on an unimaginable scale. Imagine the power a billion windmills would provide. The Dyson swarm transfers the energy it collects back to earth, where I believe it is collected by the giant towers on the horizon. Some of that energy will be consumed by the aurora on a nightly basis, to power the nano-bots that resuscitated me."

"But, surely, the energy the Dyson Swarm is collecting can't *all* be going to power the aurora?" I said.

"You are correct," Chou replied. "It would, of course, have taken an unimaginable amount of energy to bring all of us here to this planet. Even so, I estimate there is still a surplus of available energy, collecting in some kind of storage device, perhaps. Unless..."

"Unless, what?" said Edward.

"Unless that energy is being used to power other technology we are not yet aware of."

"Like what?" Tabitha asked.

"The applications would be unlimited, capable of powering vast computers, starships, and off-world ecologies." Chou rattled off.

Edward leaned forward, obviously fascinated. "But how does that disprove my theory that we have all been brought here for a second chance?"

"You have observed how bright the sun is?" Chou said.

"It does seem far brighter than our own," Edward agreed.

"And bigger," Albert said. "It's definitely bigger."

Chou smiled at the boy. "Yes, well done Albert. Both of those things are indications that this star is old; past what you could call middle-age, if you wish to use a human analogy. I believe that the star is only a few tens of millions of years away from becoming a Red Giant, which will mean the complete annihilation of all life on this planet. That observation is backed up by the fact that whatever race lived on this planet must have been extremely advanced to have built the Dyson Swarm; at least level II on the Kardashev Scale. That takes a long time to achieve."

"Hey! I know that one," I said. "The Kardashev Scale is a measurement of the amount of energy a civilization needs to power itself, right?"

"Correct, Meredith. The scale starts at Type I and progresses up to III and, theoretically, beyond. Where Type I is a civilization that can store energy that reaches it from its star. A Type II civilization would be capable of building technology that harnesses all its parent star's energy, and Type III is able to harvest energy on a galactic scale. And as the scale is logarithmic, as a civilization progresses further along the scale, so its energy consumption grows exponentially. An industrial culture such as the one Edward is from at the turn of the twentieth century would not even reach the threshold of a Type I classification. Meredith's time would be on the low end of Type I, and my own time would be getting close to Type II. To be able to construct and utilize the Dyson Swarm would place this planet's dominant civilization firmly in the Level II bracket."

"So, the question is: where is the civilization that made the Dyson Swarm?" Evelyn said quietly.

"Precisely!" Chou said. "Since our arrival, there has been no attempt by the *Voice* to contact us. There also appear to be gaps in the swarm's net, which suggests that no one is concerned with repairing it. So, where is everyone? The only conclusion I can draw is that whatever civilization once lived on this planet has either gone extinct or has migrated elsewhere. Which again suggests that this planet is far older than we suspect."

"Fascinating," Edward said. "Quite fascinating."

"In conclusion," Chou continued, "I see no reason for the *Voice* to have brought us here if the planet will be rendered uninhabitable in the near future. No, there must be another reason."

A silence descended over us that lasted until Edward said, "Well, if what you say is true, Chou, it brings us back full circle to the first question we all have: why did the *Voice* bring us here to begin with? Why save *us*?"

"That is a question I'd very much like an answer to," Bull said, more to himself than any of us.

Chou continued, "Anything we postulate is, at best, conjecture, at worst, uninformed. There is only one way for us to be sure, and that is to speak directly with the entity we call the *Voice*."

"You think the *Voice* will try to contact us at some point?" said Tabitha.

"Perhaps," said Chou.

"You don't appear to be convinced?" Edward said.

"While the intelligence behind our transportation here is undeniably advanced, I am confused by the way we were... *deposited* in such a dangerous manner the day we arrived. It strikes me as being very clumsy. Out of character with the finesse and attention to detail of everything else I have observed on this world. To bring all of us here, arriving together from our various times must have been an immense undertaking that would not only have taken an incredible amount of energy, the source of which we can now say we know, but also incredible coordination and planning. Huge computational power far beyond what was available even in my time."

"So?" Bull interjected. It was obvious he was only barely following the thread of Chou's explanation, but he seemed to get the gist of it at least.

Chou answered him. "Assuming our belief that there is some kind of a plan for us is correct, why would the *Voice* drop us so unceremoniously into the ocean? Why risk losing so many of us after going to such painstaking detail to find us and transport us here? Why not simply deposit everyone onto the beach, together? Why leave us to fend for ourselves? The idea that a plan which required such precision to bring us here could then place us in a position where our survival is left to chance, seems implausible to me."

"Maybe the *Voice* wasn't able to do any of that? Maybe their calculations were off?" I said.

"Maybe they did it that way so we wouldn't be hurt. You know, a soft landing into the ocean," Oliver said.

I shook my head. "I don't think so. I fell maybe three or four feet, and we were dropped pretty far offshore. Worst case scenario, if we'd arrived on the beach or in the shallows, would have been a few people with broken bones or bruised egos. I saw at least one woman drown and I helped rescue several more who would have died, which means not everyone knew how to swim."

"And anyone who was hurt on arrival would have been healed the first night after the aurora," said Edward.

"Exactly," I said. "As I told you before, I saw one woman drown for certain. There *must* have been others. Albert would have been one of them if I hadn't been able to reach him in time."

Tabitha, Oliver, and Evelyn all said that they had seen

people drown or swept out to sea. Edward and Bull said they had seen bodies on the beach and floating in the water.

"Perhaps that wasn't supposed to be a part of the plan. Maybe something went wrong?" said Evelyn.

"Or perhaps the plan was sabotaged?" I said.

"Sabotaged?" said Wild Bill.

I quickly recounted our run-in with the swordsman that began with Phillip's murder. "Those two men didn't seem particularly friendly and would have murdered the rest of us as well if it hadn't been for you, Wild Bill. So, maybe someone's working against whatever plan the *Voice* has for us. I mean, dropping us offshore seems like a pretty good way to screw up the plan early on."

"It vould help account for the two assassins," said Freuchen.

"What you're saying," said Wild Bill, "is that someone ain't too thrilled about us being here. Someone who ain't the *Voice*. Someone... *else*?"

"A saboteur? Meredith may well be right," Chou said. "I believe that an undertaking such as we are a part of must have been planned meticulously and would have been executed just as precisely. For something to go so obviously wrong must mean one of two things: One... the *Voice* failed to adequately account for all variables of the space/time transference or two... as Meredith has suggested, an extraneous force was exerted on the process in an attempt to kill as many of us as possible upon our arrival. Given the available information, I believe that the second option is the most likely, considering the preparation, complexity and flawless execution of the plan up until that point."

Silence descended over the group. The idea that there might be someone... or some *thing* else working against us sent literal shivers down my back. And judging by the look of concern on everyone else's face, I wasn't alone in how exposed I suddenly felt. "Great, just what we need," I whispered. This was all weird enough without the idea that someone wanted us all dead.

Edward broke the gloomy silence with an injection of optimism. "We need to remember that this is all just theory at this point. We don't know for certain that any of it is true, well, most of it, anyway. So, we need to keep our chins up. The one thing we all know is we were chosen for a reason." He smiled a broad, attractive smile. "I'll be the first to admit that I have no bloody idea what that reason might be, but we have to look after each other until we do."

There were returned smiles and even a little nervous laughter.

"Vat do ve do in the meantime?" said Freuchen. "Ve can't just sit around and act as though none of this is happening? Vat do ve do between now and ven the *Voice* decides to grace us vith his—"

"Or her," interjected Tabitha.

"Yes, or her presence," Freuchen agreed,

"We continue along the same path we are already on," Edward answered, rising to his feet. "Our priority is to ensure the garrison and all who live within her walls are safe. We continue to build the cabins and the stockade, expand the garrison if we must. We have a fine location here. If this is to be our home, then we need to be able to protect it."

"And then?" said Sarah.

"Then we canvas the island. Find out what resources there are. There must be more people; we all saw them on the beach. We need to find as many good men and women as we can and bring them into our fold. There's strength in numbers."

Chou nodded. "That seems like a reasonable plan of action."

"And after that? What if the *Voice* decides to stay quiet? What are we supposed to do then?" This from Wild Bill.

"If the mountain will not come to Muhammad, then Muhammad must go to the mountain," said Bull.

"We can cross that bridge if and when we ever get to it," Edward said. "In the meantime, we should all get some rest. We can talk more about this in the coming days."

A wave of *goodnights* echoed over the camp as everyone moved to their quarters. Albert said he wanted to sleep near the fire, something I could understand; its warmth and light instilled the only real sense of security any of us could feel at this point. "Of course," I said. "Chou and I are right over here." I pointed back at the lean-to we would be spending the night beneath, Chou already sat cross-legged under its roof.

I gave Albert a kiss on the top of his head and whispered, "Sleep well," then joined my newly resurrected friend.

THIRTEEN

THE EARLY-MORNING SUN provided little warmth, despite the sky remaining clear overnight. I exhaled pale billowy clouds as I got to my feet and stretched. Around me, the camp was gradually coming to life, gravitating one by one to the campfire. The night had been cool, but not terribly uncomfortable, and we all seemed extraordinarily refreshed despite the stress of the previous day. I thought about the sudden rush of energy I'd experienced during the aurora. I'd felt so energized, so invigorated; like I'd taken a two-week vacation. That initial surge and feeling of well-being had gradually faded, but still, this morning I felt far better than I should have after a night spent on the ground with nothing but a bed of leaves as a mattress. I *should* have aches in my muscles and pain in my joints, but I felt... great, especially so after Chou's miraculous recovery.

I walked to the fire, drawn by its warm currents. Chou was up and had already captured everyone's attention. Albert sat nearby. As I drew closer, I caught the tail-end of a question Chou was posing Edward.

"—the axes, saws, hammers and nails I see you and your people using; where did they come from?" she asked.

Edward took a handful of berries of assorted color from a bowl, his lips stained the same colors as the berries. He swallowed and said, "We found some of them washed up on the beach next to a broken wooden crate. And others came with our people, like Peter and his ax."

"I saw things falling from the sky while I was in the water," I said as I got closer, remembering those first few minutes after arrival. "Apart from people, I mean. There were parts of the bridge I was on when I..." I let my words fade away, not willing to share the manner in which I'd left Earth behind so openly. "Anyway, it was as though whatever process the *Voice* used to bring us here, couldn't bring *just* us here. It brought things that were around us, too."

"Yes," said Evelyn, "I saw that, too."

Others nodded in agreement.

"Do you think the crate washed ashore or do you think it was placed there?" said Chou.

Edward shook his head. "Hard to tell for sure," he said. "It was just sitting there. We snagged everything from it."

"Might have come from a wreck or maybe it was the contents of an airplane or something," I said.

Bull said, "Perhaps it would be wise for us to organize search parties to explore the coast, perchance there are more such crates or loot waiting for us to find. Better we locate them before anyone else does."

Edward nodded. "That's a fine idea, Doctor. We'll organize a couple of groups soon as we're done here." Edward held his words for a moment or two, then said, "And you bring up something that's been weighing on my mind: there have to be other people somewhere out there. I, for one, saw at least a hundred or more in the water upon my arrival and only a few of those faces are sitting here with us. We need to remember we're not alone on this island. And while all of you are amiable enough, let's not forget the two men who accosted Meredith's group and killed their companion as proof that not everyone is going to be as welcoming. It's only going to be a matter of time before someone wanders into camp or we encounter another group. And while I'm not saying we should treat anyone we meet as an enemy, we need to be cautious. We'll keep the lookouts posted around the perimeter, and I'll expect all of you to take your turn in watching over us. If we are going to meet others, best it's on our terms rather than theirs." As Edward spoke his gaze moved over each of us. "Now, I need volunteers to form scavenger parties to go search for anything they can find on the beach. Two groups of three should do the trick."

Chou looked at me, eyebrows raised. I nodded at her unspoken question.

"Meredith and I volunteer," Chou said.

Edward nodded and smiled. "Who else?"

"I'll go vith them," said Freuchen. He got to his feet and, stretched, the joints of his huge frame audibly popping.

Benito, Caleb, and Tabitha volunteered for the second group.

Edward nodded, looking pleased. "Well, that's sorted then. One group will go clockwise around the island, the other counter. I'd like for you all to lend a hand around the garrison today. That'll give us time to prepare supplies for you, and you'll be able to get an early start tomorrow. Okay?"

We all nodded.

"Anyone else got anything they'd like to add?' Edward said. "No? Alright then, let's get some grub in our bellies and get to work."

"Do you mind if I join you?" Edward asked Chou and me as we

finished our breakfast of wild berries together. He sat on the log with us, legs outstretched, hands folded in his lap. "If you feel up to getting your hands dirty today, we could use your help around the camp."

"Of course," I said, "what do you need us to do?"

"I'd say you could help Evelyn, but it looks to me like Albert has already usurped your job."

I laughed. Albert had really taken to Evelyn and she to him. She had asked if he would like to help her around camp and the boy had eagerly agreed.

"So, let's see what else do we have? We need someone to make sure the laborers all have fresh water. And Bull and Freuchen could use a knot bumper, or, if that's not to your liking, you could maybe scavenge branches to make sure the fire has enough fuel for the night."

I was about to ask what the hell a 'knot bumper' was but Chou spoke right over me. "That man, the one setting the stakes for the stockade, what is his name?" She pointed in the direction of the slowly growing perimeter wall of wooden stakes.

"Jorge? Why?"

"I would like to help him," Chou said.

Edward suppressed a smile. "I'm sure he'd be happy to have your company, but that's very physical labor, and I don't think—"

Chou stood up, reached down, and grasped the end of the log we had been sitting on with both hands and proceeded to lift it off the ground as if she were merely lifting a sofa.

Edward and I both jumped to our feet as, in three swift movements, she repositioned the ten-foot-long tree trunk into an upright position. I felt my jaw drop; the log must have weighed close to six-hundred pounds if it was an ounce and she manhandled it like it was nothing.

"I believe I am more than capable of helping Jorge," Chou said.

"I... uhhh... I believe you have made your point, Ms. Chou," Edward said, nodding approvingly at her demonstration of brute strength, his broad smile showing how deeply impressed he was.

"I concur," Chou said, lowering the log down into its original position beside the fire.

"So," said Edward, "on second thought, why don't the two of you help Jorge set the posts for the stockade."

"I'm down with that," I said, suppressing laughter that threatened to bubble up from deep in my chest.

"As am I," said Chou, straight-faced.

"Thank you, ladies," Edward said.

As he turned to walk away, Chou said, "Edward, wait. I have a question for you."

"Ask away."

"Have any of the group shared what they were doing immediately before their encounter with the *Voice* with you?"

"Some," Edward admitted. "Why?"

"Would you tell me their stories, please," her words were more a demand than inquiry.

Edward gave a little chuckle at Chou's directness. "Well, seeing as you asked so nicely." He lowered himself down onto the log. "Let's see. Benito told us he was a lumberjack working alone in the mountains of Venezuela. The saw he used to section a tree he'd felled hit a knot and he sliced his arm open." Edward made a cutting motion across his left arm. "He said he was losing a lot of blood and was many miles from his camp and any help. The *Voice* came to him as he was losing consciousness and asked him if he wanted to live."

"Who else?" Chou said.

"Jorge said he was washed overboard from a fishing boat in a nighttime storm and he was heading to the bottom of the ocean when he heard the *Voice*. Evelyn drowned too, though that was at her own hand; not something I believe she would want shared, so, if you would be so kind as to keep it to yourselves. Caleb said he would have surely died in the fire that took his home. And Wild Bill said he got sick after being bit by a Rattlesnake while crossing Arizona." Edward chuckled, "He was a little bit more colorful in his description, of course. And that's as much as anyone has shared with me, and I'm not the type to put my nose into other people's affairs if privacy is what they desire. You might want to speak directly with the others about how they got their ticket to Avalon."

"And you, Edward? What circumstances led the *Voice* to ask you?" Chou said, her voice still low.

Edward's eyes lost focus for a few seconds before he spoke again. "My regiment had been ordered to bolster our forces defending Ypres—that is, or was, a little village in Belgium. By the time we arrived in mid-April of 1915, there really wasn't enough left of the place to fit in a matchbox. I'd been ordered out on a reconnaissance mission to verify the location of a Hun artillery battery. Instead, the Huns, or rather their artillery bombardment found me first. I was caught in a barrage and hit by shrapnel—" Edward's hand unconsciously drifted to the right side of his chest "—and blown off my feet into a shell hole. It'd been raining heavily, and I was up to my neck in mud and muck and my own blood. I tried to pull myself out but the walls of the crater were too soft, and I couldn't get a grip. Then another shell landed nearby, and the crater wall collapsed, burying me under what I imagine must have been ten feet of mud. I was close to suffocating when I heard the *Voice* tell me it could save me." He gave a slow nod to indicate that he'd finished.

"I am... sorry," said Chou.

Edward waved off her reply. "What was one more life in

that meat grinder? I saw more death in my months over there than I ever thought imaginable. But I tell you now, *this* experience..." he shifted his gaze left then right, his eyes doing the pointing as they moved first to the caged sun, then the forest, then to the others working on their tasks, "...it's changed my view on *all* of that trouble. Now I have proof that there's something greater than all the world's petty struggles and arguments. And I have to wonder whether those lives that were so senselessly cut short aren't maybe here on this planet, somewhere. It gives me hope." He gave an emphatic nod, as if to reinforce the sentiment. "Now, I've told you what you wanted to hear, why don't you tell *me* why you're so eager to learn our stories?"

Chou took a swig of water. "Tell me, do you notice a common theme in their stories?" she said.

Edward looked momentarily confused. "Apart from the obvious one of everyone being moments away from meeting their maker when the *Voice* spoke to them?"

Chou nodded slowly.

I have to admit that I didn't see any connection other than the one Edward had mentioned.

"Well, I'll be damned," Edward said, his face suddenly lighting up, "I *do* see another connection; we all died alone, away from anyone who could have helped us."

Chou smiled, then added, "Yes, but more importantly, we all would have died in ways that would have meant there was a very high probability our remains would never have been discovered or recovered or identified. You, Edward, stated that you were buried alive. Wild Bill died alone in the desert. Jorge was lost at sea. Evelyn drowned. Benito died in the forest miles from civilization." Chou paused then looked at me, and I felt myself flinch as she said, "And Meredith threw herself into the bay at night."

"And you? How do you fit into all this? What's your story, Miss Chou?" Edward said.

"I was lost in space," she said, matter-of-factly.

Edward slowly allowed his face to turn toward the blue sky. He pointed his left index finger heavenward. "Up there?"

Chou smiled. Nodded again.

"Well, that would certainly put the kibosh on anyone ever finding your body, I suppose."

Chou seemed to appreciate the humor in what Edward said because her smile grew wider. "Of course, I cannot back my theory up with proof other than that which you have supplied me, and it is not outside of statistical possibility that the similarity shared by the few people whose stories we know of are just a statistical fluke. The only way to be certain is to gather more stories. And that means I need to speak to more people."

"Well," Edward said, "I'll leave that up to the individuals concerned. All I ask is that you respect their desire as to whether they want to share their story with you. Some of these people still seem to be coming to terms with how they arrived in this new reality of ours."

As Edward turned to walk away, his face was caught briefly in shadowed profile, and some dusty collection of neurons finally connected in my brain. I let out a short, sharp puff of surprise, "Oh, my God!"

Edward stopped, turned back to look at me, his brow furrowed. "Are you alright, Meredith?"

I felt a tingling of electricity run up my back and down my arms as goosebumps popped across every inch of my skin. I *knew* I had recognized Edward from somewhere, but it was only as he had turned away, his face caught in profile that I remembered where exactly that had been. My throat went dry, grew tight, and I had to swallow hard to get it to let the next words out. "Is your full name Edward James Hubbard?"

Edward blinked. His head jerked slightly, like he was avoiding an invisible bee, then tilted inquisitively to one side. He said, "Yes, it is. How did you—"

"And before you became a soldier were you a teacher in Manchester, England?" I said, interrupting him. "You *were* an English teacher, weren't you?" I stood up and took a step toward him.

Edward was shocked. "How could you possibly know that?" His expression changed quickly from surprise to one of suspicion.

I swallowed hard again to try and keep my voice from freezing up, unable to speak, finally, I blurted out "*If beauty sets brother against brother and causes empires to fall, is not too high a price placed upon its exquisite head—if jealousy, pain, and death are the currency for loveliness?*"

Edward closed the distance between us in two quick strides that bordered on leaps. He seized my arm just above the elbow, hard enough that I felt the blood begin to slow. He hissed, "Tell me how in God's name could you know that poem? I've never had any of my work published. Never shown a poem to a living soul. Who *are* you? Answer me!" He yelled the last two sentences loud enough that the rest of the camp would surely have heard him if they had not already moved off to their assignments.

In the periphery of my vision, I saw Chou step closer, her eyes hard and focused squarely on Edward. "It's okay," I said, turning my head long enough to give her a tight smile before turning back to look at Edward.

"Answer me," Edward hissed. "Are you responsible for all of this? Are you the one who brought me here?"

I shook my head. "No... no, I'm not."

"Then tell me how you could possibly know *any* of that

information about me?" His voice softened a little. He released his grip on my arm. "*Please.*"

I closed my eyes, allowed myself to relax a little as I reached back into my memory. "When I was in high school, I read a lot of poetry: Tennyson, Wordsworth, Blake, Keats. But my favorite poem by far was written by an Englishman named Edward James Hubbard. It was *so* good, I memorized it in its entirety. It was called *The Maiden*; one of your earliest works, I believe. It was one of a hundred of your poems released in an anthology of your work long after your death."

Edward's face turned beetroot red. "I am *so* sorry," he said, "It... I'm still getting used to the fact that we are all from different times. While I am incredibly humbled by the fact my work was read by anyone after my death, it makes perfect sense that you would have read it in what would have been my future. I am so very sorry if I frightened you—"

Now it was my turn to take Edward firmly by his arm. "No, *you* don't understand. In my time, you were seen as one of the greatest poets of your generation to write about the horrors of World War I. In *my* time, after the end of the war you became chair of the English department at Oxford University and you were eventually named Poet Laureate. Edward, in the time *I'm* from, you *survived* the First World War. You did not die until 1963."

"What?" Edward blurted. "I don't understand. Are you saying someone stole my identity after the war? My God, that's an outrageous thing for them to do."

I shook my head. "No, no. It wasn't someone impersonating you, it was *you*. There were photographs of you in the book, and there was one where you were smiling and turning away from the camera like you just did. That's what triggered my memory of you. And there were other photographs I've seen of you where you were in your uniform; the same uniform you're wearing now, I'm sure of it. There was a biography at the beginning of your book that said you married a woman named Rebecca, she was your childhood sweetheart. You had kids... children... and... and..."

I felt Chou's hand gently touch my exposed forearm and I realized from the horrified look on Edward's face that I had utterly overwhelmed the poor man, confused him beyond belief with the deluge of information I was forcing on him. I mean, who *wouldn't* be confused by some stranger from the future who knows so many intimate details of your life? A life that, in their time had not been cut short by war and one which, from your point of view, still lay ahead.

A couple of awkward moments passed in complete silence while Edward regained his composure. "Rebecca was the woman I intended to marry after I got home from the war," he said quietly, his voice heavy with emotion. "We were betrothed a week before I shipped out." His eyes suddenly became very wide. "My God," he hissed, "does this mean I wouldn't have died in that godforsaken shell hole? If I'd said no to the *Voice*, I would have been saved and made it back to my beloved Rebecca? Oh no, that cannot be. That is simply too much." Tears appeared at the corners of his eyes and slipped down his cheek.

Absolutely horrified that I'd caused him this amount of distress, I began to second guess myself. Perhaps I *was* mistaken. Maybe I had confused him with someone else? After all, the photographs I'd seen had been old and grainy. But that wouldn't account for how I knew so much about what had happened to him after the war, or that I knew his poetry so well.

"I do not believe that to be the case, Edward," Chou said.

"Given the description of your final moments, you most certainly would have died if you had not responded positively to the *Voice*. As would I. As would Meredith. As I am quite sure, would *everyone* who exists on this island and, possibly, across this planet. If you had died in Meredith's timeline, she should have no recollection of your poems at all as you would never have written them. You should have simply been one of the forty-million killed or missing by the time that war was over. Remembered by no one other than—"

"Forty... *million* dead?" Edward whispered, his voice cracking. "What folly. What utter folly." Edward seemed unsteady on his feet, and I thought he was going to faint, but instead, he allowed himself to sink to the log. He sat there in stunned silence as Chou continued to talk.

"As I have no reason to doubt Meredith's recollection of your history after the war, there are only a few other possibilities: an opportune impersonator who happens to look so like you, he was capable of fooling even those closest to you for the rest of his life, including the woman who knew you best *is* a possibility, but unlikely enough that we can ignore it."

Edward gave a mirthless laugh. "Well, that's good to know, I suppose."

"It is also theoretically possible, given the advanced technology employed to bring us here, that the *Voice* could have duplicated the original versions of us, cloned each of us, then copied our memories and implanted them in the cloned version to make it... make *us* think we were still the original. But that seems... inefficient to me and still does not account for how, in Meredith's time, you survived the war."

I said, "And if that's what happened, then why would the *Voice* feel the need to ask our permission to save us? It could've just made a copy of us, and we'd never even know about it. And why would the *Voice* even need to wait until we were looking death in the face to ask if we wanted to live? It could have just posed the question at any point in our lives, after all."

"Precisely," said Chou. "No, I don't believe either of those possibilities are the correct explanation for what has happened to us."

"Well," said Edward, "if neither of those ideas makes sense to you, what other possibilities does that leave us with?"

Chou stood silently, then, "There is a third possibility."

"And that would be?" Edward said.

"Are you familiar with the concept of a multiverse?" Chou asked.

Edward looked puzzled, shook his head.

I'd seen enough sci-fi movies to know what Chou was hinting at. "It's the theory that there's more than just one version of the universe out there. That for every choice we make, a new copy of the universe is created where we make the opposite choice, right?"

"That is a very simple explanation, but yes, the theory suggests that there exist infinite versions of the universe outside of our own, all independent of each other. The laws governing those universes may be very similar to ours... or not. There are areas in the cosmos, light years across, known as cold spots which are believed to be the result of these alternate universes interacting with our own. I was part of a mission to investigate one when something went wrong, and I was brought here."

"But that's all just theory, right?" I said. "I mean, none of it has ever actually been proven. Not where I'm from, at least."

"In your time, yes, it was still an unproven concept. However, in my time, that theory was greatly strengthened with a discovery by Professor Adrianna Drake of what became known as Vagrant Particles; extraordinarily rare sub-atomic particles which simply should not exist in the standard model of our universe. Professor Drake proved that vagrant particles could only originate from the numerous cold spots she had discovered scattered throughout the cosmos, which seemed to suggest that the cold spots were somehow connected to other alternate universes. At least, that's what we thought, but those cold spots were so distant, it was only during my lifetime that technology capable of allowing us to reach them was developed. *That* was the mission assigned to me... and my husband. We were to investigate one of those cold spots and study the anomaly over an extended period of time."

"So, these 'cold spots' are what, exactly?" I said.

"We believe they were created when our universe somehow brushed against an alternate universe. The resulting devastation ruptured both universes' spacetime continuums. You can think of the cold spots as scars that have never quite healed, and every so often they open again, allowing particles from each universe to bleed through into the other."

"My God," said Edward, for the umpteenth time.

I took a few moments to digest what Chou had said. Although the concept was mind-numbingly confusing, the idea that there could be an infinite number of other *Merediths* scattered throughout these parallel universes was a surprisingly comforting thought. It meant there might be a version of me out there that hadn't gone through the shit I'd had to suffer through. Maybe one of these other *mes* had done something meaningful with their life.

"It would explain why Edward was alive in my time and died in his," I said. "And it would explain something that's been nagging at me about Wild Bill, too. I'm sure I saw a TV show where he was shot in a bar while he played cards, rather than dying in the desert."

"I believe my theory is the most likely explanation, given the data we currently have available to us," Chou said.

Edward had managed to compose himself. He raised his

eyebrows and shook his head sharply. "I would suggest we keep this *theory* to ourselves for now. The others have enough to worry about without adding this complication. Are we in agreement?"

"Yes," said Chou, "I think that is a good idea, for now at least."

I nodded. It was hard enough for me to get my mind around, and I, at least, had been born in a time when technology was everywhere. I couldn't begin to imagine how baffling it must be for someone whose experience of advanced technology amounted to nothing more than a vacuum-tube-based radio set.

"Very well, now, if you'll excuse me," Edward said, obviously rattled by the conversation. He gave a curt nod and walked off in the direction of the cabin he had been helping to build.

We joined Jorge at the stockade. Before he could object to us, Chou shouldered one of the logs from a large stack that sat nearby awaiting his attention. Jorge watched expressionlessly as she carried it to a hole he'd just finished digging and dropped it in. He nodded once and went back to digging the next hole.

And that was how, for the next eight or so hours, we dug holes, sweated, manhandled the stakes brought to us by Bull and Freuchen into the holes (both men obviously astonished when they saw Chou's handling of the logs), and sweated some more. There was no cement to secure the stockade stakes in the ground, so we mixed mud I'd fetched from the banks of the river with gravel and pebbles. Jorge assured us it was an age-old method and would work just as well as cement, and it seemed to hold the spikes in place just fine.

By the time Edward yelled that it was 'time to knock off' I

was exhausted, but as I stood back and looked at the stockade's fresh line of new poles that extended twenty-four stakes further than when we had started that morning, I felt an immense sense of pride like I'd never felt before. I came from an age where accomplishment seemed to be measured by the latest app or the newest smartphone or how many likes you got on your Facebook posts. All helpful, life-improving (for the most part, at least) additions, but all intangibles, and with associated prestige that would vanish the second the next big thing was released. But *this*, this was something solid that would stand for *years*, protecting those within its walls. It was something *I* had helped to build. And for the first time in, well, forever, I felt a burgeoning sense of self-worth. I had *value*. And it felt good. *Really* good.

Smiling with the glow of this new-found self-worth, Chou and I walked silently back to camp.

The smell of cooking meat greeted us, wafting on a cool evening breeze, mixing with the pungent wood-smoke of the fire.

While Chou seemed absolutely fine, my muscles ached and throbbed like I was ninety years old. If I had gone to bed that night knowing that I'd have to do that kind of work all over again when I got up the next day, I think I would have cried myself to sleep. But knowing that when the aurora showed up tonight, all of these aches and pains would vanish, eased my mind.

Chou and I were the last to arrive. The dirt-streaked faces that turned to greet us with smiles and nods each showed the exhaustion they felt. Everyone was in good spirits, laughing and chatting amongst themselves as they waited in line for the food Evelyn and Albert had prepared.

"Busy day, ladies?" Evelyn said as we stepped up to her makeshift workbench, a log that had been split down the middle to give a flat surface. Albert beamed when he handed me my food.

"It was, indeed, tiring," said Chou.

I just smiled, took my food and followed Chou over to the fire.

"Good work on the stockade," Edward announced as we passed him sitting with Freuchen and Oliver.

"It was mostly Chou and Jorge," I said as I sat down on the log near them, too tired to continue the conversation.

Wild Bill sauntered over from where he'd been tending to Brute, carrying something in both arms. "I believe these belong to you," he said, placing the set of armor I'd stripped from the dead swordsman into my outstretched hands.

Had that really just been a day earlier? It seemed like an eternity ago. "Thank you," I said as I took the armor from him, trying not to notice the dried blood that still clung to the chainmail.

For the rest of the evening, we chatted quietly amongst ourselves, planning for our excursion the following morning. Albert would (grudgingly) remain behind in Evelyn's care, while Chou, Freuchen, and I set off on what we agreed would be, at most, a three-day trek to map the outline of the island and report back on anything we found.

More tired than I think I'd ever felt in my life, I eventually made my excuses and retired to our shelter to wait for the aurora's inevitable arrival.

FOURTEEN

OUR TWO GROUPS set out from the garrison not long after the sun rose over the horizon. Morning dew saturated the grass, and an ethereal mist rose from the river, drifting across our path as we walked downstream for a mile or so until we came to a spot Freuchen said we could cross.

Large boulders, the results of a rockfall or a flood that had swept them downstream, formed a natural path across the river.

We said our goodbyes to Benito, Caleb, and Tabitha, and watched them briefly as they continued downstream while we used the natural causeway to reach the river's opposite bank. The boulders were slippery with lichen and water, but all three of us made it across without taking an early morning dip. We followed the river's course toward the ocean for about five miles until the forest thinned out and we reached the estuary. The sea looked almost as gray as the pebble-strewn beach. The only sound came from the hiss of the waves lapping at the shore. As the three of us stood looking out at the ocean, Freuchen pulled a small pad of paper and a pencil from the pocket of his coat and began to draw with it.

"What are you doing?" Chou asked.

"I intend to make a map of our journey, so ve have a better idea of the size of this island," Freuchen said. "It vill be very basic, but vill be better than nothing. I vill mark any major landmarks or points of interest that ve see or find so that ve can explore them later." He finished his doodling and replaced the pad and pen back into the same pocket.

The tide-rounded rocks and shale that made up the beach were exhausting to walk on and required constant attention to where you planted your feet or risk spraining an ankle. We spread out in a line with approximately twenty feet separating us and began to walk: Freuchen closest to the trees, Chou near the water's edge, and me in the middle. The beach stretched ahead of us in a slightly undulating line for several miles with no sign of ending, as we picked our way over it, scanning for anything that might be of use.

We found the first body about thirty minutes later. It was a man in his late thirties. He lay face down against the rocks, one arm tucked under him, the other stretched above his head like he was hailing a cab. He was completely naked and beginning to bloat.

"Oh no," I said turning away, my stomach reeling.

"Looks like someone got to him already," said Freuchen, "unless he arrived here naked, of course."

I stayed back. The smell from the dead man made me want to vomit.

We found a second body ten minutes later, washed up at the shoreline. It was another man, but this poor unfortunate was still fully-clothed. The waves lifted and deposited him again and again, pushing him further up the shore, shifting his body in a macabre slow-motion dance. He was dressed in a modern-looking sweater, khaki pants, and brown shoes, one of which was missing. He too was beginning to bloat.

"Jesus!" I hissed when I made the mistake of getting a little too close. Some of the island's smaller aquatic life had begun to pick at the corpse's pale water-wrinkled flesh. Small crabs scuttled about his hands and head. This time, I couldn't contain my reaction. I vomited the remains of my breakfast onto the shale.

"Sorry," I said sheepishly, spitting away the remnants of vomit and wiping my mouth with the back of my hand.

Freuchen chortled. "Don't vurry, I had the same reaction ven I saw my first body up close." He moved closer to the dead man, prodded him with the tip of his boot.

"I don't think it vould be a good idea to take his clothes," said Freuchen, squatting to examine the body more closely. "Vithout any vay to sanitize the poor fellow's things, ve could be opening ourselves to any number of diseases."

"That might not be a problem," said Chou, seemingly unperturbed by the sight or smell of the body.

We both looked at her for a second not comprehending, then Freuchen said, "Oh, you mean the aurora?"

"I believe that the nanobots inside us will also prevent us from contracting any disease. It would seem like a logical addition for the *Voice* to ensure we remain healthy," Chou said.

"But all we know for certain is it cures physical injuries and poison," I said. "We can't be sure it works against viruses or bacteria."

"Time will prove me correct or not," Chou added.

"Still, I don't think it vould be a good idea to test that theory, just yet," Freuchen insisted.

"I agree," I said, "but shouldn't we at least bury him?"

Freuchen shook his head. "Better safe than sorry, yes? Besides, the sea vill take care of him, given enough time." He took out his pad of paper and with a few short strokes of his pencil added details to his map. We left the body where it was and continued onward.

A quarter-mile later and Freuchen stopped. "Here! Look at

this," he said, excitedly. Bending down, he picked up something jammed in between several rounded stones. "Do you know vat this is?" Freuchen said, offering the object out to me and Chou.

"It's a cellphone," I said, examining the old-style flip-phone Freuchen held in his hand. When I saw the blank look on his face, I added, "A kind of communication device; like a radio," which seemed to do the trick. I took the phone from Freuchen and opened it up. The screen was blank. I pressed and held the power button for a few seconds to see if it would turn on. It didn't. "It's dead," I said. "Not that it would matter; it isn't like the reception's going to be any good out here anyway." I giggled at my own joke and handed the phone back to Freuchen. "It's just junk."

Freuchen examined the phone, flipping it open then closing it again a couple of times, which seemed to amuse him. Then he dropped it into his pants' pocket and walked quickly to catch up with us.

I found a leather wallet with what I think were probably Australian dollars in it. The oldest date on the notes was 2004. There was no ID inside. A little further on, I found a wooden hairbrush which I pocketed. Chou found a single red-accented white sneaker, a woman's, and then a discarded blouse which we rolled up and placed in Freuchen's backpack.

"Perhaps we should look and see if the owner of the sneaker and blouse are nearby," Chou said.

"Good idea," I agreed, and we paused our beach-combing for another hour while we moved into the forest a quarter-mile or so in all directions, searching for any signs of life, but found nothing.

It was sometime in the early afternoon that we finally saw the beach begin to curve to our left. When we reached that point, we found that we had indeed found the furthest Southern point of the island. The shale had been growing less and less as we had progressed further south, and within a half-mile of reaching that point, had been replaced altogether by dark, almost black glass-like sand, which made walking much easier.

Freuchen made notes on his map, and began walking again, "Ve should probably continue on for another couple of hours before ve make camp for the night, I vould suggest that ve—" He stopped, dead in his tracks, staring up into the forest.

"Peter? What's wrong... oh!" Following the direction of Freuchen's gaze, I saw what had caught his attention. About a mile or so away, a tower jutted out of the forest's canopy. Actually, it was the *ruin* of a tower; its gull-white walls rose in a gradual spiral like a twist of licorice, but there were ragged gaps here and there on the exterior. The tower projected upward at an odd angle. It reminded me of pictures of the Leaning Tower of Pisa. It must have had some kind of addition at its top, but that was long gone, leaving behind only a broken web of what I took for support beams and pieces of ragged material that could have been the remains of a floor or another wall, it was impossible to tell from here.

"Vat do you think?" Freuchen said, over his shoulder to us. "Should ve make a detour?"

"Hell, yeah," I said, with honest enthusiasm. "This is the first sign of any civilization on the island. We can't just ignore it."

"I would not be too hopeful," said Chou, "It is obviously in an advanced state of disrepair. And we should also be aware that other survivors may well have made their way there already... it is hardly inconspicuous."

Freuchen tossed his ax from one hand to the other three times, as if relishing the idea of a fight. "If ve pick up our pace, ve should reach it before evening," he said. "Ready, ladies?"

"Better mark this one down on your little map," I said, as Chou and I stepped past him and walked into the forest.

"I vill take that as a yes," Freuchen chortled and set off after us.

I had badly underestimated the distance from the beach to the tower. Rather than the mile I'd first guessed, it turned out to be closer to three; all uphill, too. My calves were burning by the time we found the first debris from the tower strewn across the forest floor. We spotted several pieces of what looked like highly-polished aluminum or steel poking up from the layer of dead leaves covering the forest floor. Kneeling, Freuchen wiped the leaves from a large piece of it that was easily as tall and just as wide as the man himself, and at least five inches thick. There was no sign of rust or scratches or any kind of weathering or degradation.

"I think it's some kind of metal," Freuchen said. He placed his legs in a wide stance and lowered his butt to the ground, sliding both hands beneath the huge sheet of metal, bracing himself as he started to lift the piece of the shattered tower.

Freuchen's eyes widened as he easily lifted the large sheet off the ground.

"Wow!" I said as he waved the sheet in front of him like it was made of cardboard.

"It is impossibly light," Freuchen said, tossing the sheet from one hand to the other. "And look at these edges."

He offered the piece of the tower to me, and I braced myself to have to drop it but, as Freuchen had said, it was *incredibly* light, given its size, weighing no more than a half-pound, if even that. The edges were fringed, uneven, like a sheet of paper torn from a spiral notebook with no visible sharp edges or burrs, not at all like how normal metal twists and deforms when it's put under stress. It didn't look like any kind of building material I had ever seen.

Chou picked up a second piece of the tower, this one about the size of a shoebox and began to examine it. "We have similar metamaterials in my time," she said, "but this is definitely more advanced. Although it looks like solid metal, it is in fact constructed of very precise nanotrusses which account for its incredible lightness. The nanotrusses are then layered with an outer covering of material such as aluminum or ceramic, then coated in a weather-repellent or self-cleaning finish." Chou turned to Freuchen. "Try and bend it or break it," she told him, with a nod of encouragement.

Freuchen shrugged, smirked as if he had been given an easy task and tried to do what Chou had asked, placing his hands on both of the short sides and squeezing. The piece flexed outward slightly but that was all. Next, he tried to break it over his knee, but it refused to bend more than an inch. Freuchen continued to apply his considerable strength in an attempt to warp the metal, his face growing more and more red from the exertion until, finally, he gave up and tossed it to the ground. It instantly sprang back to its original shape.

"Another characteristic of nanotrusses are their incredible strength," Chou said, with a little chuckle that brought a smile to my face too.

"Ve should continue on to the tower," Freuchen said, obviously a little put out.

We followed the growing debris field up the hill until, at long last, we emerged into an area that had probably been a clearing at some point in the distant past judging by the younger trees that populated the large circular area. Although bushes and grass had pushed up at its edges, an uninterrupted pathway of what looked like wet silver ran down the hill and disappeared into the forest twenty feet to our right. The path was connected to the base of the tower, a bulbous fifty-foot-circumference section made of the same strange metal material. The tower gradually tapered in on both sides, vase-like at its mid-point, which I guessed was about one-hundred-fifty to one-hundred-seventy feet above us before expanding outward again until it was just as wide at the top as it was at ground level.

The overall effect reminded me of an hourglass. Spaced at regular gaps around the circumference of the tower, large, flat, tulip-shaped protrusions jutted out horizontally. They were made from the same material as the rest of the tower, and I wondered if they were observation decks or if they maybe served some other purpose.

The top section of the tower was, as I had thought when we first spotted the building from the beach, nothing but a latticework of crisscrossing beams and remnants of what, I surmised, had once been floors and walls and ceilings. There had obviously been *something* up there at some point, but the remnants of it now lay all around us. Despite the evident destruction up top, as my eyes moved up the outside of the tower, I saw that it remained pristine, unblemished in any way. No lichen grew on it. No vines or ivy wound up its sides. No weathering of any kind at all.

"If it wasn't for the mess up top," I said, "you'd think this thing had just been built today."

"Look," said Freuchen, pointing toward the rear of the base of the tower. "There's the reason it's leaning at such an odd angle."

At some point in the past, a slab of the mountain had broken away behind the tower, sending an avalanche of boulders ranging from SUV-sized boulders to smaller rocks the size of my head smashing into the tower. A rocky debris field lay all around it, covered in lichen and other plants, which seemed to indicate the rockfall had happened a few seasons ago at least. A large amount of that rockslide, millions of tons, had flowed past the tower, leaving a huge drift of rock piled up around the base of the structure.

"If that had happened to a building in my time," Freuchen said, "there vould have been nothing left but matchsticks and dust. He knelt and pulled a piece of the tower from between two rocks. "But this incredible material the tower is made of must be vy it has only tilted instead of toppled."

I pressed the flat of my hand against the side of the tower. "It's very warm," I said, "especially given how little sunshine it must get."

Chou and Freuchen did the same.

"You're right," Freuchen said. "Very strange."

"It is possible that there is some kind of thermoelectric system built into the structure still gathering energy," Chou mused. "Perhaps the outer layer is a kind of solar collector, or there may be a subterranean heating system that is still operational."

We scouted the circumference of the tower's base for as far as we could, climbing over and around the rubble. There was no obvious entrance in the tower's wall, but it could just as easily be hidden behind the sixty-percent or so obscured by the rockfall.

"At least there's no sign that anyone else got here before us," Chou said.

"Yes," said Freuchen, "if there is anything inside it, then it should be ours... if ve can find a vay in."

I took a few steps back from the tower, just to get a better look at the higher section when a flash of something metallic in the rocks and boulders of the debris field caught my eye.

"Hey!" I called back to Chou and Freuchen. "Come take a look at this."

My two companions picked their way over to where I stood.

"What do you think that is?" I asked, pointing toward a thick tangle of vines twisted between a tightly clustered group of trees off to our left. "See, right there in the rock pile between those two trees." I pointed as best as I could. "Can you see it?" Through a few gaps in the twisted, snake-like vines and the rocks that had accumulated around them, the rays of the afternoon sun reflected off of something gold and glittering.

"Vat *is* that?" said Freuchen. He scrambled over the boulders and picked his way toward the trees, Chou and me right behind him. We began tugging at the vines but quickly figured out it was useless; they were too tightly wound together and incredibly strong.

"Stand aside," Freuchen said. He leaned his ax against the trunk of the nearest tree, pulled the machete from his belt, placed a boot on the rough surface of a large boulder for balance, and set to work, slashing at the vines with short, powerful, precise cuts. He sheathed the machete and began pulling some of the smaller boulders from the pile and tossing them away. A couple of minutes later, he stepped back, perspiration and bits of vine peppering his hands and face.

I gasped in amazement. "I think it's another robot," I said breathlessly. I couldn't be absolutely sure because most of it was still hidden beneath the vines and rocks, but Freuchen's work had revealed enough of the golden body that I was confident what lay beneath the rocks was the remains of another robot.

"You mean like the vun you said you saw on the beach, the day ve arrived?" Freuchen said, nodding toward the space he had cleared while grimacing as he wiped the sweat from his face with the back of an arm. "Two mechanical men!"

I leaned in to get a better look. Through the gap Freuchen had cleared I saw a black lattice-work of metal and the smooth curve of a gold surface I was pretty sure I recognized as the robot's chest. I smiled at Freuchen and nodded. "Yes, I think so. But how on earth did it get stuck here?"

"The rockslide must have caught it unavare and trapped it," Freuchen said. He stood back and eyed the debris piled up around the robot. "Ve could clear the vines avay in a matter of an hour or so... probably. It vould give us a better chance to examine it." He let his words hang in the air, more question than statement.

"You think it might give us a clue as to who made it?" I asked, turning to face Chou.

"I hardly think it would have a manufacturer's stamp on it, but who knows," she replied. "It might yield some clues."

Freuchen looked dubious, despite having made the suggestion to clear the vines in the first place. "The question is, do you think it is a good idea to uncover it? It could be dangerous."

"The one I saw on the beach was..." I searched for the right words to sum up the feeling I'd gotten in my gut as the robot had walked by me into the ocean. I settled on, "...confused. It was like it didn't understand why it was doing what it was doing. I know that sounds weird, but that's the impression I got. I don't think it had any intention of hurting us. Truth is it could have grabbed me and drowned me if it had wanted to. It's no threat... probably."

Chou shook her head. "It's been buried under all that rock for a very long time. If it was going to get up and do anything, I think it would have done so by now. But it leads me to another question. Look at these trees." She pointed at one of two trees that stood about twelve feet tall, young by comparison to the others that towered skyward around them. "Do you see how they are growing out of the space between the boulders?"

I nodded, not seeing the point Chou was trying to make.

But Freuchen apparently did. "They are growing from the rock pile that buried the mechanical man," he said, "vich means that they must have started growing *after* the rocks were deposited here. A tree grows at a rate of about one to two feet a year, given the right soil conditions. That vould mean these trees have been here for a minimum of twenty years and perhaps longer. Vich also means the mechanical man has been buried here for at least that long, too."

"Exactly," said Chou. "But that raises another question. If this is a robot and it was trapped here decades ago, why did the one Meredith encountered on the beach choose the moment we arrived to walk into the sea?"

"You think it was just waiting there, on the beach? For all that time between whenever *this* happened..." I swept my hands over the rockfall "and when we arrived? That just doesn't make sense."

"Yet another question on a very long list of senseless events, I fear," Freuchen said. "But perhaps if ve vur to free our metal friend here, he could give us some answers. Are ve agreed?"

Chou nodded.

"Sure," I said, shrugging. "What have we got to lose."

"Vunderful," Freuchen said, his concern over the robot apparently alleviated. "Let's get to vurk, then."

For the next hour and a half, Freuchen hacked away at the vines while Chou and I pulled the severed creepers from the body of the robot. Bit by bit, the huge golden form of the robot was revealed. By the time we pulled the last vine away, there was less than an hour of daylight left, and we were all exhausted and soaked with sweat.

The three of us took a step back and stared at what had been revealed. The robot was trapped in a sitting position on the ground, its segmented arms clasped tightly to its sides. Its left leg extended straight out in front of it, the right leg trapped beneath a heap of rock. Several large boulders had piled up behind the robot, pushing its upper torso forward at its waist, like it was bowing. The robot I'd seen on the beach had a concave bar that floated just in front of the mound between its shoulders I assumed was its head. Two piercing blue lights had glowed on the bar and had moved to look at me as I floated in the water. I had *assumed* they were its eyes. The bar on *this* robot was firmly attached to the mound of its head, and there were no lights. No indication of 'life' at all.

"It must have been here for a long time for the vines to have grown so thickly over it," Chou said.

Freuchen nodded. "Yes, but look, there is very little sign of veathering or any kind of corrosion on its body. Not even any scratches from the boulders. Is it made from the same material as the tower?"

Chou ran her hand over the golden chest. "I believe this is *actual* gold," she whispered. "Gold is the most non-reactive of all metals which would account for the lack of corrosion, but to be this strong it can't be pure; it must be some kind of alloy." She rapped the knuckles of her hand against the robot's chest. "It's as hard as steel." Chou maneuvered around the robot, climbing over tree roots and boulders, inspecting the machine as minutely as she could, given the forest's advancing shadows as afternoon edged toward evening. "I do not see any kind of port or activation switch; no interfaces of any kind," she said after completing her inspection.

Freuchen looked skyward, to the patches of darkening sky visible through the trees. "I have no idea vat you're talking about but ve should ready a camp for the night. I vill prepare a fire."

Chou reluctantly joined us, her fascination with the machine obvious.

We gathered extra wood and piled it next to the campfire Freuchen had built near the robot, ate some of the smoked salmon and jerky we'd brought with us, then sat around talking quietly to each other as evening edged toward night. The forest was alive with the sound of birds and other creatures I couldn't identify, almost as if the animals that lived within the trees knew we were there and were warning each other about the strange interlopers on their territory. But gradually, as night descended through the trees, even that noise died away, leaving only the crackle and snapping of our fire.

"I vill take the first watch," Freuchen volunteered, positioning himself atop a large nearby boulder. Chou and I bedded down near the fire to try and get some rest before the aurora inevitably woke us again. I was exhausted, and I felt myself slipping easily into sleep the second I closed my eyes.

I awoke just as the first streaks of the aurora filtered through the forest's canopy. Freuchen and Chou were already up and about, sitting around the campfire talking in low voices.

The sky crackled and glowed as bolts of energy shot across the black sky. The nano-particles did their nightly dance, and I felt the cool rush of energy coursing through my body and the welcome feeling of regeneration as the aches and pains of the previous day's trek and toil were erased from my body. When the show was over, I stretched and took over guard duty from Freuchen.

"I don't think I vill ever get used to that," Freuchen said, referring to the aurora. "But it is very velcome." Without another word, he lay down in the spot where I had slept, closed his eyes and started snoring almost immediately—a strangely high-pitched sound for a man of his size.

"Wake me in a couple of hours," Chou said, and she lay down too.

I walked over to a tree close to where the robot sat, the machine's golden body reflecting the orange light of the fire, bouncing it around the forest. I sat down between the tree roots, my back resting against the trunk, and looked at the robot. The campfire illuminated the front of the mechanical man, casting a long shadow behind it that shifted with the flames, creating the illusion that the robot was swaying back and forth. A pile of dead leaves, pine needles, gravel, and pinecones had collected in its lap. Grass sprouted from between its long metal toes. My eyes had just begun to wander to the forest when something caught my eye. Something about the robot had changed, I was sure of it. I just couldn't put my finger on what it was exactly.

I got to my feet and edged nearer to it. I looked closer... and gave a little gasp of surprise. The robot's eye-bar that earlier I was sure had been firmly fixed to its head now floated an inch or so in front of it, just like the one I'd seen on the robot on the beach. I moved to the robot's left shoulder to get a better angle. Sure enough, I was right, the eye-bar *was* floating in front of the mound between its shoulders.

"What is going on?" I said quietly.

As if my words had triggered some mechanism within its golden body, two tiny blue points of light materialized at the center of the eye-bar and quickly grew in size. I was suddenly looking directly into two electric-blue orbs.

I stumbled backward, an involuntary cry of surprise caught in my throat. My heel clipped a rock, and I fell hard on my ass with an *oomph*! The blue orbs followed my movement.

It was *alive*! The robot was alive.

I started to push myself to my feet but froze as the robot's right arm flashed toward me, grabbing my wrist in a strong but not painful grip. Surprisingly, its long metal fingers felt as warm as a human's hand against my skin.

"*Candidate 13, I have a message for you,*" the robot said in that same calm, humanesque voice I'd heard from its twin during my arrival on the beach. The tone was non-threatening, soft, welcoming; the kind of voice you might expect from a counselor or a psychiatrist. The timbre, resonance, and rhythm of its words articulated in such a way I couldn't tell whether the voice was male or female. It was quite beautiful to hear. The robot tried to lean in closer to me but was unable to free itself from the rubble that had trapped it. Its eye-bar moved left and right then up and down as if it was assessing its situation. I looked back over my shoulder to where Chou and Freuchen were still asleep, thought about yelling for their help, but something told me I wasn't in any danger. Not yet, anyway. When I turned back, the robot's electric-blue eyes were focused on me again.

"*Candidate 13, humanity is in peril. The plan has been compromised by an external entity. This interference has introduced multiple patterns of disorder; the effects on the outcome have moved beyond predictability. Agents of chaos will be unleashed in an attempt to stop what I require of you. You must travel to the Collector immediately and locate Candidate 1. They must know that the field is collapsing, and the void follows behind.*"

I sat there in the dead leaves and rock and twigs, staring at the robot. "I... I have no idea what you're talking about." I finally managed to splutter. "What plan? What external entity? What do you mean? Who *are* you?"

"*Candidate 13; humanity is in peril. The plan has been compromised by an external entity—*"

It took another recitation of the same short speech for me to realize that I was listening to a recorded message. It was in the process of delivering the message for a third time when it suddenly stopped mid-sentence and released its grip on my arm.

From behind me, I heard Chou and Freuchen scrambling to their feet, registering the shock in their voices as they saw that the robot was awake.

"Vat? Vat is that?" Freuchen hissed. He was standing next to me now, his open hand extended toward me, but his eyes fixed on the robot.

"Did you do something?" Chou said, as I took Freuchen's outstretched hand and allowed him to pull me to my feet.

"I was just looking at it and—"

A sudden high-frequency whirring sound, like the noise a generator makes when it's starting up, filled the air. At the same time, the robot's eyes glowed momentarily brighter and then turned to look directly at the three of us. The whirring sound grew louder and higher in pitch, then either stopped or the frequency passed outside of our hearing range. The robot spoke again: "*Welcome children of Earth. Do not be afraid,*" it said in that same calm voice. "*I know you are confused and have many questions. I am here to help you assimilate into your new surrou* —" The robot's words tapered off. The eye-bar moved left then right, then back to where the three of us stood watching it, our eyes and mouths wide in astonishment.

"*Please excuse me. An error has been detected. This does not appear to be my assigned reception point. Please stand by.*"

"It can talk?" Freuchen said, very quietly, turning to look at Chou and me. "No one told me it vould be able to talk." Despite Freuchen's huge size, right then, he sounded like a scared little boy.

"When it first woke up, it said something about a plan, a collapsing field. That I had to find someone or something called 'Candidate 1.' I..."

"It has to be the aurora," said Chou. "It seems that the same energy which powers the nanites also powers the robot. The question is why didn't it activate when we first arrived? If it's been here long enough for the vegetation we had to cut from it to have grown as profusely as it had, then why didn't it just free itself and leave?"

I answered her. "There was something wrong with the one I saw on the beach. It walked right out to sea and barely even registered that I was there. If this one was far enough inland that it couldn't make it to the water, maybe something else was done to it..."

With a sound like ancient, unoiled hinges, the robot suddenly tried to get to its feet, spilling the leafy debris that had collected in its lap.

Freuchen yelped and jumped back, pulled the machete from its scabbard and raised it above his head. I gulped and took an involuntary step toward Chou who did nothing more than cock her head to the left and continued to stare inquisitively at the golden automaton.

Unable to free its right leg from the pile of boulders that pinned it, the robot collapsed back into its sitting position with a heavy thud that sent a puff of dead leaves and dirt spiraling into the darkness. "*System diagnostics indicate significant degradation of multiple modules. Memory system corruption detected. Main power is at zero percent. Battery backup at two percent. Attempting to establish Neuro-net link...*" There was a three-second pause, then, "*Neuro-net link connection failed. Free roam status activated. Power level now at one-point-nine percent.*"

Again, the robot's electronic eyes moved to me, Freuchen, and Chou.

"*Welcome children of Earth. Do not be afraid.*"

For a second, I thought it was about to go through the same spiel we had already heard. I was wrong.

"*Hello. I am Standard Instruction and Learning Servitor 762. You may call me Silas. This message is being broadcast simultaneously in Multi-Speech. I apologize for the inconvenience, but I appear to be suffering from an undiagnosed malfunction. I will shortly return to conservation mode, but please do not be concerned; I have activated my assistance beacon, and another* SILAS *unit will be with you promptly. In the meantime, I will remain active as long as—"*

"The other SILAS units are all deactivated," Chou said quickly, stepping in closer to the robot... to Silas. "There will be no help from *anyone*. We need you to stay online for as long as you can and help us to comprehend what is happening. Do you understand me."

Silas' blue eyes moved over each of us in turn. "*Candidate 13, Meredith Gale; Candidate 20078, Weston Chou; and Candidate 207891, Peter Freuchen. Please elaborate.*"

This wasn't the first time I'd been referred to as a candidate; the *Voice* had used the same terminology when I was on the bridge. I looked at Chou, hoping she'd caught the reference. She glanced in my direction nodded as though confirming my assumption, then continued, "Silas, can you tell me how long you have before your power is exhausted?"

"*I have approximately seven minutes and thirty-one seconds. Please elaborate on your last statement.*"

We humans exchanged glances.

"We need to know if he is the *Voice*," I whispered to Chou. Freuchen nodded his agreement.

Chou turned back to Silas. "Silas, are you responsible for bringing us to this planet?"

"*I did not bring you here,*" Silas said.

"Then who did?" I shot back.

"*The Architect.*"

Three sets of human eyes locked with each other then turned back to the robot.

"Who is the Architect?" I said, pronouncing the words slowly.

Silas hesitated for a couple of seconds. "*I... I am sorry, I cannot remember that information. My memory modules appear to have been seriously compromised."* Silas tried to raise its right arm but only managed to move it a few inches from its side before it fell back again. The robot's eyes travelled over the boulders trapping its right leg. *"Do you know what has happened to me?"* Silas asked.

The robot's confusion was almost heartbreaking. I'd interacted with computers that gave the appearance of being able to talk like a human, but this, this was on a whole new level. This machine seemed, well, *truly* alive. There was real emotion behind Silas' words, and I couldn't help but feel sympathy for its situation. It appeared to be just as puzzled about what was going on as we were.

"I'm sorry, we don't know what happened to you. We don't even know what has happened to us," I said. "But when we found you here you were... turned off and buried under rocks and vines. Lots of them."

Chou added, "It was obvious that you have been here for a *very* long time."

The robot's eye-bar moved slowly left and right as if it was only now becoming aware of its surroundings. "This is not my assigned reception location. Have you interacted with any other Silas units?" His blue eyes dimmed momentarily, then brightened.

"I saw one of..." My mind stuttered over the correct personal pronoun, and I cringed as I settled on "one of your kind... on the beach the day we all arrived here. It walked out into the ocean and... and it did not stop."

Chou spoke up. "Silas, can you do a full self-diagnostic and tell me what's wrong with you?"

"Yes, I shall begin at once." Silas sat motionless for about ten seconds, then: *"I have limited power available to me, and my diagnostic report indicates that my memory has been severely corrupted. I am suffering from what you would classify as severe*

brain trauma. I have attempted unsuccessfully to contact other Silas units via the Neuro-Net. My diagnostic system informs me that my interface is functional which means that the Neuro-Net must be down. I have also detected unauthorized code additions within my main programming. It would seem there was an attempt to override my ambulation module. I have purged that code." The robot paused for a second or two. "*Please tell me everything that you can about your arrival.*"

We quickly recounted everything that had happened to us since we'd been dropped into the ocean.

"If it had not been for the ruined tower, ve vould never have found you," Freuchen said.

"*Ruined tower*?" Silas asked.

"Yes," Chou said, "The tower behind you. It looks to have been abandoned a long time ago. It's badly damaged, but it must have been impressive."

"*The habitat? That is troubling,*" Silas replied. His eyes dimmed again then brightened. "*Given what you have told me and my current location, I can only assume that something has gone catastrophically wrong with the Architect's plans for your arrival. My internal power source was designed to last for approximately three centuries. As I am currently running on auxiliary battery power and I can detect no problems with my internal power system other than it has been exhausted, I have reached the conclusion that I have been at this location for a minimum of three hundred years. I have tried to reach out to my sibling units, but the Neuro-Net has vanished. That, in and of itself, is of great concern, but when I include all of the information you have given to me, I find it... disconcerting.*"

"You think this Architect's plan you spoke of was somehow sabotaged?" Chou said.

"*Perhaps,*" Silas murmured. "*There is also the slight possibility of a confluence of natural phenomenon having caused these events, but I have calculated the possibility of that occurring as being low enough to discard as highly improbable. When all the events you have described are considered together, and my own predicament is also added to the equation, along with the corrupted code I detected, I can only assume that, yes, an outside force has purposely disrupted the Architect's plan. The question is who would do such a thing? If only I could remember...*"

Chou interrupted, "Silas, can you tell us what you were supposed to do for us when we arrived."

"*Yes, of course. Once the great transference is complete, it is my role to assist candidates in any way I can. I understand that the transference will have left you confused and that you have many questions. I will be happy to answer all of those questions but first... but first... but first...*"

Silas repeated those last two words for another minute, jumping back and forth like a skipping record. Then, abruptly he stopped.

"*Extensive memory corruption detected. Two minutes and fifteen seconds until shutdown. I hope that has answered your question. Is there anything else I can help you with?*"

"Ummm, okay," I said.

Chou met my gaze and raised her eyebrows momentarily. "Silas, is there any way we can help you recover your corrupted memory?" she asked.

The robot processed the question in silence, then said, "*Yes. There are several options. If you can contact a repair facility that would be of great help.*"

"Okay," I said, "now we're getting somewhere. Where can we find a repair facility?"

There was another pause. "*I... I am unable to access that information.*"

"Vunderful," Freuchen mumbled.

"Okay, okay," I continued. "You said there were several options. What else can we do?"

"*If you can locate an inactive Silas unit I would be able to transplant modules and replace my own damaged components and memory.*"

"How the hell are ve supposed to do that?" Freuchen wondered aloud.

Chou said, "Silas, if we freed your leg from the rocks do you think you would be able to walk?"

"*Yes. My diagnostic system indicates that there is minimal damage to my legs.*"

"And if we freed you, would you be willing to come back with us to the garrison?" Chou continued.

"*Of course. My primary purpose is to assist you in any way that I can.*"

Chou turned to face Freuchen and me. "I think the best thing we can do is get him back to camp where we can examine him without all of this..." Her hands fluttered to the forest.

"That makes sense," said Freuchen, "but how?"

"He's going to run out of power soon, but I think that tomorrow night, when the aurora returns, his backup battery should recharge sufficiently that he'll be able to make it some of the way back to the camp. What do you think?"

I nodded. "Can't say I've had much experience with robots, but it sounds like it makes sense to me."

"Only one vay to find out," said Freuchen.

Chou turned back to the robot. "Silas, your power is going to be exhausted soon. While you're in shutdown mode, we're going to free your trapped leg. That way, when the aurora recharges your emergency battery tomorrow, we'll talk more. Do you understand?"

The robot's eyes had been slowly losing some of their brilliance while we discussed the situation. Now they were only a little brighter than the sparks that had first alerted me to him being awake.

"*Yes*," Silas said, his voice an electronic slur.

"You can shut down, now," Chou said, laying a comforting hand against the robot's metal chest.

"*Thank you...*" And with those final words, the robot's eyes dimmed, then were extinguished, and there was only the three of us once again.

"Tell me again about the robot you saw walk into the sea on the first day," said Chou. We had settled around the campfire, huddled close to its flames, more for the sense of security than warmth, I thought.

"There's not much to tell," I said. "It looked identical to this one and walked from the beach into the sea. But it just kept repeating 'Welcome children of Earth' over and over. It felt almost like it had no control over its actions. Like it was being forced into committing suicide." I didn't tell them about the sense of panic I thought I sensed from the robot as it disappeared beneath the surface of the ocean.

Freuchen gave a subtle nod to where Silas sat beneath the pile of rocks. "Do you think this one could be the *same* mechanical man?" Freuchen asked.

"I don't think so, no. No, in fact, I'm sure it's not; Silas has been trapped beneath that rockslide for a long time. It wouldn't make sense that they could be the same."

I felt a sudden thrill of excitement at this latest development. A golden robot! And all we had to do was free it. *Maybe* it could give us answers to the questions we had. A thought struck me: in all the excitement of our discovery of Silas, we hadn't *actually* given any consideration to whether it was even a good idea to free the robot. I said so now.

"But what if it's not really friendly?" I said. "What if we free it and it tries to kill us?"

Freuchen gave a deep growl, like he was considering the possibility of my words, but said nothing. Instead, he looked to Chou.

"There is always that risk," Chou said. "But if his intent was to harm us, why greet us so warmly when he first encountered us? And why would the one you saw walk into the sea not try to harm you?"

"You're right," I said and quoted Silas' opening line: "'Welcome children of Earth, do not be afraid,' isn't exactly a threat. And that's what the other robot kept repeating when it walked past me. I think it was supposed to help keep us calm. To show it's not a threat."

"Still, we should have a plan," Chou said. "In case we are wrong. Although I will admit, I don't believe we will have much chance of either overpowering or doing damage to it. Perhaps it would be best if we agree that if Silas proves aggressive, we should simply run away."

"Yeah, because running from a killer-robot *always* works out," I said. I felt it safe to assume Chou had never seen any of the Terminator movies. "So, if it comes down to it," I continued, "it's going to be a race between me and you, Peter, because I've seen how fast Chou can move."

Chou was right, though; we had no weapons capable of harming Silas. Running away *really* was our only recourse at this point.

"I don't believe it will come to that," Chou said, all business again. "Now, earlier you said Silas gave you a message..."

"Mmm hmm," I said. "Right after it first woke up."

I've always had a pretty good memory but, now, as I recalled the moment, I found I was able to remember Silas' words *exactly*: "Candidate 13, humanity is in peril," I recited. "The plan has been compromised by an external entity. This interference has introduced multiple patterns of disorder; the effects on the outcome have moved beyond predictability. Agents of chaos will be unleashed in an attempt to stop what I require of you. You must travel to the collector immediately and locate Candidate 1. They must know that the field is collapsing, and the void follows behind."

A long silence followed.

"There was nothing more than that?" Chou asked.

"No," I said, "that was everything. When you and Freuchen woke up, the robot stopped talking and went through his... I don't know, I guess you'd call it a start-up process? Like booting up a computer." I paused, unsure whether I should say what I felt but decided I should. "It felt like the message was recorded. It just didn't feel spontaneous to me."

"We will ask Silas what he knows of it tomorrow," Chou said. "But if what you say is correct it seems obvious that the message was meant for you, Meredith. That suggests whoever left it *knew* you would be the one to find Silas and gave him the message specifically for *you*. It *must* be the Architect Silas spoke of. Do you know who Candidate 1 might be?"

I shrugged. "Not a clue. You?"

Chou shook her head. "No, but whoever it is, they must be key to all of this. If we assume that the originator of this message is the Architect, then we can also assume that the 'plan' is the reason we were brought here and what was supposed to have taken place after our arrival."

"And I think we've already met a couple of the 'agents of chaos,'" I said.

"The two men who murdered your friend and almost killed Chou?" Freuchen asked.

"Exactly," I said. "But what about the last line? What do you think 'the field is collapsing, and the void follows behind' could mean?"

Chou considered the question. "I do not know," she said finally.

"I guess that's one we'll need to ask this Candidate 1 when we find them. But why would the Architect leave such a short, cryptic message? Why not just give the exact details of who and where Candidate 1 is and how to find them?"

Freuchen said, "Perhaps the Architect could not risk that information falling into the hands of one of these agents of chaos? Vun thing appears clear: this message *is* a varning. And if ve're correct, and the two men who killed Phillip ver agents of this unknown entity, then it means your location is known, and more vill surely follow."

"Well, thanks for that, Peter," I said. "That makes me feel *so* much better."

Freuchen continued, "Ve should make Edvard avare of the situation as quickly as possible. It vould not be right for him not to know."

Freuchen didn't have to say it, but the implication was clear: *our friends' lives are in danger because of your presence, Meredith.*

I nodded my agreement. "We'll do it as soon as we get back to the garrison. The last thing I would ever want is to put their lives at risk."

Freuchen snored quietly next to the fire, one arm raised, his wrist limp as he dreamed of wrestling polar bears or whatever occupied his slumbering mind. Chou could have been asleep or awake, there was no way for me to tell. She rested on her side facing the fire, perfectly still.

I lay awake, my mind leaping from thought to thought like a needle skipping across a record: *Who is the Architect? Where was Candidate 1?* Who *was Candidate 1? What was the void? How was I supposed to get off this island?* And last but not least, *Why choose me?* Why out of everyone on this island had I been singled out?

Round and around my thoughts spun, feeding a growing sense of restless anxiety that kept me firmly in the waking world. If our assumptions about the message were correct, then I had to find a way off this island as quickly as possible. But where was I supposed to go? The only other land was the distant coastline visible from the beach. But I had no way to reach it or any idea if that was even where I was supposed to start looking for this Candidate 1.

And the idea of walking away from my new friends and the security I'd found with them to set out on my own was *deeply* frightening, terrifying even. Less than a week ago, I had been a strung-out junkie intent on ending her life. And now, by some ludicrous cosmic rolling of dice, I was at the heart of a mystery that was so utterly crazy I had to stop myself from laughing at the absurdity of it.

And yet...

Beneath the feelings of helplessness and fear, a part of me I had not known existed had awakened, a growing desire to turn my face toward the unknown, to square my shoulders to the darkness and say '*Bring it*' to whatever lurked within the shadows.

I have never thought of myself as brave, but I knew that was going to have to change. I was going to have to find that courage within me, and I was going to have to find it fast.

FIFTEEN

EARLY THE NEXT MORNING, good to Chou's word, we began clearing away the rocks and debris that trapped Silas. The back-spill of boulders and gravel behind the robot proved the most difficult to deal with... and the most dangerous. Each time we removed one of the larger boulders, an avalanche of smaller ones slipped down from the scree above. More than once we had to jump away to avoid being crushed by a rogue rock we inadvertently dislodged and brought tumbling in our direction. And, of course, when we'd set off from the garrison the previous morning, we hadn't exactly anticipated having to dig a robot out of the side of a mountain, so we had no shovels or other tools with us, which meant we had to rely on our bare hands. My nails were soon little more than a shredded mess, my hands cross-marked with cuts and grazes. Then, as the hours of lifting passed, we added blisters that split and bled to our growing list of wounds. But by noon, we had managed to clear away three-quarters of the rock that had trapped Silas. Two hours later, only a few smaller rocks in the fifty to sixty-pound range remained along with one large boulder that even Chou and Freuchen's combined strength couldn't budge.

"We need something for leverage," Chou said, after the three of us, panting and dripping with sweat, had tried for the umpteenth time to roll the boulder away.

"I can fix that," Freuchen said. He walked over to a young Fir tree, a quarter the size of the others; spat into both palms of his dirt-and blood-streaked hands and took a mighty swing at the tree's trunk with his ax. Five similar swings later and the tree toppled to the ground. Freuchen quickly stripped all the smaller branches from a length of the trunk then separated that denuded section from the rest of the felled tree, creating a respectably straight eight-foot-long pole. He hefted the cleaned pole in both hands and carried it back to us. "Leverage," he said, his eyes twinkling.

I got on my knees and used my hands to dig out a hole beneath the boulder large enough for the tip of the pole to fit snugly into, then, together, the three of us took hold of it.

"On the count of three," Freuchen said. "Ready... and three!"

Grunting and snarling, we levered the boulder off Silas and cheered in unison as it rolled away, gaining speed as it bowled down the incline before crashing violently into a tree and coming to a halt in a shower of leaves. We yelled whoops of satisfaction, and I raised my hand to high-five Chou and Freuchen. They both looked at me quizzically. Freuchen raised his hand mimicking my own, and I slapped it hard. We made our way back to the fire, ate some of our provisions and chatted about our lives before our arrival on this weird other-world. The shadows grew longer, as we waited impatiently for darkness and that night's coming aurora.

I volunteered for first watch, but despite the fatigue of the day, none of us slept, the idea of actually getting some answers too exhilarating, I think.

When the aurora finally lit up the night sky, I watched the

cuts and grazes I'd collected while we'd worked at freeing Silas heal over, and the tension in my muscles vanished.

"Are we ready?" I said, turning to face my companions when darkness returned.

As one, the three of us got to our feet and walked over to where Silas, free of his rock prison, now sat slumped on the ground and waited for him to wake up. For a minute or so, nothing happened.

"Do you think it is broken?" Freuchen whispered. As if he had uttered magic words, Silas' eye-bar floated free of its fixture. A second later, the two sparks of blue light that would become his eyes appeared.

"Hello Silas," Chou said, as the blue dots expanded.

"*Welcome children of Earth. Do not be afraid. I know that you are confused and have many questions. I am here to help you assimilate into your new surroundings...*" Silas stopped. "*I am sorry, there appears to be a problem. System diagnostics indicate significant degradation of multiple modules. Memory system corruption detected, main power is at zero percent. Battery backup at seven percent—*"

I interrupted, "Silas, it's okay, we've been through this with you last night, remember?"

The robot's eye-bar moved in my direction. "*I am Standard Instructional—*"

"Silas, stop," said Chou. "Do you remember us?"

"*You are candidate 20078, Weston Chou. Your friends are Candidate 13, Meredith Gale and Candidate 207891, Peter Freuchen.*"

"Yes, but do you *remember* meeting us last night?" Chou continued, her voice hesitant.

"*I am sorry, but that would be impossible. Today is transference day, and we could not have met...*" Silas' words tapered off again and his eye-bar began to move left and right, up and down as he cast his electronic gaze over the trees and rubble strewn ground. "*This is not my assigned reception location. I apologize for the inconvenience, but I appear to be suffering from an undiagnosed malfunction. I will shortly return to conservation mode but please...*"

As Silas continued to run through the same lines he'd spoken to us the previous night, Chou turned to face me, a look of abject dejection on her face. "I think its memory problems might be a bit more complicated than we first thought."

"Oh, that's just great," I sighed. "That's just freaking great."

"Silas, stop," Chou demanded, as the robot continued the same speech it had given the night before. When he did as she asked, Chou added, "We know this is confusing for you, but your memory has been damaged. We spoke last night, so we know you only have a short amount of time before your systems begin to shut down again; what we need to know from you is how can we help you so that you can help us?"

"Yes," Freuchen said. "It is time for us to sit crooked and talk straight."

"*If you could locate a repair—*"

I took a step toward the robot. "There is *no* repair station. There is *no* neural net. *None* of the other SILAS units have survived on this island that we are aware of. Nothing has gone according to the Architect's plan. There is only *you*, Silas. We don't have time to explain everything to you. What we do need to know is if there is any other way to keep you powered up before your backup battery is depleted?"

As if he was waiting for someone to admit that what I had just said was a joke, Silas' eye-bar dipped on the left side, giving the impression of an eyebrow raised in disbelief.

"*I have a photoelectric charging system built into my outer skin,*" Silas said after no one contradicted me. His eye-bar moved to look up at the forest canopy. "*It will prove sufficient to keep my main systems active. There is insufficient sunlight here. Please direct me to the nearest open area."*

"The beach," Freuchen said. "Ve should get him to the beach."

"I don't think he'll make it that far," Chou said. "Not at night. His backup batteries are only going to last him twenty minutes at most. Then we'll have to wait until tomorrow's aurora, and we'll be a day later back to the garrison than we said we would be."

"Maybe we should just get him into the clearing near the tower," I said. "At least there's open sky. Maybe it will be enough to keep him charged long enough to get to the beach."

Chou nodded. "Yes, it's worth a try." She turned back to Silas. "Silas, will you follow us please?"

"*Of course,*" said Silas. The robot slowly extended both of his legs until they were directly out in front of him, his joints grating and creaking like stressed metal. At the same time, he flexed both of his arms, like someone at a gym warming up before hitting the weight machines. He did this several times, each time the grating sound grew less and less until, finally, he pushed himself to his feet.

We walked back to the tower, an unobstructed view of the star-speckled sky above us, the robot, looming over us.

"This will do," I said. "Silas, wait here, please."

The robot obeyed.

"What should we ask him?" I said, thinking back to the previous night and all of the questions that had gone left unsaid.

Chou shook her head. "I don't think we should ask him anything tonight. We need him to conserve as much energy as possible to get him to the beach tomorrow morning. If we ask questions, it will use up his energy reserves."

"You're right," I said, even though the questions I had were ready to spill from me.

Silas said, "*Weston is correct. If I enter standby mode soon, I will conserve ninety-eight percent of my available power.*"

"It's the best course of action," Chou said.

Both Freuchen and I agreed.

"Silas, shut down until we reactivate you."

"*Shutting down. Good night.*" And with that, the robot's eyes dimmed and went out.

SIXTEEN

WE SPENT the rest of the night camped at the base of the tower. At some point, I'd fallen asleep and awakened to the sound of birds chirruping in the tangled wreckage at the top of the tower. The sun was still too low in the sky to illuminate much of the clearing, instead, sending shadow emissaries creeping ahead of itself, gradually shrinking harbingers of early morning's approach.

The robot was in the exact same position we had left him.

"Silas, wake up." No sooner had I said the words than the two blue spots of electronic light sparked into life on the robot's eye-bar. I half-expected to have to go through the same welcome speech, but his battery-backup appeared to have held.

"*Good morning,*" the robot said, rising to his full height.

Silas looked around. "*Oh, the habitat!*" he said, surprised when he saw the ruined tower behind him.

"You mentioned the tower... the *habitat,* as you call it, when we spoke with you the first night we found you. What was it?" Chou asked.

"*A residence for this island's candidates. A home for all of you. I built it in preparation for your arrival.*"

"You built it?" Freuchen said, obviously impressed.

"Yes, with the help of another SILAS unit."

"Do you think there is anything of use to us in there?" Freuchen said, nodding at the tower.

"I do not believe so. The habitat was just that: a place for you to rest, shelter. It was to be furnished and stocked at a later date."

"Silas, do you know why we were brought here?" I asked.

"Here?" the robot said.

"To this planet."

"I apologize, but the information is lost to me."

"That's okay," I said. "Silas, the night we found you, when you first woke up, you relayed a message to me. Was the message from the Architect?"

Silas' eye-bar swiveled in my direction. *"I'm sorry, Meredith, but I have no recollection of relaying any message to you."*

I quickly repeated the message back to him: "Candidate 13, humanity is in peril. The plan has been compromised by an external entity. This interference has introduced multiple patterns of disorder; the effects on the outcome have moved beyond predictability. Agents of chaos will be unleashed in an attempt to stop what I require of you. You must travel to the collector immediately and locate Candidate 1. They must know that the field is collapsing, and the void follows behind."

Chou asked, "Who is the 'external entity'? And what did you mean by the 'void'? Can you tell me?"

Silas' eye-bar tilted quizzically. *"I have no information or memory of ever relaying that information to you, Meredith. Perhaps this is a product of my memory failure?"*

"Okay," I said, "can you at least tell me who Candidate 1 is? Or who the Collector is? Where I can find them? And what does this collector... collect, exactly?" Visions of bad horror movie villains sprang unbidden into my mind.

"I... there appears to be a block on that information."

"You mean you've forgotten who it is? When we met, you knew who I was, who Chou and Freuchen were? Why would you forget who they are?"

"No, I have not forgotten the information, that part of my memory appears to be fully intact. Access to information relating to the first five candidates appears to have been placed behind a barrier that I am unable to breach."

"You mean, it's password protected?" I said.

"In a manner of speaking, yes. I know the information is there, I just do not have the authorization to access it."

I tried not to let my growing frustration show, and while Silas may have been correct about having forgotten the message he had related to me, it just didn't *feel* right. I mean, how could whoever had sent the message know it was going to be *me* who would be the one to find Silas? And why would the first words out of his mouth have been a message for me, only to then deny having any memory of it? It just didn't make sense. But at least now I knew that the robot had some answers. How I was supposed to access that information was a whole other question.

"Can you tell us who the Architect is and what it wants from us?" I asked.

"That memory is fragmented. I do not remember who the Architect is, but I do know that he wants you to survive."

"Survive? Survive what?" Chou said.

"I do not know."

"Then vy did the Architect choose *us*?" Freuchen said. "Vy vould the Architect choose me? Or Meredith? Or any of us?"

"Your wasted potential," Silas said, as if those three words were self-explanatory.

"Wasted potential?" I repeated back to him. "That makes no sense at all."

"Please, explain what you mean," Freuchen urged.

The robot repositioned himself, his eye-bar slowly moving to each of our faces in an equivalency of eye-contact. "*Each of your lives was cut short; whether by your own hand, as the result of an accident, or by some other event. With your death, everything you would have ever achieved was lost. It is that wasted potential which drew the Architect to you. You were chosen because of your probability for achievement, or for your specific knowledge, or the skills which you possess that would prove useful in ensuring the continued success of humanity.*"

"I knew it," I said, throwing a smile at Chou. "There *is* a plan, and we're all a part of it."

Chou leaned in. "But how could the Architect know what our potential was? That suggests it possess some way to observe or predict what we could have achieved."

"*I'm sorry, I have no data available on that.*"

"Oh, shit," I said, with a sudden understanding of where Chou was going with her line of questioning. "There's really only *one* way the Architect could know what our potential was."

With a subtle nod, Chou encouraged me to continue.

"It *had* to have had something to compare our lives against. A version of us whose potential *wasn't* wasted."

"Yes," said Chou, a smile parting her lips.

In my excitement, I grabbed both of Chou's hands in mine. "You were right about Edward. You've been right all along. Parallel universes. That explains it. Not only are we not from the same time, we're not even from the same *universe*, are we?"

Chou nodded, her smile widening. "I believe that is correct."

Freuchen looked completely perplexed. "Vat on Earth are you talking about? How can ve *not* be from the same universe? Vat other universe is there?" He sat down hard and began to caress his temple with one meaty hand.

I crouched down beside him. "I know it's confusing, but I'll try to explain," I said, placing a hand on his knee and squeezing gently. "When Wild Bill first brought us to the garrison, I was sure I knew Edward from somewhere. It was only later that I realized I *did* know him, or rather, I knew *of* him."

Freuchen's brow furrowed but he did not interrupt me as I explained it all.

"Are you saying that our Edward is an imposter?" Freuchen asked when I was through. "I do not believe you."

"No, no. I'm not saying that at all. Our Edward *is* Edward. But the Edward I read about in my time, the one who survived the war and went on to become an esteemed poet, is *also* Edward. There's a theory that suggests there's not just a single universe, but an infinite variety of them. That, for every choice you make, another version of you makes a different choice and creates a new off-shoot of that universe. And while both versions of you share a common past, at the point they diverge, they branch off into their own, unique version of the universe."

It would be easy to look at Freuchen and think that because of his size he was not a smart man, but that would have been a grave underestimation of him. Behind that humongous beard and the bear-like frame was a sharp mind. "You mean that the Edward Hubbard you say you knew from his poetry books is our Edward, but also not him?"

"In a way, yes," Chou said, taking over the explanation. "The Edward from Meredith's universe shared our Edward's life exactly, right up until Meredith's Edward made a choice that saved his life, sending him down a different path and creating a new version of the universe. An alternative version.

"Perhaps in Meredith's timeline, her Edward delayed leaving the trench to reconnoiter the enemy's position a minute later. Perhaps he was on some other battlefield that day, or the task was given to another unlucky soldier. Whatever the reason, Meredith's Edward made different choices and lived. He *is* Edward and also not Edward. Do you understand?"

Neither Chou nor Freuchen noticed the quiet gasp of realization that slipped from between my lips. I understood now *exactly* where *my* life had diverged; the asshole in the Ford F150. That night, if Oscar and I had left the party just a minute earlier or later than we had, we would never have been t-boned by the truck. And if that accident had never happened, then Oscar would still be alive, and I would not have set off down my own dark path that led to me sitting here with this bizarre group of reluctant interdimensional time-travelers.

Freuchen said, "It is enough to make your head spin. I have always understood that the mechanics of our universe ver complex, it vould seem that I grossly underestimated just *how* complex."

"Look on the bright side," I said, leaning against Freuchen, "it also means that in some of these alternate universes, we're alive and happy, and living normal lives. We probably have families. And in one of those lives, we achieved something so astounding that the Architect came looking for us."

Freuchen smiled a sad, enigmatic smile. The idea was, I am sure, as appealing to all of us as it was to me, that there were other versions of us out there who were happy, successful, living their lives in blissful ignorance of the crazy reality of our multiple existences. It was... comforting.

Freuchen broke the silence. "Vile this answers one of our questions," he said slowly, his voice a low rumble, "it also creates others: vy vould the Architect choose to contact us ven ve ver staring our mortality in the face? Vy not simply ask the question ven ve ver safe in our beds? Or choose a version of us that vas never in peril to begin vith?"

Chou sat cross-legged in front of us. "I believe I understand why." She gathered her thoughts then continued. "Although we all originate from very different times, we do all share one commonality: after we died, our bodies would never have been found. I would have drifted for eternity through space. Meredith's body would have been carried by the tide out to sea. Edward would have remained buried beneath the battlefield. And you, Peter, you said you would have frozen to death, lost in a blizzard. Our stories *all* end the same way."

"But that still doesn't explain why the Architect would wait until we were about to die. Why hold out until then?" I said.

"If the Architect had taken us at any point *before* it was sure our lives were over, it could have changed the course of the timeline. It had to be certain its actions would leave the timeline unaltered. The only way the Architect could be certain of that would be if it contacted us at the *exact* moment our lives would have ended if it had not intervened."

"It does make a fantastical kind of sense," Freuchen said, nodding in agreement.

I wondered just how long it must have taken for the Architect to find a version of me that met whatever criteria it had judged us by. How many timelines must it have searched through? How many lives had it observed? And what kind of an intelligence could be capable of such god-like feats? It was at once awe-inspiring and absolutely terrifying.

"Yes, yes. I see it now," Freuchen said, his enthusiasm gathering steam. "And by the same logic, your theory also explains vy the Architect did not harvest us from a universe vare ve ver not destined for an early demise." Freuchen was following Chou's logic better than I was, apparently.

"How so?" I asked, uneasy with his choice of words; the idea of having been *harvested* was... creepy.

"Consider the shockwaves that vould have reverberated through your friends' and relatives' lives if..." He made an explosion with his fingers. "Poof! Suddenly you are no more... vanished... gone vithout a trace from a vurld vare you vould have lived a full and productive life. It vould irreversibly alter the chronology of that universe into one that vas never meant to be."

Chou nodded in agreement.

Freuchen kept going, on a roll now. "Imagine for a moment all the people you vould have met, talked to, befriended, loved, all the ripples of influence that your presence vould have made over the course of your natural life. None of those things vould ever happen if the Architect meddled in a timeline vare our lives ver not destined to end prematurely."

"But if there are infinite timelines, why would altering one of them have even mattered?" I said, my mind trying to grasp all of the implications.

Chou answered. "It would only matter to an ethical intelligence."

There was a long pause as we allowed that information to sink in.

"You mean the Architect chose us because it *cares* about us?" I said, slowly.

"Not necessarily about us as individuals," Chou explained. "But it suggests that the Architect *is* concerned about humans as a *species* and will carefully consider the effect its actions would have on us and humanity in general."

Chou took a step closer to Silas. She reached into her pants' pocket and pulled something from it, held it in her closed fist. When she unfurled her fingers, she held the remains of the mechanical bug she had killed that first night. "Can you tell me what this is?"

Silas swiveled his upper torso to face her and leaned down to inspect the bug. Gently, the robot lifted the remains from Chou's hand and held it close to his eye-bar (whether this was an affectation to mimic a human response or whether he really needed a closer look, I have no idea).

"*Fascinating!*" Silas whispered. "*I do not recognize this unit.*

It appears to be a beautifully crafted mechanism designed specifically for surreptitious observation."

"You're saying that thing was designed specifically to spy on us?" I said.

"*Yes, I believe so.*"

Silas placed the broken bug back into Chou's hand. "*How did you acquire it?*"

"During the first night we arrived," Chou said. "It attempted to infiltrate our camp. Why would you say it is designed to spy on us?"

"*There would be no need to have it mimic an insect unless it was designed to blend in and avoid detection. As you can see from my own appearance, the Architect does not seek to disguise his creations.*"

"If it's not a tool of the Architect then who is it spying for?" Chou continued.

"*I can only surmise that whoever is responsible for interfering in the Architect's plan must also be responsible for that exquisite mechanism.*"

"Are you saying someone is vurking against your master? Against the Architect?" Freuchen interjected.

A lightbulb suddenly lit up in my head as I made a connection that had been right in front of us. "The message Silas gave me, it warned about an 'external entity.' Maybe *that's* who made the bug."

"Then our suspicions ver correct," Freuchen said. He snapped his fingers loudly. "The message also mentioned 'agents of chaos.' That could explain the two men who murdered your friend and I believe may vell have done the same to you and your companions if Vild Bill had not found you."

"*Murder*?" Silas gasped, as though he had been startled. "*That is impossible. The Architect anticipated that there would be confusion after the great transference, but efforts were made to ensure that your natural human proclivity to strike out during times of stress was abated for several days."*

Freuchen stroked his huge beard as he answered. "Vell it looks like vatever 'efforts' you're talking about came to nothing, because if our friend Vild Bill had not found Meredith, Chou, and Albert, they vould surely have been killed too. Vat do you have to say to that?

"*It does not make sense.*"

"It *does* if you include this mysterious entity from the message in the mix," Chou said. "But why would they target us?"

"Maybe it's because I was the one who was going to receive the message from the Architect?" I said. "But that would mean that this other entity knew about it ahead of time. None of this makes any sense to me, either."

"This other... adversarial entity," Freuchen said, "it seems apparent that it does not share the Architect's good vill toward us."

Chou nodded. "Just the opposite. It appears to have its own agenda. And how we factor into that agenda, if at all, I do not know. But it is obvious to me that it does not share the same ethical values as the Architect."

I said, "So the Architect has our best interest at heart, but we don't know what it wants from us. And this other entity—what did you call it, the Adversary?"

"The Adversary seems an appropriate name for it, yes," said Chou.

"The intentions of this Adversary are completely unknown to us," I continued, "but it does appear its agents are willing to kill on its behalf, assuming our theory is correct."

Freuchen leaned forward, stroking his beard. "It seems that venever ve unravel vun mystery it is immediately replaced by another that is just as perplexing."

"Silas, what do you say about all of this?" I asked the robot.

"I wish that I could confirm or deny your theory. I know that there was a plan. I was created to help educate you as to its purpose, and assist you in achieving its goals, but that is as much as I can remember. I am sorry. Please, believe me when I say that this is almost as frustrating for me as it is for you." Silas seemed honestly broken up about it.

"That's okay," I said, "it's not like it's your fault. But is there anything else, anything at all that you can tell us about what the Architect wants from us?"

"I am sorry, but no."

Chou said, "Silas, if you don't know *who* the Architect is, can you at least tell us *where* he is located?"

That question hadn't even crossed my mind. I hadn't given a thought that the robot might hold the key to the whereabouts of the Architect.

"Regrettably, I do not have that information."

Well, so much for that idea, I thought. There was a brief period of silence.

"I have a question," Freuchen said. His voice had grown quiet. "Can the Architect send us back?"

"Back? To where?" Silas asked.

"Back to our planet. Our home. Can this Architect, if ve find him, can he send us back to vare ve came from?"

"I am sorry, but, no, I do not believe that would be possible."

"But you said the Architect brought us through time to *here*... varever *here* is," Freuchen continued. "If he brought us here, vy can't he just reverse the process?"

"The exact process of how your translocation was achieved is unavailable to me. But I know that the procedure by which the Architect brought all of you here was not truly time-travel, it was something... else. What that mechanism was, exactly, is lost to me. I am sorry, but there is no going back."

"Vell," Freuchen said, a note of exasperation entering his voice as if he already knew he would not receive an adequate answer in this ongoing exercise in exasperation. "Can you at least tell us *vare* ve are exactly? What name should ve call this planet of yours?"

Silas's eye-bar tilted in a display of surprise. "*I apologize. Had I not made it obvious? This is planet Earth.*"

You could, quite literally, have heard a pin drop for what seemed like minutes.

Freuchen finally broke the silence. "But that cannot be. The sun? The moon? How can this be Earth?" His voice was tremulous, only just above the volume of a whisper.

I suddenly realized that of all the questions we had asked so far, we had missed the most obvious one. I asked it now: "Silas," my own voice barely under control, "*When* are we? What *year* is this?"

Silas's eye-bar swiveled in my direction. "*As I cannot account for the exact period of time during which I was deactivated, I cannot calculate with any degree of accuracy what—*"

Freuchen leaped to his feet and strode toward Silas until he was eye to eye-bar with the robot. "For the love of all that is good, vould you just give us a straight answer you metal monstrosity!" he hissed.

"*The year is approximately 420,353,745; plus or minus several hundred years, allowing for my period of inactivity.*"

"What?" I sat down. *Hard*. When I lifted my eyes again, my two friends looked to be in just as much shock as me.

"How can that be?" Freuchen said. "How?" His eyes drifted to Chou and me as if we might hold the answer.

"Holy shit," I whispered, my eyes dropped to stare at the

tufts of grass between my feet. I suddenly felt very, very tired. "*Holy. Shit.*" I managed to lift my head and look at Silas. "Half a billion years?" I whispered, my voice trailing off into an unrecognizable squeak that would have sent any nearby dogs into a howling frenzy. "We've been brought half a... *bill... billion* years into the future?"

"*Approximately,*" Silas said brightly, obviously happy he could finally give us an actual answer to a question, blissfully unaware that he had just delivered a hammer-blow to all three of us. It felt as if a cord I didn't know I was connected to had been stressed beyond its breaking point and suddenly snapped. And now I was... adrift. I felt incredibly vulnerable, which was strange when you consider everything else that had happened to me since my arrival here. Could I even call it an arrival when I had, apparently, never even left Earth? But this new information from Silas only served to ram home how distant my old life was, and, even though this was still my planet, how very, very alien *this* Earth was.

"But if this is Earth, vare are all the other humans? The countries and civilizations? All our great vurks and vunders?" Freuchen's voice trailed off.

"*I have no data available on that, Peter.*"

Chou, who seemed the least affected by the latest news, said, "Silas, why do you refer to us as Candidates?"

"*That is your official designation, assigned by the Architect.*"

"Yes, but candidates for what?" I said.

"I have no—" Silas began, but I cut him off.

"Available data on that," I snapped, finishing his sentence. "Yes, we get it. Well, can you at least tell us how many candidates there are?" I said, expecting the same answer.

Silas processed the question then said, "*There were one billion nine-hundred-million five-hundred-thousand-and-eighty-*

nine candidates who agreed to be relocated here from their home timelines."

My mind reeled again, trying to take in the enormity of the number. It was *staggering*. I had grown used to the idea that this little island was all there was. That we were it.

Obviously, there couldn't be *that* many people on the island, which meant they had to be elsewhere. The distant coastline I'd seen from the beach was the only logical place. It *had* to be part of a larger landmass or continent; large enough to accommodate almost two-billion temporal-gypsies, all so very far from home. Two billion people thrown together with no direction, no answers, and no understanding of who or what had brought them here.

It sounded to me like a recipe for disaster.

The first few days on this island had been insane, but now I counted myself lucky to have arrived here rather than the mainland. I could not begin to imagine the chaos that must have been magnified a million times across the mainland. How could anyone possibly be expected to build from that? How would we make it?

And yet... the kindness I had witnessed in my time here; the drive to begin over, to build something worthwhile from the ashes of destruction seemed... unstoppable. I'd come to realize that the will to succeed, to create something bigger than ourselves was a basic drive woven deep within the very fabric of our humanity.

We had all been given a second chance. A chance to try again. To make something... better.

And so what if the Architect was AWOL? Who cared if there was no roadmap to follow? And as for the Adversary; well, it wouldn't be the first time humanity had come face-to-face with a tyrant intent on subjugating all of us to his will. Throughout the history of our race, we had confronted those same trials and beaten them, time after time.

There were two billion humans on this planet. Two billion hand-selected souls who shared the same drive and determination that had brought our species to dominance over every other living thing on this planet. *This* was our chance to build that brave new world that had haunted our species' dreams for millennia. To rescue humanity from whatever fate had swept it from our rightful home.

The Architect had chosen *me*. Had told me that I was the one it trusted. And if our theories were true, then the Architect knew more about me than I did. So, who was I to question its choice?

Still, the fact remained, somewhere out *there,* amongst those two billion strangers, was the key to all the mysteries: Candidate 1.

"Ve vill need to be on our vay if ve vish to be back at the garrison before sunset," Freuchen said, breaking me free of my thoughts.

"If you are sure there's nothing worth salvaging from the habitat then there's no reason we should remain here any longer," Chou said. "Silas, do you think you have sufficient energy to make it approximately three miles through the forest to the beach or should we wait?"

"If we leave soon, I will make it."

"The sooner ve are on our vay the better. All this standing around is making my feet itch," Freuchen said. He kicked dirt over the smoldering campfire, then said to the robot. "Follow us."

SEVENTEEN

THE SECOND DEAD man had vanished from the beach. All that remained to show he'd ever existed was a lone shoe and a shallow indentation in the shale starting where his body had lain and ending at the edge of the forest.

"Did something drag his body away?" I said, not wanting to hear I was right. My mind flashed back to the saber-toothed tiger that had stalked us over those first two nights.

Freuchen bent over, picked up the shoe then dropped it quickly when he saw the foot still in it. "Something big, for sure," he muttered.

"And hungry," Chou added, scanning the forest. "Best we keep moving."

"No argument from me," I said. Despite having the giant robot as a deterrent, I couldn't shake the thought that whatever had dragged off the decomposing body of the man was following us, camouflaged within the trees.

"*Many animal genera were brought here by the Architect,*" Silas said. "*A wide variety of species from Earth's timeline were needed to ensure an adequate food supply and maintain the biological fecundity of the planet. These include carrion eaters.*"

"Oh-kay," I said, "Well, thanks for that reassuring tidbit, Silas."

"You are welcome, Meredith."

The first body we'd passed was, however, still there. We smelled it long before we saw it, thanks to a breeze that set the forest rustling and the stench of decay wafting in our direction. After two more days in the sun, the dead man was evidently too far into the decomposition process to draw larger carnivores and had, instead, attracted birds, crabs, and a mass of insects that now treated the rapidly decaying cadaver as either food, a new home, or both. I gave the body as wide a berth as possible, covering my nose and mouth with a hand while trying hard not to repeat the embarrassment of losing my breakfast again.

Silas, on the other hand, appeared to be completely immune. He walked over to the body and knelt next to it. "*The number of candidate deaths is disturbing*," the robot said. "*Losses were expected during the Great Transference, but those were anticipated to have been due to shock induced by the translocation of candidates from their timeline to this one.*" He leaned in closer, his eye-bar scanning the corpse. "*Losses of this nature should never have occurred; it was all but impossible. Provisions were made by the Architect to reduce fatalities to as close to zero as possible.*"

"What *kind* of *provisions?*" Chou said, also seemingly unperturbed by the stench of the dead man.

"*Some minor adjustments were made to your bodies to ensure the release of elevated levels of key chemicals such as serotonin, and oxytocin upon your arrival.*"

"Wouldn't that bring on a sense of well-being, happiness?" I said, being somewhat of an aficionado on highs until a couple of days ago.

"*Yes, Meredith, along with feelings of closeness for your fellow candidates,*" Silas replied. "*This would help mitigate the shock of your arrival long enough for my fellow SILAS units and I to educate you on why you had been chosen and to help assimilate you into your new home."*

"Figures," I said. "Well, we certainly didn't feel anything like what you described during this Great Transference. In fact, it was the complete opposite. Almost everyone panicked. But we *definitely* feel something like it every night during the Aurora."

"*Curious,*" Silas said. "*I wish I had access to more information on the subject.*"

"Is there anything else you *can* remember? Anything at all?" Chou said.

"*No, that is as much as I am able to recall. I am sorry.*"

Noon had come and gone by the time we reached the estuary. I was pleasantly surprised at the feeling of 'coming home' that blossomed in my chest at the idea of reaching the garrison and once again seeing the people who I now called my friends. And it had been oddly quiet without Albert. The kid had grown on me.

"Ve should take a break," Freuchen suggested, stopping to lean against a tree and empty several pebbles from his shoes.

"Oh, God, yes please," I said. We'd been exposed to the full force of the sun for the last couple of hours, so fifteen minutes dangling my sweaty feet in the river sounded delicious.

"Very well," said Chou, "but remain close by."

"Don't worry, I'll stay within screaming distance," I said, only half-joking.

Freuchen excused himself and headed for the privacy of a row of trees to do what he had to do. I walked to a cluster of boulders just a little further upstream, perfectly positioned in the shade of six coconut palms. I splashed cold water over my face and washed some of the sweat from it. I stripped off my shoes and socks, rolled up my jeans and dipped my feet into the water, and leaned back. Through half-closed eyes, I watched Chou climb atop a large boulder that reminded me of a giant turtle's shell, where she watched over us like some mother duck guarding her ducklings.

In the distance, semi-obscured by haze and clouds, the monolith guarded the horizon. My eyes drifted from it to Silas.

I watched him climb nimbly down to the riverbank, then wade out into the fast-flowing water, his eye-bar moving back and forth, searching the water for something. Eventually, he reached down, lifted an object from the river, scrutinized it, then placed it in a metal pouch on his hip. A few more minutes passed, then he stooped down again and pulled a second object from the water, held it in his hand and examined it closely. Apparently satisfied with whatever it was, he put the second object in his pouch and waded back to shore. He sat down on the river bank and took one of the objects he'd collected from his pouch and held it in front of him. It looked like a flat piece of rock or wood, I couldn't tell. The robot raised his other hand, pointed an index finger at the object, and I saw a bright beam of light emanate from it. It was a laser, I was sure. Silas' hand moved in a blur for several seconds back and forth across the object. Then the light went out and Silas, seemingly satisfied, placed the object back in the metal pouch on his waist. He got to his feet, looked around and began to walk to where I lay watching him.

When the robot reached me, he stood for several moments, his eye-bar moving back and forth across the scenery. "*It is so very beautiful here,*" he said.

"It's almost paradise," I said. "All it needs is a Tiki bar, and I'd die happy."

Silas' eye-bar tilted oddly as if he were assessing whether I was joking or not, then he said, *"May I ask a favor of you, Meredith?"*

"Of course." I propped myself up on both elbows and gave him my full attention.

Silas reached into his pouch and pulled out a flat, gray piece of rock about eight-inches wide by four.

"It is slate," Silas said. *"I would like to give this to you now, to ensure that you know what to do tomorrow."* He offered the rock to me.

"Okay?" I said, taking it from him, puzzled as to why he would want me to have it. I flipped it over and saw rows of finely inscribed markings neatly etched onto its smooth surface. The markings reminded me of a UPC barcode like you'd see on something you bought from a store, except this was much longer, easily several thousand tightly packed lines long. The code took up about half of the available surface of the one side of the piece of slate.

"What is it?" I asked, wondering at how perfectly the lines had been etched into the slate's surface.

"In anticipation of the memory loss I will undoubtedly experience when my battery is exhausted, I have inscribed all pertinent information of the events leading up to today onto the slate in machine-readable code. It includes your names and everything you have told me, and that I should trust what you tell me without question. It will save us all time, I believe. I will update the slate on a daily basis until I am able to find a more permanent solution to my memory loss."

"Wow!" I said, honestly impressed. "What do I need to do with it?"

"When you reactivate me tomorrow, simply hold it in front of my eye-bar. I will automatically recognize it and assimilate the information."

I nodded at the robot. "Will do."

"*Thank you, Meredith.*" Silas dipped his shoulders in acknowledgment.

I leaned back against the rocks. The clouds that had earlier obscured the monolith had moved on, so now most of the huge mega-structure was visible. It was hard to look at it without feeling uneasy; it was just so massive. But it was also beautiful. The reflected sunlight shone like a distant beacon.

A sudden realization hit me like a slap across my face. I jumped to my feet.

"*Are you okay, Meredith?*" Silas said.

"I'm fine," I replied, then, "Come on. We need to talk to Chou and Freuchen." I jogged to where Chou stood on her rock, casually chatting with Freuchen.

"The collector," I said, not waiting for them to stop talking. "What if it's not a person?"

Both of my friends looked at me quizzically.

"From Silas' message: You must travel to the collector immediately and locate Candidate 1." I pointed over their shoulders to the monolith.

"Oh!" said Freuchen. "Vell, I suppose that vould make sense, vouldn't it?"

Chou took a few moments before she replied. "It is the most prominent landmark. But why not one of the three others?"

I took a moment to consider her question. "It's the only one of the four that we can be certain is located on land."

Chou nodded slowly.

"It *vould* be the logical place to start looking, at least," Freuchen said, with a dip of his chin. "If you could get off the island, at least."

I felt my mood drop a little. He was right. I would have to find some way to get to the mainland. But if the Architect was as smart as it appeared to be, and if it wanted me to locate this

Candidate 1 so badly, then there *had* to be some way for me to escape the island. I just had to find it.

Chou stared at the monolith for a while, then said, "Time to move on."

Together we set out on the final trek back to the garrison.

We retraced our original path up the river, crossed from one bank to the other, then continued following the river through the woods toward home, chatting happily amongst ourselves.

The acrid smell of woodsmoke wafted downwind to us; stronger than I remembered from the garrison's campfire, but still a welcome reminder that we were almost home. But as we drew closer to the garrison, I noticed more smoke, a lot of it, reaching between the trees like ghostly fingers. I felt a moment of unease, then we stepped out of the forest and into the garrison's clearing, and for a brief moment, I felt a distinct sense of relief.

"Stop," Chou said suddenly, throwing up an arm to bar our way. "Look."

The feeling of relief evaporated as I caught sight of what had brought Chou to such an abrupt stop. Edward's cabin was nothing but a smoking ruin, and most of the lean-tos had been reduced to little more than splinters. There was no sign of anyone working in the camp or the forest. The garrison was deathly quiet. Deserted.

"No, this cannot be," Freuchen hissed and ran toward the camp.

"Stop," Chou hissed. "Whoever did this might still be in the camp."

Freuchen ignored her.

Chou exhaled a long sigh then motioned we should follow

too. By the time the three of us caught up with Freuchen, he was circling Edward's cabin.

"I do not see any bodies," Freuchen said, turning to look around the remains of the camp.

Edward's cabin was a smoking ruin; a skeleton of blackened logs and ash-gray burned planks. But here and there, a few pieces of the outer walls remained untouched by the fire. There was something odd about one of them.

"I think these are bullet holes," I said, running my fingers over several missing chunks that had been gouged out of the wood.

Freuchen examined them too, then walked away from the cabin, his eyes scouring the ground. After a minute, he bent over and picked something up from the scorched grass. He bent over four more times in quick succession. "You are correct, Meredith," he said, holding out his hand to show us five brass bullet casings.

"Oh no," I heard myself say. "Why would anyone do this?"

No one answered me, but Freuchen said, "There are a lot of tracks leading tovard the north gate. I think whoever is responsible for this has kidnapped all of our friends and spirited them away."

"Why though?" I said. "What could they possibly want with them?"

Chou shook her head. "There are many possibilities. None of which are good. We will need to locate our friends quickly if we have any hope of freeing them."

"How long do you think it's been since whoever did this left the garrison?" Chou asked Freuchen.

"It's difficult to be sure, but I vould say no more than a few hours judging by how the cabin is still smoldering."

Chou nodded. She looked skyward. "We still have several

hours of daylight left. I would suggest we gather whatever supplies we can find and follow their trail immediately."

"I agree," Freuchen said.

Five minutes later, we began to follow the trail of footprints through the north gate of the stockade. We had refilled our water bottles and found a few scraps of food, including several salmon bricks left behind in the ashes of the campfire.

"Vell, at least they vill be easy to track," Freuchen said, nodding at the ground and a muddy furrow that marked the route where our friends had been marched away, presumably in single file. "They should be slower than us, too. So as long as ve keep our pace up, ve should catch up vith them quickly."

"Let's move," Chou said, she began walking briskly in the direction the tracks lead.

"*Look, there,*" said Silas. He pointed at several sets of footprints laid down parallel to the deeper tracks of our people. "*There appear to be four others walking alongside the main group; two at the front and two more at the rear.*"

"Guards," said Freuchen. "So ve know ve are not outnumbered."

The tracks continued north initially then curved west, back into the woods, in the direction Wild Bill had found us. We were about to cross from the clearing into the woods when Silas came to a halt. He raised himself to full height, and his torso moved slowly left then right. His eye-bar moving rapidly as though it were scanning the forest.

"What is it?" I asked.

"*There is a single human. Approximately fifty-seven feet in that direction.*" He sliced the air with a gold arm at an angle away from the tracks we were following. "*They appear to be in some distress.*"

"It could be one of the kidnappers," Freuchen said, his jaw set. I could tell he was spoiling for a fight.

"If that is so, we might be able to learn something from them," said Chou. "We should approach carefully. If it is one of the people who attacked the garrison, they may still be armed." She turned to the robot. "Silas, I want you to lead the way. Be as quiet as you can." She looked back at me and Freuchen. "We will remain behind you."

We followed Silas as he picked his way carefully through the forest. "*We are nearing the location*," He whispered. "*Should I go ahead and ensure that there is no threat*?"

All three of us humans found cover behind the wide trunk of a Redwood.

"Yes," Chou whispered, crouching next to me and Freuchen.

"Be careful," I added, kneeling beside her.

The robot dipped his eye-bar in acknowledgment and began to creep forward, while we all held our breath in anticipation.

Seconds passed with only the background noise of the forest to cover our deep breathing, then Silas said "*Candidate 812139, it is a pleasure to meet you. You are injured. May I be of assistance to you?*"

There was a momentary pause then an unmistakable voice said, "You come one step closer, and I'll blow that excuse for a head right off your shoulders."

"Wild Bill!" I yelled, unable to hold back my relief. As one the three of us clambered from cover and rushed toward our friend's voice.

Silas' huge frame stood between two trees, blocking my view. He stepped aside as we approached, and I slipped past him, the grin on my face melting away as I got a good view of the scene. On the ground ahead of me lay Wild Bill's horse.

Brute was obviously dead; several bullet wounds along his flank a testament to what had ended the beast's life. Wild Bill lay next to his horse, pinned from the waist down beneath him,

"Well, you all are a sight for sore eyes," the cowboy whispered, through gritted teeth. "I thought I was a dead man, for sure." As he spoke, he ran his hand over Brute's mane, but his eyes did not leave Silas. "And the God's honest truth is I ain't convinced I ain't dead." He nodded at Silas "Is this... *tinman* with you?"

"Silas?" I said. "He's one of the good guys. We'll tell you all about him later."

Freuchen stepped in and knelt at Brute's head. "First thing ve need to do is get you out from under there. Silas?"

"*Yes, Peter. How may I be of assistance?*"

"Vill you help us lift Brute off Vild Bill?"

"*Of course.*" Silas moved closer, his multi-jointed legs bending in a way that allowed him to slide his arms under Brute's body. Then, in one swift yet touchingly gentle movement that did not go unnoticed by the cowboy, he lifted Brute off of Wild Bill and set the horse's body down nearby. Silas' eyebar shifted in Wild Bill's direction. "*I am very sorry for your loss.*"

Wild Bill gave a curt nod of acknowledgment, exhaled a long breath that I assumed must have been relief then grimaced as he tried to move his legs.

"How badly are you injured?" Chou asked, kneeling next to the cowboy.

"Hard... to... tell," Wild Bill said, through clenched teeth. "Damn legs are asleep or broken or both." He tried to get up, but his legs wouldn't respond.

"Just take a minute," I said, laying a hand against the cowboy's shoulder.

"Argh," Wild Bill continued. "Feels like I'm being stabbed by a million damn knives."

Chou knelt beside him and slowly moved her hands down his left leg, then his right. "I don't think your legs are broken."

"We came from the garrison. Can you tell us what happened?" I said.

Wild Bill winced. "Four men showed up around noon today. Came out of nowhere, hollering and pointing rifles at us. They was all dressed the same, some kind of uniform. They rounded everyone up before we could do a damn thing to stop them. They lined us up like they were going to shoot us right there. Instead, they walked up and down the line checking everyone real close. Like they was looking for someone. They kept asking questions, but no one could understand them." Wild Bill grimaced and spat. "Damn it all to hell that hurts," he said, wracked by another spasm of pain. But I noticed his legs were moving, which I took for a good sign. "Anyways," Wild Bill continued, "Edward said they was speaking German, what with his experience fighting them in that war he was in. Said he didn't recognize their uniforms, and their guns were like nothing he'd seen before."

"German?" I said.

"Can you describe vat they ver varing?" Freuchen said, his voice suddenly suspicious.

"Like I said, they was all dressed identical, but they had these two lightning bolts on their tunics, right about here." He reached up and fingered the lapel of his shirt.

Freuchen started to say, "They sound like—"

I finished his sentence for him, "Nazis."

"That's what Evelyn called them. Nazis. Said they were murdering cowards. That they'd been responsible for some worldwide war that killed, and I ain't sure I believe this, millions of people."

"She wasn't lying," I said.

"How the hell did they find the garrison?" Freuchen pondered.

"Benito led them here. They had him all trussed up like a pig ready for slaughter. Looked like they'd beaten him black and blue; poor son of a bitch could barely walk."

"Then they must have also captured Caleb and Tabitha, ven they left to explore the other side of the island," Freuchen said.

Wild Bill nodded in agreement. "Anyways, like I said, seemed to me they was looking for someone. Well, whoever it was, they didn't find them. That's when they made it clear they was going to march us right out of the garrison to wherever the hell they came from. Edward grabbed me, said I should make a run for it, take Brute and find you three and tell you what happened. Said you were our only hope. I wasn't right happy about leaving them all, but it seemed like the best thing, under the circumstances."

Wild Bill flexed his left leg slowly, moving it back and forth a few times. He did the same with his right leg, then continued. "Edward made a play for one of the guards, and in the ensuing commotion, I slipped past them, grabbed Brute and rode hell-for-leather toward the woods. One of them Nazis spotted us and started firing that gun of his—ain't seen nothing like it; must have fired fifty rounds faster than I could spit. I'll never forget him, an ugly bastard, had a scar down his face." With his index finger, Wild Bill made a slicing motion from his right temple across his nose to the left side of his lip. "Anyways, he hit old Brute here, but we kept on going till he couldn't go no more. And we been here ever since. I reckon them Nazis must have thought they missed, and we'd got away, so they didn't bother to track us."

"What about Albert?" I said.

"He was alright, last I saw him. Holding on to Evelyn like she was his mamma."

I breathed a sigh of relief. "And Edward? Did they hurt him?" I braced for the worst, expecting nothing but bad news.

"They beat him good, but he was alive."

I squeezed Wild Bill's shoulder. "Thank you."

"I reckon I can probably walk, if you'll help me up," Wild Bill said to Freuchen.

Freuchen offered both his hands and pulled the cowboy to his feet, then wrapped an arm around Wild Bill's waist while the two men took a few tentative steps.

"Would you fetch me my saddle?" Wild Bill asked Chou.

Chou uncinched the saddle, lifted it free of Brute's body, and brought it to Wild Bill.

"I think I'm good now," Wild Bill said, stepping away from Freuchen. "Legs feel like I spent a week in a Deadwood cathouse, but I'm pretty sure I'll survive." He took his saddle-bags and rifle from the saddle, slung them over his shoulder, then walked to his horse. "I hate to leave you here like this, old friend, but I swear I'll make that bastard pay for what he done." He turned back to us and said, "I reckon they got a good two-hour start. Best we be on our way if we're going to find our friends. And while we're at it, why don't you fill me in on who this here tinman is."

We picked up the trail again, following it into the forest while we recounted to Wild Bill the story behind how we had found Silas. Perhaps it was the time Wild Bill was from, or maybe it was a symptom of this new, incredible reality we found ourselves living in, whichever, Wild Bill accepted our explanation with a simple nod and a note that he was "Glad the tinman is on our side."

But it quickly became obvious that while Wild Bill's injuries were, thankfully, minimal, we weren't going to be able to keep up the pace we had before finding him.

"If ve're going to have a chance to catch up vith our people before nightfall, ve have to move faster," Freuchen said.

"Leave me," Wild Bill insisted. "I'll make my own way."

"No," said Chou. "We will need all of the help we can get if these Nazis are as well armed as you say they are." She pointed at the two pistols Wild Bill had on his hip, and the rifle slung over his shoulder. "Without your weapons, we will have little chance of engaging them successfully."

"So, what do we do?" I said.

"I will go on ahead and attempt to locate them," Chou said. "Once I have found our friends, I will return. Then we can plan how best to rescue them."

"I'll come too," I said.

Chou shook her head. "I will be faster alone."

I couldn't argue with that. I'd seen how fast she could move. "Well, just be careful."

Chou smiled. "If I have not returned by nightfall, make camp. I will find you. If I have not returned by morning, you should consider me captured or dead." She turned, sprinted away, flitting between the trees like a Valkyrie searching for the souls of the righteous dead.

"When he showed up, I thought Silas was a man in a suit, like them knights of yore I heard about, all dressed from head to foot in armor. Now you're telling me the tinman's a machine?" said Wild Bill "How's that even possible?"

I did my best to explain. "I don't really know how he works exactly, even in my time we didn't have anything like Silas, but we had computers... machines that could imitate people so well, you thought you were talking to a real person. You should think of Silas as an artificial person. A very, very smart person."

"Thank you for the compliment, Meredith."

Wild Bill just shook his head. "All I know for sure is that if the tinman here hadn't found me, I'd be as dead as Brute right now. So, artificial person or not, I owe you a debt."

As we walked, I told Wild Bill everything we had learned from Silas about the Architect, including his message to me and how the robot had been unable to recall it once he had lost power.

"When you found me," Wild Bill said to Silas, "you called me a candidate? Candidate for what?"

"I'm sorry," said Silas, *"but that part of my memory is corrupted."*

"Well, that ain't much use," Wild Bill said.

"We think the Architect and the voice that asked us if we wanted to be saved are probably one and the same," I said.

"Makes sense, I guess," said Wild Bill. "About as much sense as any of this can, at least. But if this Architect fellow brought all of us here for a reason, why would he bring these Nazis, too? Or the two men who killed your friend Phillip? I mean, you folks all seem like reasonable and good-natured people. Why drop you in amongst men of such low moral turpitude?"

"Chou thinks something else, some exterior force, brought them here," I said.

"The same force that caused us all to land in the vater rather than on land," Freuchen chimed in. "The same force responsible for the destruction of the building ve saw at the other end of the island."

I nodded in agreement. "It seems obvious from what we have all experienced and from the few gaps Silas has been able to fill for us that there was a grand plan of some sorts... and that this isn't it."

"Someone or something has thrown the proverbial spanner in the vurks," said Freuchen.

"Yeah, exactly," I said. "We think this *other* —which we call the Adversary—has caused the Architect's plan to go off course. But even if that is true, it doesn't help us. It just means there's an even deeper mystery to why we're here."

We fell into an almost hour-long silence.

That silence was broken when Silas suddenly announced, "*Someone is approaching.*"

Before we could even think about hiding, Chou appeared from the trees ahead of us, and I breathed a quiet sigh of relief. She jogged to us, wiping away a light sheen of perspiration from her forehead with her sleeve. Wild Bill handed her his canteen of water, which she accepted gratefully.

"I have located the Nazis," Chou said, after drinking deeply from the canteen. "They have a camp approximately three miles ahead of us in a natural clearing close to the base of the mountain."

"Our people?" Freuchen said.

"They appear safe. They are being kept with others."

"Others?" I said, surprised. "What others?"

"I counted approximately fifty more captives as well as our own people. They are being held in two separate groups. There are nine Nazis in total."

"Nine? Damn," Freuchen said.

"Yes, and they all appear to be heavily armed."

Late afternoon shadows had begun their slow crawl through the forest. I estimated we still had maybe two hours before evening caught up with us.

"Think we can make it before dusk?" I said.

"Yes, if Wild Bill is able to keep up."

"You try and stop me," Wild Bill said.

We picked up the pace, walking quickly and silently. I occasionally glanced over at Wild Bill; his face was set in a mask of determination, but his pain was obvious. Back in the normal world, the damage that had been done to his legs would have meant days or even weeks of bedrest and recuperation, maybe even hospital. But here, whatever injuries he sustained would vanish when tonight's aurora arrived. Still, his pain was obvious, and I marveled at his determination and drive. But when Chou finally held up a hand for us all to stop, I saw the relief on the cowboy's face. He sank to the ground, soaked in sweat, gasping in pain.

"Are you okay?" I asked him, but he waved me off.

"I'll be just fine once I've caught my breath."

We had stopped near to where the edge of the forest gave way to the mountain; close enough that I could see the gray scree of the mountain rising up to my right through the trees.

"Their encampment is just beyond where the tree line ends," Chou whispered, her hand following the curve of the forest's edge ahead and to the right of us. She turned and pointed up the side of the mountain. "Up there is an outcropping of rock that will give us a view of the camp, but first, I need to explain my plan."

We gathered around her. Chou turned to face Silas. "Silas, we will need your help if we are to free our friends and the captives held with them. So, it is imperative that we carry out this plan before your backup batteries die. Are you willing to help us?"

Silas' eye-bar tilted upward. "*Of course, but you should know that I am ethically unable to participate in any violence. Nor am I able to directly or by omission of action allow harm or do harm to any human; candidate or otherwise.*" I thought I detected a note of suspicion in the robot's tone of voice.

Chou nodded. "I understand, but our friends and the prisoners being held captive by the Nazis are all candidates who could be murdered at any moment. And the Nazis are, as far as we can ascertain, not actual candidates selected by the Architect."

"*Yes, that is correct,*" said Silas, "*but as I have stated, I am not permitted to hurt or cause to be hurt any human being. That, I am afraid, includes Nazis.*"

"But your ethical programming does not preclude you from entering the camp on our behalf to negotiate the handover of the hostages, does it?" Chou said, a grim smile crossing her face.

"*That is an excellent idea, Weston,*" said Silas. "*It would be my pleasure to negotiate a peaceful resolution to this situation and secure the release of the candidates.*"

Chou spent the next few minutes explaining to Silas how she wanted him to enter the camp. "I will leave the exact details of the negotiation to you, Silas. Now, if we can—"

Chou's words were abruptly cut short by the unmistakable boom of a single gunshot echoing through the forest.

"Someone's shooting at us!" I hissed.

"No," said Wild Bill, "that shot was close by, but not close enough that it was aimed at us."

Chou turned to the robot, "Silas stay here and alert us if you see anyone. Everyone else, come with me."

Chou raced away in the direction of the outcropping she said she had scouted earlier, with the rest of us scrambling behind her.

We scrambled up the side of the mountain, clutching at

boulders and vegetation, anything that would give us traction or a handhold.

"There," Chou said, leading us toward a slanted sheet of rock that at some point in the last thousand years had cleaved away from the rest of the mountain. Over time the rock had tilted further and further away from the mountain until it rested at an angle that created a **V**-shaped fissure wide enough for all of us to slip into. One after the other, we stepped in and pulled ourselves up until our heads were above the rough edge, our bodies hidden from view to anyone who might happen to glance in our direction.

Below our hiding spot, less than a quarter-mile away, the forest gave way to a large grassy clearing. Smoke rose from several campfires. Two large groups of men and women sat or lay on the ground in the clearing, separated from each other by a hundred feet. Each group was guarded by three tall men wearing the distinctive uniforms of World War II Germans. The soldiers carried machine guns or rifles cradled in their arms as they walked slowly, almost nonchalantly it seemed to me, back and forth around the groups.

"They've split the prisoners into two groups to ensure they can't all rush the guards at once," said Chou, "but look at the guards, they're too relaxed. These are soldiers who are used to being in charge of prisoners they know won't resist. They're not expecting a fight."

"Do you see our people?" Freuchen asked.

"There," I said, keeping my voice low so it wouldn't carry. "In the second group. Toward the rear, I think I see Edward. And that might be Oliver and Sarah with him, it's hard to be sure from here." My heart gave a little jump when I spotted Albert lying with his head in the lap of a woman who surely had to be Evelyn. "Yes, I think I see everyone... except for Benito."

The man Wild Bill said had led the Germans back to the garrison was nowhere to be seen.

"He could be in the other group," Wild Bill said.

From the edge of the forest, hidden from our view until they stepped into the clearing, came two more soldiers. One of them was tall and wore a crisp looking uniform with a peaked cap, his trousers tucked into knee-high black leather boots. He was obviously an officer. The second was another soldier, and he dragged the lifeless body of a man behind him.

"Oh my God!" I hissed. "They shot that man. They just shot him." I felt a surge of horror and revulsion rush through my body.

"That's the scar-faced son of a bitch who murdered Brute," said Wild Bill, pointing at the soldier dragging the dead man behind him. "I'd recognize him anywhere."

The scar-faced soldier dragged the man's body over to what I had taken to be just a pile of rocks near the first group of detainees and unceremoniously dropped the body next to it. I squinted to try and get a better look at who the dead man was and sucked in a deep breath as I suddenly realized that what I had thought was a pile of rocks was something else entirely.

"Those are more bodies. They've been executing prisoners," I whispered.

There were at least five dead bodies in the pile, limbs twisted and stiff; men *and* women. While our horror at the realization that these bastards were murdering prisoners in cold blood sunk in, the Nazi officer strutted along the edge of the group holding our people. As he walked, he slapped a pair of black leather gloves against the palm of his left hand. He stopped abruptly and pointed at one of the prisoners cowering on the ground before him. The scar-faced soldier waded into the group and grabbed the woman the officer had pointed at and pulled her roughly to her feet. I saw Edward struggle to get to his feet, but one of the other guards stepped up behind him and cracked him on the shoulder with the butt of his rifle. Edward collapsed to the ground again and stayed there.

The scar-faced soldier pulled the struggling woman out of the group to where the officer waited, presenting her to his superior as if she were up for auction.

"Dear God!" Freuchen hissed. "Is that...?"

"We have to move, now," Chou snapped and instantly began scrambling down from our hideout, closely followed by the men.

I remained where I was for just long enough to see Evelyn's struggling form as she was dragged kicking and screaming into the trees.

EIGHTEEN

THROWING any reserves of caution to the wind, I sprinted down the side of the mountain after Chou. She had already reached Silas. Panting for breath, I ran to her side in time to hear Chou tell the robot, "You have to go now, Silas. Quickly."

"*Of course*," Silas said. He turned, and with quick loping steps, covered the hundred or so feet to the edge of the forest. We ran after him. Chou angled to the left, darting between the trees. She stopped several trees back from the edge of the clearing in a position that placed us between the two groups of prisoners.

Chou turned to Wild Bill, "I need you to provide covering fire for me," she said.

Wild Bill nodded, grabbed his rifle and levered a round into the chamber, then bent low at the waist, ran to a line of trees capping a nearby hillock.

"Cover for what?" I hissed.

Chou ignored my question. "Stay here," she ordered. She turned to Freuchen, said, "Come with me," then the two took off through the woods, winding through the trees in the direction our people were being held. Suddenly alone and completely out of the loop of what was happening, I turned back to face the clearing just in time to see Silas step out of the forest and into full view of the Nazis.

The response to his sudden appearance was, initially at least, shocked silence.

Silas walked closer, raised a hand in greeting and I recited the first few words of his now familiar salutation, "*Welcome children of Earth—*" The rest were drowned out by panicked yells, screams of fear and surprise, and gasps of amazement from the Nazis and prisoners alike. The three stormtroopers guarding the group nearest to Silas dove for cover, the three others guarding the second group reacted similarly a second later.

And then everything went to hell.

Five of the prisoners from the group closest to Silas jumped to their feet and dashed for the woods.

One of the stormtroopers, a grizzled-looking soldier with a week's worth of blonde stubble on his jaw, pointed his weapon at the back of one of them and pulled the trigger. Bullets tore through the man, sending gouts of blood into the air. He crumpled to the leaf-strewn ground as though his soul had been ripped from him.

Silas froze as the violence unfolded around him.

The Nazi continued firing, cutting down another two people in as many seconds. Several of the prisoners who still sat obediently on the ground flopped over sideways or screamed in pain as stray bullets from the soldier's automatic weapon slammed into them.

His synthetic voice ragged with horror, Silas yelled, "*No! What are you doing? Please, stop... stop...*"

I stifled a gasp of horror as a woman dressed in a peasant's woven blouse and skirt staggered backward, three red spots suddenly appearing on her chest, raked by a burst of gunfire. She collapsed motionless to the ground. Another man spun and dropped, blood streaming from a leg wound. He began to pull himself hand-over-hand toward the nearest tree for cover.

Quickly, I scanned the rest of the camp. The Nazi officer and the soldier with the scar were crouched behind a tree, less than fifty feet from where I hid. Kneeling next to the officer, his pistol pressed against her temple, was Evelyn, her pale face speckled with dirt and streaks of blood. I felt a surge of anger well up inside me when I saw the skin around Evelyn's left eye swollen shut, hidden beneath folds of bruised skin. The bastards had beaten her!

All three were oblivious to me, their attention focused on the violence unfolding in the clearing, their mouths simultaneously falling open in disbelief when they saw Silas.

Thankfully, the other stormtroopers seemed too shocked to decide who to shoot: the fleeing prisoners, those who still cowered on the ground, or the huge mechanical man who had suddenly walked into their camp.

Silas did something I never expected; he rushed the Nazi shooting the prisoners. The soldier's face paled as he saw the huge golden robot bearing down on him. He swung his machine-gun in Silas' direction... and fired a sustained burst at the robot until his magazine was empty.

Small dents appeared on Silas' chest, and I heard the ping of bullets ricocheting away. Silas reached the man and slowed to an almost instant stop.

"*No*," the robot said, his voice pleading. "*You must stop this carnage.*"

The stormtrooper stumbled backward ten feet, fumbling another magazine into his weapon. He raised his gun and fired another burst of automatic fire into Silas, adding more dents. Then the air was suddenly filled with thunder as more Nazis opened fire on the robot.

"*No!*" Silas bellowed. "*This is not a part of the plan.*"

He bounded across the space separating him from the Nazi, reached down and yanked the machine gun away from the soldier's hands and tossed it away. The weapon skidded to a stop about ten feet from me.

"*This is not a part of the plan*," Silas repeated, enunciating every word as if speaking to a child.

The stormtrooper stood as stiff as a petrified tree. Silas loomed menacingly over him. And even though he had no face to express it, I swear I could feel the disappointment and anger raging through the mechanical man's circuits.

"*You were all chosen for a reason*," Silas yelled, standing erect, looking at the clumps of humans scattered in disarray around the clearing. "*You are the only hope humanity has to—*"

The rest of the stormtroopers opened up on Silas again.

Bullets zinged through the air as they bounced off the robot's body. I ducked down as one thudded into the trunk of the tree I had hidden behind, sending shards of bark into my arm.

When I looked up again, I spotted Chou. She'd circled to the rear of the clearing until she was behind the guards. Now she raced out of the forest toward the furthest stormtrooper guarding Edward and the rest of our people, all of whom had thrown themselves to the ground when the shooting started, their faces pressed into the grass.

With five paces left between her and the guard, Chou leaped into the air, her right hand held above her head, and I saw the glint of the dagger she'd taken from the swordsman she'd killed. She brought the knife down with the force of all her weight behind it, driving the ten inches of blade into the Nazis' neck up to the hilt. The man crumpled instantly to the ground, trailing an arc of blood as he dropped.

Chou grabbed the dead man's machine gun and tossed it to Freuchen who was running from the trees toward her. He caught it deftly and ran to the group of captives. He knelt, but didn't fire, so as not to draw the other guard's attention, I presumed.

While Freuchen watched over our people, Chou was already rushing toward the next stormtrooper who she quickly dispatched with similar economy as the first. She was bearing down on her third target when I heard four fast single shots ring out one after the other. Two more Nazis dropped, shot by Wild Bill, one of them was the stormtrooper Silas had just disarmed. The man spun away as if he had been punched in the face, splattering blood across Silas as he fell lifeless to the ground.

Movement in my peripheral vision pulled my attention back to the officer and Scarface; they were on the move... in my direction. Scarface grabbed Evelyn by her forearm and dragged her toward the tree I was hidden behind, running in quick bursts from tree to tree, cover to cover.

A short distance from where I lay, the ground formed a natural concavity, and the two men pushed Evelyn toward it. They dragged Evelyn down into it with them and lay still, completely invisible to anyone who hadn't seen them on the move.

"*Stop*!" Silas pleaded, his eye-bar shifting quickly left and right across the unfolding carnage.

I think I was probably the only one who heard him because the world was chaos now; tendrils of smoke from the automatic weapons drifting through the air like lost spirits, people screaming in fear and panic, the smell of cordite mixing with the stench of terror. The wounded cried out in pain, and the dead added their own coppery smells. Machine gun fire crackled through the air and in between came the random snap of Wild Bill's rifle, as he targeted the remaining Nazis.

Chou's next target must have sensed her approach because just before she leaped at him, the stormtrooper turned and dove away, bringing his machine gun up. He fired a short burst at her, but Chou dodged at the last moment, rolling to her right. There was no cover for her to hide behind, so the second she hit the ground, she was up again with that amazing almost inhuman agility she possessed, just as another short burst of gunfire smacked into the ground she had momentarily occupied. The soldier's magazine now empty, he ripped it out and dropped it to the ground and fumbled for a fresh magazine from his belt.

Chou, seeing her chance, lunged at him, her knife curving upward. But the stormtrooper was fast too; he dropped his weapon and pulled a wicked looking dagger from his jackboot, slashing the air in front of Chou, missing her by what must have been a hair's breadth. Chou brought her right foot up and kicked the man in the solar plexus, sending him staggering backward, then she leaped inside his guard and dropped to avoid a meaty fist aimed at her jaw. As Chou hit the ground, she swept her left leg around in an arc across the dirt and knocked the stormtrooper's feet from under him. He slammed into the ground, his head smacking so hard I winced, and before he could have realized what was happening, Chou was on him. She brought the blade up fast and hard into the soft flesh of his chin.

I looked away, not willing to watch this man's ugly death. When I looked again, the soldier lay spread-eagled on his back, blood pooling around his shoulders, his head tilted in my direction, sightless eyes staring at me accusingly.

The Nazi officer watched Chou from the safety of his hiding place. My breath caught in my throat as Scarface began to raise his machine gun at Chou, but the officer pushed the barrel of the gun down. He shook his head. It was obvious to me he saw the writing was already on the wall for his men and was hoping to go unnoticed long enough that they could slip away into the woods unnoticed.

Silas was moving again, bounding across the field before

throwing himself between one of the remaining Nazis and a group of cowering people just in time to take a burst of automatic fire that would have cut them all down.

Chou started to run at the soldier while Silas stepped in closer to him, completely blocking the view of his intended victims with his metal bulk, focusing the soldier's attention completely on him.

"*Stop, please,*" Silas begged. "*You must stop this madness.*"

I wasn't sure if Silas was talking to the Nazi or the rapidly approaching Chou. Either way, it didn't slow Chou. She stepped up behind the stormtrooper, grabbed him under his chin with her left hand, pulled him backward until he was off balance, then drove the blade of her knife into his back with three quick, vicious jabs. I felt myself about to vomit, fought it back long enough for me to bury my face as close to the ground as I could to ensure Evelyn's captors would not hear me.

The fertile scent of the forest, wood, and brier, pungent wet moss and lichen, filled my nostrils. I allowed myself a few moments to simply ignore everything happening beyond this tiny little bubble of false safety I found myself in. My heart thudded against my ribs like a crazed rabbit caught in a trap. Even allowing for how I got to this world in the first place, I can honestly say I'd never been so frightened in my whole life. I took three deep, slow breaths, held the last one for a few long moments then exhaled.

That Chou was capable of such unerring, precise acts of brutality wasn't what made me throw up. It was the cold precision with which she set about carrying out her murderous task. That and the knowledge that at some point in the future of humanity, from my perspective at least, someone had gone to the trouble of hard-wiring how to eviscerate another human into her genetics so successfully that her body seemed at its most perfect when it was occupied with the act of taking a life. Even in the far-distant version of the future Chou came from, there was still a need for murder. And my friend was very, very good at it. That all of the destruction and bloodshed she was capable of seemed so incongruously out of place with the beautiful vessel that carried out these acts of death, made it all so much more obscene.

The sound of shooting had stopped, I realized, almost as abruptly as it had started, replaced now by the pained cries of the wounded and dying, and the pathetic whimpering of men and women who had survived the attack unscathed. I raised my head slowly and looked into the clearing.

Silas moved to each of the many bodies that lay strewn across the clearing. He stopped at a wounded man who had been among the first to be shot. The man was terrified, digging his hands into the dirt as he tried to push himself away from the robot. I couldn't hear what he said to the wounded man, but it didn't seem to do any good, the man continued to back away. Silas followed him.

Edward helped Albert to his feet as Freuchen rushed to them. Edward embraced Freuchen then began urging everyone else in his group to stand up. I saw Bull, Jorge, Oliver, Sarah, and Tabitha. They all seemed unharmed. Caleb, Evita, and Jacquetta were in the other group but were making their way over to join the rest of our friends. Caleb was being helped along by the two women, who supported him as he limped toward Edward. Caleb's left pant leg was stained with blood, and someone had wrapped what looked like a scarf around his thigh to slow the bleeding. Chou hugged Albert tightly, then began to encourage everyone to follow her in my direction... right toward where the two remaining Nazis hid, the officer's pistol still held to Evelyn's head.

From my vantage point, I saw the Nazi officer tap his subordinate's shoulder, then nod in the direction of Chou who was backing up toward them, urgently beckoning to any of the captives not from the garrison to follow her and our group to the cover of the trees, oblivious to the trap she was walking herself and them into.

If I yelled a warning, the Nazis would open fire immediately, and it was almost a guarantee that they would hit Chou and some of the other captives. They would, I was sure, also immediately shoot Evelyn. There was only one way to stop this.

Carefully, I crawled from my hiding place on my belly, pulling myself hand-over-hand toward the machine gun that had landed a few feet from me earlier; I could see its black outline still propped against the roots of the tree where it had fallen. I glanced in the direction of the two Nazis; their attention was entirely on Chou and the civilians, waiting for them to reach a spot where they would be nothing more than target practice for the experienced soldiers.

Slowly, ever so slowly, I reached out my arm and managed to touch the grip of the machine gun. Crawling forward another two inches, I was able to wrap my fingers around it and pull it to me. I had never fired a gun in my life, not even a pistol, so my entire knowledge of how to shoot came from cop shows and watching Bruce Willis in *Die Hard* on TV at Christmas. With the gun in both hands, I began to crawl commando-style through the leaves toward the two Nazis, hoping their attention remained focused on Chou and the approaching survivors long enough for me to get close.

Less than ten feet separated me from them when Evelyn saw me and gasped loudly.

Scarface turned in my direction, his eyes growing wide. I jumped to my feet, leveled the barrel of the machine-gun at the officer and screamed, "Don't move. I swear I'll shoot."

"My God!" the officer said in perfect English, spinning to

face me, shock registering on his face. "It's *you*! Where did *you* come from?"

For a moment I was confused, then realized that my talent had apparently kicked in now that I was close enough to them. The officer seemed frozen, taken aback even, a look of surprise and, was that *recognition* on his face? He turned to look at his superior.

"Grab her!" the officer screamed.

I pulled the trigger.

Nothing happened.

Scarface raised his weapon and pulled the trigger just as Evelyn landed a right hook that connected with his cheek. The machine gun barked, and I recoiled as a swarm of angry bees zipped past my head. Evelyn roared and lunged at Scarface, locking her arms around his upper torso, throwing him off balance and sending the both of them to the ground. The Nazi officer swore, drew his pistol, and pointed it at the two writhing bodies.

Now, I might not know how to shoot a gun, but I am resourceful. I held what felt like ten pounds of metal in my hands, scrambled the few remaining feet to the officer's side, and, with a banshee scream, swung the machine gun by its barrel like a baseball bat. The metal stock of the machine gun connected with the officer's temple, sending his cap spinning away. He dropped to the ground like a stone, unconscious or dead, I couldn't tell which. Neither did I care at that point, either.

I turned back to help Evelyn. Scarface had her pinned to the ground, her arms trapped beneath his knees. He'd grabbed the officer's fallen pistol and now had it aimed at me.

I realized I was about to die and closed my eyes.

I heard, "Hey, asshole, anyone ever tell you your face looks like a dime's worth of dog meat?" I opened my eyes in time to see Wild Bill step out from behind the tree he'd used to hide his approach.

The Nazi swept the pistol toward the cowboy, but he was too slow.

Four gunshots rang out in quick succession, and four corresponding holes appeared in the soldier's belly. The gun fell from his hand, and he collapsed backward off of Evelyn, his hands grasping at his stomach, his face a mask of agony.

Smoke rose from the barrels of both of Wild Bill's pistols as he walked up to the mortally wounded soldier. For a moment, Wild Bill stared down at the dying German. "Those four were for my horse, Brute," he said as he raised his right hand and pointed the pistol at the Nazi's head. "This one's for me, you son of a whore."

I managed to turn my head away a fraction of a second before Wild Bill pulled the trigger and shot the man between the eyes. But there was no escaping the sickening crunch of the bullet entering his skull or the coppery smell of blood that filled my nostrils.

I stumbled toward where Evelyn lay on the ground, semi-conscious. The swelling over her left eye looked even worse now, the skin around the socket so badly bruised and swollen it was sealed completely shut, her right eye was half-closed too. Scarface must have managed to get in a punch or two while I was dealing with the officer, because Evelyn's lip was shredded and bleeding, and she had an inch-and-a-half-long laceration on her cheek. Splotches of blood and mud had tangled her hair into clumps in several spots. She was whispering what could have been a prayer through her bloody lips.

Panting from the exertion and the gallon of adrenaline rushing through my veins, I bent down and picked up the machine gun and tossed it to Wild Bill, then took the officer's pistol and stuffed that into the waistband of my pants. I couldn't tell if the officer was still breathing, but there was a three-inch gash on his forehead where I whacked him with the machine gun, and it was bleeding quite badly.

"Meredith, are you hurt?" Chou asked, running to my side. Behind her stood Edward and a horrified Albert. Behind them were the shocked faces of the rest of the Garrisonites and twenty or more men, women, and children I did not recognize.

I nodded and gave Chou a weak smile. "I'm okay, but I think Evelyn could use some attention."

A sudden collective gasp of fear escaped from the stunned group as Silas strode across the clearing toward us.

"*Excuse me. Hello. Excuse me,*" he said, easing himself between people.

"It's okay," I said, "don't be afraid. This is Silas; he's on our side." I turned to Edward. "I'll explain it all later."

Silas stooped down next to the officer and began examining him.

My hands began to shake as the realization of what had just happened hit me—of just how close I had again come to dying. I flopped down hard onto the ground, and dug my fingers into the peaty soil, gulping in air.

"Did I... did I kill him?" I said, watching Silas examine the officer.

"*No, thankfully you did not, but this man has a serious concussion,*" the robot said after a few seconds examining the unconscious man. Silas' voice, if you can believe it, sounded as shaky as mine, as though he were barely able to hold back his own feelings.

It's funny really, isn't it? Human arrogance. We think that emotions, feelings—both positive and negative—are an explicitly human trait. I doubt most of us have ever even considered the possibility of a machine being capable of love, fear... hate. But here was Silas, the product of some unbelievably advanced intelligence, expressing more compassion for the man who lay unconscious before him than any human I had ever met. It was nakedly beautiful, however misplaced it might appear to be to me.

Silas moved to Evelyn's side. "*This candidate is severely dehydrated and has deep tissue damage, but her wounds are not life-threatening.*"

"Is it safe to move both of them?" Chou asked.

"Yes," Silas answered.

Edward handed Albert over to Tabitha, then walked to my side and placed a gentle hand against my back. "Are you alright?" he whispered, kneeling beside me.

"Yes, I think so."

Edward smiled and stood back up, surveying the carnage.

"What do you want to do with this fellow?" Wild Bill asked, kicking the officer's leg with the toe of his boot.

Edward turned his face to the sky and stared into the darkness as though he were expecting some sign. "It's getting late," he said. "We need to secure the camp and help the injured make it to the aurora. Let's find something to tie him up with. We'll decide what we're going to do with him later."

NINETEEN

WITH THE SMOKE of battle dissipating, Edward, Chou, Freuchen, and Wild Bill moved through the clearing like ghosts, checking the bodies of the dead soldiers, collecting their weapons as they went. Silas carried the half-unconscious Evelyn to the campfire where Albert was given the task of watching over her. Bull and Silas did what they could to stabilize the wounded.

I was the one who found Benito.

He lay with the twisted bodies of the five other men and women the Nazis had executed before we arrived.

"Oh, God!" I whispered, my hand thrust over my mouth. All had been shot once in the back of the head. There was less blood than I had expected, but if anyone ever tries to tell you the dead look peaceful, they are liars; every face was frozen in a rictus of pain, the horror of their final moments captured in their sightless, dead eyes.

It was... a nightmare.

I sensed someone walk up beside me and turned to see Wild Bill. He stood over Benito's corpse, sweat or tears running down his cheeks, I couldn't tell which, his face an expressionless mask.

"Are you okay, Bill?" I asked softly, afraid that if I spoke too loudly, I might force the stoic exterior of this cowboy to crack and he would come pouring out in a flood of grief and anger.

Wild Bill continued to silently stare at the body. "The one in the fancy uniform did this?" Wild Bill's words were even quieter than mine, his usual drawl gone.

"Yes, but Bill—"

Wild Bill pivoted on the heels of his boots, simultaneously drawing both pearl-handled pistols from the sash around his hips. He strode toward the unconscious body of the Nazi officer, his murderous intent written large across his face.

"Wild Bill, no!" I yelled and ran after him. "Bill, please. Stop."

Freuchen looked up, read Wild Bill's intention, shot to his feet and placed himself between Wild Bill and the Nazi.

"Now, Bill vill you please think about this," Freuchen said, a hand held up like he was a cop ordering a car to stop.

The cowboy ignored him too.

"Stop!" I yelled again, loud enough that it caught Edward's attention. He spotted Wild Bill trying to force himself past Freuchen and immediately understood that he was a man set on vengeance. Edward sprinted over and placed both hands on Wild Bill's shoulders, stopping him in his tracks.

"Bill, no. You're a better man than this," Edward hissed.

Wild Bill's rage bubbled to the surface, and for a second, I thought he was going to do harm to Edward.

"Did you see what that bastard did to Benito?" Wild Bill said, pointing at the officer with one of his pistols. "Did you see?"

"I see," Edward said, glancing back at Benito's body. "I see. But we're better than him, Bill. *You're* better than him. Put the guns away, please. Put them away. There's been enough murder for one day."

Wild Bill looked torn, then he glanced down at his hands and the two revolvers they held, and I saw his eyebrows rise with surprise; I don't think he even knew he had drawn them. Slowly, ever so slowly, he slipped the pistols back into his sash.

"That man might hold answers to why we're here," Edward said. "We have to find out why he wanted us all kept alive long enough to question us. He has to live. You understand me?"

"And when you've gotten everything from him that you need?" Bill said.

"Then we put him on trial and decide what we do with him after that."

Wild Bill's rage bubbled up again, momentarily reaching the cowboy's eyes, then it faded away, and I saw the man who had rescued me, Chou, and Albert that first morning return.

Wild Bill nodded as though he were agreeing with some unspoken question. "I'm going to bury Benito," he said, then he turned and walked away without another word.

"Make sure you tie it good and tight," I told Edward. He was in the process of securing the officer's hands and feet together with two leather belts we had taken from the dead soldiers. We had wanted to tie him to a tree, but Silas had insisted that he would not allow that.

"*The man is badly injured,*" Silas said, "*it is my duty to look after him.*"

"This *man* is a *monster*," I replied. "He shot those people in cold blood, would have killed everyone else, too, if we hadn't stopped him. Why would anyone do that?"

Freuchen stepped forward, "He's lucky ve don't just let the others have their vay vith him." When the Nazi officer's former prisoners had realized their captor was still very much alive, several of them had tried to reach him, even if he was effectively comatose. I think they would have torn him apart with their bare hands if Freuchen hadn't fired a warning shot over their heads, scaring them into silence and then placed his substantial bulk between them and the helpless Nazi.

"I understand your feelings toward him," Edward said, cinching the belt tighter around the officer's wrists. "When his men brought us here after they raided us, Evelyn told me about the atrocities men like him carried out in the next war. If they're true, well..." He shook his head in disbelief as his words trailed off. He pulled the belt tight around the officer's ankles and tied the loose end into a knot. "Peter, will you please watch over our... guest?"

Freuchen nodded, "It vill be my pleasure."

Bull and a couple of others had volunteered for the gruesome job of gathering the bodies of the soldiers and disposing of them, but not before they had been stripped of all usable clothing and equipment. Each had carried a dagger and either a machine gun or a rifle, along with ammunition. That considerable arsenal was now being guarded by Wild Bill, partly to ensure no one made a grab for them but also to give him something to do other than brood about the Nazi officer.

Each dead soldier also had a backpack, a first-aid bag with bandages, gauze, and ampules of morphine, along with a metal canteen of water, and various utensils and tools, all of which were a welcome addition to our supplies.

"We can't just leave them lying there," I said when I saw that Bull had dumped the almost naked bodies of the dead soldiers unceremoniously in a pile in the woods.

"I'm inclined to leave them for the carrion eaters," Bull replied. He was streaked with dirt and sweat and other people's blood. In Bull's defense, it had been a stressful couple of hours.

He and Silas had tried valiantly to save as many of the wounded as they could, and the pressure of working on so many patients, dealing with wounds unlike anything he'd dealt with before, had taken its toll on Bull. The human doctor and the robot had settled on a simple improvised triage system. Those with minor wounds were handed off to Evita and Tabitha to watch over. Those who'd suffered more serious injuries but would likely survive at least long enough for the aurora to restore them to full health were treated, dosed with morphine where needed, then told to wait quietly. Those poor unfortunates with mortal wounds were made comfortable and watched over until they expired. There had been too many of the latter and not enough of the former, so, tempers were, understandably, short and spirits low.

Edward shook his head slowly. "No," he said, the tone of his voice allowing no room for argument. "We bury them, like the decent human beings we are. We are not like them. Remember that."

Bull was not happy. "These men were murderers, nothing more. I say we burn the bodies and be done with it."

Edward shook his head again, "If we burn them there's always a chance we'll start a fire we can't extinguish that could spread across the island. The last thing we need right now is to set the woods aflame. And no matter what you or I might think of them, these men were soldiers and they deserve a decent burial."

Bull grudgingly agreed then walked away to carry out his task, grumbling and cursing to himself.

"What *is* his problem? He seems permanently disgruntled," I said as I watched Bull round up Jorge and Jacquetta to help him.

"He's a man who is used to being at the top of the intellectual food-chain, who now finds himself out of his depth and out of his time." Edward gave me a sad smile, "Which is one thing he and I have in common."

I looked at Edward for a moment. "Yes, but the difference between you and him is you've accepted this is where you are and where we'll all be for the foreseeable future. Bull seems like a man who is, pardon the pun, stuck permanently in the past."

Edward laughed gently; it was a pleasant sound. "He's a good man at heart, Meredith. I don't think he could be in his chosen profession and not want to do good, despite his protestations to the contrary. And I think that that's why he's here."

I thought about that for a moment. "I think that might be why all of us are here," I said.

Edward, Chou, Silas, and I volunteered for the ghastly job of burying the unfortunates the Nazis had murdered.

We found a spot of clear ground at the furthest end of the clearing, scraped away the layer of decaying leaves, and began to dig a mass grave using small foldable shovels we took from the Nazis' backpacks. The soil was soft after all the rain, but even with Silas' mechanical strength, it still took us well over an hour to dig a hole deep enough and wide enough for all fifteen bodies.

As we dug, Edward listened to us explain everything we'd learned since we found and freed Silas, commenting only to acknowledge that he understood what we were telling him. I think it's a measure of how much he trusted us that not once did he ever question the validity of what we were telling him as we relayed what we knew about the Architect and its plan, Silas, the message I had been given, and, of course, the fact that there was some unknown entity working against us we had named the

Adversary. When we were finished, he nodded grimly and said, "I'll make sure everyone else knows once we're done here."

"*I will inter the deceased,*" Silas said when the mass-grave was finally complete. The robot had remained silent throughout most of the excavation, and I got the distinct feeling that something was not right with him. He seemed... off-kilter.

It could just be that his energy was running low, but I decided to stay behind and talk with him, just to be sure. I told Edward and Chou I would join them in a few minutes then, when they were out of earshot, turned to Silas. "How's your energy holding up?" I asked as cheerfully as I could considering the job at hand.

"*I have sufficient power to carry out this final task, Meredith. The continued exposure to sunlight has helped me immensely.*"

I nodded, paused for a second but couldn't find the right words to describe the disquieting feeling I was getting from him. Maybe I was just projecting my own emotional turmoil onto Silas, but I didn't think so; I mean how do you quantify a feeling of empathy with a machine... a machine that has no face or human body-language to convey those feelings?

I nodded again and said, "Okay, well, thank you for doing this."

I started to follow the others back to the camp, when Silas said, "*May I ask another favor of you, Meredith?*"

"Of course. Shoot," I said, and felt my cheeks grow warm at my poor choice of words.

Silas did not seem to notice. He held a piece of slate about the same size as the one I had in my pocket, and I remembered that I had seen him fish two of them from the river earlier that day.

"*I have updated this new slate with the events of today. Please replace the first with this one.*" He held the slate out in front of him, so I could see it. Its gray surface contained substantially more code than the first.

"What does it say?" I asked quietly.

Silas remained silent for a few long seconds. When he spoke, it seemed to me he chose his words extra carefully.

"*My emotional and empathic systems were created from human genomic data, that much I know, but the emotional pain I have experienced during today's brutality was unexpected. My programming has an understanding of humanity's ability to inflict horrors on each other, but it was an understanding—until today. I have been overwhelmed by the cruelty I witnessed earlier... and by the deceit and manipulation. I would never have imagined it possible for candidates to behave in such a manner. It is imperative that I do not allow such carnage to occur again, at all costs. So I have recalibrated and attenuated all of my systems to take today's events into consideration, but once my battery is expended, those settings will reset, and I shall forget. I* must *make myself aware. But that requires that I trust you to carry out this task for me.*"

I stepped in closer, my instinct to place a reassuring hand on his shoulder, but he had no shoulders to speak of, and there was no way to tell whether he would understand the gesture.

"What happened here isn't indicative of humanity overall. Those men were from a time where that kind of barbarity was accepted. It doesn't reflect the majority of humanity." Even as I spoke the words, I knew I wasn't convinced that I believed them.

"*And yet, Chou, who is from a substantially more advanced and distant future than your own, seemed very effective at slaughtering those men.*" Silas edged closer to me, placed his hand on my arm and gently turned me around to face the camp. "*Look, there,*" he said, pointing to where Edward and Bull were enthusiastically examining the machine guns they had gathered from the dead soldiers. "*Do you see? Even now, they are excited by those weapons. No, I must remember this event. I must learn from it. I must protect you and the others from yourselves.*" He handed me the new slate. "*Will you do this for me, Meredith?*"

"Yes," I said.

"Thank you," said Silas. He reached out and touched me on the arm. I was sure I could hear relief in his synthetic voice.

I watched the robot walk back to help tend to the wounded, leaving me to wonder which of us was truly the more human.

We had relocated the uninjured and the walking-wounded to the opposite end of the clearing, away from the gruesome work of tending to the dead and dying. Jorge, Oliver, and Sarah had volunteered to watch over them, trying their best to keep the group of sixty-plus people calm, but the language barrier was making it difficult to keep it that way.

"They're behaving themselves for now," Oliver said, "but we shouldn't expect them to stay that way."

"You're right," said Edward. "Food has a wonderful way of helping people feel better. Seeing as the Nazis were kind enough to leave us their rations, why don't we see about getting them distributed to our new friends? Once they've got some grub in their bellies, I'm sure they'll feel better." The German soldiers had been well supplied, and that included several large boxes of military rations that contained canned meats, crackers, and even chocolate. There was more than enough to feed everyone for several days, longer if we rationed it. Edward called Sarah over and had her begin distributing the food to the frightened survivors.

"These people are all still so scared and confused," I said. "Edward, I think you really need to talk to them. Calm their nerves and make them understand that they're safe. Right now, they have no idea what's going on or whether they're any better off than they were under the Nazis. And I bet as soon as darkness falls, some of them are going to either make a break for it into the woods or do something stupid that's going to get them or some of our people hurt."

Edward considered my suggestion, then said, "You're right... again. Come on, better sooner rather than later, eh!"

The former captives were a geographically and temporally diverse group, with ethnicities ranging from, judging by their clothes, ancient Roman, through Dark Age Greek to twentieth-century African and European. They ranged in age from five or six to late-thirties and early forties. But despite their ethnic and chronological diversity, they all shared the same fearful look.

"Hello," said Edward, raising a hand in greeting as we approached the group. The look of shock on the faces staring back at us was unanimous and almost instantaneous. Before Edward could utter another word, a man in his mid-thirties wearing a green toga with a leather belt around his waist and a brown cape thrown over one shoulder jumped to his feet and ran to him. He grabbed hold of Edward's hands.

"You speak Latin?" the man said. "Thank the gods. I have not heard another of my people since I arrived in this place. Tell me, my wife, Maretta, and my son, Plennius, I lost sight of them after the eruption, have you seen them?"

A few faces turned in the man's direction.

"Latin?" a slimly built woman dressed in a peasant's skirt and tunic said. "Both he and you are quite obviously speaking Russian."

"No, no," a deeply tanned man, wearing a dirt-streaked gray suit and clutching a Trilby hat to his chest said "You are all speaking French. Why did you not say so earlier? I..."

"Ah, shit," I said, low enough no one would hear me. I

stepped in front of Edward. "Quiet down," I yelled, waving my hands above my heads. "All of you, be quiet." A couple of questions were thrown my way, which I ignored, and waited for everyone to shut up. "Good, that's better." I took a deep breath and continued. "Hello everyone. My name is Meredith Gale. As you all have probably figured out for yourselves by now, we are all in a *very, very* strange place. I'm sure you, like me and all of my friends, were brought here when you were facing certain death. I'm also sure you all heard the *Voice* and answered 'yes' when it asked you if you wanted to be saved."

I paused to let the information sink in.

There were gasps and more questions, which I continued to ignore. I waited for everyone to quiet down again.

"For a reason I don't understand, the *Voice* that brought us here also granted me a..." I searched for a word that would translate well for everyone, no matter what time they came from. "A *boon*. And that boon allows me to translate languages for anyone who is standing near me. Which is why you can all understand me, and we can understand each other."

More questions were hurled at me, and a couple of men jumped to their feet but sat back down again when Edward and Oliver stepped forward.

"Quiet... quiet," I yelled over their collective voices. "Right now, you all need to calm down and listen to what Edward here has to say to you. So, everyone, please sit back down and shut the hell up."

I turned and smiled at Edward. "They're all yours, boss."

Edward dipped his head in a show of playful deference, then said, "Let me start by saying that you are all safe and it is neither mine nor any of my people's intention to hurt you. The men who held you captive were evil beyond words, but we are not like them." He paused for a second, and I saw the rows of faces looking back at us relax just a little, enough that I could tell Edward's words were having an impact. "We have a camp less than a day's walk from here. There's fresh water, enough game and fish to easily feed all of us for years to come. Any of you who wish to join us are welcome. If you choose not to, then you will be free to leave and find your own way whenever you want. For tonight though, I ask that you stay here with us for your own safety and take advantage of our hospitality and protection. In the morning, if you choose to leave, we will give you what supplies we can spare, and you may go on your way. For those of you who wish to join us, you'll get a roof over your head and become a part of our community."

I saw a few smiles cross faces that had up until then been tight with fear.

"Now, eat your food. Settle in for the night and know that you are safe. Edward smiled back and leaned in close to me. "I should check on Evelyn," he said and walked off.

"Right," I said, eyeing the remaining supplies, "who else is hungry?"

I spotted Edward, Freuchen, and Bull standing in a small group, and also, to my surprise and delight, Evelyn who was sitting up and talking with the men.

"Well, you look better," I said rushing to her side, forcing a smile to my lips. It was a lie, she still looked like shit. The left side of her face was horribly bruised, which made it look like spoiled meat. She tried to smile through her shredded lips, but instead, winced, and spat a gobbet of blood onto the ground next to her, giving me a glimpse of several gaps in her upper teeth and at least two more broken teeth in her lower set.

"You're a terrible fibber," Evelyn slurred.

I bent over and took her hand in mine. "Not long now until the aurora. Then you'll be good as new," I reassured her.

Everyone else was suspiciously silent, and I thought I detected an air of discomfort.

"What?" I said.

The men refused to meet my eyes, which did nothing to relieve my growing sense of paranoia.

"You might want to sit down," said Edward.

"Ohhhkay, now you're starting to freak me out." I sat beside Evelyn, cross-legged.

"Well, go ahead, tell her," Bull urged Evelyn.

Evelyn took a swig from a canteen of water, winced in pain, then began to talk. "Just before you showed up, that Nazi son-of-a-bitch dragged me into the forest. The officer asked me all sorts of questions in German that I didn't understand. I didn't say a word, just stared at the bastard... which is when they did this to me." Her hand fluttered up to her ruined face. "They were about to shoot me like the rest, so I may have yelled something unpleasant about his relationship with his mother at him." Evelyn shrugged, gave a lop-sided smile that was more of a grimace and continued. "This smug smile comes over the head honcho's face, and he put his pistol away, then he leans in close to me and tells me in perfect English that he was very happy to make my acquaintance, like he was some kind of Lord or something. He said he was looking for someone. Someone very important. Then he started to describe a woman to me. A very specific woman that he had been told to find."

"Told to find by who?" I said, feeling my heart begin to sink.

Evelyn shook her head and grimaced in pain. "He didn't give a name, but he was *real* specific about describing the woman he was looking for, like he was describing a painting or something."

"Okay?" I said, hoping that this wasn't going where it looked like it was heading.

She glanced at Edward.

Edward gave an ever so perceptible nod.

Sucking in a big gulp of air Evelyn said, "It sounded like you, Meredith. *Exactly* like you, even down to the clothes you are wearing. The woman the Nazis were looking for is *you*!"

"Now let's not jump to conclusions just yet," Bull said. "Just because the description *sounds* like Meredith, doesn't mean that it is her he was looking for."

I nodded slowly, not really listening to him. My mind was elsewhere, running back over part of the message Silas had given me: *Agents of chaos will be unleashed in an attempt to stop what I require of you. You must leave this place immediately.*

"Bull's right," I lied. "Has to be a mistake. Why would a Nazi from sixty years before I was even born be interested in finding me?"

"It doesn't make sense at all," Edward added. "But then, nothing has really made any sense since we arrived here, has it?"

"Vell, there is only vun vay to be sure," said Freuchen, his beard bobbing with each nod of his head. "The officer is still unconscious, but ven the aurora comes, ve vill have a chance to ask him directly."

TWENTY

CHOU INSISTED we keep the new arrivals corralled together for the night and under armed guard. "Not just for their protection, but for ours too," she insisted to Edward. "We do not know these people or what their motivations may be. It would be safer for us all."

Edward was not particularly happy about the idea. "We're supposed to be open, welcoming. What kind of message are we sending if we force these people to stay here while someone with a gun stands watch over them? We are not the Nazis."

"And what kind of a message will you be able to deliver if one of them decides to slit your throat while you sleep?" Chou said, matter-of-factly.

In the end, the group of former prisoners made the decision for us. Exhausted both physically and emotionally from their time under the Nazis' jackboots, they huddled together in a group, their innate natural fear of the gathering darkness and the unknown things that lurked within it, winning over any distrust they felt toward us.

Still, Chou's concerns had pricked Edward's attention, and

he grudgingly assigned Wild Bill and Caleb to surreptitious guard duty over our guests.

I grabbed some food and joined Chou where she sat alone near one of the campfires, silently watching the group of newcomers. She glanced up when she heard me approach.

"What a day," I said, lowering myself down next to her, the warmth of the fire taking the chill off what was turning out to be a cooler than normal evening. "Fight a few Nazis. Rescue a bunch of innocent people from certain death. Just another day for the lost boys and girls here in Neverland."

Chou smiled back at me. "I am as bemused by it as you, Meredith."

We sat quietly, watching the flames dance as the logs crackled and spat.

"I have a kind of question for you," I said, eventually.

"A *kind* of question?"

"Well, I guess it's more like I need some advice from you."

"Very well."

I thought for a moment how best to pose my question, then said, "I have a dilemma. After the battle today, Silas confided in me how shocked he was by today's violence. And how hurt he was by what he called our betrayal of his trust."

Chou nodded. "Whoever designed him did an exemplary job integrating emotions. He does seem very empathetic. I am sorry I had to deceive him to achieve my plan."

"Yes, but it's all just programming, right? His emotions? I mean, he doesn't *really* feel sadness, happiness, anger. He can't *really* be hurt... like on an emotional level... right?"

Chou paused for what seemed like a minute but couldn't have been more than a few seconds. "In your era," she began, "artificial lifeforms are limited to simple automatons and computational devices that mimic human responses and emotions. But in my time, lifeforms such as Silas, albeit not as exquisitely designed or as advanced mechanically, are a part of our everyday lives. They are as ubiquitous as automobiles or pets of your time. The biological systems required for the level of emotional connection I have seen exhibited by Silas are above and beyond any of my time, but only by a few generations in my estimation. It would be very easy to look at Silas as merely a machine as he is so different to you and me. At least, externally. But in here and here," with her right hand she tapped her forehead, then her heart, "he is *exactly* like you. *Exactly* like me. So yes, I do believe that Silas is more than capable of feeling emotional pain and distress, perhaps more so than you or me even."

I gave a long slow sigh. "Well, that complicates things."

"How so?"

I recounted the rest of my conversation with the robot, just before he shut down, showed Chou the new slate he had entrusted to me. "My dilemma," I added, "is that if I give him this new slate, he will be permanently changed, and it will be our fault. I'm thinking it might be better if I just conveniently lose it."

Chou considered my idea then said, "Do you really think that a machine as intelligent as Silas would not have thought you might do that, possibly even hoped you would?"

"What? Why on Earth would he do that?"

"Perhaps because he is ethically unable to *not* allow that information to change him. He may have no choice but to assimilate the experience, despite wishing he did not have to."

"So, giving the slate to me, forcing *me* to make the decision for him could just be a way for him to circumnavigate his programming?"

Chou nodded. "Perhaps. He knows that you will do the right thing. It's an act of ethical mercy on your part. After all, he will never know that he was complicit in the deaths of those who were killed today… even if most of them were genocidal maniacs. It would be an act of mercy that he cannot ethically ask for. After all, his remit is to help all candidates, and if by learning about our propensity for violence helps him to understand us it would be merciful to deny him that knowledge; an act of mercy that he ethically cannot request."

"But if I don't give it to him, I'll betray his trust."

"Yes, you would. It is a dilemma, isn't it?"

"What would you do?" I asked.

"I would do what I thought was right," she said, predictably evasive.

"Lot of use you are," I grumbled.

Chou fired that enigmatic smile in my direction and said, "I am glad to have helped." I wasn't sure if she was being serious or not.

Eight of the twelve most seriously injured made it to the aurora. And as the first streaks of light crackled across the sky, igniting the pixie dust into a snowstorm of tiny glowing dots, Chou, Edward, Bull, Jacquetta, and I got a front-row seat to experience the nightly phenomenon's incredible healing power.

"Wow!" I whispered in sheer awe. I was watching a young black man, dressed in bloodstained jeans and a blue t-shirt as he lay on the ground, unconscious thanks to a liberal dosing of morphine we'd found in the dead Nazis' medical packs. He had taken a gunshot wound to his upper left arm that had splintered the bones and torn away a disturbingly large amount of the flesh and the muscle but miraculously missed any major arteries. It had been hit or miss as to whether he would live long enough for the aurora to work its magic, but he was strong and managed to hang on. I had seen the incredible benefits the aurora-powered nano-bots we called pixie dust were capable of—I'd been on the receiving end of it, after all—but those wounds had either been internal or comparatively minor, at least in comparison to this man's injuries. Now, beneath a shimmer of heat produced by the pixie dust as it worked away at the young man's wounds, I watched as bone and sinew and muscles then skin regenerated and knitted back together over the course of just a few minutes, leaving just mocha-colored hairless flesh. The same thing was playing out with the other seven patients; bones knitted, wounds healed, fevers subsided. Life bloomed. It was... miraculous.

"It relegates me to little more than a nurse whose sole job is to keep people alive until the aurora each night," Bull said, less a complaint and more a statement of fact.

"A hell of a problem to have, Doctor," said Edward. "But one I'm glad we have, considering the alternative."

As the aurora's light faded, one after the other, the injured sat and looked around. It reminded me of one of those old horror movies where the vampires or zombies come back to life at nightfall. But these weren't the undead, they were the *almost-dead*, saved by a technology so advanced I couldn't even begin to comprehend the intelligence behind it. How did that quote by Arthur C. Clarke go? "Any sufficiently advanced technology is indistinguishable from magic," I whispered the words reverently.

"Magic indeed," Bull said.

"I wonder, if we had possessed this technology in my time whether we would have continued to fight?" Edward opined. "Or whether we would have ever started those damnable wars in the first place. It seems to me that only infinite enlightenment could have created such a technology as this."

"It doesn't matter what time or where," I said, "humanity has a habit of turning everything good into a weapon. I'd bet this technology would not have stayed benign for very long once humanity got its dirty little hands on it."

"That's rather pessimistic," Edward said. He sounded honestly surprised at my dark tone.

I threw a sad smile in Edward's direction. "I've seen way too many people screwed over for a buck to have much faith in the chance of technology ever truly enlightening our species."

"But someone has faith in us as a species," Jacquetta added. "Otherwise, what are we all doing here?"

I couldn't really argue with her on that. I stepped toward the revivified and said as reassuringly as I could, "It's alright, you're safe. There's nothing to be afraid of. You were injured, but the aurora has healed you. You're among friends now."

We spent the next fifteen minutes calmly explaining who we were, what had happened to them, and that they were now safe and had nothing to fear from us. By the time I saw Freuchen striding out of the shadows toward us, the formerly injured were up on their feet and being handed food and water.

"The Nazi, he is avake," Freuchen growled, before adding with a chuckle, "And he is not very happy vith his predicament."

"It's okay," said Jacquetta, "I'll handle things here. You go deal with him."

"Perhaps it would be a good idea for you to stay back a little so he can't see you," Chou whispered as we drew closer to where the restrained Nazi officer was being watched over by Wild Bill. "If you are who he is looking for, it will allow us some time to interrogate him before he knows you are here."

"Okay," I said reluctantly. I wanted this particular mystery put to bed as quickly as possible. The idea that this man and his band of killers had murdered all those people in an effort to find out whether they knew me seemed preposterous. But the message Silas had relayed to me had predicted this might happen; there were people, bad people, who would be looking for me. And there had been that moment of apparent recognition when the officer had first seen me. It was terrifying, if I was honest, because there was no reason whatsoever I could think of why I should be of interest to them. I was just a student who'd taken a wrong turn and become a junkie. The *Voice* had offered me a second chance here on this alternate future Earth, and I'd taken it. But I hadn't asked for *this*. It had been forced on me. So, if we could learn more about the reason behind it from this man, then I was all for it. Still, as I watched my friends approach the restrained officer from the shadows, I felt a flutter of anxiety wing its way into my stomach.

"Are you comfortable?" Chou said stepping into the officer's field of view, her face soft, relaxed.

The officer shook his head.

"Would you like us to loosen your bindings?" Chou asked next. "Perhaps that would make you more comfortable."

The officer did not utter a word; he only nodded.

Chou crouched down in front of him, her hands hovering above the belt that secured his hands. "Perhaps you would do something for me, first? Tell me, what is your name?"

"My name is Obersturmbannführer Otto Weidinger, Commander of the 4th SS Panzer-Grenadier Regiment, and I demand you release me immediately."

A few years older than me, if I were to guess, Obersturmbannführer Otto Weidinger was an undeniably handsome man. His aristocratic features had looked a little bruised after I'd clobbered him with the machine gun earlier, but that had disappeared along with his concussion, thanks to the aurora, and now his classic German features were restored. There were still blood splatters on his cheek, and his military-cut black hair had mud or dirt clumped in it, but his pale skin, piercing green eyes and dashing good looks still couldn't make up for the whole homicidal Nazi vibe. In fact, the more I watched his arrogant, smug answers to the questions Chou asked him, the more he reminded me of one of the rich frat boys I'd had the misfortune to run into at parties during my time at Berkeley. He was a grade-A asshole.

"Why were you interrogating and executing your captives?" Chou asked nonchalantly.

"Your German is impeccable," the officer replied, avoiding the question.

Chou ignored him and said, "Please answer my question."

He repeated his first answer again, "My name is Obersturmbannführer Otto Weidinger, Commander of the 4th SS Panzer-Grenadier Regiment, and I demand you release me immediately."

Chou persisted, her voice losing some of its softness, "We have already established that, now answer my question: Why were you interrogating and executing your captives?"

"My name is Oberst—"

Chou's hand flashed out and slapped Weidinger so hard across his face his head turned directly toward where I hid in the shadows less than ten feet behind him. I stifled a gasp of surprise, thinking he might see me, but Weidinger's eyes were glazed, his face slack with shock. He blinked a few times, then turned slowly to face Chou.

"You will pay for that, you insolent whore!" Weidinger spat. "I will—"

I flinched when I heard the crack of the second slap connect with Weidinger's face. Blood began to drip onto his tunic's lapels from a newly sliced lip.

Chou's head tilted first to her left shoulder then, ever so

slowly, to her right as though she were trying to see the whole of this man who sat seething with anger and embarrassment before her. "I had taken you for a smarter man than this Obersturmbannführer Otto Weidinger. A man of your... *profession* should realize the situation he now finds himself in." She stood, allowed herself to look around as though she were taking in the surrounding forest for the first time. "You are, I am sure, aware of the restorative power of the aurora. I thought that someone like you would have realized its potential."

I had absolutely no clue what she was talking about, and neither did Weidinger, apparently, as he looked up at her, he said, "What are you babbling about, you fool?"

Chou knelt again, this time she was eye-to-eye with Weidinger. "I can keep you alive for days, months, *years* if I wish. And I can make every single hour of each day excruciating." She took his chin in her right hand. The man tried to shake free, but she was too strong for him. "Perhaps tonight I will take an eye. Tomorrow, a couple of fingers, or perhaps a leg. Who knows? But what I do know, what we *both* know, is that every night your wounds will heal and then I will begin again. Over and over and over again. That *will* be your fate. Unless... you give me what I want. Do you understand me?"

"Threaten me as much as you like. I will answer none of your—"

Chou slapped him again.

I'd had enough of this. I stepped out of the shadows and made my way casually into the light of the fire. The Nazi glanced up at me as I passed by his shoulder and stopped next to Chou. He started to look away then his head snapped back to me.

"You! It is you, isn't it?" Weidinger hissed, a look of utter astonishment shattering his arrogant demeanor. He struggled against his bindings, but the leather belts Edward had used to secure his wrists and ankles did their jobs. He thrashed impotently for a number of seconds then stopped, then he raised his head, jutting his chin out imperiously. "You are younger than I expected but that red hair... it is unmistakable. It *is* you."

"My God!" Bull hissed. "Evelyn was right. It is Meredith he wants."

I felt almost everyone's eyes turn to me at the same time I felt my stomach plummet to the ground. "Who sent you?" I said, trying to keep my voice steady. Weidinger just stared back at me, an arrogant smile on his lips.

Chou's gaze became steel as she turned her attention back to Weidinger. "Answer her," she said. "Now!"

"I will say no more until you release me."

"I'll bet my last penny he's working for the Adversary," Bull said, stepping up to stand next to Chou.

I saw a moment of confusion flitter across the Nazi's face, then the same arrogant mask descended over his features.

"I'll wager that he doesn't even know who the Adversary is," said Edward.

"Or the Architect, either," Wild Bill growled.

Confusion spread across Weidinger's face.

"I believe, you are all correct," Chou said. "I think he knows less about what is happening than we do."

"I... I..." Weidinger stuttered.

"Tell us who sent you. What do they want with Meredith? Now!" Chou yelled.

Weidinger's facade was beginning to crack under the mounting pressure.

Freuchen stepped in closer to the prisoner, his huge bulk adding to the implied threat. "If you know vats good for you, you vill answer us, Nazi."

"Alright, alright, I will tell you," Weidinger said finally, his eyes wide with fear as Freuchen leaned in close, his huge hands balled into sledgehammer-sized fists.

"Very good, Otto. Here, have some water." Chou raised a canteen to Weidinger's lips, and he drank deeply from it, water spilling over his chin, washing the blood away from his split lip. The area around his right eye was beginning to bruise and swell from Chou's last slap. "Take your time," Chou cooed.

"My unit was stationed in Poland. While we were traveling, our transport was caught in the open by an American bomber and attacked. We should all have been blown to pieces but as the bomb exploded... everything... stopped. I was surrounded by frozen fire and pieces of my staff car and my men, all suspended in midair as if by some magic."

Weidinger had an almost dreamy look in his eyes, as though he were recalling something that came close to a mystical occurrence or perhaps a brush with the divine.

"It was then that I heard the voice of the Führer telling me he was willing to save me and my men, save us all so that we could serve him in a very special capacity..."

"Wait a second, just wait a second," I said, interrupting him. "You're telling me that you were contacted by Hitler? *Adolf Hitler*? *That's* who you heard talking to you?"

Weidinger thrust his chin out, indignantly. "Yes. I have met the Führer on several occasions. His voice is unmistakable."

I looked at Chou. She met my eyes, her brows raised inquisitively for a moment then she turned back to Weidinger and told him to continue.

"My Führer told me he had a special mission to assign us—that from all of his armies he had selected me and my men. He would save us from the attack in order to send us here to this island where we were to use any means necessary to track down and detain a very specific woman. That if I did not achieve my goal, this woman would bring about the downfall of our beloved

Reich. She would destroy *everything* he had planned, which was why she must be found and stopped. That I would find you on this island, but if you somehow eluded me, I must go to the mainland where I would meet with more of the Führer's agents, and together, we *would* find you. And if I completed this special task for him, I would be assured of a seat at his table and help him govern over the thousand-year-Reich. But first I must accept his offer."

"To which you said 'yes,'" said Chou.

"Of course, I accepted. I am not a fool. My loyalty will always be to the Führer and the Fatherland."

"That's very good, Otto," Chou said. "Now, tell me, how did you know what Meredith looked like?"

"It was very strange." Weidinger looked up at me and his forehead furrowed as he spoke. "When the Führer spoke of you, I suddenly had a very clear image of you appear in my mind, like an old memory I had suddenly recalled. It was as though I had met you at some point in my life and forgotten you until that moment."

"Describe this image," said Edward.

"In the image... in the *memory,* you are surrounded by hundreds of men and women, all smiling. You are standing on a dais, in front of a microphone, your arm is raised as if you have just won a great victory. You are older, perhaps in your late thirties, but it is definitely you, I know it."

"That doesn't make any sense?" I said. "I'm twenty-seven, how could the image you have be from the future?" As the words left my lips, I already knew the answer.

"Because the memory that was implanted in his brain is not of you, it is of a *version* of you. A version which did not follow the same path you took," Chou said, without taking her eyes off of Weidinger. "What else can you tell us about this memory of Meredith?"

"I don't—" Weidinger winced as Chou took him by the wrist and squeezed.

"Tell us anything that you can remember," Chou whispered.

"There was a sign behind her, on the wall," Weidinger said.

"What did the sign say?" Chou asked.

"I don't know what that—"

"Answer the question," Chou insisted. Her grip tightening on Weidinger's wrist.

"It said, 'America Together—Meredith Gale for President 2028'."

I felt the world spin, then Freuchen's steadying arm around my waist. When my vision cleared, Weidinger was staring at me, and I said, "Are you sure that's what it said?"

Weidinger scowled, "I am not a fool. I have told you everything I know. Now I demand that you let me go free."

I shook my head. "There's got to be some kind of a mistake. Why would that *version* of me be running for president? I mean, I was interested in politics, sure; but president?" As I spoke, I noticed movement near the epaulet of Weidinger's tunic on his left shoulder. There was something—

"Watch out!" I yelled, as I suddenly recognized the glowing green eyes of a mechanical beetle, identical to the one Chou had destroyed that first night. It scuttled from Weidinger's back onto his shoulder. Before any of us could make a move, the beetle leaped onto the collar of Weidinger's tunic; there was a glint of something metallic and a needle-like rod shot from between the beetle's jaws, puncturing the officer's throat. Weidinger flinched as though he'd been stung, and his eyes immediately rolled back into his head, and he began to convulse. Froth bubbled from between his lips and nose. His jaws snapped shut, his back arched against his restraints and a keening whistle escaped from between the Nazi's clenched teeth. A moment later, he slumped sideways to the ground and stopped moving, white foam tinged with red leaking from his mouth onto the ground.

Chou was the first to react, lunging toward the mechanical assassin. But this time, the beetle was too fast even for her. It leaped from Weidinger's shoulder onto the ground where it stopped for just a second and looked right at me before it raced into the darkness beyond the light of our campfire and vanished amongst the trees.

"My God!" Edward said, moving to Weidinger's side. He placed a hand against the German's neck. "Stone cold dead!" he announced after a few seconds. His eyes drifted to where the beetle had disappeared.

Bull stuttered, "Am I imagining it or did that... that *insect* seek him out and kill him specifically."

Chou looked in my direction and said, "This isn't the first time we've encountered one of those beetles. Our first night here, one of them came into our camp before the very first aurora. I killed it and discovered it was not an animal, but a construct, a mechanical beetle."

"Mechanical? How can that be?" Bull said, incredulously.

Chou answered him. "It is merely a device, finely crafted and integrated into a body designed to not draw attention. An agent, I suspect, of the Adversary."

"But why *kill* him?" Bull asked. He looked nervous.

"Maybe because he was about to reveal something more?" Edward said.

"You mean something more incredible than the idea that Adolf Hitler sent a bunch of Nazis to kidnap me? Or maybe the fact that in some alternate universe I'm running for president? Spoiler alert: it *can't* get any weirder than that!" I hissed, still unable to believe what I had heard.

"I do not believe the message he received was from Hitler," said Chou.

"You think it was the Adversary, pretending to be Hitler? That's why it had to ask him to accept the offer to come here," I said.

"Yes. There is no reason to believe that any version of Hitler, in any timeline, would have had access to the technology required to bring Weidinger and his men or anyone else for that matter here."

"Tell that to some of the conspiracy nuts from my time," I mumbled then added, "So the Adversary was just impersonating Hitler, to get Weidinger to do what it wanted?"

Chou nodded. "It would be a simple way to control someone like him, someone used to blindly and unerringly carrying out orders."

Bull scowled. "Perhaps you are correct, I do not know, although the idea of a woman running for president strikes me as an outrageous fabrication in and of itself. Regardless, the next question is: if that mechanical insect was truly an agent of the Adversary, as Ms. Chou has postulated, and it sent the late Mr. Weidinger to capture her, why did the beetle simply not attack one of us? Specifically, why did it not simply kill Meredith?"

For the second time that night, all eyes turned to look at me.

Chou gave us the answer. "Weidinger said that he and his men were here to *capture* Meredith. He was very specific that we should turn her over to him. If he had wanted her dead, I do not think he was the kind of man who would have balked at saying so. I believe that the Adversary has plans for Meredith that can only be accomplished if she is alive."

"Is that supposed to make me feel better?" I spluttered. Right about then, the weight of everything that'd happened over the last few days came crashing down onto me, and I felt as though it would crush me. "All I wanted to do was get my law degree. Maybe start a family sometime, have a great life. And if it hadn't been for the car accident, I'm pretty sure that's what I would have gotten, too, because I'm smart and tenacious, but the one thing I'm not, is the key to some existential *thing's* plans to conquer whatever world *this* is. I mean, *come on*! I'm just an *ordinary* woman." I was almost hysterical at this point, my voice rising to a shrill screech filled with panic and fear. My words choked off.

"Looking on the bright side: at least you know the Adversary does not vant to kill you. Vich is more than any of us can say," Freuchen said, grinning his gentle smile.

I exhaled a breath I had not realized I was holding, laughing sadly as I did so. "There is that, I suppose. I feel like I've just seen myself on *America's Most Wanted* and I have no idea why."

All I got back was questioning stares of bemusement.

"Don't worry about it," I said. "I... I just don't know what I'm supposed to do now? I mean, I'm being stalked by an unknown entity that has no problem sending history's worst killers after me and killing them if they fail. How am I supposed to deal with that?"

"Perhaps," Bull said with an uncharacteristically kind tone in his voice, "the best thing for all of us to do is get some rest."

Edward nodded his agreement.

"What about Weidinger's body?" Chou asked.

"We'll handle that," Edward said. "You take care of Meredith."

Exhausted by their encounter, our new arrivals slept soundly. By contrast, none of the Garrisonites seemed capable of sleep this night, the adrenaline and horror of the day hanging around in our blood like a triple-espresso. Those of us who weren't assigned to babysit the newcomers or on guard duty, sat around the campfires talking quietly amongst ourselves, or stared into the flames of the fire, each working through the events of the day in their own ways.

Evelyn, now fully recovered from her assault, at least physically, sat to my left, Albert's head resting in her lap. She gently stroked the sleeping boy's hair while Edward sat between Chou and me, reminiscing about his hometown of Hastings, a small village on the southern coast of England where he had grown up. It was fascinating to listen to this man, talking quietly so as not to wake the sleeping. His voice tinged with a profound melancholy, he spoke fondly of how he'd spent his youth wandering the town cemetery while composing his poems or sitting beside a tombstone reading Shakespeare or Tennyson. Of how he met Rebecca, the woman that, in his other life, he would have gone home to from the war and led a perfectly normal life with.

A shadow moved through the semi-darkness separating us from the sleeping forms of the new arrivals. The shadow transformed into a fire-giant as Freuchen passed from darkness into the umbra of the flames of our campfire. A second man, who I did not recognize, followed just behind him.

"Forgive me, Edvard, but I need to interrupt you."

"No need, my friend, I'm sure I've bored these ladies half-to-death already with my stories."

"Meredith, this is Captain Joel," Freuchen said, gesturing to the man standing next to him. I guessed the stranger was in his early forties. He was stocky with a slight paunch around his middle and a week or so's worth of salt-and-pepper beard on his chin. "I think he might be able to help you," Freuchen said.

"I'm sorry," I said, "I'm confused. Help me how, exactly?"

"Mr. Freuchen says you need to get off this island," the man said. "I can help you with that." He stuck out a meaty hand. "Captain Joel, at your service."

I took his hand, feeling the calloused skin of a working man against my own, and he shook it enthusiastically.

"Captain of what, exactly?" Chou said, suspiciously.

"Of the *Sea Wraith*," he replied, then sat himself down next to me.

"And she would be?" I pondered.

The captain smiled a broad, warm grin. "My fishing boat."

I felt my eyes widen and my heart skip a couple of beats. When I'd arrived just offshore of Avalon, I'd seen things also come through with other candidates, including bits and pieces of the bridge, but I'd not heard of or seen anything larger than Wild Bill's horse Brute. The idea that a boat could've come through opened up all kinds of possibilities; first-and-foremost, getting my ass to the mainland.

"You have a boat?" I said. "Here? On the island?"

Captain Joel nodded. "Yes... well... kind of."

Uh, oh. I felt my enthusiasm start to dwindle toward disappointment. "Kind of?"

The captain's face took on a pained expression as though he was thinking about the death of a loved one. "Well... most of the *Sea Wraith* came with me. Now, I've heard others talking about how they arrived here, so I'm assuming it's a given that you all got asked the same question as I did by that *Voice*?"

We all nodded.

"My boat was on her way to the bottom of the ocean just off of Montauk, swamped by a huge bastard of a storm, and I was going down with her when the voice asked me if I wanted to be saved. That's when we found ourselves... here. Two days after I arrived, I was still trying to figure out where *here* was exactly when those Nazis grabbed me."

"Did they find your boat?" I asked.

"No, luckily. I was in the forest when they found me."

"Now I'm confused," I said. "Is your boat—"

"The *Sea Wraith*," Captain Joel interjected.

"Is the *Sea Wraith* seaworthy or not?" I continued.

"I managed to make some headway in those first few days, but she's still a bit beat up. Nothing a half-day's worth of work with the help of anyone who can follow directions and is handy with a saw and a wood chisel won't make right. I've got the tools stowed onboard her. All I need are the extra hands," Captain Joel said, effusively.

I was beginning to get the impression that far from being the eponymous dour sea captain that books and movies tend to paint men of his profession Captain Joel was one of those people who was permanently chipper. I had warmed almost instantly to him. When he smiled, it was a full-on grin. And I suspected that when he laughed, it would never be anything as mundane as a chortle but only a belly-laugh.

"And if we help you repair the *Sea Wraith* you'll take me to the mainland?" I said.

Captain Joel (I never thought to ask if Joel was his first or last name) leaned back and smiled at me. "I'm a man who has spent the better part of his life at sea, Meredith. After more than a few days on land, I get fidgety. And after what you and your friends did for me and the rest of those people you rescued, the least I can do is give you a ride to wherever it is you need to get to."

I felt a swell of excitement bloom in my chest. I looked across to where Edward sat. "Can you spare a couple of our people?" I said, unable to keep the excitement out of my voice. Since learning that I was a target of the Adversary, I'd felt like I was the proverbial sitting duck. The idea of getting off this island (even though it was the only safe haven I knew) was enticing... and scary at the same time.

Edward nodded. "Of course, I'm sure Peter and Caleb would be happy to go with you. Will that be enough, captain?"

"That'll do nicely," he said.

"How far away is your boat?" Chou asked.

"She's beached about six miles north of here, I'd guess. We washed up in a cove. I'm pretty sure I can find my way back there."

"Sounds good to me," I said. "We can leave first thing tomorrow morning."

TWENTY-ONE

I'D THOUGHT I faced a difficult choice over which of the two slates I should present to Silas that morning, but as I stood in front of him, dawn's early light kissing the back of my neck, I found that my doubt was evaporating as quickly as the morning mist that clung to the ground.

I held both slates in my hands, their slick gray surfaces cold against my fingers. I tucked the one I had decided to keep under my right arm then lobbed the other slate high into the air and watched as it sailed off into forest, before hitting a distant trunk and shattering into pieces.

I turned my attention back to my friend. "Good morning, Silas," I said, raising my chosen slate to eye-bar level.

"*Welcome Children of Earth...*" His electronic eyes spent a few seconds scanning the slate then moved to look at me. "*Hello, Meredith. Thank you.*"

"You're more than welcome," I said. "Say, why don't you go and help Albert." Silas got to his feet and walked to where Albert was helping to distribute breakfast among our new guests, wishing each person he saw a good morning.

In the end, the decision had been an easy one. Blame my

indecision on the time I was from, if you want to, an era where machines were little more than tools designed and manufactured to enhance our lives, whose value was measured not in the amazingness of their uniqueness, but in what *they* could do for *me*. A self-centered view that, if I had applied it to any other cause that meant something in my life, I would have been ashamed for ever having thought that way. I had made the mistake of considering Silas as nothing more than a mere machine, something that had been created with no other use than to help me, us, humanity. But still, at his core, just a tool that was capable of holding a great conversation. Inhuman. Not like us. Not like me. Different. And if I was truthful, a little bit frightening. It's easy to make the right choice when the right choice has already been decided on by the majority but, as I was now finding out, it was harder to make the decision when you were the first one to have to make it. *That* kind of decision always comes down to your personal sense of morality, I think, your innate human compass' ability to guide you, to help you make the right decision over the wrong one.

Silas' constant striving to understand us just that little bit better, how we ticked, his expectations of what we, as a species could be had seemed so *expected*. After all, *we* were the humans and *him,* the machine. But I'd gotten it all so wrong. If anything, that walking tower of glittering metal was more human than *any* of us gathered together in the clearing. *He* was what *we* should all be determined to be more like, not the other way around.

And so, in the end, my choice had been easy. I'd thrown the new slate away because it was us who needed to try harder to be more like him, not the other way around. We were the ones who needed to change, not Silas, and I vowed to be more like him from this day onward.

I inhaled a deep, satisfying breath of the cleanest air I had ever breathed, allowed my eyes to drift first to the trees as they whispered in the breeze, then to the people laughing and chatting amongst themselves all around me. A smile creased my lips, and I stood for just a minute taking it all in before finally I set off to find Captain Joel.

The *Sea Wraith* was beached close to where the low tide lapped against the sandy shore, her prow angled toward the forest, listing far enough to her right that the afternoon sun reflected off the wood of her deck and pilothouse. A blue tarpaulin hung from her port rear quarter, fastened to two tall branches planted in the sand to form a basic shelter. A corner of the tarp had broken free from one of the branches and now flapped gently in the breeze blowing in off the ocean.

It had taken just over three hours for Chou, Freuchen, Caleb, Captain Joel, and me to hike to the small cove where he had beached her, while Edward and everyone else made their way back to the garrison.

"All we're missing is a couple of mojitos and bathing suits," I said, which brought a guffaw of agreement from Captain Joel and nothing but blank looks from everyone else.

I can't say I'm an aficionado of boats in general, but the *Sea Wraith* was the finest looking vessel I'd ever seen, even more so now that I understood that she would be the key to getting me off of Avalon and to the mainland.

"She's a 1969 Derecktor, sixty-eight-footer," Captain Joel said. "An absolute classic. Refitted and renovated her myself right after I bought her, and I've never had a day's trouble with her." He laid his hand against her aluminum hull and allowed it to drift over the boat's curves, like he was tracing the outline of a lover. "I missed you," I heard him whisper.

The *Sea Wraith* was sleek and obviously well-maintained.

She reminded me of something you'd expect 007 to pilot in one of those old sixties' *James Bond* movies. She really was beautiful, and I told Captain Joel so.

"Thank you," he said, his pride for her shining in his eyes. "Took me twenty years and two wives to pay for her, but she was worth every red cent."

"She doesn't look damaged to me?" Freuchen said as we drew closer.

"Starboard side," the captain said, leading us to the opposite side of the boat.

"Ah!" said Freuchen when he saw the two-feet high and three-feet wide section of hull missing from halfway up the side of the *Sea Wraith*'s hull.

"I was so confused when we dropped out of the damn sky, and the fog was so thick I didn't see those rocks," the captain pointed to a reef of ugly looking gray rocks jutting out from the far wall of the cove. "Ripped her up good. Now, if I was at port, repairing her would be simple, but out here..." He ran his fingers over the uneven edge of the gash in her side. "It's not fatal, I suppose, but it's big enough of a hole to stop me putting her back to sea. What I need are some planks that are large enough to fit over the hole. I figured if you can fell one of those oaks over there and turn out a few boards, I'll have the material I need to get her patched up and seaworthy," Captain Joel said. He turned to face Freuchen. "What say you, big man?"

Freuchen nodded. We dropped our packs and provisions under the tarpaulin, while Freuchen grabbed his ax and made straight for the forest with Caleb.

When they returned almost a full hour later, they carried a six-foot-long log between them. Both men were covered in wood chips and sweat. Freuchen took a long chug from his water bottle and poured some of it over his face. Then, while Caleb held the big log upright, Freuchen raised his ax and with more finesse than I would have thought possible, split the log down the middle, then split each piece again until the log lay in quarters at his feet. I watched with fascination as Freuchen took one of the quartered pieces and fashioned several wedges from it with his knife. He used the wedges to split apart the other quartered sections into rough but serviceable planks.

"I hope you have something in mind to fasten these beauties," Freuchen said when he was done, standing back and tapping the six planks with the tip of his boot, his caterpillar eyebrows raised questioningly.

Captain Joel gave an appreciative full-throated laugh and nodded. "It just so happens I do. Let me go get my tools."

Captain Joel retrieved a large toolbox from below deck and set it down next to the *Sea Wraith*. He fished out a metal hand-powered drill and attached a large drill bit. Then he set about carefully measuring and marking several spots above, below, and on each end of the hole in the *Sea Wraith*'s hull before marking corresponding spots on Freuchen's planks. He drilled two holes a half-inch apart at each point he had marked on the planks and the hull. Setting aside the drill, he picked up the largest plank and handed it to me and Chou.

"If you ladies would be so kind as to hold the plank right... there. Perfect," he said, after maneuvering the holes in the plank over the ones in the hull. He had Freuchen and Caleb hold the two other planks in position, while he checked the tear in the hull was completely covered by them. He lifted a spool of manila rope from the toolbox, measured then cut the same number of hand-to-elbow lengths that there were sets of holes, then began to thread the rope through each hole, so the loose ends hung on the inside of the hull, while we held the planks steady.

"Don't go anywhere," he told us with a grin, then hopped up onto the deck and vanished into the cabin. Soon after, we heard the sound of him removing whatever paneling lay between him and the interior of the hull.

"Hold those planks tight," I heard him yell, then he systematically drew each length of rope taut enough that it pulled the plank snugly against the hull before, I presumed, he must have tied the rope off. He reemerged from the pilothouse and dropped down beside us. He inspected his handiwork, nodded happily, and said, "You can let go now."

We stepped away. Nothing fell off, which I took as a good sign.

"One last touch," said Captain Joel. He picked up a can from the toolbox, pried open the lid with a flathead screwdriver, then used a brush to paint a thick black tar-like substance over the planks until all the seams were sealed. "We'll be all squared away in an hour or so once that sealant's dried," he said and stepped back to admire his handiwork. "The bilge pumps'll be able to handle any leaks. Now, all we have to do is wait for the tide to come in and then you can point me in the direction of the garrison."

I was on a pleasure ship cruising up the coast of California.

At least, that's the little fantasy I told myself as I sat in the cockpit of the *Sea Wraith*, just behind the pilothouse, watching the coastline of the island we had come to call Avalon drift by. We were serenaded by a minimalist soundtrack courtesy of the *splish splash* of waves breaking across the hull of the *Sea Wraith* and the rhythmic *chug-chug-chug* of her engine.

To a person, we all sat and just... *were*, silently taking advantage of this momentary respite, this little chunk of normalcy, floating within a sea of the weird and absolutely screwed up.

"We should probably wait at the pointy end, make sure we don't miss our stop," I said when I guessed we were getting close to the estuary of our river.

"It's called the prow," Captain Joel corrected from the pilothouse, but I saw a wry smile cross his face, and I smiled back.

Freuchen and I were the only ones who'd actually seen the estuary of the river leading up to our little enclave, which, I suppose wasn't going to stay so little for very much longer. The people we'd rescued were going to more than triple the numbers of the Garrisonites and, if the guesstimations we'd made of how many people we'd seen dropping into the ocean when we arrived were accurate, there were easily a hundred or more souls spread across Avalon. Of course, any one of them could be an agent of the Adversary, which made getting off the island even more imperative for me. At some point, Edward was going to have to find those time-lost refugees and try and bring them into his fold. He wanted so much to create something new here, something magnificent; a utopia where everyone was equal and valued. I did not envy him in his task, but I had never met anyone more capable of achieving that dream than him.

But that wasn't going to be my job or my problem. I wasn't going to be *here* for any longer than I had to be. And now that the probability of leaving Avalon was all too real, I felt a weird mixture of fear and anticipation. I was going to have to leave my new friends behind me and strike out on my own to try and find this mysterious Candidate 1. I was going to embark on an adventure the likes of which no one had ever experienced before; all on a version of earth that was so different to my own that it may just as well have been a completely different planet. Vast. Unknown. Alien.

"There!" Freuchen called out, pointing ahead of us. "The mouth of the river is dead ahead. I recognize that outcropping of rock."

Captain Joel took a second to look where Freuchen pointed then guided the *Sea Wraith* toward the estuary and drove the prow into the shale beach.

"It's not pretty, but it beats getting wet," he said, "All ashore."

We clambered over the *Sea Wraith*'s gunwale and dropped onto the rocky beach, and once Captain Joel had finished securing his boat we set off upriver toward the garrison.

"How are you holding up?" Edward asked. We'd been back for a couple of hours already but, other than a wave and a yelled 'welcome back' Edward's attention had been focused on helping the new arrivals settle in.

"Nervous," I said, surprised at my own candidness. "Really, really nervous."

Edward smiled. "Understandably so. But are you sure you really want to go ahead with this? You know that you're more than welcome to stay here. We could use you."

"Trust me, leaving Avalon is the furthest thing from what I want to do, but there's no doubt the Adversary knows my whereabouts now. It's only a matter of time before it sends another assassin, or I end up like that Nazi officer." I mimicked the bug crawling on my shoulder with my fingers.

Edward nodded.

"And the longer I stay, the more danger I put the garrison in. If the Adversary is as smart as we think it is, it'll send more than just a crew of Nazi murderers. We had the upper hand this time; next time we might not be so lucky. The sooner I'm out of your hair, the safer it'll be for everyone."

"As much as it pains me to agree, I know you're right. Do you know when you plan to depart?"

"Tomorrow, soon as the tide allows. Captain Joel thinks it should be sometime around dawn, so we're planning to set out then, but the tides are strange here, so we're '*playing it by ear.*' The Captain's words, not mine."

Silas approached us. "*I will be accompanying Meredith on her journey, too,*" he said. His eye-bar focused on me. "*If that is acceptable to you?*"

I smiled and nodded. I'd considered asking if Silas would like to join Chou and me but wasn't sure how Edward would take it. The robot would be such a great asset to the community and could have helped grow the garrison in record time. Now, of course, there would be plenty of extra hands and his help would be missed less.

"I think that's a good idea," Edward said, his words encouraging but his face couldn't disguise the look of disappointment at Silas leaving.

I saw Freuchen talking to one of the newcomers. He spotted me looking at him, excused himself and walked over to us.

"I vas vaiting for an opportunity to get you two alone," he said, looking first at Edward then me. "I think it vould be a good idea if I accompany Meredith on her journey."

Edward looked aghast but said nothing.

"Of course, I'd love to have you along," I said, "but I certainly don't want to drain the garrison of its best human resources. Are you sure?" I glanced at Edward and gave him my best 'sorry, I didn't expect this to happen' face.

"Yes," Freuchen said, "I have thought hard about it, and neither you nor Ms. Chou—"

"Silas is leaving, too," Edward interjected.

Freuchen glanced at the robot. Nodded in a 'that's good to hear' kind of a way and continued. "Neither, you or Ms. Chou—or Silas—are experienced explorers or outdoorsmen... vimen... you know vat I mean. I have spent all of my life traveling the vurled. I vould not be able to rest knowing that you ver out there vithout me. Besides, I vould very much like to see this new Earth that avaits us."

I could see Edward was vacillating between giving his approval and begging Freuchen to stay, but the truth was, I needed him more than Edward did.

"You still have Jacquetta," I said.

After a few seconds more mulling it over, Edward nodded his approval.

"Thank you," I said. I hugged him and stepped back.

"Wait here for a minute," Edward said, then walked over to where Wild Bill was storing the last of the equipment we had liberated from the Nazis beneath the remaining intact lean-tos. They chatted for a while, then the two men made their way back over to us. Both carried a large bundle of equipment in their outstretched arms. Edward dropped his at our feet. "These will probably be of help," he said. It was four of the backpacks we had taken from the dead Nazis. Wild Bill brought canteens, extra military provisions, a first aid kit, and a pair of binoculars that had belonged to the Nazi Officer. He laid them down next to the backpacks. Edward also had two of the German machine guns, one slung over each shoulder. Wild Bill had another. Edward unslung one of the weapons and offered it to me, "You should probably take these too," he said.

I shook my head. "No thank you. We're going to need people to trust us. If we walk into a community armed to the teeth, it's going to give the wrong impression. People might just decide to act against us first rather than listen to what we have to say. I'll stick with this." I tapped the sword that rested against my thigh. Honestly, the idea of having to use that machine gun terrified me. It was a risk to leave the firearms behind, no doubt, but a calculated one, given Chou's lethality, Silas' size, and Freuchen, who was almost as imposing as the robot.

Edward offered the weapon to Chou who similarly declined. "I have no need of it, thank you. As Meredith said, we do not want to appear to be a threat, and it will only serve to act as a magnet for those who want it. Better to not place temptation in the way of the weak minded who will covet it."

Freuchen said, "I'll take the Luger, if I may." He nodded at the pistol taken from the Nazi officer which Edward now wore around his waist. Freuchen turned and looked at me and Chou. "I vill keep it in my backpack, that vay it vill be hidden from prying eyes and sticky fingers."

I nodded, it could come in useful if we ever got into a pinch and as long as Freuchen kept it well hidden, it shouldn't prove a problem.

Edward unbuckled the pistol and handed it to Freuchen. "Pick up a box of ammunition from me before you leave," he said.

Freuchen said that he would.

"Evelyn is preparing supplies for you?" Edward asked.

"Yes," I said. "She's thrown together enough jerky and smoked fish to feed a small army. It's not exactly an In-N-Out Double-Double with a strawberry shake, but we won't be going hungry anytime soon. And when we need to, we'll hunt the rest of our food."

"Good," said Edward.

"People vill be able to smell us a mile off," Freuchen said through a grin.

Albert ran over to us from where he had been helping Evelyn.

"I'm packed," he said breathlessly, the light of expectation in his eyes shining brightly. He picked up one of the backpacks. "What do you want me to carry?"

As if sensing that I would not do well with what had to happen next, Chou stepped forward, knelt in front of the boy and said, "You will not be coming with us, Albert. The road ahead will be dangerous. It is better that you stay here with Edward, Wild Bill, and Evelyn, where it is safe."

"But... but you *promised* we'd stay together," Albert said, looking at me, his voice trembling with emotion, close to tears. "You promised we'd look after each other."

I knelt, so I was at eye-level with the boy. "I did, Albert, but we don't know what's beyond the island. It's going to be so dangerous. *Too* dangerous." I reached out a hand to wipe away the tears that had begun to run down his cheek, but he took a step back out of my reach. "You promised!" he said.

"I know, but we can't—"

Albert turned around and ran off in the direction of the river.

I took a step after him.

"Let him go," Wild Bill said. "You've got enough to keep you occupied. I'll go take care of him." The cowboy pinched the peak of his hat and set off after Albert.

I felt Edward's hand on my arm and turned back to him. "Don't worry, we'll take good care of him."

"I know," I said, but still felt pretty shitty for abandoning the kid. It was for his own good though, at least, that's what I told myself.

Edward cast his eyes over all of us. "Well, I suppose I had best leave you to finish your preparation," he said. "I have our new guests to help.".

"How many of them do you think are going to settle here?" Freuchen asked.

"They've all said they want to remain with us," Edward

replied. "It'll be a bit tight until we get some more accommodation built for them. Shouldn't be too much of a problem with all the extra hands though, so no need to worry." He smiled and walked away.

Chou picked up a backpack and began to sort through the equipment. Freuchen did the same. I watched the camp for a few seconds, the people buzzing here and there making themselves useful or standing around chatting. It was all so normal, if you ignored where we were. Just humans... being. Then I joined my two friends and began preparing for the journey ahead of us.

PART THREE

ONLY THE DEAD GO FREE

TWENTY-TWO

I ROSE A LITTLE AFTER DAWN. Chou was already up and going through her backpack one final time. Around us, the garrison was slowly coming back to life as people woke, shuffled to the latrines and then made their way to where breakfast was being readied.

"Has anyone seen Albert?" I asked, joining Chou, the dewy grass cold against my bare feet. Since the boy had found out he wasn't coming with us, Albert had fastidiously avoided me and Chou, going so far as to spend the night sleeping next to Evelyn.

Chou glanced up at me, looked around. "I saw him earlier."

I still felt terrible about leaving the kid behind, but there really wasn't any other option. I picked up my backpack and checked it again, fastened it back up and tested its weight, then set it back down beside Chou's.

Freuchen appeared like Bigfoot, striding across the encampment, a grin on his face that could have swallowed a 747, his backpack in hand. He dropped it next to ours.

"Vell, are ve all ready for our great adventure?" he said, then took a bite from a strip of jerky and proceeded to chew it vigorously, only adding to my internal image of the legendary mountain creature.

"I'll go wake up Silas," I said, unable to muster the kind of enthusiasm that was on display by the Danish man.

I walked over to where Silas sat, cross-legged like a metal Buddha next to our lean-to. Dew shone on his metal skin, glistening in the warming light of the rising sun. I took the slate from where he had left it, held it in front of his eye-bar and said, "Good morning, Silas." He went through the usual start-up routine, analyzed the code on the slate, and then listened patiently while I filled him in on the events that it didn't cover.

"*Good morning*," Silas said, nodding at everyone as we walked back to join Chou and Freuchen. Captain Joel was chatting with Chou. He raised a hand in greeting as we approached.

"Here, take this," Freuchen said, hefting the heaviest backpack containing most of our provisions and handing it to Silas. Silas swung the pack over his shoulders as if it was nothing, and we all followed suit with our own packs.

"I see you're all about set," Edward said, appearing from behind me. "Is there anything else that we can do for you before you leave?"

"I think we're good," I replied, cinching my backpack tighter.

"Come on then, I'll walk you out."

Evelyn, Wild Bill, Tabitha, and Caleb stopped what they were doing and came over to us and, after a flurry of well wishes, hugs, handshakes and a few tears, escorted us to the garrison's northern exit. I looked around for Albert, but he was nowhere to be seen.

"Don't worry, we'll take good care of him," Evelyn said, clasping both my hands in hers. "His tail feathers are just a little ruffled right now. He'll be fine, I promise."

I pulled her in close and hugged her tight, whispered "Thank you" before releasing her.

"Well," Edward said, "I'm not one for speeches, but I want to thank you on behalf of all of us for what you're doing. We wish you all the very best of luck, and know we'll see all of you back here again when your journey is successful." He paused, then said, "Oh, I almost forgot. Here, I wanted you to have this, Meredith." He handed me a folded piece of paper torn from his notepad. "Just something to remember us by."

I unfolded the paper. It was a handwritten copy of my favorite poem by him *The Maiden.*

"You know, an original copy of one of your poems would probably fetch enough from a collector of your work to buy me a house back when I'm from," I said. "It's beautiful. Thank you. I will treasure it forever." I leaned in and gave Edward a kiss on his cheek, lingered for a second and when I pulled back he was bright red.

"Go on now, all of you, before we change our minds and scuttle your boat," Edward said.

"See you soon," I managed to get past the lump in my throat. And with one final glance at the place I had come to think of as home, we turned and began to make our way to the *Sea Wraith.*

Captain Joel had estimated the rising tide almost perfectly, and we only had a half hour to wait until it was high enough for him to fire up the engines. With a puff of black smoke from the exhaust to mark our departure, he turned the boat in the direction of the distant mainland and headed out to sea while the rest of us sat on deck, watching our island home recede gradually into the distance.

"Do you have any idea where you want to go exactly?" Captain Joel called back to me from the pilothouse, when Avalon had receded to little more than a distant blob of green and brown behind us.

I rose and wobbled my way to him as the boat pitched and rolled on the ocean swell. "I haven't really given it much thought," I told him, truthfully. I stared out through the windshield of the pilothouse, past the prow and the mist of sea-spray as the boat cut through the waves, dipping and climbing. The smell of ozone was heavy in the air. "I say we aim for the monolith, as that's our ultimate destination."

Captain Joel nodded. "I'd guess it'll take us about three hours or so to reach the mainland. So, you might just as well sit back and enjoy the ride."

I thanked him and retook my place next to Silas, the rhythmic pulse of the *Sea Wraith*'s engine reverberating up through the deck like a heartbeat, and for the next forty-five minutes or so, we stared out at the open sea and the ever-nearing coast. We were still miles away, and all I could distinguish of this new land were great swaths of green and brown that suggested that the mainland was as heavily populated with trees as Avalon. But rising above everything like some unimaginable petrified creature was the monolith. Its faceted trumpet-shaped body glowing in the early morning sun. The closer we got, the more terrifying it became.

"It is an astonishing feat of engineering, isn't it?" I hadn't heard Chou's approach. She stood on my left, steadying herself with one hand on the bulwark, her face turned toward the monolith with a look of outright admiration on her face.

"I can't even begin to imagine how something like that would be built," I said.

"I would not even hazard a guess," Chou admitted quietly, in a rare moment of technical ignorance.

"It is just like a leisurely boat ride on a Sunday afternoon," Freuchen said, only half joking.

I playfully elbowed him in his ribs and laughed. "Sure is," I said, "if you ignore the robot, the woman from the far-flung future, and the mega-structures built by some long forgotten unknown hand."

"Vell, ven you put it like that."

We all laughed.

"It *is* a pleasant change," Chou said, a smile playing across her lips.

Freuchen stood up, placed a foot on the gunwale, and leaned against the roof of the pilothouse, his eyes fixed on the ever-nearing coastline. "Ve are like the Argonauts," he said, his tone suddenly reverent. "Sailing toward Colchis, in search of our own Golden Fleece."

Silas suddenly leaped to his feet. "*Captain, I sense something approaching on your starboard side.*"

We all turned to look in the direction Silas indicated in time to see a huge shape break the surface ten boat lengths off the *Sea Wraith*'s starboard side.

"It's a whale!" I yelled, as the unmistakable form of the whale rose majestically into the air, then fell sideways back below the surface, in that seemingly slow-motion way they have, sending an enormous wave of water rushing our way. The *Sea Wraith* bounced over the wave and continued on even as the whale dove again.

"Well, that's a sight for sore eyes," Captain Joel said, as ecstatic to see the cetacean as I was.

"A blue vale," Freuchen yelled. "I hunted them for food in the Antarctic."

"*It is a truly remarkable specimen,*" Silas said. "*I believe that they number in the tens of thous—*" He stopped abruptly and said, "*Something else is approaching from port.*"

"Maybe it's another whale?" I said, straining my eyes against the glare bouncing off the water.

"I don't see anything?" Captain Joel called back, his head and shoulders hanging out of the pilothouse window.

I saw the dorsal fin break the surface of the ocean fifty feet off the port side of the *Sea Wraith*. "There!" I yelled, pointing. Then, "Oh, shit!" I'd had encounters with sharks off the coast of California, seen them closeup at Seaworld too, but whatever *this* thing was, it dwarfed even the couple of Great Whites I'd seen. The dorsal fin was at least as tall as Silas, and he was eight feet, it cut through the water like a speedboat, leaving a wake of roiling water behind it, and it was heading straight across our path.

"Grab on to something!" Captain Joel yelled.

I saw him spin the *Sea Wraith*'s wheel hard to the left. While the boat was long at sixty-eight feet, it was also narrow, which made it unstable in the water churned up by the two behemoths, and she slewed sharply, the right side tipping dangerously upward. Chou grabbed the gunwale. Freuchen stumbled backward, his arms flailing. He collided hard with the side of the pilothouse which was the only thing that stopped him from falling overboard.

I wasn't so lucky.

I flailed for the gunwale, missed and felt gravity take hold of me. I stumbled backward. My leg hit something hard attached to the deck that sent me airborne. I was suddenly dropping toward the ocean. I screamed... and felt a metallic hand grab me by the arm and hold on tightly as the starboard side reached its apex. I swung like a pendulum, caught a momentary glimpse of the sea frothing and foaming beneath my feet, then Silas reeled me to him like he'd just hooked a mermaid. The *Sea Wraith* gave a violent shudder, the wooden deck creaking and complaining as the giant shark sideswiped us and scraped along our keel, buffeting us like we were riding over rapids. Then it was past us, and the boat slipped back to its natural position, leaving us bobbing on the ocean like a cork.

"What *is* that thing?" Freuchen gasped.

"Judging by the size of its dorsal fin, I believe it to be a megalodon; one of the largest shark species ever to have existed. It must be hunting the whale we saw. It should not be here," Silas said.

"What do you mean it shouldn't be here?" Captain Joel yelled.

"Predators were to be strictly limited to very specific sizes to ensure balanced bio-diversity. I am sure that something of this size was not a part of that plan."

"Jesus!" I yelped as the whale breached again, astern of us this time, a stream of blood arcing behind it from a ragged wound on its underbelly. The gigantic shark followed right after it—seventy-feet of pure death—then disappeared as both creatures presumably dived toward the bottom of the ocean. Nothing was left behind as evidence to the titanic struggle that had just taken place before our very eyes but churned up ocean and a slowly spreading slick of blood on the surface.

We stood in silence for several minutes our eyes fixed on the receding spot where the two creatures had vanished, but they did not resurface. Finally, I turned to Silas and said, "You said the shark shouldn't be here. But if the Architect didn't bring it here...?"

"I can only assume this is more work of the Adversary. Another attempt to disrupt the Architect's plan."

Nobody spoke, but I'm convinced that we were all thinking the same thought: if something as big as that shark could be brought here without the Architect's knowledge, what other unpleasant surprises lay in store for us courtesy of the Adversary? Ahead, the sun rose higher into the sky, sparking off the monolith, which now seemed less mysterious and more menacing, looming over the world, its presence an inescapable reminder that we were nothing more than participants in a game played between two unknown and unseen gods.

TWENTY-THREE

O wonder!
How many goodly creatures are there here!
How beauteous mankind is! O brave new world,
That has such people in't.
—William Shakespeare, The Tempest

A FOG-BANK SHROUDED THE COAST, oozing through fang-like spikes of basalt jutting up from the base of a sheer cliff which stretched for miles and miles and miles to the north and south. Trees lined the top of the cliff like lemmings waiting to leap to their death. At its base, years of broken and rotting pine and oak and yew lay scattered across a narrow littoral of jagged rock. Others teetered on the very edge of the cliff, their roots gradually exposed by the slow but constant erosion of tide, wind, and rain. Pockmarked black rocks surrounded by white foam peeked through the ocean's surface, making any approach by the *Sea Wraith* treacherous to suicidal.

"No chance of getting you ashore here," Captain Joel said. He had throttled back the *Sea Wraith*'s engine, and now we drifted with the current parallel to the shore.

Chou turned to face Silas. "Do you have any idea which direction we should take?"

"I have no data on this area, I'm sorry."

"North or south?" I asked Freuchen. "Pick one."

The big Dane leaned against the rail, his beard shifting with a gentle sea breeze, his eyes moving over the landscape, while overhead gulls screeched and wheeled, occasionally diving beneath the surface only to reappear with a fish between their beaks. "South, skipper," Freuchen called out with an assuredness that almost convinced me he knew what he was talking about rather than taking a wild guess.

"South it is," Captain Joel said, throttling the engine up.

It proved to be a good choice. Less than an hour later, the cliff began to descend to a tree studded headland that formed a u-shaped cove with a black-sand beach run through with streaks of saffron colored silt. A boulder strewn incline rose steeply from the beach, ascending into the forest, but it didn't look like anything we couldn't handle.

"How's this?" Captain Joel said.

"Looks good to me," Freuchen said, leaning over the bow to get a better look at the approach. Chou and I echoed his assessment.

"Let's see how close I can get you," Captain Joel said. He swung the *Sea Wraith* around, so the bow faced away from the beach, then threw the engines into reverse, carefully increased the boat's speed, edging the craft backward toward the beach while we scanned the water for any submerged obstacles.

"This is about as far as I can get you without risking running aground," Captain Joel announced when we were still roughly fifteen feet or so from the beach.

"I'll go first," Freuchen said. He grabbed his backpack, walked to the stern, and swung himself over the gunwale, dropping down into the water up to his thighs. "Give me another backpack," he said, beckoning with both hands. I handed him mine, and he proceeded to wade to the beach. He stood on the beach and waved for us to come ashore.

I turned to face Captain Joel. "Thank you," I said and hugged him tightly.

"You all come back to us," he said, solemnly.

I smiled, nodded, and followed Chou and Silas over the side of the *Sea Wraith* and dropped into the water. We waded ashore, the day warm enough that our clothes wouldn't stay wet for too long. Standing on the beach, we watched as the *Sea Wraith*'s engines churned the water and the boat edged away. Captain Joel turned once, his hand raised in farewell.

I started to turn my attention back to my companions who were already shouldering their backpacks when movement at the stern of the *Sea Wraith* caught my attention. I couldn't be absolutely sure, but I thought I had seen something drop off the boat into the water. I shaded my eyes to try and get a better look.

"Shit!" I hissed. "Silas, I need you. Now!"

"Vat is it?" Freuchen said, looking where I pointed. "Oh!" he said when he spotted what was bobbing in the water, heading slowly toward the beach.

It was Albert. The kid had somehow managed to stow away aboard the *Sea Wraith*. He was using something to stay afloat, his legs kicking furiously as he tried to swim to us.

"Would you please go and pull him out of there?" I said to Silas.

"*It would be my pleasure*," the robot replied and strode out into the water. He took hold of Albert and lifted him above the water, holding him easily in his arms. With his other hand Silas picked up the object Albert had used to stay afloat, and I saw now that it was an orange life preserver. The boy had probably never seen one before, so he hadn't worn it when he jumped overboard, but he was smart enough to use it as a buoyancy device.

"What were you thinking?" I snapped, barely able to contain my anger at Albert's stupidity as Silas placed the dripping wet kid on the sand in front of me. "If I hadn't seen you, you could have been swept out to sea, drowned, or we could have gone on without you, and you would have been left here all alone with no way back." I took two steps back, afraid I might be tempted to throttle him.

"*That would not have occurred,*" Silas said.

"What? Which one?" I said, utterly confused.

"*Any of those scenarios.*"

"What?" I repeated.

"*I was aware of Albert's presence on the* Sea Wraith."

"What!" I exploded. "You knew he was right there and you didn't think it would be a good idea to tell us? Jesus!"

"*I'm sorry,*" Silas said, "*did I do something wrong?*"

"Wrong? Nooooo, nothing's wrong. You just allowed the kid to stow away without bothering to let any of us know. What could possibly be wrong with that?"

"*But Albert instructed me not to tell you. He said it would be a surprise. I assumed you would be pleased at learning of his presence.*"

I could feel my eyes growing bigger by the second, my face flushing red. "You know," I said, staring right at Silas, "for a robot with an IQ of, what is it? A gazillion or more? That was pretty stupid."

"*I apologize.*"

I closed my eyes, sucked in a deep breath, held it... slowly exhaled. It had been twelve days since I'd been unceremoniously dumped into this world. In that time, I'd been miraculously cured of my drug addiction, had men try to kill me, seen my first dead body then seen more than I should ever have, joined together with a group of people pulled not only from different times but from different freaking dimensions, fought and beaten Nazis, counted a robot as one of my friends, and found out that I was the key to solving a mystery that held the future of humanity in the balance. I guess it was understandable if I was a little short-tempered. But like I said at the beginning, even if I could go back and change everything that had happened, I wouldn't. Not now.

When I opened my eyes again, the *Sea Wraith* had vanished around the curve of the headland and with it any chance of returning Albert back to Avalon. How did that prayer go? *God, grant me the serenity to accept the things that I cannot change, the courage to change the things that I can, and the wisdom to know the difference.*

"I placed a hand on Silas' metal shoulder. "Sorry," I said, embarrassed by my outburst.

"*Apology accepted.*"

Chou said to Albert, "How did you go undetected?"

"I hid in the hold," Albert said. "I just... wanted to... be with... you." His words hitched as he tried to hold back his tears.

I shook my head in mock disbelief as my anger began to subside. I placed my hand on the boy's hair, then slipped it to his back and pulled him close to me, wrapping my arms around him. When I let him go, I said, "Listen closely: from now on, when any of us tell you to do something, you do it? Understood?"

Albert nodded. "Does that mean you're not going to leave me behind?" he said, wiping the snot and tears from his face.

"Leave you behind? Here? God, no. No, no, no." I paused then added with a smile, "So long as you do as you're told, at least."

Albert snuffled then smiled meekly.

"Very good then," Freuchen said. "I think it's time ve ver on our vay."

I grabbed my backpack and shouldered it. We stood abreast of each other; five travelers from different times and different realities, strangers from very different shores, bound together now as comrades, all facing the same great unknown. Above us, the sun had almost reached its zenith, creating doppelgänger negatives on the ground ahead of us, and I wondered for a second whether, in some alternate version of *this* universe, a copy of me would make a different choice than the one I was about to.

"Okay, are we all ready?" I said, turning to look down the line to acknowledge everyone's nod of confirmation. "Well then, what are we waiting for? Let's go see what's out there."

A NATIVE OF CARDIFF, Wales, Paul Antony Jones now resides near Las Vegas, Nevada with his wife. He has worked as a newspaper reporter and commercial copywriter, but his passion is penning fiction. A self-described science geek, he's a voracious reader of scientific periodicals, as well as a fan of things mysterious, unknown, and on the fringe. That fascination inspired his five-book *Extinction Point* series, following heroine Emily Baxter's journey of survival after a very unconventional alien invasion.

The Paths Between Worlds, the first book in Paul's new *This Alien Earth* trilogy is now available.

You can learn more about Paul and his upcoming releases via his blog at DisturbedUniverse.com or facebook.com/AuthorPaulAntonyJones

GREETINGS, Earthlings,

I first began working on this new trilogy close to seven years ago. Back then it was called *Otherworld Chronicles*, but in the years between now and then, the name has changed and the story has gone through some major alterations. The result is the book you have just read.

So many talented individuals worked on taking the original raw manuscript I sent to my editor, pruning off the dead story-twigs (and, occasionally, entire branches), fact checking, polishing, and finally, tying it all together and presenting it in a beautiful package for you guys.

I'd like to thank Rhett Bruno and Steve Beaulieu of Aethon Books. I'd also like to thank April Taylor, Kelly Graffis, Beverly Lewallen Knobel; Britanny Lee, and Victoria Clemensen.

Special thanks go out to Emma Burns, Steven and Beth Lewis, and Becky and Darren Fleming who helped solve some nautical problems for this desert-bound landlubber.

And, as always, my greatest thanks go out to you, dear reader. I hope you'll join Meredith and her crew for the rest of their journey.

— PAUL JONES

THANK YOU!

THANK you so much for reading *The Paths Between Worlds* by Paul Antony Jones. We hope you enjoyed it as much as we enjoyed bringing it to you. We just wanted to take a moment to encourage you to review the book on Amazon and Goodreads. Every review helps further the author's reach and, ultimately, helps them continue writing fantastic books for us all to enjoy.

If you liked this book, check out the rest of our catalog at www.aethonbooks.com. To sign up to receive updates regarding all new releases, visit www.aethonbooks.com/sign-up.

SPECIAL THANKS TO:

ADAWIA E. ASAD
BARDE PRESS
CALUM BEAULIEU
BEN
BECKY BEWERSDORF
BHAM
TANNER BLOTTER
ALFRED JOSEPH BOHNE IV
CHAD BOWDEN
ERREL BRAUDE
DAMIEN BROUSSARD
CATHERINE BULLINER
JUSTIN BURGESS
MATT BURNS
BERNIE CINKOSKE
MARTIN COOK
ALISTAIR DILWORTH
JAN DRAKE
BRET DULEY
RAY DUNN
ROB EDWARDS
RICHARD EYRES
MARK FERNANDEZ
CHARLES T FINCHER
SYLVIA FOIL
GAZELLE OF CAERBANNOG
DAVID GEARY
MICHEAL GREEN
BRIAN GRIFFIN
EDDIE HALLAHAN
JOSH HAYES
PAT HAYES
BILL HENDERSON
JEFF HOFFMAN
GODFREY HUEN
JOAN QUERALTÓ IBÁÑEZ
JONATHAN JOHNSON
MARCEL DE JONG
KABRINA
PETRI KANERVA
ROBERT KARALASH
VIKTOR KASPERSSON
TESLAN KIERINHAWK
ALEXANDER KIMBALL
JIM KOSMICKI
FRANKLIN KUZENSKI
MEENAZ LODHI
DAVID MACFARLANE
JAMIE MCFARLANE
HENRY MARIN
CRAIG MARTELLE
THOMAS MARTIN
ALAN D. MCDONALD
JAMES MCGLINCHEY
MICHAEL MCMURRAY
CHRISTIAN MEYER
SEBASTIAN MÜLLER
MARK NEWMAN
JULIAN NORTH
KYLE OATHOUT
LILY OMIDI
TROY OSGOOD
GEOFF PARKER
NICHOLAS (BUZ) PENNEY
JASON PENNOCK
THOMAS PETSCHAUER
JENNIFER PRIESTER
RHEL
JODY ROBERTS
JOHN BEAR ROSS
DONNA SANDERS
FABIAN SARAVIA
TERRY SCHOTT
SCOTT
ALLEN SIMMONS
KEVIN MICHAEL STEPHENS
MICHAEL J. SULLIVAN
PAUL SUMMERHAYES
JOHN TREADWELL
CHRISTOPHER J. VALIN
PHILIP VAN ITALLIE
JAAP VAN POELGEEST
FRANCK VAQUIER
VORTEX
DAVID WALTERS JR
MIKE A. WEBER
PAMELA WICKERT
JON WOODALL
BRUCE YOUNG